SON OF
Sherlock

SON OF
Skylark

SON OF
Sherlock

Amanda C. Raymond

EpiphanyMill Publishing

Published in the United States by EpiphanyMill Publishing, a division of EpiphanyMill LLC. Mesa, AZ

EpiphanyMill Publishing is a registered trademark and the balloon colophon is a trademark of EpiphanyMill LLC.

Visit us on the Web! EpiphanyMill.com

Library of Congress Cataloging-in-Publication Data
Raymond, Amanda C.
Son of Sherlock / Amanda C. Raymond. – First edition.

ISBN 978-1-947691-00-1 (intl. tr. pbk.)
ISBN 978-1-947691-01-8 (ebook)

[1. Detective-Fiction. 2. Mystery-Fiction. 3. Classic-Fiction.]
I. Title.
Library of Congress Control Number 2017917931

The text of this book is set in 11.5 Baskerville Old Face.
Book design by Rod R. Garcia
Edited by E. M. B.
Cover Design by Whendell Souza

Printed in the United States of America

10 9 8 7 6 5 4 3 2 1
First Edition

For Allison, who IS Holmes

Acknowledgements

Allison Lang
Mikio Moriyasu
Brooks Watchel
Claire Stephenson
Mark Wallis
Kathy Nolan
James Raymond

PART I: JONATHAN

CHAPTER 1

JONATHAN EATON

In the London borough of Merton, the young lads of Rutlish School House for Boys eagerly scrambled from their classes for a well-deserved break in their studies. It was late May, and with the summer of 1901 quickly approaching, the impatience and enthusiasm of the students for the school year to end was palpable.

Within minutes, each had decided upon his various activities for the afternoon. Some gathered in the large grassy area for football; kicking the grimy ball back and forth within makeshift boundaries; while others played rugby, blind man's bluff, or hide and seek. With their navy blue, nautical-inspired uniforms, it appeared as though a ship's crew of young sailors had invaded the school grounds during shore leave.

One tall, lanky boy remained back by the schoolhouse entrance, and after finding a long, gnarled stick, sat down on the back steps and began drawing math equations in the dry dirt. His concentration was broken when a large shadow fell across his quadratic equation.

He looked up as a Humpty Dumpty of a boy holding a rugby ball had positioned himself just so, in order to block out the sunlight. The intruding boy grinned, then brushed back greasy bangs.

"Think you are too good for the rest? Is that it Eaton?" he asked.

"What would cause you to speculate that Mr. Twitchell?" the boy on the steps asked, as he scratched the word 'bête' off to the side in the dust.

"You never play rugger with the chaps, so are either afraid, or think you are above us."

"But playing would first require an invitation, would it not?"

Neville Twitchell shifted on his feet, and turned back to look at a group of boys who were watching him, waiting for a show.

"You want to play or not Eaton?" Neville said coldly, kicking dust towards the boy.

Jonathan Eaton coughed and brushed the dirt from his blonde hair. "I shall accept the invitation, but only if you correctly solve a riddle."

"A riddle? Easy enough."

Jonathan smiled, then flung his stick to the side. He rose to his feet, briskly patted the grime off his knickers, then folded his arms over his chest. Though only a child of twelve, his adult manner and height made him appear years older. "Very well then. What goes on four legs in the morning, on two legs at noon, and on three legs in the evening?"

Neville looked off to the side and scrunched up his face with a 'hmmm', presumably giving the answer considerable thought.

Jonathan's brown eyes remained fixed on Neville. "I am awaiting an answer."

Neville thought for a moment longer, then angrily threw the rugby ball into a patch of white lace flowers with spotted leaf stalks. "That doesn't make sense. Nothing does of course. It is a trick question."

4

"Wrong. A man. A human being crawls on all fours as a baby, walks on two legs as an adult, and walks with a cane in old age."

"You said morning, noon, and evening! Not different years!"

"If you ever managed to retain information from our lessons you would have known that the question and answer was presented to us not a week ago whilst reading Oedipus."

"You are just a bloody genius then, aren't you?!"

"My supposed accelerated intelligence is only magnified by *your* failure to comprehend or care, about your schooling."

With a huff, Neville snatched up his ball from the flowerbed, thrust it under his arm, then moved back towards the circle of boys who were now laughing hysterically.

"Oh, and Mr. Twitchell?" Jonathan pointed at Neville's hand, "I would advise appropriating some rubbing alcohol or baking soda at your earliest convenience, for the flower bed you were previously rifling through is filled with Heracleum mantegazzianum."

Neville stared at him blankly.

"Or, its more common name is Giant Hogweed, which is highly toxic."

Pure spite flashed in Neville's dark eyes. "Sure it is." His mouth opened to continue speaking but then his hands twitched. He winced, and examined his palm. It was quickly turning a patchy pink. "Blimey!" he shrieked.

Before Neville could muster a retaliation, Jonathan had already moved from his position and was now safely inside the schoolhouse walls.

"Eaton, sedecim, Twitchell, nihil," Jonathan smiled, making a zero with his fingers and squinting at Neville through it.

"What!?" Neville shouted.

"The score is sixteen to nothing, respectively."

"One of these days Eaton, one of these days," Neville spat, making a fist.

"I do hope I will live long enough to see it."

CHAPTER 2

THE LODGER

When school broke for the day, Jonathan tied up his books in his leather strap, then sprinted down the long alleyway beside the school's physics lab, which always smelled of pungent chemicals and rotting cabbage. As he slowed, passing by the school's front gate, he groaned, remembering what today was, and quickened his pace home.

From Dorset Rd, Jonathan turned right onto Sheridan Rd, and pushed through the gate of number 1 that was on the corner of Sheridan and Church Lane. It was a lovely Victorian brick home built in 1875, with stone steps that lead up to the green front door with light blue stained-glass windows. He peered through the bay window of the conservatory on the left of the house, and seeing no one, gently placed his schoolbooks in a pile on the door matt and climbed atop the stack to look through the stained glass. No activity. He sighed, then climbed down.

"Father, is he here?" Jonathan called, as he opened the door and stepped into the vestibule.

He glanced at the family portrait on the mahogany sideboard and focused on his attention on his mother's image in the center. He'd been dreading this day for weeks.

His sister, Frances, three years his senior, was asleep on the red chaise lounge against the wall in the drawing room. He was tempted to make a loud noise and wake her, but decided that today was not the day to make trouble.

As he tiptoed through the room and under the curved archway that led to his father's study, he heard footsteps upstairs. He froze. Hearing it was only one pair of shoes clomping around on the hardwood floors and not the two he was anticipating, he changed directions and moved from the drawing room to the staircase, and climbed up the narrow steps.

His father, Francis Eaton, emerged from the guest bedroom with a stern expression. He was portly, with thin grey hair and an equally grey beard, which conversely, was thick and full, and could have easily hidden a nest of linnets.

"Jonathan, our new lodger is to arrive shortly and I would like you to welcome him. I have business to attend to, so he may wait in the drawing room."

"I wish we did not need a lodger," Jonathan sighed.

"As the costs of the sanatorium for your mother are excessive, I am left with no choice. I shall not speak with you on this again."

Jonathan turned and headed towards his room down the hallway. He grabbed a blue book with gold lettering off the bookshelf over his bed, then trudged back downstairs.

His mother's illness should have been treated at home. There was no excuse. His father's best friend was a doctor, and his father's profession as a botanist afforded him infinite knowledge on healing herbs and plants. It was completely illogical.

"And Jonathan?" his father called.

8

"Yes, Father?"

"Remain decent if you wish to visit your mother this weekend."

"Yes, Father."

Jonathan stepped out the front door with a grunt, and dropped onto the cold stone steps to wait.

As he blinked through the sunlight, he attempted to speculate what their new lodger would be like, based on the few facts he had already been given. The man was a barrister of fair age, from Brighton, and had no living relatives.

He then frowned, realizing what little information that was. He opened his book to read but then heard the front gate creak open. He looked up as a thin, older gentleman trotted towards the house carrying a brown leather suitcase, and a brief bag. He was perhaps mid-sixties, tall, loose-jointed, and had a white fluffy beard that matched his wild, disorderly hair. His eyebrows were thick, like clouds pasted onto his forehead, which were a stark contrast to his piercing eyes.

"Hello sir," Jonathan stood up, as he held out a hand, "you are our new boarder, are you not?"

The man extended a long skeletal hand and shook Jonathan's. "I am indeed, young man."

"And, you are from Brighton, very religious, and have recently spent a great deal of time in the sun."

The man paused, then smiled. "And... how do you know all that?"

9

"As the address written on the outside of your carry case says Brighton, I deduced you were from Brighton. The skin on your finger by your ring is significantly lighter than the rest of your hand, therefore the sun has clearly browned it, which could only result from being outdoors in direct sunlight. The gold cross around your neck signifies the importance you place on religion. Were it not as meaningful to you, you would have had it tucked underneath your collar."

The wire-rimmed spectacles that were tightly embedded on the man's hawk-like nose, lifted as he smiled. "Deduced? Really? Strange word for a boy your age."

"I have seen it appear in detective stories, and I read quite a few of them."

"So you enjoy detective stories, splendid."

Jonathan proudly held up his book. "First edition of the Memoirs, limited to only 10,000 copies."

"Ah, so you like Sherlock Holmes in particular. I haven't read anything on him I'm afraid, though I hear he's an eccentric fellow, quite peculiar." The man set down his suitcase, and stretched out his back. With his matching black jacket and waistcoat, with grey pinstripe trousers and black bowler, the man looked more like an undertaker than a barrister.

"Now what might your name be lad?" he asked.

"Jonathan. Jonathan Alexander Eaton. And yours?"

"Charles Dickens."

Jonathan smiled. "Sir, that is silly. He is an author."

"And a very good one at that! You are a voracious reader I see," the man pointed to Jonathan's almost finished novel. "One can learn much from reading. Possibly even catch new bits of information upon reading the second or *third* time around, eh?"

Jonathan froze. How did this man know it was his third time reading the book? He glanced down at the dog-eared pages, then understood. Second time around, he had folded over a corner of the page ever so slightly, and the third time around, he had begun folding it down further, as the creases hadn't stuck as well with less paper. *Easy enough to infer.*

"What else do you find engaging, son?"

Jonathan tapped his chin. "Music. Bach, Wagner, Mozart, Chopin."

"Do you engage in the practice of playing an instrument?"

"The piano, like my father. I have been told I play well."

"I had heard that your father is musically inclined. Have you ever been to the Opera, Jonathan Alexander?" the man leaned in.

Jonathan recoiled from his nearness. "No, sir."

"Then perhaps your father will take you!"

"You do not know my father, sir. He is not one for outings." As if his father would take him anywhere, except possibly the dentist.

"On the contrary, I know him quite well."

Jonathan was puzzled. He thought this man had answered an advertisement in the *Daily Telegraph.*

11

As if reading his thoughts, the man laughed, "That is, I know your father through his published scientific works."

"Oh."

"Well my boy," he lifted his suitcase, "I had best see to my room and discuss matters with your father. Where might I find him?"

"He is in the study, but you are to wait until..."

Before Jonathan could finish, or offer an escort, the man had hopped up the front steps, and passed through the door. He turned back with a slight smile, then bowed dramatically, "'twas a pleasure to meet you Jonathan Alexander, I am quite sure that we'll get on splendidly." He turned left in the vestibule, then vanished under the archway.

That night at supper, Jonathan learned that the man's real name was Henry Stevenson. He had recently established a private law practice in the city of London, and precisely where, he preferred not to divulge. Upon Jonathan asking what sort of law, he re-directed the conversation. As apprehensive as Jonathan was, he was also finding this man intriguing.

One hot and humid Sunday afternoon, Jonathan sat playing Beethoven's "Moonlight Sonata" on the grand piano in the parlor. It was his favorite room, as the lime green and gold-flecked wallpaper reminded him of the meadow at his grandmother's farmhouse in Downe.

Just as he began thinking about the giant white farmhouse on the hill, Henry Stevenson appeared holding two paper tickets in his right hand.

"Sorry to disturb you Master Jonathan, but as my companion for the afternoon is ill, I find I have an extra ticket for the performance of Shakespeare's *Twelfth Night* at the Theatre Royal in Drury Lane. I wondered, might you care to join me?"

After a delightful performance at the theater, Jonathan and Stevenson spent the journey home discussing all aspects of the play; the plot, the dialogue, the acting... Although Jonathan was unaccustomed to being so chatty with another adult, something about Stevenson's presence soothed him, and before long, he began discussing all sorts of things he'd never related to anyone; how his family had lived in Down House in Kent until his grandmother's death in '96; how he missed the countryside and his tutor, Mr. Sherwood, and his greatest confession was admitting that he was barely tolerated by his schoolmasters and the students at Rutlish. He believed this was largely due to their envy of his intelligence and wit, and therefore felt it was pointless to attempt to remedy the situation. He had been angry when they were forced to move, and life in the suburbs was so very different and dreadful compared to life in the country.

"Have you expressed any of this to your father?" Stevenson had asked, as the passed by Merton Park.

"I really only have my mother, who's now ill, or my Uncle John to talk to. But he's always so busy."

"Never your father?"

"My father does not care."

"I am certain that is not true. Who is your Uncle John?"

"He's not really my uncle. He's my father's closest friend."

"And you call him 'uncle' do you?" Stevenson asked as a smirk drew across his face, "how intriguing."

"I feel as though my father resents me at times and I wonder if I were an unwanted mistake after my sister."

Pain flickered in the old man's eyes. He carefully rested a hand on Jonathan's shoulder.

"I am sorry if you've never felt a connection with your father, Jonathan. Truly I am."

For the next five months, Jonathan's mother remained ill, and he found himself relying solely on Stevenson for companionship. Although Stevenson's schedule was erratic, and he could disappear for days or weeks on end, Jonathan valued whatever time they had together. The man had become the grandfather, or perhaps even father, that Jonathan had never known.

His new friend generously bought him a year's membership to the library and they would visit several times a month. Jonathan would confide in Stevenson about his trials and tribulations at school, and Stevenson would respond with words of encouragement and advice. He confessed that he had also suffered from being an outcast, and Jonathan was grateful to finally have someone who understood him.

14

In July of 1902, Ellen Eaton's health worsened, so Jonathan's father decided to take the family to France to escape for the summer.

As Jonathan was packing his suitcase, Stevenson lightly knocked on the door to inform him that he was being sent away, and was not to return to the Eaton household. When Jonathan demanded to know why, Stevenson's only response was, "It is, as it should be."

"This is not fair in the least," Jonathan had sniffed, as he hugged Stevenson close.

"*Life* is not fair Jonathan, not ever. Why do bad things happen to decent people? Why do villains live on in the lap of luxury while their victims suffer the consequences of their crimes? We cannot say. However," Stevenson's eyes twinkled, "We *shall* meet again, and soon, but I predict it will be under different circumstances. Until then, I bid you adieu."

CHAPTER 3

MISGIVINGS

With his mother's increasing illness, and Stevenson's forced estrangement, the hole in Jonathan's heart had swelled to an abyss. The two people who had come close to understanding him, were gone.

After spending a miserable summer in France, he made himself a promise, to never get close to anyone again. He avoided contact with people whenever possible, and preferred to live in his books of fiction, rather than in the melancholia of his bleak existence. Nothing and no one mattered anymore.

One gloomy, Wednesday afternoon, when the heavy rain from the morning had left the ground soft and spongy and slick with dew, Jonathan sat perched in an oak tree behind Bowling Clubs Pavilion during recess, engrossed in one of his favorite books *The Time Machine*. He was busily traveling through the ages of man with the Time Traveler to 802,701 A. D., when a rugby ball smacked him in the leg, and jolted him back to reality.

Neville Twitchell pranced over to retrieve his lost item, and sneered at Jonathan as he scooped up the ball.

"Terribly sorry, but you *were* in the way," he said, tossing the ball in the air and catching it. "Oh, and by the by, I heard that Ellen Eaton is in horrid shape. Babbles like an idiot now. So very tragic."

Jonathan turned a page.

"What I can't seem to understand, is why you would be so upset? After all, she isn't really your mother."

Jonathan paused. He glanced at Neville, then went back to his book.

"You don't believe me? My mum's a nurse, and I overheard her telling my father what your mother said. 'I worry what's to become of Jonathan if I am gone, for he's too much like his parents. They would have known better how to handle him than I'."

As Jonathan continued to ignore him, Neville reached up on his tiptoes and pulled away Jonathan's book. "What do you think that means?"

"Hand me my book," Jonathan sat up angrily.

Neville grinned, then threw the book across the lawn into the flowerbed with the giant hogweed. "You had best be careful getting that book out I'd say."

"Then maybe I will just have you pull it out with your teeth."

"You think *I* am scared of *you*?" Neville laughed. "Your real parents probably left you, and the Eatons adopted you out of pity. Even that lunatic old man left you!"

Jonathan dove from the tree onto Neville and knocked him to the ground. He began punching the boy's fleshy face without realizing what he was about, or knowing his own strength.

Neville clawed to get him off, and managed to shove Jonathan to the side, only to have him pounce again. The two scuffled in the dirt of the courtyard, pawing and pulling at each other. The other students came running and a loud 'rip' was heard as Jonathan torn off the arm of Neville's jacket.

"Now see here!" a voice boomed into the fray, "that is quite enough!"

Mr. Pryce, the balding, bulbous-nosed mathematics teacher came banging out of the schoolhouse and yanked the two muddied boys apart.

"Jonathan Eaton, what in the world has got into you!?"

"He's the one that instigated it!" Jonathan pointed a shaking finger at Neville, his voice elevated and cracking, "He was spouting out vicious lies--"

"I wasn't lying Mr. Pryce, sir," Neville said, as he assessed the damage to his tattered jacket, "ask Mr. Eaton."

Mr. Pryce pushed the boys towards the schoolhouse, nearly tripping over his black robes in anger. "You are to collect your things and head home. Mr. Draper, the Headmaster, will be notified immediately, and your parents shall be contacted to determine the proper disciplinary action. This nonsense will not be tolerated at Rutlish!"

Once home, Jonathan slipped through the front door, sneaked past his sister in the drawing room, and scurried upstairs to his bedroom. He quickly changed his muddied clothes, and stuffed them under his bed. This was a positively wretched day, and it promised to only get worse.

He was rinsing the mud from his matted hair in the water basin in the washroom when his father stormed through the door.

"Have I not groomed you with better manners, boy?!" he boomed.

"I did not instigate it father, Neville is the one..."

"Hold your tongue!"

"Yes sir, sorry sir," Jonathan looked to the floor.

"For what reason would you behave in such a fashion? Explain to me, unless you want a good slating!"

Jonathan tensed, then swallowed. "He said you are not really my father."

His father paused. "Oh?"

"It is... not true, is it?"

Mr. Eaton pulled on his black waistcoat in irritation. "Absolutely not, and you are to go to bed without supper. We will discuss further punishment later," he said, then turned with a huff and tromped back downstairs. "Am I not really his father," Jonathan heard him mutter, "hmph! Can he be so ungrateful?"

The next day Jonathan was forced to remain at home and have lessons with his sister. He would have rather endured the slating. At the end of the schooling day, Jonathan plopped down on the front steps and began mechanically bouncing a grey rubber ball on the walkway. He felt the urge to hurl it at the pied wagtail that was eating from the birdfeeder on the lawn, or at one of the innocent pink roses in the front garden, but instead, he pocketed it, and cupped his chin in his hands with a frown. He couldn't put his mind off what Neville had said.

Just as he was contemplating heading back inside, he spotted his Uncle John walking through the front gateway. Jonathan's face lifted as the man ambled up the cobblestone pathway towards the house.

'Uncle John', was a middle-aged doctor with a thick, strong neck, and a small moustache that was slightly greying. He was of average girth, and was wearing a tan and black striped suit with a brown bowler.

"You look rather glum lad," he said, sitting down next to Jonathan. "What seems to be the trouble?"

Jonathan took a deep breath and sighed. "I was in a row, and was sent home from school."

The man's jaw dropped, but then he smiled, and chuckled. "You had me there for a moment."

"I am afraid I am quite serious. You see, someone at school claimed my father is really *not* my father."

His uncle's smile faded.

"Now I know that Neville's a nasty little snipe, but I cannot help but wonder." Jonathan paused. "You would know if it were true, wouldn't you?"

Uncle John drummed his fingers across his thigh. "Jonathan, the stories I write that you enjoy so much, the ones about my friend and roommate.... Do you think him a good man?"

"Why?"

20

The doctor pulled a handkerchief from his jacket pocket, and dabbed at his forehead. "Bit warm out today."

"I adore his character, but I only know of him through your books as I've never been permitted to meet him. Why are you changing the subject? *Is* Neville right?"

His uncle looked away as a hansom carriage wheeled by, and stopped outside the house. A man stepped from inside the carriage and Jonathan's concern shifted to elation as he recognized the caller.

"Mr. Stevenson!" he shouted, as he raced past his uncle and hugged Mr. Stevenson tightly. "I thought you weren't ever to come back? Has my father relented?"

Stevenson brushed Jonathan's hair fondly. "I might ask you the same. You are home a bit early from school, are you not?"

"Yes, well..."

"And to answer your question, no. There was a slight complication in the matter of expenses with your father, so I am here to resolve them." He then nodded towards the doctor, "Evening Doctor."

"Mr. Stevenson," Uncle John replied.

"Now then, why are you returned so early from Rutlish this afternoon? Are you well?"

Jonathan sat down harshly on the steps. "I am being schooled at home. Punished you see, for a boy at school said my father is really *not* my father, so I gave him what for."

Stevenson gave John a puzzled look, who responded by shrugging his shoulders.

"As I will assume this 'boy' is Neville, you know from previous experience he will say anything possible to provoke you. I am surprised that you succumbed to his taunts this time Jonathan, for such a fabrication could not possibly be..."

"No, Neville is right," Uncle John blurted.

Jonathan and Stevenson stared at him in shock.

"What?!" they chimed in unison.

The doctor stood, closed his eyes, and took in a deep breath. "Jonathan, I cannot lie to you any longer. This is intolerable!"

Stevenson glared at him and grabbed him by the collar. "Good God man," he whispered, "what are you about, hmm!? How can you feel this information is yours to tell?"

Jonathan stepped back from Stevenson. "You knew? You knew--and—and didn't tell me?"

"Jonathan, I..."

"Francis Eaton is *not* your father," John said, pushing Stevenson away, "he should have told you ages ago."

Jonathan felt the world around him melting, like a sidewalk chalk drawing in the rain. If he wasn't Jonathan Eaton, then who was he? The torrent of information given from that one sentence struck him so, that he began to hyperventilate. He had shared everything with Stevenson, why hadn't *he* told him this very important bit of information? Is that why he was sent away? He was going to tell him the truth?

"Then, who *is* my father?"

22

"Your... your father is well--"

"Sherlock Holmes," Stevenson interrupted coldly.

Jonathan breathed in, and nearly choked on his next words. "That is impossible."

"Jonathan," Stevenson said gravely, "it is the truth, though I wish you did not have to be told under such circumstances."

"How in the world did you know?" Uncle John gasped.

"For heaven's sake Doctor, are you still so easily duped?" Henry asked angrily, "I am not so perfect a shapeshifter as to remove every last trace of character!"

"What?"

"And incidentally, you just broke your promise to me, Watson," Stevenson said in a lower pitched voice. "Or should I also call you 'Uncle John'? A secret given away is a confidence lost."

The wheels in the humble man's mind appeared to be turning then his eyes bulged in recognition. His mouth seemed paralyzed, for though it stood open, no words were forthcoming. He then placed his hand over his chest, and breathed in with a gasp. "Holmes! Good lord, you will be the death of me yet!"

There was a searing pain in Jonathan's gut as the realization of who Stevenson actually was hit him like a battering ram. He blinked through the tears that were beginning to stream down his face.

"This is a cruel joke to play," Jonathan said, attempting to breathe, "the both of you. You should be ashamed."

23

"There is no deception here, Jonathan," John Watson sighed, "at least, not anymore. Although Holmes, you *should* be ashamed of yourself!"

Sherlock Holmes placed on hand on Jonathan's shoulder. "Calm yourself Jonathan. As you may have guessed, I am not Henry Stevenson. I am Sherlock Holmes."

Jonathan brushed him off. "And... you are my father."

"That is correct."

Jonathan wiped his eyes, then bolted behind a large shrub in the garden. "I want you to leave, both of you!" he cried from behind the bush.

"Son, listen to me..." Sherlock began.

"Sherlock Holmes never had a son!" Jonathan snapped. "I read all your stupid stories, *Watson*. Holmes does not even like women! He hates them! The only one he was ever close to caring about was that American opera singer who died."

"Your last name is Holmes, Jonathan, not Eaton," Sherlock said, "now please come out."

Jonathan gripped a small branch of the shrub as his hands shook. His brow sweated as he tried to come to terms with the information he'd just been presented. Suddenly things made sense. The disconnect with his family, the inherent differences in their personality and physicality, the feeling of never being understood or belonging, because frankly, he didn't. He should have deciphered this sooner, and cursed himself for his own ignorance.

24

Jonathan took a deep breath, then carefully stepped from behind the shrub.

"Why did you lie to me?" he demanded coldly, "and where is my mother?"

The man formerly known as Stevenson reached up to his face and carefully peeled off the white beard from his jaw. He removed his hat, the bleached white wig, and the pasted-on eyebrows as he said softly, "Your mother died after your first year." He then yanked out a white handkerchief from his breast pocket, and proceeded to wipe off the beige and grey make-up that had aged him.

"Then you abandoned me," Jonathan said curtly. His mood had shifted from shock to anger. His once beloved friend wasn't real at all, and was just another of the countless characters that Holmes had created over the years to get what he wanted. Jonathan had been played. He felt cheated and bitter, and no longer cared about this man or his feelings.

"It is not quite so black and white," Holmes said as he ripped the remaining cosmetic putty from his chin and eyebrows, and placed them into the handkerchief.

"No? Well then who was it you bedded? The sister from Stoke Moran? Miss Hunter, the governess? That America opera singer before she died? Irene was it?"

"No!" Holmes said sharply, folding up the handkerchief and placing it in his pocket. "Mrs. Norton was never an interest, and she certainly never left me a photograph that I 'cherished' and 'displayed as a reminder of her' as Watson had implied. I also never referred to her as 'the woman'. After my departure in '91, Watson felt inclined to create

25

many unnecessary and damaging truths regarding our cases in an attempt to produce dramatic effect." He gave Watson a sidelong glance. "The only woman *ever* Jonathan, was your mother, and the only photograph of a female I possess, is of her."

"You did not answer my first question," Jonathan narrowed his eyes, "how did she die?"

Holmes' face tightened. "That is not important."

"I deserve to know!"

"Some secrets exist for a reason..."

An avalanche of emotion caused Jonathan to kick over the birdfeeder, which resulted in a mountain of birdseed spilling out onto the grass. "So you couldn't bear the thought of having me around? Is that your excuse for leaving me?"

"There are reasons which I cannot reveal Jonathan, not yet."

Jonathan sniffed, as the weight of the situation came crashing down on him. "The man in the stories I learned to admire wanted nothing to do with me, even though I was his son, perhaps even less so because of that."

"Would I have come to you as Stevenson, were that true?" Holmes asked, as he maneuvered around the destroyed birdfeeder.

"Watson thought it true, which is why he never wanted me to meet you! Then behind his back you reenter my life, earn my trust, and abandon me *yet* again? What sort of sadistic villain are you?"

"It was not my choice, as you recall. Francis sent me away."

Exasperated, Jonathan began to bawl. "I don't care! I want nothing to do with you. I hate you!"

Jonathan ran towards the front door, but Holmes grabbed him by the arm, and pulled him back. "There is far more to this puzzle than you can imagine, my boy."

Jonathan violently fought to break free, but Holmes' grip was too strong.

"I beg you to listen..."

"NO!"

Jonathan punched his fists into Holmes' forearm until he was able to escape, then scrambled to the front door. He grabbed for the doorknob, but Holmes reached it first.

Jonathan backed up.

"I know you to be a rational boy, are you not?" Holmes said quietly, slightly winded.

Jonathan paused.

"Will you allow me to explain?"

Jonathan nodded slowly.

As soon as Holmes had stepped away from the doorknob, Jonathan quickly ducked under his arm, twisted open the door, then slammed it shut behind him, bolting the top lock to keep them out.

"I wish you *had* died at Reichenbach Falls!" he shouted through the door, "we would all be better off!" He flew up the stairs to his room, shut the door, and dropped onto his bed. He gulped back tears finding it hard to swallow. His throat was sore from shouting, something he was unaccustomed to doing.

He grabbed up the gold-framed portrait of his supposed family from his bedside and stared blankly at the now foreign faces. They were nothing to him. He threw it against the wall causing the frame to shatter, and splinters of jagged glass skipped across the hardwood floor.

Suddenly, a loud thump sounded on his door, and Francis Eaton stepped through the doorway. He was dressed in his grey sack suit, with scuffed black oxfords, and had an infuriated expression on his face.

"What in the world has got into you?" he fumed, looking down at the shattered glass. "Slamming doors, running upstairs, throwing portraits?"

Jonathan shifted onto his back with a grunt, and stared up at the ceiling.

"Jonathan Alexander!"

"I *know* you are not my father," he said coldly.

"I thought we had discussed this..."

"My real father is just downstairs now," Jonathan sat up, "chatting away with his roommate, Dr. Watson, or should I say... my real father, *Mr. Stevenson?*"

Francis' eyes went wide. "You... you... cannot mean...?"

"Yes, Sherlock Holmes and Henry Stevenson are one and the same. Might be good of you to say hello."

"That is impossible! Long ago he... Jonathan, we will speak on this later, when you have calmed."

Jonathan turned his head. "The hypocrisy of one who so firmly totes honesty, and is in fact a liar, is vexing at best. Therefore, I have nothing further to say to you, *father*."

Francis sighed heavily. He quietly closed the door and the sound of his footsteps slowly faded down the hallway. Jonathan heard the familiar creak of the front door open so crawled off his bed, flipped the latch hook, and carefully pushed the windowpane forward to listen in on the jumble of heated voices below.

"I cannot believe this! What the devil...?" he heard Francis ask. "How could you do this? Especially to him? You had no right...!"

He tilted the windowpane closed in repulsion, no longer caring what anyone had to say. He inched over to his oak wood dresser, and began to rummage through its drawers, removing articles of clothing, and throwing them onto the floor.

He slid his faded brown leather suitcase out from underneath the bed and threw the clothes inside. "I will bid you *all* adieu."

He glanced around the room for a final inspection and then noticed the thick blue novel with gold lettering on the shelf over his bed. He grabbed it down and began violently ripping out the pages, scattering pieces of paper across the floor until he was physically and emotionally exhausted. After a few moments of calmed rage, he tossed the wounded novel into his closet, causing it to collide with an old, grey and white spotted rocking horse with thin black hair and a red saddle. As the book smacked into the horse's wooden frame, its velocity prompted the toy to teeter back and forth, causing it to crush down on the battered object

29

beneath its bow rocker. Jonathan's once prized and cherished possession, '*The Memoirs of Sherlock Holmes*', now lay discarded and abandoned at the bottom of a closet, and left to endure the wrath of a rocking horse.

CHAPTER 4

RUNNING AWAY

It was nearly midnight, and the Eaton household was asleep. The only sound was the rhythmic snore of Francis Eaton, and the ticking clock in the upstairs hallway. Jonathan flung his suede satchel over his left shoulder, tightly gripped the small suitcase, and took a deep breath as he crept downstairs.

As he moved towards the front door, he glanced at the initials 'J.E.' that had been sewn into the upper left corner of his suitcase and frowned. Making a quick detour into the kitchen, he swiped a knife from the countertop, forcefully lifted the 'E' off his case, then dropped it into the middle of the floor.

Jonathan Eaton was dead. In fact, he never existed.

He slipped into Francis' cave-like study which overflowed with books and randomly strewn about papers, then grabbed up the hollowed-out Bible from the shelf near the writing desk. He knew that a large stash of pound notes and ring of keys was kept inside. As the Eatons had no use for religion, it gave the book a practical purpose. He used the smallest copper key to unlock Francis' gun cabinet, and grabbed up a small 4-barreled silver Sharps derringer.

He held it in the palm of his hand.

It felt cold and heavy, much like his heart.

He pocketed the pound notes, opened the front door, then breathed in the night air. He hadn't a clue as to where he was going, but it didn't matter. All he knew was that he never wanted to hear the name Francis Eaton or Sherlock Holmes, ever again.

Sometime later, in the early hours of morning, ravenous and exhausted, he found himself in Shoreditch on the east side of London. He mechanically noted his surroundings as he passed by a soot-covered, hulking industrial plant with a sign that read 'Beckton Product Works' and reeked of ammonia and sulfur. Quickening his pace to avoid the smell, he came upon a crossroads post with two white signs that read, 'Shoreditch High St.' and 'Hackney Rd.'.

Shoreditch, brilliant. The place which serves as a byword for crime, prostitution, and poverty.

He trudged along until his legs began to twitch from exertion. He scouted out a small niche underneath a platform between several large wooden barrels, and situated himself between two of them. It smelled of urine and gin.

A two-story building with a marquee sign was on his left. The letters on the yellowed board spelled out, 'The London Music Hall Shoreditch'.

Jonathan wrapped his arms around his knees, and shivered. He had no one, and *was* no one. He picked up a filthy cigar butt from the dirt, and angrily threw it into a metal dustbin near the music hall's side entrance where a young blonde girl was standing, talking to a wizened old woman.

It resonated with a *thud,* which caused the girl to jump.

"Watch it there!" she said.

"Sorry," Jonathan mumbled. He froze as the girl took a large gulp from her pewter tankard of beer, then began to approach him as the other woman stepped inside.

She appeared about eighteen, and was dressed in an orange coloured, knee-length dress, with layers of white lace and petticoats underneath. Curly golden locks fell loosely around her face, and she wore entirely too much make-up; thick rouge on her cheeks, and bright pink over her eyes. Her lashes were long and thick, and her lips a deep red. She reminded Jonathan of the ladies he'd seen on a tobacco card in the Wild Woodbine cigarette boxes Francis used to purchase. She was obviously a 'performer,' as they liked to call themselves, for the music hall theater.

"Hello, you are... not from around here are you?" she asked, eying his beige boys' suit and shiny black boots with curiosity.

"*However* did you know?" Jonathan said testily.

Clearly not understanding his sarcasm, she laughed. "Your clothing!"

"Brilliant deduction. You should consider detection as your profession."

"Where are you from, ducky?"

Jonathan shifted his body to the side to avoid her. "It does not matter."

"What brought you here?"

He scooted backwards then winced, as a sharp stone rubbed uncomfortably into his buttock. "I do not wish to say, thank you."

"Sorry. Are you hungry? I could take you to where there's food."

Jonathan sighed, and shook his head.

"Should you change your mind, come find me. I am Abigail," she held out a hand, "Abigail Hopkins."

Jonathan forced a smile as he shook it. "Jonathan."

"Well, be careful, Jonathan. It can be beastly out here."

As she turned and walked away, Jonathan bit his lip. He *was* terribly hungry. He picked at a loose thread on the silver button on his trousers, then paused. "Wait?" he called out, "I *will* come, if such an answer is still acceptable."

Abigail stepped over, helped him up, then dragged him inside the half-lit dining area of the pub next door to the dance hall. She circled around to a table where a small tin plate of food was resting amidst stacks of dirty dishes, and plopped down her tankard.

"You can have this if you like," she said, picking up the plate, "I have no stomach tonight."

Jonathan eyed the crust of bread and piece of pressed beef that sagged on the plate. Normally he wouldn't have had the stomach for such unappetizing fare either, but it wasn't as if he had other options.

"Abby, we're closing up in 'ere!" called a heavyset man, who was perspiring down his dirty apron as he moved a chair atop a table. "Take that back to the 'all would ya?"

"Yes sir! Thank you Nelson!" Abigail turned to Jonathan. "I'll take you where you can sit."

They exited the pub and she led him around towards the back of the music hall. As she reached for the backstage door handle, Jonathan pulled away. "Forgive me, but am I allowed in there?"

"The ladies will like you," she winked, as she pushed him inside.

Jonathan clumsily stood in the doorway and surveyed the women in front of him who were preening before their next performance. Most of them were older than Abigail and seemed oblivious to Jonathan's presence. They sat on frayed, red velvet cushions adjusting their stockings, or stood leaning against the rose patterned wallpaper as they tightened their colourful corsets and smoothed out their ruffled skirts.

"Girls!" Abigail said, immediately drawing everyone's attention. "There's a poor boy here who's needin' something to eat, now don't give him no trouble."

"Amber, you bringing in more o' them urchins?!" said a short, snaggle-toothed woman who was dressed like a clown. "Before you knows it, they'll be swarmin' around 'ere like a pack o' vultures!"

A venue of vultures, Jonathan thought, *and why did she call her Amber?*

35

When the woman noticed Jonathan's fitted suit with the pressed white collar and polished boots, her bright red lips curled into a grin and she whistled, "Ohhhhh, we have a little gentle 'ere. *They*, on the other 'and, is always welcome."

The other girls giggled.

An older, round gentleman in a dated black tux with a thick black mustache and bald speckled head suddenly poked his neck through the doorway and growled, "Girls, you have three minutes 'til curtain! Now shut the 'ell up, and get out 'ere to wait in the wings!"

"Yes sir, Mr. Ball!" the gaggle of girls and women replied, as they frantically danced around with last minute touches to their make-up and inspected their fractured reflections in the cracked mirror in the dressing room. As they rustled out the door to the backstage, Abigail leaned back in and whispered to Jonathan;

"You can sit here and eat, but stay hidden. I would like if you stayed, but you do not have to."

Jonathan nodded. Where else would he go?

He sat atop his suitcase against the back wall, close to a blue satin curtain, and took a bite of the pressed beef. It was cold and gamey. He nearly gagged. The bread wasn't much better, but could be stomached.

After several hours, a fluster of skirts, ribbons, and bells came prancing back into the dressing room. The girls were chattering and giggling, and guessing as to which patron might want to sponsor them, or take them off to a better world to perform on a real stage. They were seemingly oblivious to Jonathan, who had nearly drifted off.

Jolted by the noise, Jonathan jerked his head, and looked around for Abigail. Not finding her, he shrugged, and walked towards the backdoor. Just as he was about to leave, a warm hand wrapped itself around his wrist.

"Sorry," Abigail said, out of breath, "I was held up."

"I should go."

"To where?"

"I... do not know."

Abigail pressed her index finger to her lips, then took his hand and led him outside. Sitting down on the mud-crusted curb, she prompted for him to do the same.

"Have you *anywhere* to go?"

Jonathan shook his head.

"Not even a friend's?"

"I haven't any friends."

"Why not?"

"Because they leave you, or lie to you, or both."

"Sounds like you've been hurt, good and proper." Abigail then thought for a moment, and smiled, "you ah... you could stay with me tonight."

Jonathan jumped up anxiously.

"Don't be takin' it the wrong way, Jonathan," Abigail laughed, shaking her head, "I just feel like I should help you. I know how it is to feel cut, and betrayed. I do not know your plight, but don't turn your back on *everyone*. Not all people are evil."

Jonathan considered this for a moment, then sighed. "Where do you live?"

"Right down the street at Plough Road and Bowl Court."

Abigail led Jonathan to a three-story brick building. She unlocked a white door and took him from the ground floor up to the first, then unlocked a door numbered '26'. There was a low kitchen with white-washed walls and a fireplace, a tiny washroom, a common sitting-room with a single worn sofa and armchair, and a wooden table with benches that was positioned against the back wall. Two bedrooms split off from the sitting-room.

Abigail opened the door on the left, and led him inside the room. She turned up the lantern resting on a rickety old dresser next to a square window, and gestured for him to have a look around. The room was small but clean with wood floors, white walls, and a shelf on the back wall. A chipped water basin with towel was positioned underneath a square mirror. There were two beds, neatly made, and one had a white lace pillow and large, carved, oak trunk at the foot of its steel frame. The trunk looked expensive, and out of place with the rest of the furnishings. A thick turquoise curtain was pulled back against the wall, and a long metal curtain rod extended through the room's center, hung by two rings bolted into the ceiling. The curtain must serve as a divider of sorts, Jonathan thought.

"Yours is the bed on the left," Abigail said, "I had another roommate until a fortnight ago, but she got engaged, and moved out when they married. I'm lucky, the others here share three to a room."

Jonathan dropped his things onto the empty bed and yawning, wearily sat down then laid his head upon the flat pillow. The bed squeaked as he lifted his legs onto the grey, pilled blanket. He tightly gripped his suitcase's handle in his fists, and closed his eyes.

Abigail reached for the curtain, and pulled it across the room. "Do you need anything?"

"Just rest please."

Abigail shrugged, and blew out the lantern. "Then sleep good Jonathan, good night," he heard her hop into the creaky bed.

"Sleep *well*, that is," Jonathan sighed. This girl was far too trusting to be living in an area filled with such immorality and villainy. Was she daft? Or perhaps, one of them? A common thief who had lured him here to rob and kill him? No, he would have sensed that. Perhaps she was naïve, or had come from a better background initially, like him, given the ornate trunk. It was a difficult reality to stomach, the fact that until yesterday, he'd had a family, a home, and an identity... but all that had vanished up in a giant puff of smoke. Smoke and mirrors, isn't that what magicians' tricks were referred to as? And magicians, those charlatans who deceive, swindle, scam the mind... those men who are liars of an epic proportion.... Francis, Watson, Holmes... they were all that, all conspirators in the awful plot to fool and mislead a young boy, and for what reason? Why the fabrication? He supposed he could have allowed himself to calm enough to simply ask them the question, but it was too late now, and there was no turning back. Who knew what would happen to him at this point if he did. Whatever the outcome of his rash behaviour, at least he had his freedom, and if he'd been lied to about his birthright, what else had been false? There could be dangers lurking even deeper, and heartache even more devastating. More than likely, he escaped in the nick of time. Or so he tried to convince himself before drifting off to sleep.

The next morning, Jonathan's nostrils were awakened by the smell of bangers and eggs. The delicious aroma was inviting and as he kept his eyes closed, he wondered if the previous day was nothing but a bad dream, a horrible memory that wasn't real. As he blinked his eyes open, to his disappointment, he was lying in a small room with a curtain drawn across, and his father was apparently the world's most famous detective.

He slid off the bed and peered around the curtain. Abigail was gone, and her bed was made. Jonathan rubbed his eyes and stretched. Just as he opened his suitcase to grab a fresh shirt, Abigail walked through the doorway holding two tin plates. Each had a thick sausage, mound of eggs, and a wooden fork resting on top. She was wearing a plaid, brown dress with a black satin sash tied around the waist. She looked younger, and without the excessive makeup, her face glowed with natural beauty.

"Bangers?" she smiled.

Jonathan closed up his suitcase. "Where did you get those?"

"Once a week, I have breakfast with the girls at the pub next door to the hall. Today I managed an extra plate!" she beamed. "Nelson was feeling generous."

Jonathan then remembered her conversation with the heavy-set, aproned man from the night before. "Why did you not stay and eat with them?"

Abigail handed him the steaming plate. "I see them all the time. I might only be seeing you this once." She sat down on his bed and patted the mattress. "This all right?"

"The mattress, or your seat upon it?"

Abigail blushed and stood up.

"No no, sit please," Jonathan said.

Abigail did so, but this time closer to him. She smelled like rose petals and talcum powder.

"Why the interest?" Jonathan asked, as he took a bite of the sausage. It was good, and still warm.

"Something about you Jonathan... just... well, eat up!" Taking her own advice, Abigail scooped up a bit of egg with her fork, then smiled. "You should live here you know."

Jonathan laughed. "They do not allow opposite genders to cohabitate in lodging houses."

"The deputy keeper won't care, I will just give him a little extra and he'll turn a blind eye. A male roommate for a slightly larger fee is better than having to pay for a room entirely on your own."

"If I did decide to stay on... how?"

"You would have to pay your share of the doss money. We all split it."

"How could I earn my keep? I am an amateur, I haven't a professional trade to work at, and nor would I fancy factory employment. I hear tell what they do to children."

Abigail laughed. "But you are not a child."

"Quite right, at thirteen, I am anything but a child."

Abigail's face fell. "You are thirteen? Well I'll be if you don't act older. Might change things a bit. Hmm... the hall owner, Mr. Ball, pays boys to run errands or deliver letters. That is an option."

"I could manage that."

"And, also, when people leave the pubs completely stacked, they tend to be careless and easy pickins really, especially round Saffron Hill."

Jonathan eyed her. He was familiar enough with Oliver Twist to know of Saffron Hill's reputation as an area of pickpockets and thieves.

"Just don't get caught, or it gets wicked," she added.

One would assume, he thought.

Jonathan pondered her offer. It wasn't terribly appealing, but what other choice was there?

"Though I do not condone thievery, survival of the fittest I suppose," he shrugged, then held out his hand. "Thank you, Abigail, I will stay."

Abigail eagerly shook it. "Brilliant! Welcome Jonathan... ah, Jonathan... what did you say your surname was?"

"I did not say, and nor do I wish to, if you please."

Abigail nodded in understanding then slid her plate to the side and hopped off the bed.

"You do not have the proper clothing for Hoxton, have you?" she asked, as she inspected his suitcase.

Jonathan gave her a puzzled look.

"Clothing that will not raise issue or interest in your actual station. If you are truly escaping from something or someone, you will have to blend in with the blokes around you in both look and speech. Can you talk cockney? Or something equally End East like?"

"Well, er..." Jonathan unlocked the suitcase and held up a new, green velvet suit jacket. "I would say that is an accurate appraisal of the situation," he nodded, as he looked over at her worn and dated frock, "and no, but I learn dialects quickly."

"Then first thing tomorrow, I will take you to Camp Field Manchester, a clothing reseller. Threadbare garments to be sure, but wearable. Petticoat Lane has good used topcoats as well. You will need one as soon as it gets colder. And just listen as much as you can to folks for now, and don't talk so good."

"I do not understand why you are helping me, but am grateful Miss Hopkins."

"I had someone once help me," she smiled, "so just repayin' the favour."

"What do you do on stage, if I may ask?"

43

"Did you hear the patter song last night called: '*I'm One Of The Ruins That Cromwell Knocked About A Bit*'? That songbird was me! I be a singer I is, mister Jonathan!" Abigail giggled, "my stage name, is Amber Gaslight."

Jonathan did as Abigail suggested, and began running errands for the music hall's owner, Mr. Baxter Ball. He also occasionally helped with stage set up and ticket sales. With Jonathan's genteel demeanor and polite nature, it wasn't long before Mr. Ball became rather fond of him.

When the crowds had emptied the theater one evening, and Jonathan assumed the hall was deserted, he sat down at the piano by the stage and began playing Beethoven's 'Moonlight Sonata'. As he played on the melancholy tune, he heard someone gasp;

"Jonathan, you are amazing!"

It was Abigail, who had just poked her out from behind the red curtain and hopped off stage. "Where did you learn to play like that?!" she asked, as she sat next to him on the bench.

"I took a few lessons, taught myself the rest," he stopped playing. "I rarely had much else to do. It was better than fighting with my sister, or father..." He then frowned, and resumed his playing, but now pounded more fiercely on the keys.

"Anything the matter Jonathan?"

Before he could answer, the main curtain was hastily pushed aside from the left wing and Mr. Ball stepped onto the apron of the stage. "Didn't I tell you urchins never to touch that there piano?!"

Jonathan jumped to his feet. "Yes sir, I am sorry sir. It will not happen again."

Mr. Ball then stepped from the stage with a chuckle, "Forget that Jonathan. You, my boy, may play it whenever you'd like. Do you know 'ow to play any of them tunes we use 'ere in the music 'all?"

"No sir, but I do read music."

"Then 'ow'd you like play a song tomorrow night? I will pay you twice yer normal wages."

"That would be wonderful, sir! Thank you!"

Mr. Ball lifted the piano bench's seat and reached inside. He removed a yellowed sheet of music, and handed it to Jonathan. "Now study this 'ere one and 'ave it ready by nine o'clock Friday night. You can practice in the daytimes when the 'all is empty."

From then on, for a few nights a week, Mr. Ball allowed Jonathan to play a song or be the musical accompaniment to various acts that graced the stage. Though the money was decent, and his talents appreciated, there were parts of his old life that he missed. His own room, good food, a warm house, and even the ability to attend a high profile private school, were all luxuries he had taken for granted with the Eatons. His mind was under-stimulated, and he was becoming restless. He longed for culture.

Sensing this, on a Saturday night in the middle of October, Abigail asked if he'd like to attend the Royal Opera House in Covent Garden. When they reached the building that evening, Jonathan watched in awe as a procession of six footmen and a chef marched through the main entrance.

"King Edward must be coming tonight," Abigail explained. "He always brings a chef you see, to set up a banquet table outside his box seats, and what a chef indeed!"

"However would you know?"

She cupped her hand over his ear. "I have sampled some of his food."

"You pinched food from the Royal Family?" Jonathan pulled back, "Now *that* I *must* object to-!"

"Well cart me for six, it is not as if he needs it! I hear he is 16 stone! Now follow me."

Abigail led him through a back door in the alleyway. They climbed a rung ladder to the catwalks, and successfully avoided several stagehands that were busily knotting the ropes and setting the stage with the last bits of scenery. Abigail sat down on a metal rail, and dangled her feet over the edge. With her black dress and boots, she practically blended into the background. She gestured for Jonathan to join her.

Jonathan gulped. "I cannot say I like heights."

"They do have a net below. But best not fall, else the game is up."

A few moments after Jonathan had carefully situated himself on the catwalk the house lights went down. He held his breath and tightly gripped the rail. His heart beat like hummingbird wings. But then the stage lights flicked on, and he observed an actor in an elaborate Viking costume enter from the left wing and take center stage. Jonathan sat transfixed as the man suddenly burst into an aria.

Abigail elbowed him. "Pretty fantastic, eh?"

"I have always wanted to see an opera," Jonathan whispered, "but my father, er, Francis, would not take me."

Abigail stared at him curiously. "You call your father Francis?"

"Yes well... wait a moment," Jonathan listened carefully. "I know this opera. It is The Ring Cycle, by Wagner."

"What language is it in?"

"German. It took him twenty-six years to write."

"That is a long time for one opera!"

"It is actually four operas that tell a complete narrative, much like the ancient Greek dramas. This is the third segment, called Siegfried."

"What is it about? I just like the costumes and singing, I never know the story."

"It is essentially based on Norse mythology, and centers around a particular ring that would allow the owner to rule the world. Everyone desires its power, so it is the legend of the battle of the ring. In Siegfried, his father..."

"Oh, you were to tell me why you call your father by his Christian name."

Jonathan sighed, then loosened his grip on the rail.

"Jonathan, anything wrong?"

He took a deep breath. She was certainly his only friend. The least he could do was be honest with her. "Abigail, have you... ever had people in your life that you loved?"

"A few yes."

"How would you feel if those people had been lying to you, all your life, and your entire existence was proven to be nothing but a deception?"

"I cannot even imagine such a thing."

"That is why I say Francis. You wanted to know why I left where I came from. That is the reason."

"Well strike me dead! He wasn't really your father?"

"No, and my actual father is still alive."

"And your birth mother?"

"Gone."

"How do you know?"

"My father came into my life disguised as someone else entirely. When I discovered the truth, I... I left."

"Who was he?"

Jonathan paused. What would she think if she knew? He shifted his focus to the stage below where Siegfried was having a scene with his foster father, Mime. Jonathan frowned, and closed his eyes. "Sherlock Holmes."

Abigail gasped. "That detective? I did not know he was married, or had a son."

"Neither did anyone else."

"Do you know who your mother was?"

"No, nor do I care."

"What if she was someone famous as well?"

Jonathan crossed his arms. "What does it matter, if she's dead?"

They watched the opera in silence. Abigail folded her hands between her knees, and sighed loudly. "Jonathan, I am just curious..."

"How they decided on such a ghastly wig for Mime?" Jonathan pointed to the actor on stage with a very fluffy white wig. "So was I actually."

"About your mother."

Jonathan waved a hand dismissively.

"Are you not curious who she was? What happened to her?"

"I *was*. But Abigail, she died."

"Maybe you have family still. What if they have money? Jonathan, you are so smart, and so well read. I am sometimes jealous. Everything you know, everything *I* have learned *through* you, has made me think there is so much more for you, and now knowing what I do, I am certain of it."

"What if there is not?" Jonathan asked sincerely.

"I saw something in you Jonathan, that first night we met. I did not know what it was then, but now I do. Do you really want to be playing in a music hall the rest of your life?"

"If I discover my mother's identity, what then?"

"You're Sherlock Holmes' son. Surely that means *something* to *someone*."

Jonathan sighed testily. "It is not as though he's the King of England."

Abigail defeatedly crossed her legs and folder her arms.

Jonathan watched the scene below him where Mime the dwarf was telling his son Siegfried that he was really not his father, and that his true paternal parent was murdered after his mother died. He suddenly stiffened, and began to reflect on his own situation. What harm would there be in finding out who his real mother was? Perhaps he had a grandfather, or a grandmother on her side? An aunt or uncle even? What if they had been wondering about him all these years?

"On second thought," he turned to Abigail, "it might be interesting to know the truth after all."

Abigail brightened. "Who would know?"

"Dr. Watson, but he cannot be trusted."

"Do you think we might find something in the doctor's home?"

Jonathan snorted. "You mean Baker Street? Where Sherlock Holmes lives?"

"I did not know they lived together."

"After Mary Watson died, Dr. Watson moved back to Baker Street. Touching anything in that mousetrap would be the kiss of death. Sherlock notices everything, down to the newest layer of dust on the windowsill."

Jonathan rested his chin on his laced fingers, and closed his eyes. "I would need to slip in quickly, and leave not a trace. If only there was a way to get through the window..."

"I will handle the window bit!" Abigail poked him, causing him to open his eyes. "Friend of mine is a chimney sweep. He works around Baker Street, so people are used to seeing him on the rooftops. Just stuff up the chimney he will, then they'll have to open the window for sure."

"It cannot seem intentional, and would have to be timed properly. Not too early, and not too late."

"He can block it up just enough to make things unpleasant."

"Perfect," Jonathan purred. "Now may I watch my opera?"

CHAPTER 5

ATTACK ON BAKER STREET

Jonathan sketched out a rough floor plan of 221B Baker Street based on what he remembered from Dr. Watson's narratives, and planned on scouring the doctor's room for information. As Holmes was not the type to keep a personal journal, Watson was his only hope.

After a few days of careful planning, they decided to enact their assault on Baker Street on the 5th of November.

Abigail sent Sherlock Holmes a letter, pretending to be a wealthy English heiress in dire need of his protection from her murderous and unfaithful husband. Fearing that the police would not take his death threats to her seriously, she begged for Holmes' help, but dared not venture to Baker Street. Instead, she requested that he and his partner meet her at Hyde Park at noon to avoid suspicion. She would be carrying a yellow parasol.

"That should be vague and interesting enough to intrigue him," Jonathan said, as he dangled his legs between the iron bars of their room's balcony. "He will more than likely suspect it is a trap and come armed, but it will not be the type of trap he anticipates, as the real threat is to Baker Street." He took a last bite of his red apple, and squinting one eye, aimed the core at a dustbin on the street below. It landed inside with a clunk.

"Suppose they do not leave? Or they come back too quickly?"

"Do not worry so much, my dear 'Mrs. Allison Parker'," Jonathan winked. "Just drop the parasol in the park, then meet me at

Baker Street to be my lookout. As someone will undoubtedly pick it up, they will then become our decoy, and serve as a distraction for Holmes and Watson. I will need some sort of sound alert though, if they return early."

"How about a dog bark?"

"Oh? Let's hear it!"

Abigail looked embarrassed, but then barked loudly, and finished with a howl.

Jonathan was in fits. "So in truth, it is you out there, three in the morning, singing through the window?" Abigail smacked him in the ribs. "Your bark is lovely, we shall use it."

As planned, Watson and Holmes left at half-past eleven. Moments later, Jonathan quickly climbed in through the upstairs back window from the alleyway. It was only open a sliver, but it was just enough to sneak inside. The rooms were still smoky, so Abigail's friend had done his job well.

Jumping down from the windowsill, he readjusted the wooden planks that were buckled to the bottom of his boots, then ran into Watson's room, and frantically began rummaging through papers and desk drawers. He lifted the mattress, the chair cushion, and looked under the Persian rug. He tapped the floorboards, moved aside paintings, and pried open anything with a lid. Nothing. He consulted his pocket watch. Noon. He was wasting precious time.

There must be something! He thought, pulling at his hair.

53

As the clock ticked on, he discovered a large black box buried under several suitcases and crates of clothing underneath Watson's bed.

There were copies of *The Strand Magazine* starting from 1891 resting inside, with Watson's hand-written notes stuffed in the back cover of each issue, but they were all of stories that Jonathan had read, and that had been published. He felt a tinge of bitter nostalgia as he remembered how much he had once loved the reminiscences of the dear doctor, and now, how he hated them.

His pocket watch read quarter past noon. Time was running short.

Sweat ran down his forehead as his gloved hands shook, fumbling through the yellowed pages. He paused when he reached a bound portfolio wrapped in twine near the bottom, and pulled it from the box. The cover read, '*Unpublished Works*'.

Curious, Jonathan discarded the twine, and pulled back the top flap.

The first hand written page was dated 1887. These writings were obviously from before The Strand Magazine's first publication on Holmes' adventures.

Jonathan shoved the portfolio into his satchel, unsure of what'd he found, but without any time to decipher it further.

Before climbing back out the window, he did a visual scan of the room. The floor looked clean, and any observable marks would be that of the long planks, not his footprints. He chuckled, remembering Abigail's confusion.

"Why are you putting wooden boards on your shoes? You going skiing?"

He explained to her that it was to cover his footprints. As Holmes had written an entire monograph on how one can deduce height, weight, and disposition based on those alone, it was an attempt offset and thwart his methods.

Jonathan ducked out the window onto the ledge, then leaned against the far-left side of the building. He removed the boards from his shoes, and tossed them into his wide satchel.

Running from the back courtyard around to the side, he met up with Abigail and they dashed off down Dorset Street.

"Did you find anything?" she asked, when they were halfway home.

"I hope so."

"Then I shall call you the Boy who Broke into Baker Street," she smiled, putting her arm around him, "for that was no small job!"

CHAPTER 6

THE HIDDEN TRUTH

Once they were home, Jonathan stared at the first full page of the stolen portfolio.

"1887 was the year it began..." it read. It was penned in a different coloured ink than the rest of the entry. *An afterthought.* Jonathan crossed his legs, cradled the papers in his lap, and took a deep breath as he prepared to read...

~ ~

It was early summer. I was saying my final farewells to my friend and roommate of many years, as I had recently married and was off to a new and more stable life.

"I wish you the best Watson," Sherlock Holmes had said, as I grabbed up the last of my belongings, "although it is a pity you are moving from one officious living companion to another."

"I shall miss you Holmes," said I, "even in all your eccentricities. Will you be all right? Have you found a new flatmate?"

"I have indeed. A recent student of Cambridge whose interests lie in criminology."

"Splendid! Do you think you will get on? Is he a chap that is up to snuff?"

"*She* is quite capable and responsible. The timing is impeccable as she was searching for a mentor in her field of study, and what better way to learn and be taught, than be completely immersed in one's work around the clock. I believe it shall be a very amiable relationship." Holmes then took my hat from the floor where I had dropped it in my shock, and handed it to me with a chuckle. "You needn't be so astonished doctor! It is a perfectly acceptable and might I add, sterile, situation."

I was not convinced.

"Come now Watson! You see it quite frequently these days. Most cannot afford to reside singularly in London, and will take on any boarder possible, regardless of sex. Besides, as repairs are being made to her father's estate, she was in need of lodgings elsewhere for the interim."

"I say Holmes," I began slyly, "do you think that perhaps she might..."

He lifted an eyebrow predicting my next question. "You can put your hopes of me finding any amorous companionship with this woman to rest. It is purely a mentor/student arrangement, as well as one of convenience. And fear not, it shall indeed remain that way, or Mrs. Hudson would have my head." I eyed him curiously. "The girl is the third cousin of Mrs. Hudson's niece."

I sighed. "Then is she a Scot?"

"No, English."

I then had a disturbing thought. "Will she be accompanying you on cases?"

"In time, but for now, I will keep her occupied with file sorting, sifting through the agony columns and newspapers for criminal activity, and research. Her father will be temporarily supporting her whilst she is in training."

I was not at all in favour of the situation, but could only muster, "Will you smoke less with a lady present?"

"My habits are my habits."

"What is her name?"

"Scarlett, Scarlett Tennyson."

I laughed. "In all seriousness Holmes," said I, as my novel, 'A Study in Scarlet' was soon to appear in the November issue of Beeton's Christmas Annual, and Holmes had never cared for its title.

"Odd coincidence, isn't it? Though the spelling is different. Perhaps it is a sign? You do believe in those, don't you old boy?" he asked sarcastically, for if anyone did not believe in the supernatural, it was Holmes.

"Is she at least attractive?"

"Ghastly."

"Dear Lord! What an awful mess you've got into!"

"Haha, Watson! You are as predictable as always! If you are indeed so curious, stay and meet her. She should be here presently."

A few moments after the warning, there was a knock.

"Come in!" Holmes called jovially.

It was Mrs. Hudson. "She is here Mr. Holmes."

"Please! Quench Watson's thirst of curiosity and show her in!"

"Yes sir," she nodded, as she returned downstairs.

She later returned with a pale, beautiful girl. I say girl, for she could not have been more than three and twenty, certainly no older. She was tall and slender, and dressed in a deep red satin bustle dress. She had small, dainty hands and sparkling eyes that were a deep shade of umber with a twinkle of green. Her black hair was pinned atop her head, and sprinkled down wisps of curls that framed her oval face. She gingerly stepped towards us with a smile. What a magnificent creature she was! Ghastly indeed! Holmes did not even blink.

"Miss Tennyson, may I introduce my close friend and previous associate, Dr. Watson? He has been very anxious to meet you," Holmes gestured towards me.

He then curled into his basket chair to observe the situation with an air of amusement.

Miss Tennyson blinked her dark lashes and smiled. "Dr. Watson," she held out her hand, "It is a pleasure to make your acquaintance. Mr. Holmes has told me much about you." Her fingers were soft and cool as I shook them, and even the black lace around her wrists could not hide their delicacy.

"Indeed I have," Holmes said with an enigmatic smile, as he rose from his chair. He moved to the mantle for his Cherrywood pipe and the Persian slipper with the tobacco inside, and after lighting a match across the stem, he jovially puffed away, then eyed me knowingly. He was only too aware of my interest in his new companion. I felt a red blush sweep across my cheeks.

"I wish you luck, Miss Tennyson," I said graciously, wishing to end the awkwardness. "This is your dominion now, so I will take my leave."

"You are welcome any time old friend," Holmes said, as he came over to shake my hand, "that is, if you are permitted out by the missus," he teased, poking me with the bowl of his pipe.

"I should say!" I said indignantly.

Miss Tennyson smiled uncomfortably. She was not yet accustomed to Holmes' dry sense of humor, nor our constant banter. I am certain she was unsure of how, or if, she should respond.

I decided to make it easier for her, as I for one, had had enough. I bowed, and bid them both a good night.

As I walked down the stairs into the balmy summer evening, I looked to the window of my old rooms. I would miss him, certainly. Though I cannot deny I was anything but in favour of him choosing a female boarder. I hope this girl will be good for him, and perhaps look out for Holmes as I had done. He could be his own worst enemy at times and a handful, both in his moments of excited passion during a case, and in his melancholy states between them, I only prayed his moods would be less cyclical with her than they had been with me.

As I closed my eyes and again tried to envision her, I caught myself smiling. Could she be just the thing to cure Holmes of his mistrust of women? Teach him to embrace them perhaps? I shook my head at the absurdity of such a thought. Holmes was right, I knew him better.

And no offense to my friend, but what woman in her right mind would ever want, or could stand, Sherlock Holmes as a companion?

6th September 1888

I just returned from an odd, and what I would have previously thought, highly unlikely conversation with my friend Sherlock Holmes. I had been summoned by Holmes to his rooms. The reason he said, was of the utmost secrecy. I brought my service revolver as a precaution, for with Holmes, you never knew what might materialize in the course of an evening.

I was aware that he and Miss Tennyson had been working as partners since December of last year, and that she had been accompanying him on numerous cases. However, you can imagine my surprise when I walked through the doorway, and the first words he uttered were...

"I want to marry her, Watson."

I paused, shocked, but then, laughed long and hard. "Holmes, for perhaps an instant, you had me!" I slapped my knee. "I congratulate you on your supreme creativity, but even you go too far on such a fib. Now then," I smiled, "what is the issue?"

"I am afraid I am quite serious," Holmes said softly.

He had been standing with his back to the fireplace in his blue dressing gown, but then dropped to his armchair seeming tired, and subdued. His normally piercing eyes had softened, and the fire that so often filled them, had all but been extinguished. He cradled his head in his hands and woefully stared at the floor.

I blinked, waiting for the punch line.

61

"Enough charade Holmes, why have you summoned me? Although," I chuckled, "the thought of you marrying is rather amusing."

"I am in love with her."

I hesitated, slightly uncertain now. "Can this be true?"

"She is the most vibrant, elegant, and inspirational individual I have ever met. I have never known a woman so perfect, and yet so flawed by society's standards. I cannot be without her."

At that point, I froze. Was he being honest? Or would he, in another moment, admit to leading me on, and again comment on my gullibility. Taking a leap of faith, I asked, "This young lady has stolen your heart?"

He nodded his head.

I stood silent, absorbing this new information. Was this the same keen-witted man who had so despised love and romance, had snubbed his nose at the very prospect of marriage, and now, was courting a lady?

"This is not a situation I ever imagined," Holmes said quietly, "It very near terrifies me."

"Are you concerned she might not return your favour?"

"No, our mutual affection and relationship has already been well established, like oxygen to hydrogen, gears to sprockets..."

I nodded, then my eyes went wide, understanding his meaning. I could not have been more stunned if you'd hit me over the head. "I think I need sit, else I might faint," I grabbed for the sofa, as my legs buckled beneath me. If Holmes had had relations with Miss Tennyson,

I now understood the severity of the situation. He must absolutely marry her.

"Now you see," Holmes said, confirming my fears. "My only hesitation, is that I am fearful for her safety should our relationship become known. Suppose that in an attempt for vengeance on me, someone assaults her? What would be more satisfying to a villain I've thwarted then to prey upon my wife? There could be positively nothing worse. No Watson, should I make this decision, our marriage must be kept an absolute secret, which is why I summoned you." He stood, then approached the sofa and loomed over me. "Can I count on you? There must be no mention of her in any further narratives of yours about my adventures. For the ones of which you are not a part of, I request that you refrain from discussing them entirely."

"But Holmes," I gulped, feeling a bit cornered, "as I am aware you have been working together, surely I am not the only one? Will you no longer continue your partnership, given the circumstances?"

"That would be an unacceptable option," he returned to his chair, "besides, she is useful to me, in ways you could not be."

"I see," I said, somewhat stung.

"Oh come now old man! I was simply alluding that her being a woman has allowed her access into such areas in which neither you nor I could ever infiltrate. However, I do not want all of London to know of her unless they are directly involved in a case of ours, and not even then, if I can avoid it."

"So what you are implying... is that I can never mention her existence at all?"

"In regards to your publications, that is correct. It is most essential that you do not."

"What of Scotland Yard?!"

"I will answer any and all questions. You are to feign ignorance, my dear friend, as you do so well. Do we.... have an accord?"

Something about this seemed wrong, horribly wrong. But, he was my friend.

"I do not condone the idea of withholding information from the public, or people we know and trust, but I will do as you ask, whether or not I approve."

He sighed with relief.

"Do you think she will be in agreement?"

"Not a doubt."

"Very well Holmes, this goes against my better judgment, but I only wish for your happiness."

Holmes paused with an enigmatic smile. "I believe I am, for the first time in my life."

~ ~

There was a side note on the page, hastily written in red ink. The spaces between the words were peppered with splatters, undoubtedly from pressing too harshly on the pen.

It read:

"The day he confessed to loving Scarlett was the day the deceptions began, and never ended, for any of us."

Jonathan lowered the page. Had his mother lived, he would have existed within a world of secrets, of lies. It would have been a worse existence than he'd had with the Eatons. He was tempted to stop there, but his curiosity got the better of him and he flipped over the next page...

19ᵗʰ September 1888

A day I never thought I should witness. The afternoon that Sherlock Holmes married his beautiful fiancée, Scarlett Tennyson. It was small and secretive, as they wanted, and was held at St. Mary-Le-Strand Church in Westminster. To avoid suspicion, she did not even wear a white gown. According to my wife, it more resembled the silver Coronation gown of Maria Feodorovna of Russia from '83, but with shorter cap sleeves that exposed her thin ivory arms, and several layers of trimmed lace at the front. Only myself, Mary, Mycroft, Mrs. Hudson my former landlady, and Scarlett's closest friend Celeste Whalley, were present. Though had it been left to Holmes' discretion, Miss Whalley would most certainly not have been invited, as they were known to come to verbal blows.

We were all sworn to secrecy, and Holmes even demanded that Celeste sign an agreement, for Scotland Yard was the last organization he wanted knowing anything of his personal affairs. Clearly she was insulted, but her bond to Scarlett must be as strong as mine to Holmes for her to agree to such terms. I believe we share a mutual disgust as to how things are being handled.

When asked how they were to go about their practice, Holmes responded that their relationship would remain hidden from their clients. I questioned about the wedding ring, and he informed me that she was not to wear it in their presence.

I felt sympathy for Scarlett, but I suppose it was her choice as well? At least, I did hope so, though the whole thing seemed entirely wrong and dishonest, whether or not it was for her protection.

19th October 1888

Now that Holmes and Scarlett are married, I see little of them. As Holmes has never experienced life with a female companion, I do not believe he has the ability to successfully balance Scarlett with other people in his life. He seems under a spell, and has become a man I no longer know. The few times I've had the off chance to see him for tea or sherry, the talks and visits have been brief and barely graze the surface.

I am also of the opinion that as Scarlett is the only woman he has been with; passion and love are new and fascinating concepts to him. It could be akin to introducing a child to chocolate. First time around they simply cannot get enough and tend to overindulge until they are ill. But yet, it does not discourage them from wanting more once they have recovered. Holmes, I fear, is no different.

Since these records are for my eyes alone, I feel I can be brutally honest. Is Scarlett some magical siren who's put an enchantment on him? I have never seen a man so drunk with love and desire that he cannot focus on anything else. She must not be of this world. Perhaps she is an angel? And angels, being ethereal, are creatures that no human hand should ever touch for the consequences are unknown. Who knows what type of power a creature built to perfection, would have over a human being as they are so imperfect? I am being metaphorical, but the point is made.

Or, am I too harsh on my friend? Is it that I want Scarlett for myself? I must confess there are times I have thought of her. The images I've had concerning her I will not commit to paper. But oh, to have one night with her! How exceptional she must be! No, I will no longer allow myself to entertain such ideas. I am pledging this here and now. I am not, nor will I ever be, an unfaithful man.

In my entire relationship with Mary, I have never even been tempted, until I met Scarlett. But in all honesty, how is it that a man who has never expressed interest in women, nay, one that was conversely considered asexual, is able to marry the most impressive woman in the country? And I, whom am every bit your typical masculine specimen, cannot?

Imagine that one has been riding horseback your entire life, and is ultimately left with a Shetland pony. Yet on the other hand, someone who has 'never' ridden, one who expresses little if any attraction to the sport, one who quite generally loathes the animal in general, decides to give it a bash, and is handed a prized Arabian.

Should I not be happy for him? Who am I to set limits upon whom he is worthy of? I suppose what they say is true, 'how bitter a thing it is to look into happiness through another man's eyes.'

I wonder how it is to hold her. She appears soft, and her skin smooth like fine china. I imagine she wears silk and lace to bed, as well she should! Oh Holmes is a lucky man indeed! To be with such a woman every night, to have his way with her... just envisioning her figure, how she moves, how she feels... No! Enough of this Watson, pen down!

28th October 1888

It was recently brought to my attention that on numerous occasions, Scarlett had donned a man's attire for their cases in London. I am certain that many mistook her James Mumford for me, which explains why I was often times stopped and questioned about the details of a case of which I had no knowledge.

Though I insisted upon having no involvement, I now understand their confusion. Apparently Holmes has kept much from me, the one person he claimed to have trusted the most. I have even been asked to lie about certain cases, and claim I 'was' involved, even when I was not. My only response to such cases were... 'they were of such a secretive nature, that I was implored 'not' to reveal the particulars to anyone'. For how could I possibly volunteer information on a case of which I had no knowledge?

On their assignments outside the city, I have heard that he allows her to remain as Scarlett, for as Holmes had said, he wished to keep her as much of an unknown in London as he could control.

"For her safety of course," he always emphasizes.

But is she truly happy? Or is she remorseful of her decision to be involved with such a private and duplicitous man? I sometimes wonder. Most likely, I give it far more thought than I should.

8th November 1888

Holmes and Scarlett came to my practice today in Paddington. When I asked the reason for their visit, I was told that over the past two weeks, Scarlett had been awakening with nausea, and was occasionally becoming ill during the day. Additionally, she was having frequent headaches and spells of dizziness. She was constantly tired and easily fatigued. Holmes was concerned.

Upon assessing her condition privately, I had no doubt of the diagnosis. She was with child. My dear friend was about to become a father!

When I informed Scarlett of the news, she burst into tears, and immediately demanded that Holmes be brought in.

Though initially stunned, Holmes' reaction surprised me. He walked into the room, requested I leave, then shut the door. What I wouldn't have given to be a fly on that wall! After a while he emerged, shook my hand, and stated that all was well.

I casually inquired as to whether she would be in need of a doctor, and Holmes jovially replied that they would be delighted to have me care for her. I was pleased, for various reasons, but I would of course be professional.

Monday, 24th June 1889

I curse myself and am bitterly ashamed. Scarlett is a month away from delivering her child, and had popped by my office today for her final check in. She was in a state, and bemoaned how 'awful' and 'monstrous' and 'disgusting' she had become. She was resentful that she could not do what she loved, and was positively bored as Holmes had repudiated her request to continue on any cases until after the child was born. She loathed herself and 'life was intolerable'.

The theory I created, that she might be unhappy with Holmes, resurfaced in my mind. What did he say to her when they were alone? I had never honestly asked her. Was he causing her to feel this way? I suddenly became protective, and patted her shoulder to assure her that she was as beautiful as ever.

She said I was 'terribly sweet', but accused me of false praise. I protested that I meant what I said, but then... I did something terrible. I hugged her close, and as I released her, gently brushed her cheek. Though I did not act beyond that, my intentions on her were clear, and she pulled away and jumped to her feet. She demanded that I find her another doctor immediately. I agreed I would. 'What am I to tell Holmes?' I had asked. I was to claim that I had become too busy, she said, and knew of someone who was more experienced in such delicate matters. If I did not, she would reveal to Holmes the true reason she was uncomfortable.

I blame myself and should never have offered in the first place, but I did not know until today, that I had fallen in love with her. Oh Mary, please forgive such thoughts. I shall never be unfaithful to you, I swear it. I shall write no more of her.

Saturday, 14th February 1891. 3:30am

I was awakened by a knock in the early hours of the morning. It was Wiggins. He begged me to come to Baker Street. As his normally resilient face was ashen and afraid, Holmes, Scarlett or their son must be in a great deal of trouble. I quickly packed my bag and revolver.

It was worse than I could have imagined.

70

Upon arrival at Baker Street, I entered into an ungodly sight. Scarlett was carefully laid down on the sofa and a blanket covered her body. Her arms were folded over her chest, and her eyes remained closed.

Even from where I stood, I knew she was dead. There were red stains on the carpet that had been scrubbed to the best of Holmes' ability, but they could not hide that something dreadful had recently occurred.

Holmes was perched in the basket chair with his knees drawn up to his chest and his arms wrapped around them. His gaze never left Scarlett's body. His eyes were bloodshot.

"What in heaven's name happened Holmes?" I asked, holding in my own emotions.

He slowly turned towards me and sighed, although he did not appear to see me at all.

"I... I... took Jonathan out this evening to give her peace," his voice and lips shook, "I returned to find..."

"You needn't revisit it," I said calmly, though I was anything but. "Do you suspect anyone?"

"Yes, but I must first speak with Miss Whalley," he answered quietly as he uncurled himself.

"Holmes, what could Scotland Yard possibly do? You are far more competent! Do you not think..."

"I am well aware of that, Watson!" he snapped, "but," his tone softened, "there is something I must look into, and she is the only one who can help me, loathe as I am to admit it. It is not merely a question for Scotland Yard, or I would simply ask Lestrade. But there is something deeper, something, from her college years, that I must inquire about," Holmes' voice trailed off as his eyes shifted the side.

"What is it that we are discussing?"

As if he had not heard me, Holmes remarked, "Miss Whalley is my only hope of discovering its whereabouts."

"*Its* whereabouts? Holmes, you are being horribly vague."

"I can say no more," he sighed, then stood. "My friend, I must ask a very large favour of you. Could you and Mary keep Jonathan safe until I have more information?"

"Absolutely."

"I could be a few weeks to a few months. Should you discuss this?"

"Jonathan is a very well-behaved child, and anything I can do, well, it would not be enough."

"I fear for his safety at present, else I would not trouble you."

"I understand," said I, wondering whom he suspected, but knowing that now was not the instance to ask.

"I simply need time."

"If there's anything else..."

"That is more than enough," he fiercely shook my hand. "Jonathan is in his crib. All necessary items are with him." He then moved to the sofa, and sat next to Scarlett's body. He took one of her limp hands in his, and kissed it.

"Now, if you will excuse me."

He then became much affected, and for the first time in our long association, I witnessed Sherlock Holmes weep.

~ ~

Jonathan stopped reading, even though there was one page left in the portfolio.

"She was *murdered*?! Why did he not tell me?"

Jonathan dropped the page to the floor, an emotional cyclone. He hurled the portfolio into the corner and glumly flopped onto his bed. Why would someone kill his mother? Why did Holmes give Jonathan to Watson? What danger was he concerned about? Or... was it a ruse, a way to get rid of Jonathan if his mother was no longer alive to care for him? And when did the Eatons step in?

Swiping the lone page from the ground, he held it above his head, and stared at it.

"Did Holmes ever find you?" he asked the page. "Are you dead now? Why did you kill my mother?" He closed his eyes and let the page fall to his chest. "I must know."

Jonathan visited the library that evening to search for his mother's obituary. She may not have existed in Watson's stories, but proof of her existence must be available somewhere. He flipped through the records from February 14, 1891 until he found it. It read:

73

The death is announced of Scarlett Lillian Tennyson, on Friday last at home in London at the early age of 27. Only child to Clara and Alexander Tennyson of Cavendish Square. Survived by relatives in Long Island, New York, America. There will be a private ceremony for friends of family only.

Jonathan frowned. No mention of him or Holmes. There was only one person he could think of who might be able to help him with discovering the truth, if he dared pursue her. Celeste Whalley, the woman Holmes had wanted to speak to. However, she was also a risk, for who was to say he could even trust her, or that she wouldn't turn him in?

It was too late in the day for any more theorizing, so he returned home.

There was one page left from Watson's letters, so he pulled it out and sat down.

~ ~

Friday, 24th April 1891

A few months had passed since Scarlett's death, and I'd heard little from Holmes, save for two notes from France, one from Narbonne, and one from Nimes. This morning he entered my sitting room unannounced, looking paler and thinner than I'd ever observed.

"Watson, I apologize for calling so late. It is not fair to you in the least."

74

"No apology necessary," said I. "I saw in the papers that you were employed in France? Have you been able to determine who Scarlett's..."

"I believe this to be the work of Professor Moriarty. Therefore I must find and destroy him. You understand why now, more than ever." He lowered his eyes to the ground. "I... do not know if I will return from this venture."

"But what of Jonathan? You have to think of your son and what is best for him."

"That has already been arranged. He will be with Francis Eaton, a friend of Mycroft's from Cambridge. He and his wife Ellen will retrieve Jonathan from you tomorrow morning, and take him to their home in Bromley. He is well esteemed by my brother, so I trust him completely. You needn't be burdened any longer. Again, I apologize for inconveniencing you for a greater time than I hoped."

"Mary's grown quite fond of him, but Holmes, is this really the most suitable option...?"

"He will be in good hands. They have two children of their own and claim they would gladly welcome another. Watson, as long as Moriarty is free, Jonathan's life, as well as mine, is in danger. Therefore I must ask you to inform those who are aware, that Jonathan is with me."

I nodded solemnly. This seemed positively dreadful. I did not wish to be the sole keeper as to the secret whereabouts of Jonathan, yet, what was I to do?

"As for the rest of the public, I must again reiterate my profound need for secrecy. You may reveal that I have awayed in pursuit of Moriarty, and as I've noted your negligence in mentioning his existence thus far to your readers, so that should keep them entertained enough for now."

"You had strictly prohibited me from doing so!"

"But now, you may. I actually require that you claim this is the very first I have ever discussed him with you. However, the true reason for my pursuit must not be disclosed."

"Then what reason am I to give?!" I asked in frustration, unsure of whether I would adhere to his demands.

"That he discovered the Holy Grail and wishes to live forever unless I prevent it. Tell them he plans to sink England into the ocean, or burn down Baker Street.... come now Watson, you are a writer, make something up! Perhaps... 'given their turbulent history, current events had led to the need to finalize the battle, for Holmes' career had reached its crisis, and no possible conclusion could be more congenial than this...' In all seriousness, you may fabricate whatever you'd prefer those events to be, as people will believe whatever you tell them. Say you came along. The story matters not, though I implore you to omit any mention of Scarlett or Jonathan. Can I count on you, old friend?"

"Yes Holmes, I promised you years ago."

"Good man, good man. There is too much at stake, most importantly, Jonathan's safety." Holmes entered the parlor, and carefully scooped up his sleeping son from the sofa. Never before had I seen such sorrow in a man.

"May I, see him from time to time? If... anything should happen?"

"Of course! But neither my identity nor his must ever be revealed, least of all to him. I wish him the chance of a normal life. If he is not to be with me, then it is best... I am forgot," he swallowed.

"Yes Holmes. I swear I'll never reveal the truth. But what of Mrs. Hudson, or Miss Whalley..."

Holmes angrily snapped his head. "That explanation is to be given to everyone Watson. No exceptions."

"Yes, yes of course." I already felt guilty for what I must now do.

"Thank you doctor, I am fortunate to have someone I can rely on so completely." He lightly kissed Jonathan on the forehead, and hugged him close.

The boy's eyes slowly blinked open. He gazed up at Holmes with a sleepy smile then yawned, and stretched out a leg. His round head turned left, then right, as if looking for someone.

"Mummy?"

"No Jonathan..."

"Mummy? Mummy?!" The child began to cry, and attempted to escape Holmes' arms, as if determined to investigate his mother's disappearance himself.

There was a tragic look upon Holmes' face, a deep-seated sorrow, though he attempted to mask it.

"Be good, Jonathan," Holmes had managed, "you will be just fine. Goodbye."

He returned his boy to the parlor and upon reentering the sitting room, his mood had changed from sadness, to sheer devastation. His eyes were foggy, and his body, limp and broken.

"If I do not see you again," he said to me, "then I thank you, for all your years of loyal friendship. The absolute best of everything to you," he shook my hand.

I sighed sadly. "To you also."

As he grabbed the door handle he paused, then turned with a smile. "I suppose you could label this 'My Final Case' Watson."

"Or problem," I said, under my breath.

"Whichever you choose. Besides, if I am dead, I cannot really object to the title, now can I?"

That was the last I ever saw of Sherlock Holmes.

~ ~

"The last you saw of him, until three years later," Jonathan said bitterly as he sat with his hands folded between his legs. Things were not making sense. "According to Watson's story, 'The Final Problem', Professor Moriarty died over Reichenbach Falls in '91. Why then, did Holmes not come for me once he returned to the world of the living in '94? And why *did* he disappear for three years?"

"Find anything important?" Abigail asked, startling him, as she entered the room and threw off her brown bonnet.

Jonathan rested the page upside down on his belly, and sighed. "My mother went to Cambridge, Holmes married her, kept their marriage *and* me a secret, then, she was murdered."

78

Abigail gasped. "All that was in those papers!?"

"Well, more than that actually."

"Were there any clues? Any leads to go on as to why she was killed?"

Jonathan rolled over onto his stomach and drew his hands up under his chin. "Only that someone named Celeste Whalley, who works for Scotland Yard, was my mother's friend, and Holmes had gone to her for information after my mother was dead."

"Maybe ask her what it was? Unless she's in good with Holmes?"

Jonathan sat up and inhaled deeply. "You may be right."

Based on the diary entries, it certainly didn't sound like they were chums, so perhaps that was a viable option. He glanced over at Abigail's bonnet, and threw it on his head. "But only if I go in disguise."

CHAPTER 7

SCOTLAND YARD

Jonathan took the Underground to the northern shore of the Victorian Embankment, which stretched between Westminster and Blackfriars Bridge.

He paused on the foreboding steps of the Gothic red and white brick building that served as the headquarters for the Metropolitan Police, or, the New Scotland Yard, and wrung his hands nervously. Could they be looking for him? Were Celeste and Holmes friendly now? Was he walking into a trap? He took a deep breath, straightened the brown curly wig under his bowler that Abigail had borrowed from a performer, then marched up the steps.

Once through the front door, he encountered an older woman sitting at the reception desk in the dark and narrow main hallway. She was severely overweight, with thick spectacles, and a crooked nose. She probably had a large cauldron and black cat at her rooms as well.

She glowered at Jonathan as he stepped closer.

"What you want?" she asked in a raspy voice.

"I am... looking for Miss Celeste Whalley..."

The woman shifted impatiently in her wooden swivel chair, causing it to squeak. She peered up at him, her spectacles magnified her eyes to twice their actual size, and asked, "Is she expecting you?"

She is still here. "No... but I simply must see her, it is rather important you see."

80

The woman was unmoved. "You are not carrying any weapons are you?"

"No ma'am."

"Show me your pockets!"

Jonathan pulled them inside out. They were empty, except for a few biscuit crumbs.

"Now, open your jacket."

Jonathan pulled back his jacket to show his waistcoat underneath.

"She is down the hall, first right, 3rd door on the left," she waved him along. "*Knock* before you enter."

"Yes ma'am, thank you ma'am," Jonathan bowed, as he headed down the hallway.

When he reached Celeste's office, he paused. His stomach churned, and his palms were sweaty. He placed his hand over his chest, took a deep breath, then knocked lightly.

"Come in," a woman's voice said sweetly.

Jonathan slowly opened the door, and a flaxen-haired, ivory-skinned woman with soft freckles was seated behind a desk facing the door. Her hair was capped on her head like a mushroom. Pompadour style, was it? And she was busily writing with a pencil.

She appeared to be in her late thirties, and wore an olive-coloured tailored suit made of serge. An embroidered shirtwaist blouse, and draped bustle skirt of the same colour, smartly shaped her voluptuous figure. Her high white collar was adorned with a small olive bow at the neck, and a gold chain bracelet with turquoise and pearls was clasped snugly around her left wrist.

Apparently, Miss Whalley followed the fashions for the more liberated and independent female, a trend and style that most men objected to. Appearance wise, she seemed like a formidable woman.

"May I help you, boy?" she said, resting down her pencil.

"Miss Whalley, have you a moment?" Jonathan asked, as he closed the door behind him.

"Yes, I..." She then eyed Jonathan intently. "You... look familiar. Have we met before?"

"I have never seen you before in my life."

"Then I am afraid you have me at a disadvantage lad, what is your name?"

"Before I tell you, I have a question. I... heard you knew Scarlett Tennyson."

Celeste prickled at the name. "We were practically sisters. Now just who *are* you and why do you want to know?"

Jonathan cleared his throat. "I have a very vested interest, and would like to know more about her, please."

Celeste's warm demeanor faded. She stared at him coldly, and folded her hands in front of her. "If you know the name, then you must also know that she is no longer with us."

He cautiously approached her desk. "Yes but, her husband is."

"She never married."

"Now I... I know that not to be true, Miss Whalley. I am surprised you are protecting him. I was under the impression that you did not get on." Jonathan prayed that was still the case, or this would be a short meeting.

Celeste rose from her desk. "Before this discussion continues, I insist upon knowing your name."

"I apologize," Jonathan backed up, "but not until I have more information. I was taking a rather large risk is seeing you today. I need to know if I can trust you."

"Trust me!?" Celeste laughed as she crossed her arms. "What do you think you know, and we'll go from there, shall we?"

"For one, I know that you are lying. You were at her wedding where you were all sworn to secrecy. You in particular, had to sign an agreement..."

"Who put you up to this, hmm?!" Celeste raged. "And who in the hell *are* you to think you can say *anything* about Scarlett Tennyson?!"

Jonathan placed his hands on his hips. "You mean Scarlett Tennyson Holmes?"

"This is rubbish! I demand to know why you would possibly suggest such a..."

"My information was gathered from a diary entry, and as there were only five of you present at St. Mary's that day, I assume you can guess the author?"

Celeste sat back down.

"Scarlett Tennyson was married to Sherlock Holmes, I know that for fact."

Celeste wrapped her fingers around the pencil on her desk, and squeezed it tightly, possibly ready to snap it. "This conversation has just ended," she said with a hiss, "unless you tell me who you are."

Jonathan stood up straight. "Very well, but you may not reveal my identity to anyone, *especially* not Sherlock Holmes, otherwise, I remain nameless."

Celeste released her grip on the pencil. "You have my word, I owe Holmes nothing."

"You promise?"

"Yes! Now who are you?"

Jonathan closed his eyes and gulped. "I am Jonathan, Scarlett's son."

"That is impossible!" Celeste gasped, nearly falling out of her chair. "He died nearly twelve years ago!"

"So you admit Scarlett had a son!" Jonathan leapt at her, no longer afraid.

Celeste covered her mouth and leaned back. "Oh dear God... it cannot be."

Now that he'd got her to admit his existence, he had a distinct advantage. It was not something she could easily take back, and she'd have to give him more information if he was to keep his mouth shut.

"Miss Whalley, I am who I say."

84

"Then you are a ghost."

Jonathan dropped into a chair to the left of her desk, and hung his head. "I am afraid I am fairly sentient. You cannot imagine what it feels like to be presumed dead, or to never have existed at all..."

"I simply cannot believe... let me look at you!" Celeste stepped over, and lifted his chin to examine his face. "You have her eyes..."

"You see, I speak the truth."

"Why? Why would Holmes lie? Why say you were gone?" she said softly, returning to her desk. "When he returned from the *dead* in '94, he told us Moriarty had you killed, and out of rage, he returned the favour." She punched her fist into a stack of white papers, causing them to fall to the ground. "It was due to *grief,* that he stayed away years longer. How could he be so heartless? What *was* he about those three years? God damn him!" she slammed down her fists.

She then sighed deeply and dropped her head into her elbows, attempting to breathe.

Jonathan scooped up the papers from the floor, and neatly placed them back on her desk. "Based on the deception surrounding their entire relationship, are you truly surprised?"

Celeste looked up and a tear rolled down her cheek. "Jonathan? Jonathan Holmes? Is it really you?"

"I shall never go by that name, but yes. Holmes spied on me for a year before revealing who he was, and quite on accident I might add."

Celeste pulled a handkerchief from her top desk drawer, and wiped her eyes. "How did you even know who I am, or where to find me?"

"You have Dr. Watson and his diary to thank for that. He doesn't know that I have it, or that I am aware of anything beyond that Holmes is my father, and I should like to keep it that way. If you please, Miss Whalley."

Celeste nodded. "Just Celeste, Jonathan. With whom have you been living all these years?"

"You swear you will say nothing?" She again nodded. "I was led to believe that Francis and Ellen Eaton were my parents."

"Well! That is why I recognized you!" She walked over to a bulletin board on her wall, and pointed to a pinned up black and white photograph of Jonathan with fair coloured hair. It read, **BOY MISSING**. "*You* are Jonathan Eaton!"

Jonathan removed his hat and wig and fluffed his hair. "I am, and I am not. I don't really know who I am. Not an Eaton, not a Holmes... it is all very unsettling."

"With whom *are* you living?"

He replaced his wig and straightened his hat. "No offense Miss Whalley, I mean... Celeste, but I don't know you. Forgive me if I cannot disclose everything."

"I understand. Though why come to me?"

"I am trying to determine who murdered my mother and therefore need your help. Was it really Moriarty as Holmes had said? Or was that also a lie?"

"Holmes said it was an associate of Moriarty's."

"I would like to assume that Holmes made *some* attempt to find him. Did he ever mention anything to you?"

"No. When first it happened, we were told it was a burglary, and he hadn't the slightest clue of where to begin."

Jonathan threw up his hands in exasperation. "He's the world's foremost consulting detective, and he did not have a *clue*?!"

"I did suspect your father was being dishonest. I certainly doubted the embroidered burglar story. He would have found any common thief immediately."

"*I'll* never call him that," Jonathan snorted. "Then he had not enlisted the help of you, or Scotland Yard?"

"No, as you apparently already knew, he and I had a very tempestuous relationship. It wasn't until after his supposed 'death' that Watson revealed how this Moriarty was the instigator of her murder."

Jonathan frowned, then began to pace the room. "That is odd then..."

"Why?"

"What did Holmes come to you for, after my mother was murdered?"

"What... ever do you mean?"

"In Watson's letters, Holmes said he needed to speak to you about something. You were the *only* one who could help him. If he did not involve you with my mother's case... then what did he ask you for?"

"He asked to see the files on Jack the Ripper."

Jonathan paused, and turned around. "Really? Why?"

"He claimed he needed a distraction from your mother, and wanted to pursue the Ripper case."

Jonathan frowned. "That is all? But Watson's note made it seem so very urgent that Holmes speak with you."

"It certainly wasn't an urgent request, more of a condescending wish to look over a case that *no one* at the Yard had the ability to solve." Celeste leaned her elbows on the desk and chuckled. "Or so he said. But then, he never figured it out either."

"He joined forces with Abberline and Dew on the Ripper case?"

"No, he wanted everyone off. He demanded complete authority."

"And you let him?"

"*They* let him! 'I' was only an assistant at the time. Edward Bradford was commissioner of Police and Lestrade was his second in command. Lestrade would give Holmes anything he desired. Abberline was a year away from retiring, so gladly relinquished any attachment to it. Sir Edward Henry, I view much more highly. It has been a far different place since he became Commissioner."

"Do any of Holmes' notes on the Ripper case exist?"

"If they do, they would be at Baker Street. Holmes *never* shared his notes, not a page, not even after a case concluded."

"Pity, I would have liked to see them."

"Good luck getting into Baker Street."

Jonathan hid his smile. He didn't know her well enough to admit he already had.

"You said Holmes failed at discovering the Ripper's identity..."

"He didn't so much fail, as lost interest. He claimed he found a lead on your mother's killer, left the country, and.... disappeared. It was only then that we were made aware of this 'napoleon of crime', Professor James Moriarty. The rest, I assume you know."

"How would Moriarty know of my mother, if their entire marriage and relationship was kept a secret?"

"Moriarty was brilliant he said, and what a fool was he was to assume he could hide anything from that man. I find his self-assessment quite valid."

Jonathan smiled. He found it comforting to know that someone hated Holmes as much as he did.

"On the subject of 'hiding' things Celeste, in Watson's diary, Holmes had also mentioned that he was looking for something, something... from my mother's college days that he wished to ask you about. What was it?"

"Her trinket box? I really hadn't the slightest why he asked me. How should I know where it is or what was in it? He claimed she had it at Cambridge, and perhaps had left it there in secret, and I would be the

89

only friend of hers who would know. But what nonsense, leaving a box hidden in a college after you've left. He was so heavily 'medicated' by his addictive vices when he came to see me, that I thought he was simply delirious."

"Cocaine or morphine? And on the matter of secrets, how did they explain my mother's, well, appearance, before I was born? What sort of story had they come up with?"

"She never showed until the end, and by then she was kept home, and tended to by Mrs. Hudson."

"I understand how my existence could be ignored in print, but surely their clients would have at least heard me if I were at Baker Street?"

"Mary Watson and Mrs. Hudson would rotate turns, watching you during the daytime hours."

Jonathan now understood why Holmes had left him with the Watsons for several months. It would not have been that out of the ordinary for them to be caring for him. He wished he could remember Mary.

"Needless to say," Celeste began, as she attempted to reorganize her desk, "I've had little to do with Holmes since his return." She then stopped, and pounded her desk again. "That horrid rat! I knew he lied! Why would he have taken a child with him to Switzerland? And Watson, oh Watson, you lying blackguard! He knew the entire time, didn't he? He is lower than Holmes."

"He was brought into my life as 'Uncle John,' my 'father's' best friend."

Celeste's face was red with rage. "So he has seen you throughout the years? I *knew* your father... Holmes... hated me. I obviously did not know the extent."

"I do not know as Holmes trusts or likes anyone. He lied to Watson as well. That is who he is I suppose, incapable of being honest about anything personal. When he returned from Tibet, or wherever in hell he was in '94, did he continue searching for the murderer of my mother?"

"Not that he said. He felt vindicated in killing Moriarty, so any mention of tracking the true murderer was dismissed."

Jonathan then thought of Holmes, and his portrayal of Henry Stevenson. Was the loving Holmes, the husband and father Holmes, just another role, another character in his repertoire of disguises? He typically donned a costume or persona to either acquire information or to get what he wanted, but if so, what *had* he wanted? "From what I've read, it is a wonder if he even really loved her at all."

Celeste's eyes were glass. "I had always questioned that Jonathan, but she had made up her mind."

Jonathan suddenly felt sorry for his mother. *Had* she been duped? Was she just a trusting, adoring, naïve girl that Holmes had taken advantage of? His skin burned.

"Did my mother have any enemies?"

"No."

"No bitter relatives, friends? No previously jilted lovers who might have been jealous, or spiteful?"

91

Celeste shifted uncomfortably. "Why would you say that?"

Jonathan's throat was dry, so he coughed into his hand, then licked his lips. "I am trying to eliminate options."

Celeste eased out of her chair and moved towards a large glass pitcher of water on the sideboard table. "Glass of water?" she asked, grabbing the pitching with her left hand and pouring water into a small tumbler.

"No thank you, I should be leaving soon."

"She hadn't any family except for her father who died in '88. She *was* seeing someone briefly before Holmes, but it was short-lived, so short-lived that she never disclosed his name. She said they separated amicably."

"Well, I do appreciate your help Miss Whalley, I will not monopolize any more of your time."

Celeste hugged the pitcher to her chest with a sigh. "Jonathan? Are you being taken care of? Are you safe? Are you well? As we were enlisted to find you, clearly you ran away..."

"When I learned the truth, yes."

"But what are you about now?" she asked, resting down the pitcher.

"I am safe."

Celeste moved around her desk and to Jonathan's surprise, hugged him tightly. "I am so grateful that you are alive."

A tear landed on Jonathan's neck. He resisted the urge to wipe it off.

"You are not going to disappear again, are you?" Celeste held him at arm's length. "You are the only link I have left to her."

Jonathan shook his head.

"Good then. If, you do discover anything, please let me know immediately."

Jonathan nodded, and just as he opened the door, he heard a familiar voice down the hallway. He anxiously peered around the corner, and saw Francis Eaton talking to another inspector. His eyes narrowed and he quickly shut Celeste's door. "What is Francis Eaton doing here?" he accused.

"Being updated on you, I presume. Quickly," Celeste pointed to the door on her right, "inside my closet if you wish to stay hidden."

Jonathan jumped into the closet behind the chair he'd been sitting in, and carefully pulled the wooden door shut. He peeped through the slats in the top half of the door as someone knocked.

"Yes?" Celeste called. "Enter, please."

Celeste pretended to be busy with a letter as the door opened, and Francis Eaton stepped into the room. The hairs on Jonathan's arms were standing on end.

"Miss Whalley," Francis said, "I am here to see if anything further has come of the investigation concerning my son."

"I assure you Mr. Eaton, we are doing all we can."

"Should you find anything, please use this contact," he handed her a calling card, "as he is also looking into things, and there should be an open communication."

Jonathan squinted to read the card. It read:

Sherlock Holmes

221 Baker Street, B, London, England

Celeste's expression shifted from cold calm, to a violent fury. "I wouldn't work with Sherlock Holmes if *His Majesty* asked me!" She slammed down the card. "He may conduct his investigation on this matter, on-his-own."

"Madame, I had been given your assurance that you were willing to take any measures necessary to..."

"Normally, you would be correct. However, this is more personal. I am sorry. Ask another inspector for assistance if you must involve *that man.*"

"He has a particular interest in this case. The boy is almost like family to him..."

Celeste snorted. "You can tell *Holmes,* that if he wants any information on *his* son, he will have to talk to me directly!"

Francis gaped at Celeste, clearly surprised that she knew Jonathan's true identity.

Jonathan leaned his head forward in frustration. She had been faring well in keeping her knowledge of Jonathan a secret, but Francis' last comment had provoked her into tripping up. This would not be good. He shook his head in irritation, and in doing so, almost lost his hat and wig, but managed to catch them right before they fell to the floor.

"As you wish," Francis bowed, then exited.

Once Francis had closed the door behind him, Jonathan slowly pushed the closet open, and poked his head out.

"I am so sorry Jonathan," Celeste sighed, "I lost my temper and it... it just slipped out."

Women. "I understand. Is it safe to come out now?"

"Not just yet," Celeste cautioned as she held up a finger. "If I know Holmes, he's likely to be close by. And, if I am predicting him correctly, he will be here straight away now that he knows I am aware of your being alive, *and* whom you've been masquerading as."

"Good point," Jonathan said, as he stepped back into the closet.

In less than a minute's time, there was another knock on the door.

"Come in!" Celeste beckoned, with a smug expression. Just as expected, Sherlock Holmes entered through the doorway dressed in a frock coat suit of black cloth.

"Sherlock Holmes, what a pleasant surprise! Why, the last time I had you in my office was before you were dead, or... was that before *Jonathan* was dead?" She folded her arms over her chest and leaned back in the chair. "Dear me I cannot seem to remember now, seeing as how you are both *alive*, and well."

Holmes sighed. "So he *has* been here."

"Though if it'd had it my way, you would have stayed deceased."

Jonathan was now extremely grateful that he had not accepted that glass of water as it would most certainly have been detected.

"Celeste, I deserve your anger and apologize for the deception, but I need to find him. If you know where..."

"You're the detective," Celeste spat, "*you* figure it out! Have you considered that perhaps he does not wish to be found? And most importantly, *not* by you?" She stepped around to the front of her desk. "And when did we become so familiar, *Sherlock*?"

"Miss Whalley then."

Jonathan observed Celeste curling her fists behind her and feared that she might punch him, but instead, she leaned forward and pointed a finger at Holmes' chest. "Holmes, give me one reason I should lift a finger to help you? Just one!"

"Because I know you care for him."

"Well now, I wish I had been granted *more* time to care about him, but somehow I was denied that chance for twelve years. Curious thing, really."

"If you will allow me to explain..."

"You lied to me!" Celeste stomped her foot. "For twelve years now, twelve! I had been made to believe that my dearest friend's son was dead!"

"I was trying to protect him."

"From me? From his mother's *closest* friend? Was I such an abominable person, Holmes?"

"Do not feel singled out, Miss Whalley. No one else knew..."

"Watson knew! You apparently had no qualms about keeping him in the loop, now did you?! And why should I help you? You never cared for me in the least. It was only too apparent how you disliked me from the very start."

Holmes threw his fist down on her desk. "Because you told her to leave me, damn it!"

Jonathan covered his mouth to avoid gasping.

Holmes' outburst had startled her and she nearly fell off balance, but she quickly regained her footing and pounced again. "And, she should have listened! I was being a friend, and as a friend, I could see how much she loved you, and how cruel and cold you were in return. What you did on her birthday was monstrous. She deserved better than you."

Holmes' face returned to its usual emotionless mask. "I never claimed to be perfect..."

"You used her! The biggest mistake that girl ever made was getting involved with Sherlock Holmes! If not for you, she would still be alive."

Though Holmes' face had turned red, his voice remained calm. "I *loved* her..."

"I loved her too! But wasn't she slain while *you* were out for a stroll?" Celeste poked him in the chest, "and by *your* arch nemesis?"

97

"I have told you... my God, how many times can I apologize to you, woman?"

"Apologizing does not bring her back Holmes."

Holmes sat in the chair next to the closet, and looked at the floor. Jonathan was too terrified to breathe.

"Did I invite you to sit?" Celeste asked coldly.

Holmes jumped up and mockingly gestured towards the chair. "These chairs are allegedly reserved for visitors, are they not? Then perhaps-"

"Yes, *welcomed* visitors, which, you are not."

All this fighting was making Jonathan terribly uncomfortable. His mind was spinning. It took him every ounce of control not to fidget and possibly give himself away.

Celeste stepped towards Holmes, which caused him to back up towards the door. "She was my closest friend in the world, and you pushed me away and kept me out while you did nothing to solve her death. And now, I shall do just as much to help you find your son." She pointed towards the door. "Now get out."

"Celeste, please..."

"You have one minute to remove yourself from my office before the world will know you had a wife *and* son!"

Holmes looked panicked. "You would not."

Celeste leaned a hand on the chair in front of the closet, and placed the other on her hips. "Would you like to test that theory?"

"Doing so could result in many dangers, Miss Whalley, especially for him."

She again pointed to the door. "OUT! And under no circumstances are you *ever* to step foot in my office again, are we clear? I would rather not have it besmirched with your presence."

"I do believe that the first words from your mouth Miss Whalley, were 'come in', but women are known for their vacillating decisions and temperaments, and you are no exception." Holmes spun towards the door and gruffly muttered 'good day' before exiting.

After Celeste had dismounted from her rage, Jonathan excitedly opened the closet door.

"That was brilliant!" he applauded.

"I do not think I have ever been so harsh to him. I am sorry you had to hear all that."

Jonathan shrugged. "I think I have said worse actually, but now, I really must go." He was itching to ask what Holmes had done to his mother, but another time. There was already too much information to wrap his head around, and it was best he leave now while he still could.

CHAPTER 8

WHO WAS SCARLETT TENNYSON?

"You are sure you do not wish to turn back?" Jonathan asked Abigail, as they quietly crept through the empty, dark hallways of the Rutlish School for Boys.

"Though we are both taking a risk, I am more concerned for you than me," Abigail whispered.

Jonathan held his lantern to her face. "I really could go about this alone."

"I am as curious about this as you are. Besides, I have been arrested before," she shrugged. "Now get that thing out of my face," she waved him away.

He swung the lantern around and continued down the hallway. "You really think this is going to work?"

"I read it in a book. You just need to grab some letterhead from the headmaster's office and a writing sample, and we'll submit a recommendation for you to properly apply for college."

Jonathan stopped, and shone his lantern ahead of them. "Look out for the rat."

Abigail squeaked as the rodent scurried past, and she bumped into Jonathan trying to avoid it. "Sorry," she said, nearly dropping her lantern.

"I do think this a waste," Jonathan muttered.

"If your mother had hidden something at Cambridge, you should take a bash at finding it. And, it would be easier to snoop around if you were a student there, and, you can see if anyone remembers her. You could also search their records for anything on her family, or her class choices, or..."

Jonathan eyed her skeptically. "I doubt I would be privy to that information as a mere student."

"Then steal them," Abigail laughed, "you are already stealing your own records."

"But I'm only thirteen, Abigail."

"You would not be the youngest to ever go to university."

Jonathan stopped in front of stained glass double doors. "This is Mr. Draper's office, my old headmaster."

He paused his hand on the doorknob. "But Cambridge is a three-hour train ride. I'd never see you."

"That is a bit of the point. As Mr. Holmes is already on your tail, it is not safe for you to remain in London. You need to stay one step ahead of him until the dust has settled and he has assumed the trail's run cold. And are you sure you can trust that Miss Whalley character? She is a copper after all."

"Yes, I should not assume that anyone involved in so many lies can truly be considered trustworthy."

"I know that going to Cambridge is a very roundabout way to discover the truth, but at least see what you can find. It is better than asking Mycroft or Watson."

Abigail and Jonathan then heard footsteps echoing down the hallway.

"I think I see someone!" Abigail whispered, as she pointed down the hallway where a faint light was moving closer.

Jonathan attempted to turn the brass door handle to Mr. Draper's office, but it was locked. He pulled a thin metal rod from his pocket that had several smaller key-like prongs protruding out from the end, and jammed one of them into the keyhole.

"What is that thing?" Abigail whispered.

"Something I pieced together hoping it would work to pick a lock." Jonathan nervously swiveled it around trying to unlock the door, but to no avail. His hands sweat as he tried several other makeshift skeleton keys until one of them resulted in a 'click'.

"Inside! Quickly!" he pushed her through the doorway. He blew out his lantern and prompted for her to do the same. Just as he had closed the door, another glow kept the room illuminated. The light from the hallway grew brighter, until it shone against the stained glass, creating a small faded rainbow on the green rug.

Abigail ducked down behind a leather armchair, and Jonathan slipped underneath Mr. Draper's desk.

The door clicked open, and a night watchman in uniform stepped inside.

"Why's this open then?" the man asked, jostling the door handle. A thick metal tube with a light at the end was in his right hand, and he shone the beam of light around the room, looking for anything suspicious. Seeing nothing, he scratched his head, stepped back through the door, and locked the deadbolt with a loud *thunk*.

Abigail released her breath, then inhaled deeply. "I think I almost fainted."

Jonathan swiped a match across the desk, then relit their lanterns.

"What was that cylinder object he was holding?"

"It is an electric hand torch. Have you not seen one? Americans call it a 'flash light'. They have such silly names for things." He examined the top of Mr. Draper's desk, then grimaced as he struggled to open the top middle drawer, which was locked tight. "What is the plan again?"

"I will write you a letter of recommendation explaining who you are, your background, your character, then all you need do is pass the entrance examination."

Jonathan rolled his eyes. "Oh, is that all?"

"And pick a new name of course."

"You do know the entire exam is in Latin, correct?"

Jonathan tried another drawer and this one opened. As he sifted through it, he picked up a folded-up letter, opened it up, then read through the contents. "Ha!" he cried, "A handwritten correspondence of some sort from Mr. Draper. This will do!"

Satisfied with his find, he snatched several sheets of letterhead from the file sorter on top of the desk, then closed the drawer. "Abby," he asked, handing her the papers, "do you, think he *is* looking for me?"

Abigail gave him a look. "Holmes? He nearly found you *yesterday* at Scotland Yard!"

"But, what if he's given up now?"

"Would that be so terrible? I thought you did not want to be chased after?"

"I don't know." Why *had* he thought to care?

"We should go, Jonathan," Abigail tugged on his hand.

CHAPTER 9

PREPARING FOR CAMBRIDGE

After successfully breaking into Rutlish to acquire what he needed, Jonathan began feverishly studying for the entrance examination to Trinity at Cambridge. He hoped to be accepted in time for Michaelmas Term, if he promised to take Easter Term in order to make up classes. His plan was to apply for one of the undergraduate scholarships, as they ranged from 150 to 600 pounds a year, and included free room and board. As student survival was estimated to cost between 750 to 1000 pounds per school year, he would attempt to find a part-time position somewhere at the college.

Meanwhile, Abigail and Jonathan tossed around ideas of what his new identity would be. They decided to say that Jonathan was the son of a wealthy British-Canadian timber merchant, and he would go by the name Jonathan *Hopkins,* in honour of Abigail.

As Jonathan endeavored to balance his school study with his work, he was finding that he was falling behind in both. One morning, after reading over manuscripts and science books well into the night before, he overslept by several hours, and was late to work.

Abigail pulled him aside when he walked in.

"You're not getting enough sleep Jonathan, and are trying to do too much. Others are starting to notice. As I cannot tell them why, I said you've been sick. The boy who broke into Baker Street has become the boy who is breaking by being bogged down."

Abigail proposed picking up extra hours at the dance hall to help pay the rent so he could cut back on his shifts and focus more on his schoolwork. Jonathan agreed, and decided to only work one day a week.

After days and weeks of studying, Jonathan struggled through Trinity's entrance examination, feeling that the odds of him passing were not in his favour. Though brilliant at observation and deduction, there were facts and formulas he simply did not know, and could not have planned ahead for. He assumed he failed.

As the days passed into weeks, and it was now late December, he determined that he had been denied acceptance. He resumed his normal shifts at the music hall playing the piano, and resolved to study harder before the next exam to ensure his acceptance in the fall. In the meantime, he would try another avenue to uncover information on his mother.

One afternoon, as he stopped by the royal mail sorting office to drop off the usual weekly packages for Mr. Ball, the front desk clerk stopped him, and told him to wait.

"Your last name is Hopkins, yeah?" the clerk asked.

"Yes sir," Jonathan said nervously, "why do you ask?"

"You just got a letter then. Curious, as anything for you only ever says 'Jonathan'," he said, then disappeared into the mailroom.

Jonathan shifted on his feet. He'd only given his box number to Cambridge, Abigail, and Mr. Ball in case Mr. Ball was out of town and needed to mail Jonathan his wages. However, only Cambridge and Abigail knew his fictitious last name, or, so he thought. This could be bad.

The clerk returned with a letter and to his surprise, it was from Cambridge.

Jonathan snatched up the envelope and raced home to Hoxton.

When he arrived at the flat, Abigail was gone. Blast! As he had promised to open any mail from Cambridge in her presence, he would have to wait. He collapsed on the floor in frustration then leaned on his side, and swished the letter around on the dusty floor with his index finger. Having an idea, he held the envelope up to the window to see if he could read through it. No such luck.

Just as he was about to give in to temptation, Abigail swept into the room dressed like a proper lady. Her blonde curls were loosely pinned up in a bun, and wisps of hair draped over her ears. He'd never seen her in white satin gloves before, and the white laced, high-necked, lilac Gibson dress made her look like one of those drawings of advertisement girls selling various products. Her pink lips glistened as she stood in the sunlight, and her eyes sparkled. Jonathan couldn't help but stare.

"You look different," he sat up. "Where were you?"

"Different? Is that good or bad?"

"Neither really, but look!" Jonathan held up the letter.

107

"What does it say?" she asked, joining him on the ground.

Jonathan quickly tore back the top flap, and pulled out the folded-up paper.

"Dear Mr. Hopkins,

We received your application to Trinity school at Cambridge for the coming Lent term of '03, along with your entrance examination. Standard school policy dictates that we do not accept first-year students except during Michaelmas term. We prefer to keep our scholars on yearly attendance to accommodate for lodgings, classes, and expenses. Only in extreme instances or out of necessity, do we deviate from that policy. Additionally, though you passed your examination, your score was slightly below the average percentile for acceptance to this college."

Jonathan and Abigail's faces fell. They could see where this was heading. "At least I passed," Jonathan shrugged, trying to hide his disappointment.

"However, due to a recent vacancy in Lent term for a first year, we shall allow for this singular exception. Due to your excellent and thought-provoking essays, and your offer to remain at the school and take additional courses for Easter term, we would like to inform you of our decision to accept you for the coming Lent term. You will be housing in Master's Lodge under partial scholarship. Further information concerning your state room assignment and class schedule shall follow.

Sincerely Yours,

Ernest Shelley, Admissions Tutor. "

Abigail squeezed Jonathan in a hug. "Oh Johnny, that is wonderful news!"

Jonathan started at the letter in disbelief. "I was accepted..."

"We must start preparing then," Abigail jumped up and smoothed out her skirt, "change your appearance, find you some nicer clothes... and maybe a wig again?"

Jonathan stood, then paced the room. "No, a wig is cumbersome, and too easily removed, as I learned at Scotland Yard. Dying it would be preferable."

"One of our patrons is a barber and works with dyes! I could acquire some for a trade."

Jonathan paused. "You conveniently have quite a few patrons with useful occupations to me. Could it possibly be that..."?

Abigail laughed. "I know what you are getting at, but I am not that kind of girl." She clasped her hands together with a smile. "But on the matter of occupations, I got a job today! How grand that letter arrived this afternoon!"

"Ah! You have given up the patter song for the aria? I have overheard you singing in the water closet."

"No, something completely different. And don't be so nosy! It is an assistant position to the housekeeper of a very prestigious man."

"Who, the prime minister?"

Abigail stuck out her tongue. "I wouldn't work for Arthur Balfour for the crown jewels."

"Who then? And how did you manage out of your contract with Mr. Ball?"

"Oh, well..." she removed her white travel gloves, then slid them in her top dresser drawer. "...it has been settled, not to worry. But I am working for a man of even *more* importance."

"King Edward?"

She turned towards him. "More important as far as *you* are concerned."

"It wouldn't be Sherlock Holmes would it?"

"No! Ha! His brother!"

Jonathan gasped. "Mycroft Holmes!?"

"I thought he would know about your parents, so said I was 'looking round the neighborhood' for a housekeeping position. It just so happened that his housekeeper's current help is leaving to be married. After a short talk, I was told to start the second week of the New Year."

"He will check your references Abby! This will never work."

Abigail unpinned her hair, and shook it out. "I already knew that. I created a story, just like you. Some of the hall's patrons and 'ladies' helped with that," she winked.

Jonathan smiled. "Do be careful though, Mycroft is even more astute than his brother."

Abigail brushed back her hair, and re-centered the faux diamond brooch pinned to her dress' neck. "While you're away, I can ring you up once a week, same day and time. There is a wooden kiosk a few streets from Mycroft's in Pall Mall. It is one of those with a coinbox, not an attendant, so I can make a three-minute call for a tuppence. I am off duty by six, so 7 o'clock?"

"I do hope that will coincide with my classes. Let us say Wednesday evenings, and I shall write you in ciphers should that time or day not be convenient."

Abigail paused. "Sorry I am so stupid, but what is a cipher?"

"It is writing in such a manner that would appear incomprehensible to anyone but the recipient." Abigail stared at him blankly. "Do not worry," he laughed. "I will devise an easy enough system that you can translate. Where should I address the letter? Even if in code, we must be secretive."

"The Farkle house. Old lady rarely retrieves her mail, as she cannot walk that good. This is exciting, I feel like a Prussian spy!"

The month of December was cold, bitter cold, and the fireplace in the common area of Abigail and Jonathan's rooms afforded little warmth to the other rooms. Jonathan saved his tips to purchase two used blankets, but found their usefulness negligible.

He missed the house in Merton, and even the Eatons to a certain extent. In his old life, he had warmth, delicious food to eat, a lovely home to live in, and occasionally, he could talk with Francis' friends and engage in more adult and worthwhile conversations, about literature or philosophy. Here, he could never stay warm, was forced to consume the cheapest and least appealing foods he could afford, and over half the people he knew couldn't even read. It was beginning to wear on him.

As Christmas approached, his melancholy grew worse. It would be his first year without the family he had known all his life, and real or not, and he debated returning to them.

After playing piano one evening for a rather rowdy group of drunken reprobates, Jonathan stormed backstage and threw his bowler hat and white gloves to the floor.

Abigail pushed through the curtain after him. "What's the matter Jonathan?"

He angrily struggled to untie his black bowtie, then giving up, he began unbuttoning his waistcoat. "I want to go home."

"Home?"

"To the Eatons. I cannot live like this anymore. I am cold, hungry, and am tired of being surrounded by putrid vermin!" He undid the last button then threw the waistcoat against the wall, "It will be my first Christmas away, and I feel wretched about it."

"Jonathan, you are a month away from Cambridge. You have worked so hard!"

"I am thirteen Abby! I should not even be *attending* college yet! What was I thinking?"

Abigail looked around nervously. "Keep your voice down, and you *did* pass the examination."

"I can handle the work, I am just... scared. I will be alone, and in an unfamiliar location."

Abigail picked his gloves from the floor and brushed them off. "Was that not what happened when you came here? And do you not want to find out about your mother?"

"A mysterious box that 'might' have some information of value... it's a needle in a haystack." Jonathan dropped to his knees, then face-planted onto a pile of sandbags.

Abigail tossed his gloves back to the ground. "Then go to the Eatons! It certainly will not be the same!"

"Why care if it is?" said the sandbag, "Many people have been adopted. *Their* opinion of me has not changed."

"So you want things as they were? Where you hated your adopted family, your school... That is better? Have you forgot why you left?"

Jonathan rolled over and absent-mindedly began to toy with a rope that hung from the curtain next to him. "I wasn't thinking rationally at the time, but now I have done." He rose to his feet. "I was angry, and acted in haste."

"You will never find anything about your real mother if you go back," Abigail shook her blonde curls, "but perhaps, it no longer matters to you."

Jonathan sighed, picked up his gloves and waistcoat, then placed the bowler on top his head. He pulled it down over his eyes. "Say there *is* nothing else Abigail?"

"This is your one chance Jonathan. Go to Cambridge. If you hate it, then return to Merton. But at least try," Abigail said, lifting the hat from his eyes and smiling warmly, "you owe it to yourself, and you owe it to me."

Jonathan knew what she meant. He nodded. "How long of a period have I to wait?"

"Let's not pick a date, just see how you fare. If you truly feel it is a waste of time, then you can crawl back and turn yourself in to Francis Eaton," she finished, pushing the hat back over his eyes.

"You needn't say it like that," Jonathan adjusted his bowler.

"And as for Christmas, Mr. Ball invited us to a party at the house of his friend, Charlie. I had hoped that you would go with me."

Jonathan sighed. "One Christmas away will not be my demise."

Mr. Ball's friend Charlie resided in Camden Town, which was a more respectable area than Hoxton.

"Wonder what this Charlie chap is like?" Jonathan asked, as they walked up to the front door and banged on the brass lion's head doorknocker. He shivered as a gust of wind whipped across his face.

A heavyset young woman answered the door.

"We were invited by Mr. Ball," Abigail announced, "we work at..."

"Oh, Jonathan and Abigail!" the woman cried, as she flung open the door. "Do come in and 'ave a bit of warm! Just make yourselves at 'ome!"

The house was small, and modestly decorated. Gone were the extravagant gowns and three-piece gentlemen's suits of parties past that Jonathan was accustomed to. Instead, the guests wore patched up jackets, hand me down frocks, and penny store bonnets. He likened it to visiting the family of Bob Cratchit from Dickens' *A Christmas Carol.*

A tall, handsome evergreen tree stood in the center of the sitting room, and the decorations consisted of strands of silver tinsel, popped corn, and bayberry candles. As Jonathan stood admiring its beauty, someone clapped him on the shoulder.

"Afternoon you two!" Mr. Ball said. "Let me introduce you to my mate, Charlie!" He walked Abigail and Jonathan over to a young, broad-shouldered man, who was already engaged in conversation with another couple.

"Charlie!" Mr. Ball pushed towards him, "this 'ere is Amber... I mean Abigail, and Jonathan. Sorry Abby, I gets so used to the stage aliases. Jonathan, meet me chum, Charlie Wiggins!"

Jonathan gulped. Wiggins? He then shook his head, throwing out the idea that this 'Wiggins' was the notorious leader of the Baker Street Irregulars who worked with Sherlock Holmes. As Dr. Watson had never mentioned his given name in the stories, it could have been anything, and most likely *not* Charlie.

Wiggins held out a calloused hand to shake Jonathan's. "Good to meet cha. Come 'ave somethin' to eat. Lots o' things to go 'round," he invited with a thick cockney accent.

"What is your line of business, sir?" Jonathan asked, hoping to dispel his fears.

Wiggins laughed and slapped his knee. "Line of business?! A real gentle isn't 'e?" he punched Mr. Ball in the shoulder. "I works at 'ay's Wharf in Tooley Street, son. Supervisin' and things o' that kind. Ya see, I grew up much like yerselves in the East End, but a good bloke took charity on me and me gang, and 'elped with buying up a good enough education to be more than just the 'common layman', as 'e always said. 'haps you could move up like too, if ya work's good."

Jonathan took a deep breath. "That... was very kind of him. Do you... stay in touch with your generous benefactor?"

"My, my, such words 'e uses," Wiggins elbowed Mr. Ball. "This one's out fer a good future, think you?"

"'e's a good kid Chuck. Soon e'll be off to a grand future, to be sure," Mr. Ball winked at Abigail.

Jonathan puzzled over this comment. He couldn't believe that Abigail would tell Mr. Ball he was going to college, so assumed it was something else.

"To answer yer question boy, no," Wiggins shook his head. "Lost contact when 'e disappeared for several years."

Jonathan spoke slowly to hide the panic in his voice. "Disappeared you say?"

"'e was this detective, best in London, but they said 'e died. Then 'e came back. Strange it was," Wiggins shrugged. "Course, always was a strange bloke 'e was! But 'e did me a good turn and should I see 'im again, I'd do anything 'e asked. Other fellow didn't care for us much though, 'dirty little scoundrels' indeed!"

Jonathan's eyes went wide, but before he could comment, Abigail took his arm. "I think we'll get something to drink. Have you any nog?"

"Ask me wife Lucy," Wiggins said, but then he stared long and hard at Jonathan. "You look familiar-like... do I know you?"

"Nice to meet you Mr. Wiggins," Abigail nodded as she quickly dragged Jonathan away. "Thank you for having us!" Once they were out of earshot, Abigail whispered, "He knows Sherlock Holmes? How does..."

"Shhh!" Jonathan frantically waved his hands. "This chap Wiggins is one and the same who served him for years. He was part of a gang called the Baker Street Irregulars. He used them on cases and always rewarded them handsomely. 'Dirty little scoundrels'... ugh. That's what Dr. Watson called them."

"Does he know about you?" Abigail asked. "He certainly was giving you a once-over."

"I believe so, but everyone was told I died, as far as I know."

"Then do not worry and have a good time," Abigail petted his hair. "Just don't talk so good."

"Talk so well."

"And *stop* that!"

CHAPTER 10

UNIVERSITY BOUND

The second week of January came swiftly, and it was time for Jonathan's departure to Cambridge. He gulped as he stood on the platform at Kings Cross Station, with his suitcase in hand, satchel draped over his shoulder, and butterflies in his stomach.

Abigail stood across from him, her hands clasped in front of her. "I shall miss you Jonathan. Be safe, and be careful."

"I will. Does the brown come off well?" he asked, stroking his dyed hair, "look alright?"

"You make a fine brunette," Abigail winked.

"Good luck with Mycroft."

"Good luck with finding your mother, or... about her that is."

Jonathan nodded nervously.

"You will be fine! Remember what we agreed to?"

"If I hate it..." A loud whistle suddenly blew as a warning. "My train's about to leave."

"Then go, Jonathan."

With a quick nod, he skipped up the train's metal staircase, moved down the main aisle, and plopped down in a window seat. He looked through the glass, and saw Abigail mouth something as she waved her hand. He pulled open the window, and heard her say,

"...be careful of those university boys, I hear they can be quite rough to new students!"

"I shall!" he waved.

Abigail sniffed sadly. "Don't forget about me, Johnny..."

Once he arrived at Cambridge, Jonathan anxiously crossed through King's Gateway to the Great Court, the main part of Trinity's campus, and looked around for any instructional signs. A pasted-up notice on a stone wall read, 'campus tours for new transfer students' and showed an arrow pointing north. Though he wasn't a transfer student, he *was* new, so followed the arrows and stopped in front of the admissions building where a group of boys were already gathered to be shown about the grounds. A lanky man with thick whiskers and peppered hair stood at the top of the staircase. He impatiently tapped on his pocket watch.

"Right then," the man said shortly, "three o'clock sharp, time for the next travel round, no time for stragglers." He walked down the steps and gestured for the crowd to follow. "This way please." He paused as he came upon Jonathan, and eyed him carefully. "Are you a *new* student here, boy?"

"Yes, sir," Jonathan nodded, "though I am not a transfer student, I am a first year."

The man raised an eyebrow in surprise. "That cannot be right. Where are your papers?"

Jonathan pulled his acceptance letter from his satchel and handed it to the man.

120

"Ah, Jonathan Hopkins. We were impressed with you, for a Canadian. Our rare exception to the rule," the man said. "A pleasure to show you about. Professor Nolan, drawing instructor," he shook Jonathan's hand.

Professor Nolan took them around campus through the Main Court, Queen's Tower, and King's Passage. As they approached the dormitories, he pointed to a long row of rooms covered in ivy.

"This is the Master's Lodge, typically reserved for the Royal Family. King Edward VII roomed there, as did his son, Prince Albert Victor, who was a student here in the mid-1880's. The staterooms are now open to undergraduates under scholarship, which I believe includes you, Mr. Hopkins," he looked over at Jonathan.

Jonathan completely missed his new name.

"Jonathan?" Mr. Nolan asked again.

Realizing he was being addressed, Jonathan nodded sheepishly. "Yes sir. That is where I was assigned."

"Quite good. Adjacent is King's Chapel, and over here we have the Great Court, and there in the centre is Queen's Tower where you'll see a statue of Queen Mary. Through that quadrangle is the dining hall. In the kitchen they cook for seven hundred persons so I advise arriving early if you want seconds. Now over there is Neville's Court, named for a master of the college who died in 1615. You will also find the library built by Christopher Wren in 1676..."

Jonathan's attention immediately shifted to the library.

"...it contains Newton's telescope and some of his manuscripts. We have over one hundred thousand volumes and two thousand manuscripts at present."

"Pardon me, Professor Nolan," Jonathan said, "but in the library, are we at liberty to research others that graduated from Cambridge? Out of historical curiosity?"

"Of course! Anyone who finished from one of our colleges, including our Prime Minister Arthur Balfour, we have records of," he said proudly, "they date all the way back to its establishment in 1546 by Henry VIII. Sir Isaac Newton, Bacon, Byron, Dryden, Thackeray, Tennyson..."

"Tennyson?"

"Alfred Lord Tennyson? Surely you have heard of him?"

"Of course," Jonathan grinned stupidly.

After settling into his new room, which thankfully, was a double he had to himself, as the other fellow had dropped out, Jonathan visited the main campus library to search through the alumni records. He pulled the year 1887 for both Newnham and Girton, and flipped through the pages until he found the name, Scarlett Tennyson.

"Library closing in five minutes!" he heard someone call.

Bugger! He hurriedly scribbled the information down in his notebook, shoved it in his satchel, then dashed to the small wooden hut phone kiosk for his chat with Abigail, as it was already 7 o'clock.

"My mother went to Newnham College," he said through the telephone receiver, "I found her, Abby! I will try to go through the other lists of alumni when next I have a chance, but in the meantime, I shall continue the hunt for my mother's box near the Newnham college buildings."

"Brilliant Jonathan!" Abigail said excitedly.

Jonathan eyed his pocket watch. "I have to go. Orientation is this evening."

"Good luck then, I will speak to you next week!"

CHAPTER 11

NEWNHAM NEWS

Jonathan returned to the main library on Thursday to search for records of students at Newnham. After finding what he was looking for in the lower library, he thumbed through the pages. There were several columns of names for women in each field of study who were present in 1887. He scrolled down the list until he came to 'Scarlett Tennyson' in the Natural Sciences Tripos and Law of England studies, but there was no other information available other than her name.

He thumped his head on the book, frustrated with himself. Why would he expect to find anything more? Did he believe he'd find her address, or letters of some sort, or a picture? He clearly wasn't being realistic with what he hoped to find.

Irritated, he headed towards the door but then stopped in front of a large bulletin board on the wall to read the various pages pinned up. Some concerned upcoming events, or rooms for rent, but the one he was most intrigued by, was the one labeled, 'Cambridge Alumni Association', for at the bottom of the page, it read...

"For further alumni information, please contact Edith Marian Leahy, class of '87, Newnham."

There was a floor number and building listed, so Jonathan jotted it down in his notebook, then raced out the door.

As he burst into the Admissions Building, he slid his finger across the directory board, looking for Edith Leahy. He groaned when he saw her office number. 221. He *hated* that number. He sighed, then trudged up the flight of stairs in the middle of the marble foyer, and turned left towards her office. Luckily, the door was open, and the faint clickity-clack of a typewriter could be heard coming from inside.

"Hello?" Jonathan knocked.

"Oh yes, please do come in!" came a woman's voice.

Jonathan timidly stepped through the doorway.

A bronze plaque that read 'Edith M. Leahy' sat on a mahogany desk cluttered with papers. The woman behind the desk wore wire-rimmed glasses too large for her face, and her pinned up brown hair was already showing strands of grey. She wasn't old, but wore a matronly high-collared black dress, and apparently spent years neglecting her appearance. Her fingernails were bitten down to the cuticle, and her lips were chapped and dry.

"Miss, Mrs., Leahy?"

"It is still 'Miss,' sadly. How can I help you, young man?" she asked in a soft lilting voice.

"I am very sorry to bother you Miss Leahy, but I wanted to ask you about a former girl from Newnham. The alumni flier in the library said to consult you for information on previous students."

She studied him suspiciously. "Are you *currently* a student here?"

"Yes, at Trinity."

"You seem young, even for a first year."

"I graduated secondary school early. I have my class schedule if..."

"Well then, you must be a very sharp lad," she said brightly. "What year at Newnham?"

"1887, and the name of the woman is Scarlett Tennyson."

Edith paused. "Scarlett Tennyson? She was in my graduating class. Now who might you be, asking about her?"

Jonathan gulped. He prayed that Edith did not know Scarlett was dead, or this meeting could go horribly wrong.

"She's my mother, and for her birthday I am putting together a book about her life thus far, with additional pages to add to later. Trouble is, I have nothing from her college years."

Edith frowned.

Jonathan held his breath.

"Well," Edith laughed, "how convenient you're attending the same school to get that kind of information. Goodness, I was not aware she had a son, let alone was married, but then, I have not spoken to her since we all left college. I always meant to find her for the alumni records, but she never responded to any of my letters. We were friendly enough in college mind you, but never as close as she had been with Bertha and Elizabeth."

"Bertha and Elizabeth ma'am?"

"Bertha Whalley and Elizabeth Jackson."

Jonathan's eyes went wide, could it be? "Any relation to *Celeste* Whalley?"

"Is that what she's going by now? I will have to update my records then. She always said she would change her name, as she thought Bertha was dreadful, though I am surprised she hadn't corrected me when she reviewed her updated contact information."

Jonathan was now very intrigued. "Bertha was in your class as well?"

"Yes well, she was your mother's roommate, and we all shared a common room. Surely she has mentioned that?"

"I... cannot say as I have ever asked her," Jonathan smiled, while underneath he was fuming. If Celeste were her roommate in college, then she *must* know more than she had let on.

"Scarlett and she were very close. They had been so long before college, but perhaps they are not now?"

Jonathan desperately tried to mask his growing anger. "They have not seen each other in 12 years."

"Things change, people change, I suppose. Well then, what exactly are you looking for?"

"Anything I could add to my book."

Edith removed her glasses and rubbed her right eye. She then took a beige cloth from atop her desk, wiped both lenses, then replaced the glasses to her face. "I am afraid I cannot help you there, as I said, we weren't that close."

Jonathan could see this would take further questioning. "Do you... happen to have any pictures or documents from that time?"

Edith tapped her chin and hummed. "I do have our major's class photo from that year. I could have a duplicate copy made if you would like that."

"Thank you!"

Edith moved over to a large wooden filing cabinet, and slid out a long drawer packed full with folders, each with a different year labeled on the faded white tab.

Jonathan glanced around the room. It very sparse in terms of decoration or furniture. A Union Jack Flag and a few framed photographs of alumni from different years adorned the wall closest to the door. A small tea tray rested in front of several large bookcases and filing cabinets pushed against the right wall, and other than the desk and chair positioned in the center, the room was otherwise empty. A quill pen rested on the far right of her desk, and ink spots had dripped onto a piece of a paper that appeared to contain stanzas of poetry. Upon analyzing the handwriting of various other notes scattered across her desk, she had obviously written the prose herself. Words like 'love' 'infatuation' and 'blind amorous faith' leapt out at him.

Various lunch wrappers were discarded in the dustbin, indicating that she worked through lunch, and often. Her boots were lightly covered with white and brown cat hairs and small claw marks. She must have more than one animal for the white hairs were longer than the brown. She seemed lonely.

After a few minutes of shuffling through the filing cabinet, Edith handed Jonathan an old photograph.

"This was everyone in our major that year. The classes were still rather small back then. Less than one hundred students in the entire school." She then pointed to a beautiful woman in the first row with dark hair and fair skin. "That girl there is your mother. She was always the most handsome of our class. It was no wonder she had so many men calling."

Jonathan blinked. This was news. "Really? Did she have many relationships?"

"Oh no, Scarlett was not like that. She never even attended any of the dances, always preferred to stay back in the residence hall. There was only one suitor she responded favourably to that I was aware of. Someone she called Jack, and he apparently called her 'Bean', some sort of silly *Jack and the Beanstalk* reference, but none of us ever met him. It was rumored that he was The Prince, but as we never saw her with anyone, some of us believed she made the entire thing up simply to chase away the other men! She was always a very private woman, your mother. I assume she has not changed?"

"She never tells me anything." Jonathan's mind was running wild with this information. She had no idea the pure gold she was giving him. He wanted to bolt back to London, but had to see if she knew anything more.

"She would get letters from him, but before we graduated they stopped. We all thought she was writing them herself."

"Do you know what happened to those letters?"

"She had always kept them in her trinket box, but who can say now? I would assume she had thrown them away or burned them. I cannot imagine she'd keep such things as a married woman."

129

"Trinket box? You mean the one she lost here at Cambridge?"

"She lost it?"

"Do you remember what it looked like?"

"Oh goodness, it was so many years ago and I only saw it a few times. I believe it was a dark wooden box with a bird motif carving on top but I could be mistaken."

"Did you ever see the contents of those letters from Jack?"

"Of course not! But Elizabeth Jackson did, which is how we knew about the 'Dear Bean' greeting." Edith shook her head. "I should probably not be telling you this, but I suppose it doesn't matter now, considering what happened."

"Happened, Miss Leahy?"

"Elizabeth was always getting herself into messes she had no business being in. She liked to put the cat among the pigeons. I suspect that is why she was murdered."

Jonathan gasped in shock, but bit his tongue. Things were getting interesting.

"She was murdered? When?"

Edith pursed her lips in an effort to remember something from years ago. "Sometime in June of '89. I cannot remember the exact date. Beastly thing it was; they chopped her to bits. The pieces of her then washed up on the shore of the Thames. They had an awful time identifying her. No one ever knew the story, and the killer was never found. So very sad."

"Indeed," Jonathan nodded with a swallow. There was more to his mother's past than he had assumed.

"Now, if you come back in a week, I can give you the copy to put in your book. I wish I had more information for you. You might want to try Bertha, or... I suppose Celeste, for anything else. Have you any idea where to find her?"

Jonathan's seethed underneath his warm smile. "I have not the foggiest."

Edith moved over to a smaller filing cabinet filled with index cards, much like a library's card catalog, and pulled out the last drawer. She flipped through a few cards before pulling one out, and placed it on her desk. "I have her most recent home address, so can give you that." She copied the address onto the corner of a piece of paper, and ripped it from the page. "Though I wish you luck with her for she can be a bit coarse and rough around the edges." She handed Jonathan the scrap of paper, then crossed out 'Bertha' on the card, and replaced it with 'Celeste'. "I will see you in a week's time Mr...?"

"Jonathan," he replied, as he stuffed the address into his pocket. "And thank you. You have been of material assistance, Miss Leahy." He then took off like a steam engine and raced down the hallway.

"Wait, Jonathan!" he heard Edith shout, "What is your father's name?"

"Sherlock Holmes!" Jonathan called back, as he scurried down the steps.

Edith laughed. "Good one. You can tell me next week then lad."

Jonathan raced back to his room to pack. He was far too angry to think rationally, or even consider his classes and responsibilities. He had to go to London, today. Celeste had lied to him and he needed to know why.

CHAPTER 12

WHO IS JACK?

When Jonathan arrived at Scotland Yard he was informed by the receptionist that Celeste had already left for the day. As he slumped down the steps, he paused, then ripped the scrap of paper from his pocket, and read it over. *Celeste Whalley, 8 Mercer St, Camden Town, Westminster, London.*

Jonathan waited around the corner from Celeste's rooms. She arrived moments later carrying several parcels from the grocer's shop in her arms. As she walked up the front steps, Jonathan quickly stepped behind her and tapped her on the shoulder.

"Evening Miss Whalley, nice night, is it not?"

Celeste spun around, and nearly dropped her packages. "Jonathan! What in heaven's name are you doing here, and how did you know where I live?"

Jonathan stepped closer, and whispered, "The more important question is, who is *Jack*, Miss Whalley?"

"What?"

"My mother's previous relationship in college was with a man named Jack. Now do not pretend this is news to you, Miss Whalley, Miss *Bertha* Whalley, am I wrong?"

Her eyes widened. "How did you know *that?*"

Jonathan's cheeks puffed up with anger. "You lied to me!"

Celeste appeared flustered, then glared at him. "No, I did not! Listen here, Jonathan. Come inside if you wish to continue this conversation."

Her sitting room was small but cozy, and impeccably decorated. Gold fleur de lis adorned the robin's egg coloured sofa, settee, and armchair, and a beige oval rug was in the middle of the room. Sleek mahogany side tables and a sideboard gave it a very elegant and tasteful appearance.

Celeste dumped her parcels onto the dining table, turned on a few lamps, then dropped her Dorothy bag onto the Chippendale secretary desk next to the door. She flopped onto the sofa against the wall, and sighed. "*All* I know of her former lover was that she *called* him 'Jack', but that was *not* his real name. She created it so he wasn't some nameless phantom, do you understand? That is why I did not tell you."

Jonathan ripped the red scarf from around his neck and threw it to the floor. "You expect me to believe that? According to your college chum Edith, not only were you her best friend, you were her bloody roommate!"

"And you think that granted me access into every aspect of her life? She always liked her privacy."

Jonathan began to pace. Celeste tugged off her leather gloves in irritation, and threw them onto the secretary desk.

"*No one* really knew who he was, Jonathan."

Jonathan walked to the fireplace, and paused. "Edith mentioned that this 'Jack' was rumored to be The Prince."

Celeste shook her head. "She would not have got involved in something so scandalous. Additionally, she liked older men. Albert Victor was younger than she. Besides, he was only at Cambridge for a year, and was at Trinity. The probability of them running into each at all is infinitely small." Celeste stood, then removed her long brown suede jacket and feathered hat, and hung them on the brass coat rack by the door. The dress she was wearing underneath was a pastel pink traveling dress, with white buttons and lace around the sleeves and collar. It seemed like an odd wardrobe choice for her, almost as if she was a different person today.

"What was in that box of hers, and why the Jack and the Beanstalk reference?" Jonathan asked.

Celeste paused. "What do you mean? And I don't know anything about the contents of the letterbox. It was always locked."

"She kept his letters in the box. He was Jack, she was Bean."

"How the bloody hell would I know that?!"

"Edith knew. How would you not?"

"Edith and I were not friendly, Jonathan. We shared rooms, that is all."

"Did it not strike you that there might be a correlation if Holmes was asking for all the case files on 'Jack' the Ripper, and also the whereabouts of her mysterious box?"

Celeste sighed. "Watson said Moriarty..."

"Hang Watson and hang Holmes! You *said* the Moriarty bit did not seem plausible. Someone who *knew* she was Holmes' wife killed her." Jonathan rubbed his hands through his hair, then chuckled in frustration. "No wonder Holmes finds the Yard so useless..." he then dropped into the blue armchair like a marionette, his body limp and exhausted.

Celeste huffed then walked into the kitchen that was adjacent to the living room, and placed a ceramic white and blue teakettle on the cooker. "You have your mother's temper as well I see," she snapped, "the few who knew of your parents' relationship were me, Watson, Mary, Mrs. Hudson, and Wiggins. Mary's dead, Mrs. Hudson is trustworthy, and Wiggins..."

Jonathan picked up his scarf from the floor and distractedly wound it around in his hands. "I met Wiggins a month ago. I sensed nothing vicious, save for his loyalty to Holmes." He leaned forward. "And before you ask, he most certainly assumes I am deceased, so never made the connection as to who I am."

Celeste shook her head then grabbed a match from atop the cooker with her left hand, struck it, then lit the burner underneath the teakettle. "Reading me already. I hated it when your father did that," she blew out the match, then threw it in the dustbin. "I know you want answers Jonathan, but you cannot create outlandish theories just to fill the holes in your life."

"But *if* no one else knew, how did Moriarty?"

Celeste wearily sat down on the sofa. "You may as well throw it up and be done with it, Jonathan, just as we all have."

"There are still unanswered questions, Celeste. Why didn't Holmes come back for me? What is he hiding? Why was Elizabeth Jackson murdered?"

Celeste stared at him blankly. "Edith told you about that? She was not a victim of the ripper, Jonathan, Elizabeth's death was categorized with the 'Whitehall Mysteries', a separate issue and unrelated. Inspector Turnbridge said it was of a different origin than the Whitechapel murders, so it was dismissed. What reason would 'Jack' have for killing Elizabeth?"

Jonathan rose up and again began to pace, but this time in a circle.

"Must you do that?"

"It helps me think. Seeing as how she'd read my mother's letters, perhaps she saw something in them that was compromising, maybe she knew something awful."

Celeste returned to the kitchen and reached up for two white and gold flowered teacups from inside the teak cupboard on the right. "How do you know she saw them?"

"Edith mentioned that Elizabeth had accessed them, hence knowing about 'Bean'. What if she had stolen a letter or two as blackmail if he *was* The Prince?"

Celeste's face paled, and the teacups rattled as she set them atop the cooker. "Elizabeth made an appointment with me at the Yard in '89. Said she had some evidence she thought we might be interested in, letters of some sort... Dear God..."

"Did you ever see those letters?"

137

"No."

"Probably best you did not, or you might be dead too."

"But why?"

Jonathan hung his head and shook it. He was completely bewildered by her lack of insight. "So even then, you did not see any connection between what she wanted to give you, and her death?"

Celeste slid a tin canister of Twining's Earl Grey across the countertop, and popped open the lid. "I did assume, but I had no proof," she said, as she scooped out the loose-leaf tea into a metal strainer, then placed it to the side. "But I never imagined it had anything to do with Scarlett or college. Your mother said she burned those letters."

Jonathan rested his cheek against the back of the chair, and closed his eyes. "Was my mother still close to Elizabeth?"

"After Elizabeth married and divorced that intelligence-of-a-turnip Franklin Edwards, she spent most of her life in opium dens. Your mother refused to have any part of that world, so they had a falling out."

"And what about you?"

"There was a sort of unspoken competition between us over Scarlett, as if we each wished her to be our friend to the exclusion of the other. But honestly Jonathan, those letters could have been about anything..."

"Then why would someone kill *and* completely dismember Elizabeth for them? Why approach Scotland Yard, but not the police?" Jonathan lifted his head, and just then noticed a framed picture of

Celeste with another girl hanging over the sofa. "Who is that?" he pointed.

"My older sister, Amy," Celeste stepped over, "but she and I are not terribly partial to one another, so we rarely speak."

"And that is my point with Elizabeth. Why would she *specifically* go to you, if you were not that close?"

Jonathan then shivered, and rubbed his hands to warm them. He sat down in the armchair and lifted his knees to his chest.

"....oh dear. Now you do have me wondering..." Celeste mused. "Tea will be ready in a moment, but are you cold?"

Jonathan nodded, then played with the tassels on his scarf that was draped across the chair. "They did not want her identified Celeste. Can you not see that?"

Celeste grabbed several fresh logs from next to the fireplace, and threw them on top of the blackened ones. She crumpled up some newspaper prints, and grabbed a bundle of twigs that were sitting near the hearth, then lit a match, and tossed it under the newspaper.

"If, Elizabeth had those letters, why would Scarlett's former lover pursue her for them?" Celeste asked, as she knelt down and blew on the smoking newspaper.

"Maybe he didn't know she had them until he was being blackmailed?"

Celeste lit another match, threw it into the fireplace, then jabbed the logs with the fire poker. "But why wait two years, and where does Jack the Ripper fit in?"

"Remember those letters the Yard received from the Ripper? Suppose he killed someone, or several someones, wrote nice little letters to Scotland Yard, and never thought anyone would be able to prove it was he. But, perhaps, he had written something to my mother that could possibly incriminate him? Maybe said something that hinted at darker emotions, or showed symptoms of psychosis? If he requested that she burn those letters that could have linked him to the murders in any way, but then discovered that they were still in existence, that would be a bit of a problem, would it not?"

"Outside of Elizabeth, Scarlett had no connection to any of those women," Celeste said, as tendrils of flames leapt higher and higher in the fireplace.

"Maybe he was biding his time, practicing, before he killed my mother. Maybe he was jealous, maybe she did something horrible to him, maybe he felt she deserved to die..."

Celeste thrust the poker deep into the burning logs causing sparks to spew out around the hearth.

Jonathan ducked down to avoid them.

"I don't *know!*" Celeste screamed, as the fire raged behind her, and the teakettle began to whistle loudly. She tossed the poker to the floor. "Why are you making me relive this?" she sobbed, her face illuminated by the now blazing firelight.

Jonathan leapt from the armchair and turned off the cooker's burner to quiet the kettle. "I have spent years of my life not knowing who my real parents were and now, I damn well want to know why!"

Celeste buried her face in her hands.

Jonathan sighed. "I am sorry I upset you."

Celeste lifted her head and wiped her eyes. "Are not the truths you've found thus far painful enough?"

"How much worse can it get?" he laughed lightly. "If I uncover the truth, I could conceivably piece my life together, so there is some semblance of coherency. May I see those files?"

Celeste stood, then dusted the soot from her skirt. "On Jack the Ripper?"

"*And* the supposed Whitehall Mysteries, yes. Aren't you even a bit curious?"

Celeste gave a slight nod, then returned to her teakettle. "I still say the Ripper is a throw-out," she said, as she steeped the tea, "she had not been involved with 'Jack' for three years."

Jonathan rubbed his temples, then gasped. "Was not Prince Albert Victor engaged to be married in 1891? To Princess May of Teck?" Celeste nodded. "And was not my mother killed in 1891?" Celeste nodded again, but more slowly. "Perhaps he had to kill her before he was married. There was talk that The Prince was... 'unwell' before he died in '92. You see, it fits!"

"But if Albert Victor died in '92, why keep you hidden?"

Jonathan sat on the settee and rested his chin on his knuckles. "I... do not have a hypothesis for that yet."

Celeste poured the steaming tea into both teacups. She grabbed some milk from the ice chest and added it to the tea, then dropped two lumps of sugar into hers. "Sugar, Jonathan?"

Jonathan shook his head, then nodded a thank you as she handed him the teacup. "Please, may I see them?"

Celeste played with handle of her teacup. "You are wrong, but yet, I cannot help but wonder. Tomorrow. Early, at six. You must tell *no one*. Or I will lose my job *and* go to prison."

Jonathan visited Abigail for the night and related *pieces* of the last few days to her. She asked him to meet her for breakfast at the Red Lion Pub after his meeting with Celeste, as she had a surprise for him.

The next morning, Friday the 23rd, Jonathan met Celeste at Scotland Yard and as promised, she presented him with the infamous files on Jack the Ripper and the Whitehall Mysteries.

He opened the one labeled, 'Jack the Ripper', but then violently flipped it shut. The first images inside the file were of the mutilated murder victims. He carefully re-opened it, purposely avoiding any photographs, and found pages and pages of notes. It was overwhelming. "I could not possibly get through this in the next hour."

Celeste rubbed her upper arms nervously. "If you *swear* to have them returned by end of day, you may take them. If you think these murders are by the same man, and he also killed your mother, then Prince or not, I am willing to chance it." She put her hand to her forehead. "I cannot believe that I am enlisting the aid of a thirteen-year-old child to solve a twelve-year-old mystery!"

"I am not your average child," Jonathan said defensively, "as I do not know many who are accepted into Cambridge."

Celeste stared at him in shock. "*That* is where you are?"

"Oh, yes... well I suppose we have to agree to trust each other. I enrolled last semester."

"That explains how you spoke to Edith. Well congratulations! Though given your heredity, I should not be surprised. Where are you staying while down here?"

Jonathan smiled. "I have a friend, best friend in fact, Abigail. I am staying with her. She's what prompted me to begin this entire investigation."

"Then she is a good friend."

"Oh, and one other question. What was your college room number at Newnham?"

"29 in North Hall, why?"

"Because any detail could be important," Jonathan stuffed the files into his satchel. "I will have these back by mid afternoon."

Celeste shook his hand. "Good luck, Jonathan."

CHAPTER 13

AN UNEXPECTED GIFT

Jonathan headed towards the Red Lion Pub off St. James Street in Blackfriars. After walking through the black timber frontage, he selected a table in the far-right corner near the fireplace, facing away from the door. Every now and then, he would turn to peer through the stained-glass windows, looking for Abigail. As he absent-mindedly twirled a fork that had been left on the table, he felt a slight tap on his shoulder.

"Are you old enough to be in here boy?" came a deep voice.

He spun around. It was Abigail. "You scared the trousers off me!"

Abigail laughed as she sat down across from him, her white maid's apron poking out from underneath her coat's black velvet lapels. "I have been practicing my male tenor; glad it came off proper." She placed an expensive looking mink hand muff down on the table, then fidgeted with something inside it.

"That a new muff?" Jonathan pointed.

"Oh this thing?" she looked up, "a present, from Mycroft."

Jonathan's mouth opened wide. "Are you sure you are *just* his housekeeper's maid?"

Abigail giggled then gave him a wry smile. "He's much too old for me."

"Oh, good then. Abby, I think I might be on to something, something big."

Abigail slid a large thick envelope from inside her muff, and passed it over to Jonathan.

"What is this?" he asked.

"It is your father's journal."

Jonathan gasped, and eyed the package as if it were made of gold. "He had a journal?"

"It was in Mycroft's office," Abigail whispered, looking around, "the folder was labeled, 'Sherlock's journal', so I assumed that's what it was."

Jonathan weighed the heavy packet in his hand. "Will Mycroft miss this?"

"The envelope appears to have been sealed shut for ages, so I do not think so. At least I hope not, or I will be sacked for sure!"

"Based on what I have unearthed to date, being sacked would be the least of your worries."

Abigail frowned. "What?"

"Oh, but do not fret! I will have this back as soon as possible. God, who knows what I will find in here," he gulped, as he stuffed the package into his satchel.

"Nothing too inappropriate I hope."

Jonathan jumped from his chair with excitement, threw on his topcoat, then draped his satchel over his left shoulder. "Oh Abigail, you are a fair treat! I have to return the files to Celeste before I catch my train, but we will talk on Wednesday."

"Are we not going to have breakfast?" Abigail asked disappointedly.

Jonathan paused. "Oh, food. Well, I do need to finish my notes on those files..."

Abigail looked at the floor. "You have not the money, have you?"

"No! That is not it in the least! I..."

"You do not need to pretend with me Jonathan. I am your friend." She reached back inside her muff, pulled out a pound note, and attempted to hand it to him. "I was given a raise recently, and it is certainly more than I need so..."

"Abby, no..." Jonathan shook his head.

"Just take it!" she snapped, "I will be offended if you don't."

Taken aback, Jonathan accepted the note and folded it into his pocket. "I will pay you back."

Abigail hugged him tightly. "I would do anything for you."

Jonathan awkwardly patted her on the back, a bit confused. "Thank you."

Once the Ripper files were safely returned to Celeste, Jonathan hopped on the first available train to Cambridge. He was frustrated. The files disclosed nothing he didn't already know, except that the killer was most certainly left-handed. The fact that entire pages and paragraphs had been blackened out certainly didn't help either. He had taken notes, so perhaps something would be revealed upon further securitization, but for now, it felt like a waste of time. He hoped Sherlock's journal would be more promising.

He sneaked up to the front luggage compartment, sat against the wall directly underneath a window, and positioned several large suitcases in front of him to remain hidden. There was still enough daylight to read by, so he lifted the seal, opened the package, and carefully slid out the leather-bound journal of Sherlock Holmes.

PART II: HOLMES' JOURNAL

CHAPTER 14

"WOMEN ARE NEVER TO BE ENTIRELY TRUSTED, NOT THE BEST OF THEM"

16th October 1887

Though I am not one to chronicle my life's adventures, save for minor details placed in my casebook, I find that with the absence of my faithful friend and biographer, I am required to pen such mundane and time-consuming notes myself. This will at least be a more straightforward and honest account of my journeys without the embellished and dramatized leeway of Watson's sketches.

Miss Scarlett Tennyson has been residing with me for several months now. She is surprisingly efficient, precise, and an extraordinarily quick study. She is a wealth of knowledge concerning culture, the arts, and history. She is also abominably stubborn.

Tennyson, as I prefer to address her, has seemingly little interest in the most common of activities for women, does not wish for children, and is altogether bored with idle chatter and gossip.

She is a woman of high breeding with a certain Pallas-like purity, and one cannot discredit her sense of fashion and charm. Though she is pleasant enough to her would-be suitors, she nonetheless expresses little curiosity in relationships or men in general. She is also a very private woman, and hides herself well.

She appears to have but one close friend, Miss Celeste Whalley, who is employed by Scotland Yard as an assistant. She sees her fairly regularly, and while I have met her but once and only briefly, it was enough time to formulate an appraisal of her personality. Miss Whalley, though dedicated to Tennyson as a friend, has an air of arrogance and demonstrates a rather cool disposition, one that is slightly off-putting. Perhaps that is one of the necessary qualifications for being a member of the Yard?

Normally, being allotted so much time and exposure to a person I would have acquired a more thorough understanding of her internal workings by now, yet there is much about Tennyson I find I cannot read, nor interpret. A temporary conundrum, of course.

She is fired by an unsentimental ambition to succeed and I see much potential. Though I am curious to observe her in action, I must allow more time before I am certain she is ready. When appropriate, I shall indeed have more words.

28th October 1887

Though it is impertinent to pass judgment without sufficient evidence, I tend to err on the side of caution when it concerns women.

I received a letter this afternoon. An engraved invitation from Buckingham Palace, addressed to myself. It read:

"The pleasure of your company and that of a guest is requested by her Majesty for the New Years Eve Masquerade Ball at Buckingham Palace on Monday December 31st, 1887.

Full evening or costume dress with mask is required. The night's events will commence at eight in the evening, and cease at midnight.

Please respond favourably by:

 December the first"

I examined the invitation and searched for any clues in the envelope or watermark, but found nothing to reveal the true objective behind its delivery. It seemed innocent enough, which is why I refused to trust it.

Not moments later, Tennyson entered the sitting room having just swept in from the door downstairs, dressed in her brown and white striped 'errand dress,' as she called it. She untied the black hat ribbons from underneath her chin, and pulled up the netting.

"Is that an invitation?" she asked, quickly eyeing the card in my hands as she removed her black satin hat, velvet cloak, and white pearled kid gloves.

She was no closer than six feet from where I stood, therefore her ability to interpret the paper's contents seemed extraordinary, and exceedingly unbelievable.

"Keenly observant of you, Tennyson," I smiled.

"Well, what is it for?" she asked, placing the hat and cloak on the wooden coat rack by the door.

I returned the invite to the envelope, and lightly tossed it to her. "Read it, if you are so curious."

"A New Year's Eve Masque Ball at the palace?!" she gasped, "How lovely! You do plan on attending, do you not?"

I smiled wryly. Her response seemed far too rehearsed. "Should I Tennyson?"

"It is an honour to be invited Holmes!"

"There is nothing privileged about a receiving a social invitation, and conversely, I would have to be in disguise. Who would know I attended?"

She threw back the card and moved towards the sideboard, which overflowed with untouched breads and teacakes. Mrs. Hudson would never learn.

"Masks are not all that concealing," she said, as she selected a bread knot from the tray, "you can still pick someone out if you are looking for them."

I raised an eyebrow. "May I assume that *you* would be looking for someone?"

"*I* was not invited," she bit into the bread.

"Let us suppose you presumed I would bring you, thus allowing you to not only attend, but also meet with this mystery someone with no one but myself knowing you were present. That could indeed prove beneficial, considering the implications."

She laughed as she attempted to chew on the bread.

I placed the invitation on the mantle next to the jackknifed letters of unanswered correspondence, and gave her a stern expression. "Then I am wrong?"

She swallowed, then sighed deeply. "Have I ever expressed interest in spending time with you socially? That is not part of our arrangement."

"The invitation specifically requires I bring a guest, who would undoubtedly have to be of the female sex. Are you aware of anyone else I could bring?"

"If you are so distrustful, then do not go. I simply would not expect another invitation from the palace, should you refuse." She dropped the reminder of her knot back to the tray.

I pointed to the bread. "You plan on leaving that there?"

"No, actually." She snatched it back up and placed it on the floor near a small hole in the wall. "I'll leave it for that little mouse that lives in the wall. There *were* two, though I believe his lodger has moved on."

"Then this invite was not an expected delivery?" I redirected the conversation.

She turned towards me and shrugged her shoulders. "You have me. I sent it."

She was playing the game well, but I would play it better. "Then one would only assume you desired to attend, therefore, I am asking you as my associate to join me, if you accept."

"I have not a thing to wear to such a party," she said, heading towards her room.

"In your entire wardrobe? The amount of frill and lace you brought in would lead me to suspect otherwise."

155

Tennyson spun on her heels. "Truth be told, I have always felt rather awkward at lavish parties."

"If you are declining, then I will not attend. I see no reason to engage in such pointless frivolities, nor do I wish to be subjected to the self-indulgent idleness of the higher classes if it can be avoided." I moved to sit in my basket chair, but then Tennyson touched the sleeve of my dressing gown.

"No, no, I... was not declining the offer. I could perhaps find something suitable to wear."

You just tipped your entire hand Tennyson. "Very well, but you must be made aware of one condition."

"Yes?"

"If you come with me, you leave with me."

Tennyson's jaw dropped open. "What type of woman do you think me Holmes?!"

"Perhaps you are ambitious. Finding a man of nobility as a suitor would benefit any young woman."

Her cheeks puffed out a bright red, and her eyes narrowed. "You think ill of me, *because* I am a woman."

"No, I am simply stating that temptations are manifest in this world, and one can easily be distracted by them, whether man, woman, or radish."

"If you are concerned I might succumb to unwanted attention, do you truly wish for me to go, or do you not?"

I laughed heartily and folded my arms. "Use your powers of observation to interpret my actions, Tennyson."

She mimicked my stance, then nodded. "Yes, I am going. However, the same rule applies. Should you go off and bed a duchess, I will be most displeased." She then slipped into her bedroom.

"But Tennyson," I called to her, "why on earth do you suppose I was invited to a private party of the monarchy? I am curious as to your opinion."

She was already behind doors and it was clear that the conversation was over, but the battle was just beginning.

CHAPTER 15

MR. AND MRS. STEVENSON

16th November 1887

The time has come to give Tennyson a trial case, so I have taken great care in selecting one. Mr. Higgins, a wealthy businessman in the textile industry in Durham, was convinced that his wife had become unfaithful, and so sought adequate proof to confirm his suspicions in order justify a divorce.

As our primary antagonist in this equation was a woman, Tennyson's involvement seemed logical. Who better to shadow and investigate a dishonest woman, than a creature of the same sex with similar faculties? Happy to have his case accepted, Mr. Higgins agreed to my conditions.

As Durham is a three hours train ride from London, we would need to arrange for accommodations within the city. To preserve Tennyson's reputation of being a single female travelling with a single male, we created the false identities of Mr. and Mrs. Henry Stevenson to avoid unwanted attention.

I donned a costume, and disguised myself as an aging lawyer from Brighton, here on business. As Tennyson assured me that she knew no one in Durham she was free to keep her appearance intact, she simply had to the play the part as dimwitted and shallow as possible. Mrs. Higgins would never suspect her of being involved in an investigation, if she believed Tennyson to be rather brainless.

Upon arrival at the Bridge Hotel on North Road, we passed through the downstairs pub to speak with the front desk clerk. I asked if he could recommend anything of interest in the area as I was here on business and 'my wife' would need to find some means of entertaining herself. After he had rattled off a variety of activities and places of note, Tennyson excitedly clutched my arm in hers and said, in a higher pitched voice than her own, "Of all those, Gilesgate sound lovely, doesn't it Henry? I would simply adore wandering about the countryside, seeing how the common folk live! So very rustic and charming!"

I sighed, as if weary of her. "Yes, dear Elaine. You will be entertained enough?"

"Oh indeed!" Tennyson bobbed her head excitedly.

She was believable. Well-played.

"Now let us retire for the evening," I said, as I lightly kissed her on the cheek, "we have had quite a long day."

I noticed Tennyson's eyes flicker as I pulled away from her. She must be more tired than she was letting on.

The room was modest with a low ceiling, and the walls were covered with a plum and olive coloured floral patterned wallpaper. There were two beds, a large purple armchair, a sideboard, and a rosewood desk against the wall. A large oval mirror hung crookedly above it, and flecks of gold had chipped off the frame, exposing the grey steel structure underneath. The right corner of the ceiling had a long yellow stain from rain damage, and the water closet down the hall was the smallest I'd ever seen.

Tennyson sat on her bedside and slowly began to remove items from her suitcase. She seemed distracted, and was more quiet than usual.

"Anything the matter, Tennyson?" I asked.

She shook her head then sighed. "I am just nervous is all." She rested her walking dress for tomorrow on the armchair, and tugged out an ivory coloured cotton nightdress and emerald green satin bath gown from her suitcase. "I... do not want to disappoint you. Or myself for that matter."

"No need for insecurities."

She stared at the nightclothes, then at the door, and took a deep breath.

"Do you, need assistance...?" I asked quietly.

Tennyson violently shook her head. "No, no. I'll manage fine." She quickly snatched up a black velvet box with shiny metal clasps and the nightclothes, then open and closed the door behind her to head down the hallway.

I took the time to remove the white wig, beard, and other accessories that I had used to create 'Mr. Stevenson', and had just finished dressing for bed myself when she returned in the nightgown and robe, the latter of which eerily matched the tinge of green in her eyes. Her hair was unpinned, and hung loosely around her shoulders.

She unlaced the gold sash from around her waist and removed the robe to rest it over the armchair before slipping into bed. Embroidery and ribbons were laced along the drawstring neckline of the nightdress, and decorative embellishments served to soften the cotton fabric around her wrists. I glanced at her briefly, but then realized I was invading her privacy so busied myself with reviewing the documents from Mr. Higgins. There was no question concerning her loveliness. I am certain that most men would be envious of my situation, whereas I was more frustrated that I could not be as free in my speech and movements as I could have been with Watson. It was damned inconvenient.

This was the first time I'd ever shared a room with a female so naturally I had my trepidations. Though we had discussed and agreed upon the terms of the case and the sleeping arrangements, I felt far less confident in my decision now being in the actual room, and sensing her uncertainty with the situation.

As if reading my thoughts, Tennyson sat up in her bed and said, "Holmes? Are you certain we should be in the same room?"

We could not deviate now. What's done is done.

"If we are to carry out the ruse Tennyson, it needs to be continuous." I then paused with a thought. "Do not relate this to Mrs. Hudson."

She nodded, then curled up in her bed.

I put the last of my things away for the evening, laid the additional blanket, sheets, and pillow on the floor next to her, then put out the light.

"Good night, Holmes," I heard in the darkness.

I rested down on the pillow, closed my eyes, and tried to sleep but found it difficult.

17ᵗʰ November 1887

The next morning we met with Mr. Roger Higgins. He was a tall, slender man in his mid fifties, with a greying mustache and a receded hairline. He was sharply dressed in grey trousers with a black frock coat, and though his business was obviously prosperous, he was clearly unhappy in his line of work. Based on the family portrait hanging from the wall, and his degree in medicine from Oxford positioned higher above it, Mr. Higgins hadn't been entirely enthusiastic about inheriting his father's business. The medical news journals in his office also indicated that his true interests lied elsewhere.

He explained to us that his wife was having an affair with the young man who managed his horse stables and gave her riding lessons. It was not out of heartbreak that he called upon us, but rather that he wished to prove her infidelity to divorce her. He requested that we gather proof by whatever means necessary.

Now knowing the precise conditions, I suggested that Tennyson pose as a new pupil and feign interest in this man. If the wife was at all aware of her husband's suspicions, the possibility of her being followed, or of her belongings being rifled through, she might anticipate and could plan for. However, having another woman vie for her lover's affections, she would not, and if she became jealous, her attachment would be obvious. Mr. Higgins agreed.

That afternoon, Tennyson arrived at the stables for her grand entrance. She wore a Nile green walking dress with pink tea rose lace, and a black ribbon choker drawn across her neck. I remained hidden from view to observe and guide her if necessary.

She approached the comely riding instructor with a wave, and smiled.

The young man paused in training a chocolate brown yearling to acknowledge her, and waved back. His blonde hair was cut just below the jaw, and he wore Blundstone boots over his Bedford cord pantaloons. Though he wore a short English lounge jacket, the Sydney gold sovereign on his watch chain gave away his heritage.

"Pardon me sir, but are you the riding instructor?" Tennyson called in her 'Elaine' voice.

"I am indeed," he said, with a less of an Australian accent than I expected as he shook her leather-gloved hand, "Nathan Wylly, how can I help you Miss...?"

"It is Mrs., and I am Elaine Stevenson. I am here with my husband and need something to entertain myself with while he works!"

Nathan gave her a once over. "Have you ridden before Mrs. Stevenson?"

"Just Elaine will do, and yes, but not since I was a child. Quite sure I don't remember a thing!"

The horse he had been training whinnied, then stomped its foot and tried to jerk away. Nathan responded by pulling the reins, but then patted the horse's neck affectionately. "Easy there, Misty."

Tennyson petted the horse's nose as it snorted, but then it calmed, and heaved a sigh.

"She likes you," Nathan smiled. "When would you like to begin?"

"Oh immediately! Have you any appointments today?"

He lifted a hunter-cased pocket watch from his left breast pocket, and popped the cover to examine the time. "I could take you at eleven," he snapped the watch shut, "in about a half hour."

"Wonderful! I have a lovely book that will subsequently be put to use," Tennyson grinned, holding up a thick red novel, "Now what is the charge per lesson? I would like to ride daily if possible. Learn quick as a wink that way."

Though already an experienced rider, Tennyson played the role of a beginner beautifully. As we had discussed, she was to behave in a flirtatious manner, but only to a point, in order to attract his interest. Her slight advances proved successful, for as he kissed her hand goodbye, I observed a look in his eyes that could mean one thing, and one thing only.

The next two days Tennyson returned at various scheduled times for her lessons, and Nathan noticeably 'helped' her a bit more than the day before, with anything from mounting the horse, to adjusting her stirrups, to holding the reins. Her performance was flawless, so much so that I feared it might not be entirely an act on her part.

20th November 1887

On the 3rd day, she wore a superbly tailored grey plaid riding habit that displayed her figure perfectly, along with a matching bowler hat. Her appointment was at eleven, and after her session, she was to ask Nathan to lunch with her, as we needed to move forward.

At first, he was hesitant, claiming that he was violently opposed to having lunch with students, as it would not be professional, but after much coaxing and eyelash batting, Tennyson was able to convince to accept. 'Violently opposed', he obviously was not.

During lunch at The Market Tavern I watched them from afar disguised as a patron, to keep an eye on Tennyson. I marvelled at her skill of creating an entire persona in the moment as she discussed all sorts of things that she loved, and wished she could do, and that made her happy. I found it ironic, as I knew that she truly despised most of her 'Elaine' fancies.

Nathan was transfixed. He had barely touched his tea nor the quail on his plate as he sat listening to her.

"However," she then sighed sadly, "The truth is, I don't love my husband. I don't even *like* him come to think of it! I am young and vibrant, and he is so very dull, and old," she shook her head. "What a dreary life I lead in London. Garden parties, teas, extravagant dinners virtually every weekend, so blasé and very monotonous, but you," she perked up, "you are free as a bird really! Come and go as you wish! Oh, what I would not trade to be in your shoes!" she clapped her hands.

"I suppose..." Nathan then smiled dumbly. "Though who says you have to return?" He quickly took a sip of his cold tea, and made a face. "I am sorry, it is none of my business..."

Tennyson also sipped her tea, then licked her lips. "As I am telling you, I obviously want an opinion, don't I? Besides, I like you being in my business."

I was suddenly anxious. Was she taking this too far? My fears appeared to be valid, for Nathan rose from his chair with a start. "I meant no disrespect Elaine, I--"

Tennyson grabbed his hand and pulled him back to his chair, causing the teacup to rattle on its white saucer. "Oh dear me, please do not go. I will behave myself. I simply was not given a choice you see," she pulled a pink handkerchief from her handbag and dabbed at her eyes, "and I am sometimes resentful."

Nathan shifted in his chair, possibly debating if he should stay or not.

She twisted her hanky between her white-laced fingertips and leaned forward. "I should be allowed to have fun and feel love, don't you agree? That cannot be considered wrong, can it? It is not perfectly horrible, is it?"

He sat back with a deep breath. "No, it is not."

"How wonderful it would be to have someone as handsome as yourself kiss me, and actually be allowed to enjoy it! Oh my!" she pretended to gasp, covering her mouth with her handkerchief. "I am getting too personal again! Terribly sorry!" She shook her head and returned the handkerchief to her bag, appearing flustered.

Nathan leaned in closer. "Don't apologize." Then much to my dismay, he kissed her. Tennyson startled, but then quickly slipped back into character and touched his hand as she sighed.

166

Nathan temporarily locked eyes with her, but then blew through his mouth and pulled back, scratching his chair across the wooden floorboards. "Now *I* apologize," he said, shifting his gaze to the table, "It is only... you are so unlike any woman I've ever met, and you are stunningly beautiful." He took her hands and squeezed them. "I... was carried away, it will not happen again, I promise. Please do not stop your lessons."

Tennyson lightly touched his cheek with her gloved hand and smiled sweetly. "I wouldn't dream of it."

As we prepared to retire that evening, I returned from the washroom to find Tennyson humming to herself as she brushed her hair in front of the mirror. I stared at her curiously.

"You are in a merry mood Tennyson. Has this riding instructor taken your fancy?"

Tennyson spun around. "Not in the least! Far too dull, characterless, and self-absorbed. Though I must admit, it is rather fun being someone I am not." She laid down the brush and gazed into the mirror. "I prefer older, more established men, if you were curious."

"Not particularly," I smiled, "but I will rest easier knowing that you shall not run off with Mr. Wylly before our case concludes."

She was a strange woman, talking about her relationship preferences as if I were one of her woman friends. There were certain things I did not know about Tennyson for a reason, and certain lines that should not be crossed. I glanced over and noticed that her reflection was frowning.

She crumpled up a tissue and forcefully tossed it in the dustbin. "Do not think that I am some silly idiot, Holmes."

"Feelings often rule women's reasoning and judgment," I said. "But if you claim you have no true interest in this boy, then I believe you." Tennyson snorted, then sat on the purple armchair and crossed her legs. "Something wrong?"

She folded her arms, closed her eyes, and lifted her chin. "If you think me so vulnerable, you should not have brought me."

What game was *this* now? Her comment made not an ounce of sense. Women are terribly neurotic creatures. If only there were a way to understand their moods and meanings, then one could possibly enjoy their company more frequently.

I placed my hands on her shoulders. "Stop being ridiculous woman and go to bed," I pushed her up and towards the bed. "I will retire shortly."

She begrudgingly crawled underneath the covers. "Do not think all women are equally senseless and impulsive."

"I promise to give your musings adequate consideration."

23rd November 1887

After Tennyson's lesson on Wednesday afternoon, Nathan lifted her from the horse then kissed her. This was the first open display of affection whilst at the stables, and was timed perfectly, as I heard a low growl coming from my left. Mrs. Helen Higgins, Roger's wife, stood rigidly by the ring's door with a sour expression. Her dark eyes flashed and her dull brown hair danced in the wind like snakes upon her head. The ever-present enigmatic smile that stretched across her face like a scarecrow's painted mouth, was now twisted into an ugly frown, slightly disfiguring her plain face.

The tiny white dog that she'd been holding in her arms was dropped, as if it had bitten her, and she headed into the stables with a huff. Now the game was afoot.

As Tennyson left the stables, Mrs. Higgins swept in front of her, handed her an envelope, then continued across the snow-covered lawn into the house, slamming the door behind her. A few icicles from the roof's overhang dropped down and stab into the ground as Tennyson stared at the letter.

"What does it say?" I asked, as I propped up my feet on the side table in our hotel room and closed my eyes.

Tennyson paced the room as she read. "Mrs. Stevenson, I am requesting that you meet with me at the house, two o'clock tomorrow afternoon. There is a very serious matter that I wish to discuss with you, and you alone. -Helen Higgins.' She gripped the letter between her fingers. "I should go of course?"

"Quite," I yawned, as I lowered my feet from the table, then brushed the mud clumps that had fallen from my boots onto the floor. "You will be protected. I shall alert Mr. Higgins at once, for if she 'wishes to discuss with you' what I am predicting, it is best he be present. She is an ugly customer indeed."

24ᵗʰ November 1887

The next day Tennyson travelled to the farmhouse while I slipped inside through the basement cellar doors in the back, and maneuvered my way through the house to the dining room, as Mr. Higgins had advised.

As Tennyson later related to me, Mrs. Higgins had been waiting at the window in a red plaid housedress and with a look that would make a gargoyle turn white. She greeted her rival at the door, then gruffly ushered her inside. She escorted Tennyson through the kitchen, past the tiny white dog slurping water out of a bowl, and into the dark wood paneled dining room, where I was waiting behind a curtain. I heard them discussing Nathan, how Helen suspected Tennyson of being involved with him, and when Tennyson vehemently denied it, Helen backed her into a corner.

"Now listen here, Mrs. Stevenson, and listen closely." Helen hissed as I peered around the curtain to observe them. "Nathan is mine. Since your arrival, he will not even look at me, let alone bed me!"

Tennyson gasped, not expecting such a frank confession to the affair. "I... was not aware that..."

"Because of you, everything is being ruined! We were to take my money and leave!"

"Surely you mean your husband's money--"

Mrs. Higgins leaned in closer. She was inches away from Tennyson's face. "It is mine! I have earned it! He would never miss it, or me!"

Tennyson slid along the wall towards to the doorway. "I am sorry. I promise to stay away. He is yours, just as you said."

"Oh no, as long as you're around, he will want you. I cannot allow that." Mrs. Higgins reached through her skirt's placket to the red beaded Dorothy bag slung around her waist, and pulled out a small silver revolver with a pearled handle.

"You cannot be serious!" the words barely managed from Tennyson's trembling lips, "I will leave, and he'll never see me again. You and I... we have both performed acts of infidelity... been unfaithful, therefore, you should not–"

Mrs. Higgins stepped back and aimed the gun. "Perhaps so, but there is only one way to guarantee your removal from the equation, so good bye Mrs. Stevenson, and good riddance!"

Before she could pull the trigger, I leapt from behind the dining room curtain, grabbed Tennyson by the waist, and brought her to the ground. The gun fired, and I heard a shriek behind me.

Mr. Higgins had entered from behind the living room door, knocked the gun from his wife's hand, and thrown her into one of the upholstered dining room chairs. Before she could fight back, he grabbed her up by the throat, and kicked the gun towards the door. "Your money you say!?" He slapped the handcuffs I had given him on her wrists, and shoved her towards the door. "We shall see what rights you have to it now!"

With the situation stable, I rolled off Tennyson, and helped her to her feet. "Jealousy at its worst," I shook my head, "are you all right Tennyson?"

Tennyson's body was shaking, but she nodded.

171

I held her by the shoulders. "Are you quite sure? You are quivering, my dear."

With trembling hands, she dusted off her coat and skirt. "Just... a bit of shock," she said nervously, "I cannot say as I have ever had a gun aimed at me, nor had someone try to kill me."

"You will adjust in time," I patted her shoulder, then picked up my cloth cap from the floor.

As we were stepping from the house, Mr. Wylly came running from the stables. He must have heard the gun shot. He approached Tennyson, avoiding Mrs. Higgins, and anxiously took her hands.

"Elaine, er... Mrs. Stevenson, what has happened?!" He looked at me then stepped back. "Is this... your husband?"

When Mr. Higgins also spotted the young man, his eyes narrowed. "You sir, are dismissed. Effective immediately! I want you off these premises!"

Nathan looked to Mr. Higgins, then to me, then to Tennyson for an explanation.

"I am sorry, Nathan, but my name is not Elaine Stevenson," Tennyson replied in her normal voice, "and this is not my husband. He is Sherlock Holmes, a detective."

Nathan nodded in understanding, then inhaled deeply, running his hand through his thick hair. "What a fool I have been."

"Apologies for ruining your plans with Helen, Mr. Wylly," Tennyson held out a hand. "No hard feelings I hope. This was not about you."

172

Upon leaving Durham by train the next day, Tennyson seemed lost in thought as we crossed over the viaduct high above the city.

"A shilling for your thoughts, Tennyson?" I asked with a smile.

Tennyson turned to face me. "I suppose I feel a bit of sadness, I believe."

"Sadness?" I asked concerned. "You are not experiencing guilt in regard to the case are you?"

"Nothing of the sort. They were dealt what they deserved entirely, yet...perhaps it is more of a pity for Nathan. The point was to lure him away from Helen in order to elicit a jealous response that would prompt her confession to the affair. I was to merely serve as a distraction, nothing more."

"And indeed you did!" I laughed, no longer worried. "You must realize Tennyson, that hardly ever does anything go precisely as arranged, and that part especially, was not within your control."

"I suppose not."

"You cannot blame yourself for other's actions," I said, as I looked out the window at the beautiful snow-covered landscape. "Besides, you had best get used to it."

"Used to what?"

"Men falling in love with you," I turned. "As you are quite remarkable and intelligent, this is only the first time of many I would presume."

"They need only get to know me before that would quickly change," she shook her head. "He was in love with a woman who did not exist, and one who was not me."

I looked at her puzzled. "I disagree, I feel it might have been *more* difficult for him in the end *had* she been you. Thankfully you are with me, where you needn't trouble yourself about such possible diversions."

"Yes, you are absolutely right," she said. "That, I need never worry about with you, which is why I enjoy your company. It is purely cerebral and I need not anticipate nor be concerned with anything else. Sometimes I think I would have been better off a man," she laughed lightly.

"You are too critical, Tennyson. I think you make a fine woman."

We talked little the rest of the journey home.

Though Tennyson performed marvelously, and I was indeed impressed, I kept my congratulations to a minimum as I wished for her to continue to work hard and apply herself in her training. However, I could see that she would be a valuable ally to me in the future.

~ ~

Jonathan lowered the journal.

"It was their first case together. That was the origin of Henry Stevenson." The train had stopped, and he peered through the iced over window. They had already arrived at Cambridge.

He scooped up the journal, climbed from the luggage compartment, and hopped off the train.

As he entered the doorway to his room his open Classics book greeted him, and a large circled, January 25th was written in red ink on a piece of paper that was covering the pages.

"Hang it," he threw down his satchel, and sat at the desk with a groan. "My first paper is due Monday. Better work first, read for personal pleasure later."

That Saturday and Sunday he worked exclusively on his studies but by Sunday evening, he was restless, so decided to continue his hunt for the elusive trinket box. *Jack and the Beanstalk... could that be any sort of clue as to where she left it?*

As he strolled through King's Court, he began to think about Holmes' journal. Holmes and his mother seemed so different. How did they end up together? As he continued his ruminations, he didn't notice another student passing by, so smacked headlong into them.

"Hello, watch where you're going, sir!" the boy said, as he massaged his nose. He was older, most likely a senior, and had a large worn satchel slung across his shoulder. He was a few inches taller than Jonathan but not as slender, and had blonde wavy hair, a square jaw, and wore a very expensive looking topcoat. Black shiny boots were partially covered by white spats, and he carried a black leather bag in his left hand. This boy certainly had money.

"Oh, terribly sorry about that," Jonathan said, holding out his hand, "Jonathan Hopkins. I was deliberating over my history paper and was rather distracted."

The boy muffled a dry cough as he shook it. "No harm done, Jonathan. Gabriel Adams, senior at Trinity."

"Natural Sciences major, emphasis on medicine, correct?"

Gabriel stared at Jonathan, perplexed. "How did you know?"

Jonathan pointed to the reddish-brown stain on Gabriel's shirt-sleeve. "You have a splash of bromine on your inner right sleeve, from the lab. I noticed the smell immediately when I tapped into you. You also have the weight and specific gravities of several gases and vapors written on the palm of your hand, possible for an exam, or simply a note given in class."

"Why not say I am a chemist?"

"You also have an anatomy book poking out of your satchel a black doctor's bag at your side."

Gabriel looked down at his left hand, and shook his head at the obvious giveaway. "Tell me more, Hopkins," he challenged.

"You also have a passion for drawing, due to the charcoal stains on your left thumb and forefinger and the pencil shavings on your jacket."

"Well yes, I had once wished to be an artist before realizing there was no money in it. Continue."

"You are left-handed though you scribe with your right, based on the large calluses on both your left and right middle finger."

Gabriel's jaw dropped. He playfully punched Jonathan in the arm. "That is quite the talent you have there! Your field of interest is in detective work?"

"Not at all, I am undecided."

"Well, I think I have discovered your vocation, Jonathan. You should be a Scotland Yard inspector, or perhaps, fortune teller."

"Scotland Yard detectives seems fairly incompetent to me."

"Then a private detective, like that Sherlock Holmes fellow. You could be his twin," Gabriel laughed.

"Or son," Jonathan said quietly.

"That is correct! Ha ha!" Gabriel then shivered, and tucked his bare neck down underneath his coat's high collar. "I say, it is beastly cold out. I was about to head to town for a drink at The Eagle. Care to join me?"

"I should return to my paper..."

"Ah yes, the one you were so distraught over when you tapped into me."

"I suppose a brief interruption is allowed..."

"Capital!" Gabriel put an arm around him, "My treat then."

During their conversation at the Eagle on Benet's Street in the city's centre, Gabriel explained that he wasn't very well-liked by his peers. He attributed it to jealousy of his wealth and brilliance, and was completely oblivious to the fact that they were probably annoyed, rather than jealous, at him *flaunting* his money and intelligence. Jonathan listened intently as Gabriel discussed his three and half years at Trinity, and how he hoped to study in Paris after graduation, as the latest in the surgical world was in France and Scotland.

As he continued to observe Gabriel, Jonathan was able to draw several parallels between himself and this boy, and was gaining a better understanding of why his fellow students at Rutlish had harbored such animosity towards him. It was not their envy of his mind, as he had once thought, but his pompous and continual boasting of it that pushed people away. He vowed to be more conscientious of that in the future.

Though he had been fully against imbibing more than a pint, Gabriel called the entire bill, and continued to offer drink after drink. Being only 13, Jonathan hadn't enough experience with alcohol to know his limitations, so wound up in sad state indeed. He stumbled back to his room and collapsed on the floor, his head spinning.

He struggled to pull a napkin from his jacket pocket with Gabriel's address scribbled across, then rested it on his bedside locker. With some effort, he managed to drunkenly drag his satchel from underneath the bed, and pulled out Holmes' journal to read. He knew enough about drinking that he needed to stay awake a bit longer in order to avoid feeling run over in the morning.

CHAPTER 16

MYCROFT'S THEORY

24ᵗʰ December 1887 Christmas Eve

I travelled to my brother's in Pall Mall on Christmas Eve as was tradition. Tennyson had gone to her father's. Though I would normally consider it a waste of ink and paper to chronicle a holiday visit with my brother, based on Mycroft's supposed theories and our agreement, I now find that I must.

Tennyson had presented me with a 'Christmas gift', and while I consider gift giving outside the family an unnecessary and pointless practice, I none-the-less felt guilty that I had not considered giving her something in return. I waved it off by saying I could not accept, and I was not one for trinkets. She refused to acquiesce. I begrudgingly accepted, but stated I would not open it until Christmas Eve, as it was improper to do so before then. I made the grievous error of informing Mycroft of her generosity, and he therefore requested I bring the package with me and open it at his apartment. As I did not see the harm *then*, I agreed.

I arrived at Mycroft's at a quarter past six. He greeted me at the door with a cheerful, "Happy Christmas Eve, brother."

His uncustomary gleeful nature made me anxious, but I calmly nodded the same. I was somewhat surprised at his girth, for though his weigh was known to fluctuate around the holidays, his general appearance was more round than I was accustomed to, and given his

179

unusual, merry manner, he reminded me of younger, beardless Father Christmas.

As I entered his dark and lonely den, he poured me a large glass of sherry and gestured for me to sit in his rather ornate, black and silver paisley armchair by the fireplace.

"You did bring Miss Tennyson's present as I asked you?" he asked suddenly.

Something was afoot, but I nodded, and pulled out the gold wrapped box with green ribbon that Tennyson had given me from my carry case, and set it on the tea table as I awaited the reveal.

"Splendid. Now before you open it, what did *you* give *her*?"

"There was not a mutual exchanging of goods."

"Have you no social etiquette, Sherlock?"

I gripped the thick arms of my chair, and leaned as far back into the cushion as the stuffing would allow. "I endeavor to avoid having my mind cluttered with useless information that is of no employ to me in my work or profession. Social 'etiquette' I believe, falls within that category. Besides, I was not aware of the gift's existence until the day she left."

Mycroft sniffed indignantly. "You had best give her something in return."

"I know nothing of women's tastes."

"Then I will educate you, but after... you open this," he attempted to hand Tennyson's gift to me.

I folded my arms in protest, but he unceremoniously dropped it on my lap. "Open it Sherlock."

I sighed, slightly irritated, then removed the paper.

Mycroft eyed me with a smug expression. "This is your first Christmas gift from a woman other than our mother, am I wrong?"

I paused. He was correct. I now felt about twelve, and Mycroft seemed far older than seven years my senior as he towered over me in his brown suit and blue velvet smoking jacket.

"Pour yourself a glass," I pointed to his empty tumbler in order to change the subject. "I am not partial to being analyzed or the sole focus of anyone's attention."

"You do it often enough to everyone else," Mycroft laughed, but obediently left the room to refresh his glass of sherry.

I tore the rest of the paper to find a straight seemed brown box underneath. I lifted off the lid and inside, were three cylinder canisters. They had a channeled rim, and a slip of paper was wrapped around each one. I slid out the white rolls of paper and printed in black ink across each page was 'North American Phonograph Company', followed by a record number and song title.

Mycroft returned with a full glass, then sat on the sofa next to me with a grunt. "Well?"

"They are phonograph cylinders," I sucked in my surprise. "One of Mendelssohn's '*Lieder ohne Worter*', Haydn's '*Symphony no. 94*', and Wagner's '*Magic Fire Music*' from *Die Walküre*." I chuckled and shook my head. "Some of my favorite composers." I removed the wax cylinder from inside Haydn's tube, and inspected it carefully. "I was

181

not aware that the wax cylinders had been perfected yet. I was anticipating another year or so. These must be first issue."

Mycroft snatched the cylinder from my hand, examined it closely, then sniffed it. "It smells like beeswax." He rolled the object in his hand and looked at me with a curious expression. "American. Sent for from overseas. That is going through quite a bit of trouble just for *you*, isn't it?"

I grabbed the cylinder from his fingers, wrapped the slip of paper around it, then shoved it back in the box. "Terribly thoughtful, yes."

Mycroft smiled. "Sherlock, I do believe that she has romantic feelings towards you."

I nearly dropped the box from my lap. "You are reading too much into nothing. Our relationship is purely platonic."

"Perhaps to you."

I dropped the box to the ground, and pushed it under my chair. "As I have given her no reason to think of our relationship as anything but professional, there is no basis for your argument."

Mycroft comfortably leaned back in the sofa, then folded his hands in his lap. "On the very rare occasion, I am proven to be wrong, but in this instance, I would wager my entire estate that my intuition is accurate."

I snorted.

"Controlling or predicting the development of another's emotions is impossible, my dear brother. Everyone has his own course, which is independent of you. Your behaviour or feelings, shall not determine hers."

"I disagree," I fought. "If you are unkind to someone, will they not dislike you? And conversely, if you are pleasant, will they not favour you? Anything can be controlled under the proper conditions, including feelings."

Mycroft took a sip of his sherry and licked his lips. "You cannot be so naïve, can you?" he said with a smirk.

"As you have met Miss Tennyson once, I say that there are no grounds for your accusations."

Mycroft crossed one thick leg over the other, and tapped down his drink. "No grounds?!" He grabbed a pen and accounting book from the side table, opened it, then pulled a pair of spectacles from the breast pocket of his jacket and placed them on his face. "Let us break this down, shall we?" He pressed the tip of his index finger to his tongue, then used the moistened finger to turn to a fresh page in the notepad. "How much does her father allot her per month for living expenses?"

"Perhaps ten guinea."

He wrote it down on the white lined page. "What is her rent?"

"Five pound eight." I could see where this was leading.

He moved his spectacles to the tip of his nose, and gave me a smile that was altogether mirthful. "Does not leave much wiggle room for frivolous purchases, now does it?" He gestured to underneath my chair. "How much would you speculate those cylinders cost?"

"I cannot guess."

"I would think two, three pounds each. Quite a singular investment, considering. Even one recording would have been more than generous, yet she went on to purchase not two, but three. Therefore, I state my case, she has feelings for you," he said, as he snapped the book shut and rested it down on the table.

"Suppose her reason is to persuade me to offer her more responsibilities, or additional involvement on a case?" I kicked the box further under the chair. "Have you never given a teacher an extra compliment or gift, to attain a higher mark?"

"I never had to, unlike my daydreaming brother."

"I sometimes forget that you are perfect."

"Indeed."

He was not accustomed to me defending my stances so but on this particular subject, I would offer every possible resistance.

"A proposition for you then," Mycroft slapped his knee. "I claim that Miss Tennyson has affections for you that stretch beyond the professional. The bet is this. If in three months' time you can prove me wrong, I will buy you another Stradivarius. But, if I am indeed correct, then I defy you to discover the formula for emotions and compassion, if they are indeed so easily controllable." Mycroft held out his hand. "I say it cannot be done."

I leaned over and briskly shook it. "I say it can. But as you are wrong about Miss Tennyson, my tasks will end once I have sufficiently proven her innocence. At the conclusion of three months, I shall call upon you for my violin, though I hardly need two."

"For your sake and hers, I hope I am wrong Sherlock. Need you a transcript for this arrangement?"

"No need to go humbugging about documentation, unless you require it."

Mycroft shook his head, and returned the spectacles to his pocket. "Now then, what will you give Miss Tennyson? What does she fancy?"

"Well, I do not know," I said sheepishly.

Mycroft grunted. "The woman lives with you, and you can tell me nothing!?"

"She is a very private, compounded specimen."

"Is she a person or a paramecium?" he laughed. "Had *I* a live-in companion, I should like to know everything about her. But as you have acknowledged in the past, we differ in our methods of reasoning."

I was tempted to acknowledge how we also differed in physicality, as he never shied away from dinner seconds nor a dessert tray, but I held my tongue. "She does not divulge much in order to decipher her leisurely pursuits. Now then, what should I get her?"

Mycroft uncrossed his legs, shifted his weight off the sofa, then reached for his wooden cigar case on the sideboard. He removed a long brown Cuban, clipped it, then silently lit it with a match. "Well, as she's not in love with you, and you have no interest in her, I would say candies and roses are out of the question."

"Quite."

"Does she socialize?" he puffed on the cigar, "parties, the races, balls?"

I grinned. "I am already taking her to a masked ball on New Year's Eve."

The cigar dropped from Mycroft's mouth to the floor as his jaw stood open. "A ball? On New Year's Eve?!" He picked up the cigar and angrily brushed the burning ashes from the rug. "Where is my brother, and what have you done with him?"

I laughed. "Oh it was entirely her idea."

Mycroft eyed me suspiciously. "This woman is turning you into a socialite, Sherlock. Be wary of..."

"Not in the least," I said. "There is a particular reason I accepted this invitation."

"Where on earth are you going?"

"Buckingham Palace."

"Remarkably amusing," Mycroft took another puff. "Jesting aside now, I promise. Whereabouts are you headed?"

"You have a solid grasp on the English language, I believe I said Buckingham Palace."

"You are visiting Buckingham Palace, for a New Year's party? Even I was not invited, and I have many dealings with the crown!"

"Would you have gone, had you been?"

He leaned against the bar's corner, and forcefully tapped his cigar into an ashtray. "That is not the point."

"I was not necessarily invited either."

Mycroft stared me perplexed.

"Should I be correct, I will give you an explanation later."

"This is most interesting Sherlock, but I know your methods and shall not ask. Now regarding the gift. Wine, or... the theater?"

I thought for a moment, then remembered my most recent conversation with Watson. "Watson had asked not a week ago if we would accompany him and Mary to see La Traviata in April. Though Verdi is decent enough..."

"Perfect, and if others are present, it cannot be misconstrued as courting."

"You are insufferable!"

"But for now, let us enjoy Christmas Eve. Perhaps there will be carolers?"

I sighed. I was not at all desirous of continuing to quarrel with my brother on this subject, so allowed him to claim the victory. But yet, *is* there any truth to it?

CHAPTER 17

BUCKINGHAM PALACE

31ˢᵗ December 1887

    Tennyson glowed with excitement before our departure to the palace. She had chosen a magnificent black satin gown from the closet of Lady Blackwell, laced with silver and gold trimmings. She wore a black half mask, rimmed with shiny onyx beads, and an elegant, pearled, feather headdress that rested atop a blonde, curled wig.

    I was less glamorous. Ordinary black tails, an open waistcoat, white tie, light lavender kid gloves, and a rather plain silver mask. Completing the look was a silk top hat.

    Upon arrival at Buckingham Palace, we stepped across the threshold into the Grand Hall, then made our way up the curving marble Grand Staircase. Portraits of previous monarchs were set in the walls, an addition I believe the Queen made several years prior. I briefly held the golden railing, and curiously examined the most recent pieces to the collection. Two paintings of the youngest princes, Albert Victor, (otherwise known as Eddy) and his younger brother George, were positioned next to their father Albert Edward, The Prince of Wales, and their mother, Alexandra of Denmark.

    Though only paintings, the two brothers could not have appeared more opposite. Albert Victor was more pallid, frail, and seemed troubled behind his waxed moustache and sleepy-eyed stare, whereas George's blue-eyed portrait sported a neatly trimmed nautical beard and moustache, and exuded an air of confidence. The paintings seemed to watch us as we travelled up the red velvet staircase and into the Marble Hall, and I felt a slight chill as we passed through the East Gallery's hallway to the Ballroom.

Three rows of elevated red velvet couches lined the walls inside, and it was buzzing with masked socialites, politicians, and friends of the Royal Family. I despised these types of soirées, but was here on business.

Tennyson brushed past me and immediately wandered over to the catered refreshments table. I overheard her ask for a glass of 'Duminy extra sec 1883,' and the waiter promptly pulled a bottle from behinds several others, uncorked it, and poured her a flute.

You are not being that careless are you?

A man dressed in a shiny silver suit, with a white powered wig and silver eye mask, suddenly appeared next to her. He was holding a nearly empty wine glass in his left hand, and leaned in to whisper something in her ear. She smiled, sighed deeply, then nodded as he seductively kissed her hand.

I surveyed this little interaction with mild curiosity, but stayed my distance. After the orchestra had finished the tune they'd been playing, he bowed, and asked Tennyson to dance. They moved to the dance floor and began to waltz with the other elegant couples across the ballroom.

I stood to the side, then at the properly timed moment, I stopped the couple as they circled nearer to me, and tapped the man on the shoulder. "Apologies sir," I said, as I inspected him carefully to determine his identity, "but might I cut in?"

The man gruffly released Tennyson's waist. "As you wish."

"Thank you," I said, taking Tennyson in my arms.

"What are you about, Holmes?" she whispered annoyed, as we rounded the dance floor.

"Can I not ask the most beautiful woman in the room to dance? When do I ever have that opportunity?" I was perhaps teetering on the edge of flirtation, but I needed to distract her.

"Yes, but not when it is in the middle of a set. Do you know nothing of ballroom etiquette?"

"Have I done something improper? Terribly sorry." *Mission accomplished.*

We danced in silence, but as we glided past the orchestra, she said quietly, "You dance brilliantly Holmes."

"Surprised?" I smiled, but then, in looking at her, something puzzled me. It was her eyes. There was something in them...an emotion or feeling I could not decipher. Mycroft could not possibly be correct, could he?

"I just never imagined you could be so... well..."

"Charming?" I asked, as I twirled her one last time then kissed her black-gloved hand before the music stopped.

"Something like that, yes." She averted her eyes to the ceiling, then frowned. "I think I should like to sit for a moment, my feet are used up." She fluttered over to one of the long red couches, and sat with a sigh.

Curious as to what prompted her reaction, I inspected the location that had so affected her. A kissing bough with a sprig of

Mistletoe hung from one of the chandeliers directly above me. Ah! This was certainly a noteworthy snippet to aid in disproving Mycroft's theory. I followed after Tennyson, and asked if she would care for a drink.

"No, thank you. But why don't you go and socialize?"

"I know no one here, save for you," I said to her. "I assume the same applies?"

She laughed nervously and looked at her wristwatch. "Of course..."

After I had stepped away, I discreetly turned to look back where she had been seated, and noted that her space was empty, just as I predicted it would be. I caught a glimpse of her rounding the doorway as she headed from the Ballroom and out to her left.

Now you are truly being reckless. I shook my head as I followed after her.

She had made her way towards the West Gallery, wandered past the four Gobelin tapestries that adorned the walls, then travelled into the first great room that overlooked the lawn and formal gardens. I remained hidden behind one of the Corinthian columns in the Blue Drawing Room as Tennyson rustled quickly through it to the next room, which was the Music Room.

The silver-suited man from the dance floor was waiting for her by the long bow window. Though I could not hear their conversation, words became unnecessary the moment he kissed her and held her in a long embrace. This was indeed trouble.

I quickly returned to the ballroom, and sought out a glass of port. After locating the couch previously occupied by Tennyson, I sat down to pass the time until she returned a quarter of an hour later.

"I have been waiting for you Tennyson, wherever have you been?" My expression was stern.

"I desired to see the lake and gardens, as I heard they were beautiful. Now Holmes, you should try to enjoy yourself." Her cheeks were slightly flushed, the reason for which I did not care to guess.

"Indeed," I said coldly, "and... were they?"

"Yes, very," she looked away. "You should go and see them."

"I think you have been out of my sight long enough tonight, Tennyson," I said sharply. "Did you happen upon anything else? Meet anyone interesting in your travels?"

She fussed with her skirts. "Not really, no."

Indeed.

I must have appeared less indifferent than I supposed for she said; "Something wrong Holmes?"

"Yes, as a matter of fact there is," I said curtly. "This port is damned awful. I will be rid of it at once." I slammed down my glass on the tray of a passing by waiter, as I truthfully could not stomach any more. Her act of betrayal had contaminated the entire evening.

Throughout the remainder of the night, Tennyson danced with several other fellows, including a few group sets with the man from the Music Room.

For the last number of the evening, I politely invited Tennyson to dance, though I wished to be anywhere but near her at the moment. She agreed, and as we twirled across the floor, I now observed something in her eyes that I *could* identify... GUILT.

"You are quite popular this evening, Tennyson. Awkward and 'out of place', you seem not. They must all truly believe you to be a Duchess, or perhaps... a Princess?" I asked with a hidden meaning.

"It is impolite for a lady to refuse the invitation of a gentleman to dance."

If she had caught my implication, she certainly did not acknowledge it.

The grand musical clock in the ballroom elaborately struck twelve, and everyone applauded, then shouted, 'Happy New Year!' and kissed their dance partners.

As was tradition, I kissed Tennyson lightly on the check. "Happy New Year's, Tennyson."

The look I could not interpret had returned to her eyes. "Thank you, Holmes."

"For what?"

"Taking me tonight. I've had a lovely time."

"Was there any possible way I could not have?"

She frowned. "How do you mean?"

I sighed wearily. "It is late, Tennyson."

As I followed behind her down the grand staircase, I again saw her man of the evening, watching us pensively.

Once inside the carriage, I closed my eyes to work through the conversation I would now need to have with her tomorrow morning. It would certainly not be a pleasant one.

CHAPTER 18

GABRIEL ADAMS

Jonathan slept in, and arose around lunchtime before his first class on Monday as he still felt slightly nauseous from the night before. As he was crossing the quad towards the main kitchen, he saw his new friend, Gabriel Adams, walking by in the opposite direction. He was wearing a grey wool cap, and carried a wooden box with a handle attached.

"Hello fellow, you feel all right?" Gabriel asked, his eyes slightly puffy and tired.

"Not too terrible, but I slept in."

"Oh I felt positively wicked this morning. Barely arrived to my ten o'clock on time! I haven't much of a stomach to eat, but thought to take it for lunch later," he said, as he held up the 'lunch' box. "Too much work left in the laboratory."

"Do you enjoy working in the lab?"

"Very much! And one will make a fine living if one is good. I certainly plan on attending the Sorbonne. Best school in Paris."

"Sounds interesting."

"Would you like to see it sometime? The lab? If you are indeed undecided, you should be experimenting with a bit of everything to see what takes your fancy."

Jonathan thought for a moment. "I have only a Classics lesson at one o'clock. I could come round this afternoon."

Gabriel reached under his cap and scratched his head. "I do have quite a lot of work actually, but...I say, perhaps you could help! You're obviously a sharp lad, and company would be welcome. I could also offer you monetary compensation if you would assist me, *and,* I could teach you a thing or two," he punched Jonathan in the shoulder with a wink.

"Is that allowed?"

Gabriel laughed. "As you are not aware of whether it is or not, neither am I!"

It sounded like a fair trade. "You have yourself an assistant, Mr. Adams!"

For the next few days, when Jonathan hadn't classes or homework, he would assist Gabriel in the laboratory. He truly wished to keep him as a friend, as there was something comforting about his company, like an older brother. In some ways, he reminded Jonathan of Bernard Eaton, whom he hadn't seen in years. And he finally found someone who viewed his intelligence as a benefit, and not an annoyance. Gabriel didn't realize how much *he* was actually helping Jonathan.

Abigail had sent a note that night that she couldn't make their Wednesday call, so suggested postponing until Friday the 29th.

Late Thursday evening, Jonathan returned to his room and accidentally kicked Holmes' journal out from under the bed. He had honestly forgot about it. After he'd readied himself for bed, he curled up under the covers, then flipped it open to continue.

~ ~

1ˢᵗ January 1888 New Year's Day

"Tennyson, I must ask you to cease your relations with The Prince, immediately," I said confronting her, as she sat in the sitting room with the paper, eating breakfast at the table.

She took a bite of her fried bread, dropping a few crumbs onto her cloud-blue day dress, then brushed them off with a huff. "Whatever are you talking about?" she asked between chews.

"Mask or no, your physical exchanges with The Prince were most telling. How long have these interludes been transpiring?"

She put down the bread, and swallowed. "Again, I do not know what you are referring to."

"Do you remotely comprehend the magnitude of danger you are in?"

Now, she appeared concerned. "Danger of what?"

"Of being in a romantic relationship with a member of the Royal Family. Your reputation could be in *very* grave danger. Have you any idea what people would speculate? You would become a ruined woman."

197

She seemed less affected, and returned to reading the paper. "What gives you reason to think I was talking to The Prince? How would I possibly be familiar with one of the Royal Family?"

"I am not asking when and where the relationship started, I am asking for it to cease existing."

She took a dainty sip of her tea. "I am sorry, but you are quite mistaken. You cannot always be right you know."

"Do not patronize me Tennyson."

"How would I have recognized him in a mask?"

I gripped the head of the armchair. "You should be able to answer your own paradoxical question, Tennyson. Did you yourself not claim that people aren't so challenging to identify with masks, if you are indeed, looking for them? And was it not the very nature of the mask's existence that allowed you to recognize your companion?"

"I may have said something to that effect, yes. But concerning the latter, I only made a statement that you took upon yourself to draw a more vivid sketch of."

"Highly original tactic, but that singular comment was delivered too off-handedly to have had no real significance."

She folded up the paper, then leaned her white-laced elbows onto the table. "Very well, let us *pretend* I recognized The Prince, spoke to him, danced with him even. As per the rules of proper social etiquette, which you are clearly unfamiliar with, a lady cannot refuse the invitation of a gentleman to dance." She tossed the paper over by the hearth, then snatched up her teacup and strutted towards the sideboard.

"Based on your snide comment at the end of the evening, you were aware of my dancing and conversing with many men last night."

"One man in particular was most distracted by you."

She poured another cup of tea, and stirred in three lumps of sugar. "I was being polite. Why the concern?" She bit on the tip of her spoon thoughtfully, then hummed. "What, were you jealous?"

Of course I was not, nor was I amused by her immature behaviour. "On the contrary, I could not be more removed from caring about your amorous affairs or your personal dealings except when it endangers your reputation, and future prospects. As long as you reside within these walls, you cannot see him again. That is my final word on the matter."

She took a sip of her tea, then watched me as a cat watches a canary. "You are convinced I am seeing The Prince are you? What precisely gave you that misguided impression, hmm?"

"You spent inherently more time with him than any other that night, and your tactile contact was most inappropriate."

Tennyson banged her cup on the side table, spilling a bit on the carpet. "Oh spare me your platitudinous observations Holmes. I do not recall physically attacking, or throwing myself at anyone last night. I hardly consider talking to someone..."

"I am of course referring to your interactions with him by the window of the Music Room. I do not think that you ventured there to play a prelude on the piano."

I had never seen Tennyson's face as red and as steaming with furor as it was now.

199

"So you were spying on me?" she shrieked. "How dare you!"

"No, how dare *you* lie to me!" I advanced on her, keeping only a few inches between us.

She stepped back, clasped her hands in front of her, then looked away.

I hesitated. I had never raised my voice to her nor threatened her personal space. I paced the floor feeling conflicted about lecturing her, but knowing that I must. "You have sought my advice in the past, so now I am giving it freely. You *must* end it."

She frowned, still not looking at me. Her mood had shifted dramatically. She seemed weak, fragile, and childlike. "You do not understand Holmes," she swallowed, as she slumped into the armchair by the fireplace, "I cannot..."

"Knowing who I am, and how I operate, you presumed I would not have the slightest of where you might be on *certain* occasions? You expect I believed you were with Miss Whalley? She is hardly one to frequent the races at Newmarket, or Doncaster, or embark on a sailing excursion at Cowes. That 'outing' was your first mistake. Nor could I then envision her attending a garden party of Lady Brooke's, or shopping at Worth's. You may as well have said you went shooting at Sandringham with the Royal Family, it would have been no less obvious!" I paused for a reaction. Tennyson made no attempt to speak or defend herself. I attempted to meter my emotions.

"Nor can you discount the certain precautions you'd take for each 'appointment'. The attentive primping beforehand, the scent of lavender, certain words you'd let fall, the vagueness of your responses to

200

my questions... and, I believe the most telling aspect, was the way you'd look at me before you left."

"Oh?" she looked up.

"With guilt, Tennyson. That is one emotion you do *not* conceal well. I observed it again last night, and only too clearly. Add in the smell of cologne, the mood you had returned in, the carefully hidden note after each visit... for heaven's sake woman! At least, vary your answers to keep me entertained with your lies, if indeed you must tell them."

Tennyson hung her head.

"And were you so bold to assume you could feign surprise when that invitation arrived from the palace? Tsk, tsk. The pith and marrow of the business indicates such an invite was meant for you, yet for obvious reasons, was addressed to me. You gave a convincing impression of sincerity, but not convincing enough. The letter you then replied with revealed all I needed to know."

Tennyson appeared flabbergasted. "How did you...?"

"Come now Tennyson! Any child is adept at holding blotting paper up to the looking glass. And as you pressed rather harshly into the page, it was quite simple to replicate. I then offered you several chances to be honest, but you failed me. Instead, I was forced to play along, and observe it with my own eyes in the lion's den."

"Holmes, I did not think that..."

"Say I did not participate in your game, and did not attend? Or what if I had, but not with you? Would you have gone regardless? Or were you supposing my curiosity would ensure our attendance, and the entire set-up was based on my inquisitive disposition? Ah, I believe I am giving a woman far too much credit. I've no doubt it was more one-dimensional in character."

Tennyson folded her arms across her chest with a sniff. "Holmes, that was very hard."

"Not too hard, for it is thoroughly merited. I am neither a duffer nor a blind mole, and I'd thank you not to treat me as such. If you've an ounce of respect for me as your mentor, you will not use these childish and manipulative tactics with me."

I felt like a parent lecturing an adolescent after she'd climbed out the window. This was the last conversation in the world I had expected to have with her. I sighed, seeing that once again, a woman had shown her true colours. "I hoped you would have been different. But I see you are like every female, and cannot be trusted."

"Do not think that being a woman constitutes being dishonest." Her voice was barely above a whisper.

"Ha! Show me one who is not and I will change my opinion of the sex as a whole! And *you,* my dear, have done little to dispel that belief. Your recent conduct has been absolutely inexcusable. Women are nothing but trouble, as anyone with a modicum of a brain is aware."

"I suppose you are quite perfect, are you?" She leapt from the chair. "You can do no wrong? Never lied in your life?"

"But have I ever lied to you, Miss Tennyson?"

She stood motionless.

"Well, have I?"

"No," she sat back down.

202

"I would expect the same courtesy then, if you are even capable."

"I did not mean to betray your trust."

"What did you expect from this? That everything would arrange itself perfectly? That he would whisk you away, sweep you off your feet, and marry you? I suppose every girl dreams of becoming a princess, but this is not a fairytale, and you are not Cinderella."

She was visibly upset, but I was too put about to burden myself with her feelings. I knelt on the floor next to her, and turned her chin towards me.

"I quite understand you are very young and have much to learn, but I assumed you had more common sense. I was under the distinct impression you were wise beyond your years, but I see that I misjudged you."

Her face was red. She looked as though I'd slapped her across the face. I stood, and breathed in deeply. Seeing her distraught was more difficult than I had anticipated so I looked away. I heard her sniff and suddenly felt beastly. She deserved a reprimand, but I seemed to be inadvertently destroying her. So much so, that I feared she would break. I needed to step down.

"I have little tolerance for the superficial, and his world is saturated in it. He lives purely for pleasure. Ah, that sad weakness of his!" I turned back to face her. "It will not be long before he tires of you, and is off to the next conquest. Men of such power and reputation can never be entirely trusted. This is one of the more invaluable lessons that I can teach you."

Tennyson lifted herself from the chair, and wiped her eyes. "Is it that you wish I be a slave to duty, so dedicated to my work and lessons

203

that I remain empty, and devoid of feeling? If that is your desire, then I will oblige, as you are the master. But you must clarify that now to avoid any further misunderstandings."

I placed my hands on her shoulders. "You are not hearing me, Tennyson. My stance is this. You lied to me about the existence of *that* relationship. Therefore, I am justified in expressing my opinions on it, as it has damaged *ours*. Does that seem fair?" I stepped away with a sigh. "Otherwise no," I waved her off, "you are free to see whom you wish."

Tennyson grabbed her cold teacup from the table and cradled it in her hands as she took a sip. "You are too kind."

"What I am generally saying is: Do not give me cause me to doubt or question your honesty again. No partnership can survive if there is not trust, and my faith in you at the moment, is minimal at best."

She toyed with her teacup and leaned against the fireplace mantle. "Then are we not partners now?"

I threw up my hands in exasperation. "Woman, why must you always read more into a situation than truly exists? Do not put words into my mouth Miss Tennyson, as that will only anger me further."

"I am sorry."

I thrust my hands in my gray dressing gown's pockets and wandered about the room. I felt betrayed, disillusioned, and out of sorts. I needed to calm. My natural inclination was to seek solace with cocaine, but instead I snatched up my black clay pipe from the rack off the mantle, stuffed it with shag from my Persian slipper, and proceeded to light a match.

I was aware of Tennyson's eyes upon me, perhaps wondering what my next move might be. Truthfully, I had not thought that far ahead. After a few puffs, I moved to the bookshelf and fervently began searching for something, anything to open in false interest to buy myself time. I pulled 'The Origin of Species' from the top shelf, and thumbed through it. I landed on the words, "Man selects only for his own good: Nature only for that of the being which she tends", and decided what my next condition would be.

"And henceforth you are not to set foot in the palace again, under any circumstances," I replaced the book to the shelf, "as I feel you need no further temptation from people who view morality and civility as contentious philosophies."

She sat stiffly, and her tiny lips formed into a pout. "But what if I am called there for a legitimate reason?"

"My position on the matter is immutable. And for what legitimate reason would *you* possibly be summoned by the crown?"

Her hand shook as she noisily placed the teacup back on the table. "How terribly foolish of me. Who am I, that I would have any justifiable interaction with royalty?" Her eyes welled up with tears. "I should like to go for walk, if I may have your permission," she wiped her wet chin with her hand.

"Do exactly as you please," I gestured towards the door. "I am establishing rules to live by Tennyson, not keeping you a prisoner."

She banged from the room and down the staircase. I heard her crying in the hallway as the front door suddenly opened, then slammed shut.

I slumped into my armchair, and stretched out my legs. What sort of tangled mess had I got myself into by taking on a woman as a lodger and student? I never trusted her sex, and now I was reminded why. I curse myself for thinking she would be any different.

31ˢᵗ January 1888

Since New Year's Day, Tennyson and I talk less, joke never, and she spends more time in her room than ever before. I do not believe we have had any true type of interaction since the 6ᵗʰ, when she wished me a happy birthday, and gifted me a new morning dressing gown, as she claimed my current was old, ratty, and smelled as if something had crawled in it and died. It was a beautiful shade of blue, with gold piping and a matching sash, far too extravagant for my modest needs. I said I could not accept, as I was aware of her funds being pinched to the inch, and I was quite contented with my dressing gown in all its ratty-ness. She persisted, though the exchange bordered on feigned politeness at best.

Tennyson's father was becoming impatient, and had refused her this month's stipend, so it became necessary for her to find a temporary place of employment. She took a position as a barrister's typist at the Inns of Court in Middle Temple. It is painfully apparent she does not favour it in the least.

As she is required in early and works long hours, our nights of talking by the fireplace into the early morning have vanished. I admit I miss them. My indulgences are more frequent these days. I am restless, rigid, melancholy... something appears to be absent from my life...

CHAPTER 19

IT WAS THE WHISKEY TALKING

5ᵗʰ February 1888

Having invested so much time and energy in a project, I decided to give Tennyson another chance. Friday evening, I sat in my new dressing gown (which I found I fancied immensely) and sipped away on a glass of whiskey whilst I waited for her to return home. When she entered the doorway in her black work dress and purple wool coat, I rested down my drink next to an empty glass on the table, and approached her.

"Tennyson, I believe the time is ripe for renewing an old conversation and question, to which, I will now expect an answer. What seems to be troubling you?"

Her face was stone. She began to rustle away from me, but I blocked the pathway to her bedroom door. She attempted to move around me, and I again stepped in front of her. "You have been quiet for weeks, and altogether unsociable. Pray tell, what seems to be the cause of this recent rift?"

"I have been working long hours, and am tired by the time I return home," she pushed me out of her way with her muff, "my apologies if you feel slighted, but I haven't cared for socializing with *anyone*."

"It is difficult to teach a student who is not present for her lessons, Tennyson."

She turned with a sour expression. "You have made no indication that you wished to continue instructing me. And, as you have not requested I accompany you on any cases as of late..."

"It has been quiet," I said. "That is no reflection on you, nor my wish to teach you."

She looked to the floor, and swung her left foot back and forth. "Yes well, I daresay I was predicting you would send me back to my father's any day now, as I feel you have been ignoring me."

I gently stepped on the toe of her black boot to prevent it from moving. "The shoe on the other foot, *you* have not seemed to care for *my* company or advice. For what reason are you so annoyed with me?"

Tennyson shook her head, then slipped her foot out from underneath mine. "My mood is not related to you, nor am I annoyed."

"Your response is a little unconvincing."

She folded her arms and frowned, her hands hidden by the bear fur cuffs around her wrists. She then lifted an eyebrow, and tried not to smile.

There you are, Tennyson.

"No cross examination," I promised. "But may I ask you to join me for a refreshment?"

She shook her head, and again tried to walk towards her room. I took her by the arm, and held it firmly.

"Please? Just... one." I moved my hand from her arm, to around her shoulders, and coaxed her over to the sofa. "A drink of good faith, that I will neither exile nor banish you. Then you may retire."

She begrudgingly unbuttoned her coat, and slid it off. "Oh, very well."

I took it from her, hung it on the rack, then poured whiskey into the empty glass on the table. I handed it to her as she flopped down on the sofa.

"You were quite confident I would agree, yes?" She pointed to the glass.

"I have ways of being persuasive when necessary. But it was more of a hope, than a certainty, Tennyson."

I had a plan on how to obtain the information I required, so began discussing unrelated and comfortable subjects with her in order to give the alcohol it's needed time to take effect. I poured her a drink, then another, and before her glass could ever be close to empty I would top it off, though she weakly protested.

In a now happier mood, Tennyson pointed to my dressing gown with a smile. "You like it then?"

"Yes," I sat next to her, "you were quite right about the other. Now then," I disposed of my glass, "what is causing your discomfort?"

She sniffed, and rested her glass on the table. "I feel awful Holmes, I really do. My life is such a terrible failure, and I know you are deeply disappointed in me. I have ruined absolutely everything because I was foolish, and now you no longer trust me. It was not my intent to be vicious, I swear to you."

"I cannot deny that your dishonesty upset me, but it is over now, correct?"

She nodded somberly.

"Then, what's done is done."

She poured herself another glass and downed it quickly, too quickly. I attempted to move the bottle from her reach but she held up a finger, indicating she wished for one more, then poured another half glass. "Cheers to you no longer hating me," she toasted, then polished it off. She struggled to plant her glass back on the table, but her coordination was lacking, and it nearly fell to the floor.

"As you were most biting and confrontational New Year's Day, I had more assumed you hated *me*," I reminded her, as I pushed her glass further back on the table.

She rested her elbows on her knees, and gingerly picked at her nails. "It was all an act. Inside I felt horrid, guilty, and ashamed. I was worried you were through with me and..." She stared at her glass. "I missed you."

Missed me? I patted her shoulder. "All is resolved. Therefore, we can resume our partnership."

Her cheeks were a bright red, and her movements were more slowed, and loosened. I was bit concerned she had taken in too much. "You seem flushed Tennyson, are you alright?"

She attempted to sit up straight, which apparently made her dizzy, as he upper body wobbled back and forth. "Oh to be sure! Though, I should apologize in advance, for I am quite drunk at the moment, and possibly capable of anything. As I am sure I shan't remember a thing in the morning, I am excusing myself now for anything ridiculous."

I suddenly remembered Mycroft's presumptuous theory unveiled at Christmas time. 'Capable of *anything'* she just said. Would she respond as he predicted, if she were not only coaxed, but relaxed enough to do so? This could be the perfect opportunity to prove him wrong, without her knowing that she was the subject of an experiment. "Tennyson, if you are indeed so uninhibited at present, do you think you would try to... oh I don't know... try and kiss me?"

Tennyson's eyes opened wide, and a panicked expression flashed across her face. "Oh no!" she laughed, shifting her gaze to the fireplace. "Why would I do such a thing?"

I slid closer to her, to see if my actions elicited any type of response. "Because often times one behaves in a far less reserved manner, when under the influence of alcohol."

"Being intoxicated does *not* necessitate provocative behaviour, sir, if that is what you are alluding to," she wagged her finger at me. "I... just as you... view our partnership in a purely professional manner. You should know me better and... well I must say, I am slightly offended."

I could not help but smile. She was rather amusing like this.

"No, I was asking a question. You are a truly sophisticated and refined woman, one with commendable values and morals."

She narrowed her eyes at me.

"Oh Tennyson!" I laughed, "come now, as I have never observed you under such circumstances, I was merely curious as to your typical patterns of behaviour." I leaned back with a contented and triumphant sigh. I had finally proven my brother wrong, *and* was going to have my violin.

"I see," she comfortably dropped deeper into the cushion of the sofa with me, "though I am not usually anything, as I am not usually drunk. But tonight, I have *you* to thank for that."

"I was merely the instigator, you carried on quite by yourself!"

She was in rare form. I was suddenly struck by an overwhelming and personal curiosity. As she had indicated, whatever I did at this juncture in the evening would more than likely be forgot. I had kissed women purely for professional reasons, yet had never felt anything but complete indifference towards any of them. Women, I always felt, were creatures I did not, nor did I much care to, understand.

However, what if I were to kiss a woman *not* out of necessity, but for recreation? Could it be different? I hardly thought so, but the question had crept into my mind and I debated testing it. Should my experiment be harmless, forgot in the morning, and have no lasting effect, wherein lied the injury? Though, should I be incorrect about her memory, I would have some rather embarrassing explaining to do in the morning.

I leaned into her. "Supposing I change my question, Tennyson. What if *I* were to try and kiss *you*?"

"What if what?" she asked in a drunken haze, now only partially coherent.

Before she could answer I reached out, wrapped my fingers around the back of her neck, and kissed her on the lips. She was very soft and warm, and smelled of jasmine. I felt her body go limp, and she sank further into the sofa. When I released her, her eyes were closed, and she was breathing heavily.

"Oh Sherlock, I... I..."

212

"Yes Scarlett... er... Tennyson?" I shook my head. She had never called me by my Christian name, and it caught me off my guard. I had never referred to her in the familiar either, and I am not sure as to why such a deviation occurred.

"You called me Scarlett, hmm..." she said dreamily. She then reached up and lightly stroked my cheek. "Sherlock, I truly... do love you..." Before she could say more, her eyes rolled to the back of her head and she fainted. She had collapsed into a drunken slumber in my arms.

I was temporarily frozen by her admission. Once my body had thawed, I gently lifted her back to her room, pulled the covers, and tucked her in.

"I cannot believe it," I closed her door. "Mycroft was right. I suppose I will not be getting my Stradivarius after all." But now I had a rather larger problem on my hands, and I frowned as I stared at her bedroom door. "I am sorry I cannot give you what you want, Tennyson," I said quietly. "That is simply not who I am."

6th February 1888

The next morning I sat in my basket chair reading the agony columns when Tennyson emerged from her room, still dressed from the night previous. She came down to the sitting room with slightly mussed hair, blush red cheeks, and half-closed eyes.

"Good morning Tennyson, did you sleep well?" I asked, already knowing the answer from her appearance.

"I was horrendously restless. I cannot even remember how the deuce I returned to my bed last night," she rubbed her eyes.

"There is a simple explanation for that. I carried you."

"My god, was I that bad off?" She held her head then swayed as if she would fall, and leaned against the wall for support. She squinted her eyes to avoid the bright sunlight that was cascading into the room, and rubbed her forehead. "I have such a head pain," she grumbled, "I did not do anything... embarrassing did I?"

"You remember nothing?"

She shook her head.

"Pity. Then you do not recall our romantic interlude?"

She covered her mouth in horror. "*What!?*" she gasped through her fingers.

I laughed heartily. "Whom do you take me for Tennyson? I would never take advantage of you in such a state, and you know my thoughts on such matters regardless. You were perfectly respectable. After you fainted, I put you to bed. That is all." I looked down at the paper to hide my smile.

She nodded uncomfortably. "That is a relief. You swear I was not absurd, and are only trying to avoid any awkwardness?"

"You made only one comment. That it is no wonder women have no interest in me, for I can be exceptionally dull and longwinded. That was the extent of it."

"Oh Holmes, if I offended..."

"Not in the least! I am quite contented with not being desired. It makes life less complicated. However, you do remember that we are resuming our partnership?"

Tennyson thought for a moment, undoubtedly pushing through cobwebs in her fogged brain to recall anything from our conversation. "Yes... you are no longer cross with me..."

"Precisely. So you must request to be part time, if you keep your position at all."

"But..."

"Your portion of the rent has just decreased by half. Therefore on Monday, do as I ask please."

Her jaw dropped in surprise. "Are you... quite certain?"

"Quite. On our next assignment, it can return to its previous amount, which you can pay for with your share of the compensation from our client."

"You... want to pay me for my work with you?" She spun in a circle causing her dress to flair up around her, and she gleefully squeezed her hands together. "Oh, thank you Holmes! I promise you will not regret this!"

In keeping with her expectations, the previous night was a blur. However, I now had the information I needed to begin my experiment.

CHAPTER 20

A STUDY IN TENNYSON

7ᵗʰ February 1888

Now that I am aware of Tennyson's affections, I wonder how their appearance, strength, and even existence can become anticipated, manipulated, and ultimately controlled. The premise is simple. If I am cold and detached, she will lose interest. If I pursue or express interest, she will respond favourably. Or could it be the opposite? Perhaps reveling in the thrill of the hunt? If I shower her with attention, will she retreat? And if I ignore her, will she pine?

If I am successful, this could revolutionize how men relate to women. To discover the mechanisms that drive and control a woman's passions, would allow one to create a guide of navigation to steer clear through their storms of emotional fury and wreckage. There must be a cycle, or systematic configuration, as everything in nature possesses one. The possibilities that encompass such a find could be inestimable.

~ ~

Jonathan closed the journal and rubbed his hand down his face. "What a callous... ugh...! Talking about my mother as if she were a lab rat. Enough for one night."

He slid the book underneath his bed, and turned down the light.

The next night, Jonathan ventured over to Newham College to see how close he could make it to the dormitories without being detected. He heard there was a large interior garden, which would have been the perfect place for his mother to hide her trinket box. However, upon seeing how heavily guarded the campus was with porters, he realized he would need a game plan first. He was scheduled to see Edith Leahy for his mother's class photograph later in the week, so decided to wait and ask her if his mother even *spent* any time in the gardens before taking on such a risk.

It was a crisp clear evening, and he welcomed the chill and bitter snap of the winter air, but he was lonely, so ventured over to Gabriel's to pay his friend a visit.

When he arrived, he could already see several other people milling about inside from his view of the upstairs window.

Not wanting to intrude, he turned to leave, but Gabriel flung open the front doorway with a cry, nearly spilling the glass of red wine that hung loosely in his hand, and shouted, "Hopkins! A few of my fellow Trinity students are here for a drink...or several," he grinned, his teeth stained with purple. "Do come inside for a bit!"

The rooms were tastefully decorated with expensive furniture, and a full bar was pushed up against the back wall. The hardwood floor had an exquisite Persian Rug that nearly reached the walls, and three large windows, framed by thick emerald drapes, gave the space a more open and inviting feeling. Jonathan noticed the distinct smell of jasmine and looked to the mantle to see the smoke plumes of incense burning.

Gabriel either had a slightly effeminate decorating sense, or his mother had dressed his living space. Based on the white lace doilies adorning his mahogany end tables, and the curvy porcelain and gold clock on the mantle, Jonathan assumed the latter.

The other five boys, all presumably seniors, smiled smugly at Jonathan as he entered the doorway.

"What's this then Gabriel, your little brother?" one darker-skinned boy laughed.

"No," Gabriel patted Jonathan on the back, "Hopkins here is a freshman at Trinity."

"Fraternizing with a freshman?" another asked with an Irish accent, "isn't that there a bit beneath ya Gabriel?"

"Hopkins has this extraordinary ability," Gabriel pushed Jonathan towards them like an offering, "he can tell you anything about yourself in a moment's time! Hopkins, do your thing."

Jonathan was confused. "Do what thing?"

"Your deductive reasoning and analytical thinking bit. Read them like you did me!"

"Why, he a fortuneteller?" asked a heavier set boy with dark hair, as he leaned back in a brown leather chair by the window.

He reminded Jonathan of Neville, so he immediately disliked him, but as he was Gabriel's 'supposed' friend, Jonathan remained polite. "I make educated guesses," he shrugged, "and sometimes I am right."

"He is far too modest, they are always right!" Gabriel said. "Come then! Show them!"

Though not partial to being treated like a circus performer, Jonathan sighed, then nodded. "Might I have names then, to properly address your friends?"

218

"You cannot just pull *that* out of thin air?" a rather small wiry boy complained.

"Introduce yourselves, lot!" Gabriel pounced, "elsewise, it is last call for drinks."

The boys grumbled.

"Danny Glavin."

"Nicholas Kwiatkowski."

"Jason Palen."

"Stafford Eaton."

"And Christopher Ryan," the last one huffed, as he lit a fag.

"And I, am Jonathan Hopkins," Jonathan bowed. He turned to face Jason Palen, and took a deep breath. "Right, Mr. Palen, you enjoy gambling though you don't often win. You practice archery, but are not particularly good. You enjoy red, as opposed to white wine, and your parents are well off, but are resistant to offer monetary assistance, due to your gambling habits. You are also a carpenter, engage in theater, and recently twisted your ankle, perhaps on the way here?"

Jason put down his glass of white wine and glared at him. "Gabriel could have easily told you any of that!"

Gabriel sauntered over with a rousing laugh. "How could I have done? Between your arrival and his, when would I have mentioned that you fell over that tree root and twisted your foot? Good work Hopkins."

Jason huffed.

219

"Don't you want to know how he figured that?" Gabriel asked.

"No."

"How about me then?" the blonde Stafford Eaton asked. "I barely know Gabriel. I'm here visiting my mates Christopher and Danny. This will be your true test!"

Jonathan gave Stafford a once over, then nodded. "Mr. Eaton, you are very athletic, and played rugby at Oxford where you attended. You were best on the team, though had several rather brutal run-ins throughout your career. You have an affinity for carrots, enjoy running, and are sentimental towards your woman friend, perhaps fiancée? Or at least appear to be to appease her."

"How in the world you know all that!?" Stafford asked dumbfounded, "and I *do* want to know!"

"The cuts and scars on your face, the wrapping of your knee, as well as the obvious nose fracture that you incurred whilst playing, are most telling. They are common rugby injuries. Oxford's coat of arms is on your jumper," Jonathan pointed to the small emblem on his chest, "and your hands are slightly discoloured with an orange hue due to the carotene in carrots, which would have to be eaten in large abundances in order to affect the skin so. Perhaps, as they are considered to have muscle strengthening properties? Your calves are quite shaped; observable even under your knee socks; and you should have to do quite a bit of running to maintain their mass and form, as is also part of training for rugby."

Stafford felt his bandaged knee and laughed. "Quite good, and my fiancée?"

"You have a thin pink ribbon in your left pocket. Your woman friend either requested that you carry it to remind you of her, or you sincerely asked for it for some sentimental attachment."

Danny and Christopher pointed a mocking finger at Stafford as a small piece of the pink ribbon Jonathan had mentioned was poking out of his pocket.

"Shut it, you two!" Stafford stuffed the ribbon deeper into his pocket. "It is not wise to refuse a woman anything, as they will have it." The boys laughed. "At least I *have* a woman!"

Gabriel put Jonathan in a headlock, then mussed his hair. "Do you gents believe me now? Is he not just like a little Sherlock Holmes?"

Nicholas poured a clear liquid into a glass tumbler, then brought it over to Jonathan. "Have yourself a drink Jonathan, you've earned it!"

Jonathan sniffed the glass and made a face. "What is this?"

"Ouzo, from Greece."

"Now Danny and Christopher," Stafford gestured to his friends. "This I'd like to see!"

Feeling more confident, Jonathan took a gulp of the clear liquid, winced, then cleared his throat. He proceeded to tell Danny and Christopher as much as he could discern, being wrong only about Danny mountain climbing the Urals in Siberia. It was the Himalayas in India.

"Now do you see why we're chums?" Gabriel said proudly, "he's my detective in training." He patted Jonathan on the back. "I say, do you know? I fancy I will call you that, just for fun."

Jonathan's eyes widened. "Call me what?"

"Little Sherlock Holmes! No wait, just Holmes! You don't mind, do you Jonathan? You will be a sport, won't you? Jonathan Holmes sounds fine?"

Before Jonathan could protest, the boys all drunkenly raised their glasses and toasted, "To Jonathan Holmes!"

How had *this* happened?! Jonathan looked around the room as everyone's eyes were upon him, eagerly awaiting a response. "I... suppose not, why... why wouldn't it be?"

The boys all cheered.

Jonathan lifted his glass to Gabriel and smiled. "But should I call *you* Watson then? My esteemed and faithful, yet highly unobservant friend?"

Gabriel pouted and put down his glass as the other boys again shouted enthusiastically with approval.

"To Jonathan Holmes, and Gabriel Watson!" Nicholas chuckled, as he sipped down the last drop of Ouzo and tossed the bottle into the dustbin. "Think you may have broken through the anti-freshman barrier in this place Jonathan. In fact, we'd trade *you* for Gabriel!"

The boys all whooped and hollered.

Gabriel sniffed. "Oh? Well, I'd trade *you* for a *cow*, and think I'd be getting the better deal."

Jonathan hoped that Gabriel would be drunk enough to forget the whole thing in the morning, but for now, he'd had enough, so headed towards the door. "Capital meeting you all, but I really should be getting on."

Jonathan staggered back to his room, now seeing double doors where there was usually one. Though still adjusting to socialization, he belonged with the college crowd. For the first time in his life he wasn't treated like an outcast. Finally he was accepted for who he was and even revered, based on Gabriel's friends' compliments.

With renewed energy he picked up Holmes' journal, grabbed a glass of water off his bedside locker, and blinked at the words on the page until they finally came into focus.

~ ~

18th February 1888

As Watson's practice thrived it became necessary to use Tennyson more regularly. As some of my older and less 'accepting of the times' clients might be opposed to my associate being a woman, we decided that in a few instances she should don a man's suit and mustache, and play the role of Mr. James Mumford. She has been practicing her character daily, and plays the part well, but I only hope she will be able to sustain her persona for the duration of a case.

CHAPTER 21

INCEPTION OF JAMES MUMFORD

It occurred to me that I would have to instruct Tennyson on how to defend herself, as women know little of physical combat.

She had not been entirely open to the idea but when I explained the necessity, she consented. Our first lesson was in pugilism. I demonstrated a handful of moves, then had her attempt each one several times before we sparred.

"I *will* be easy on you Tennyson, but you must view this as an actual fight, and not just an exercise. Remember that physical strength is not the primary factor that determines the power of punches. The quickness of moves, a person's concentration, and the correct use of body weight, are all elements that could contribute to success."

She was doing quite well for a time, but I then surprised her by pinning her arm behind her back. She writhed angrily, fighting to break free, and I warned her to never underestimate her opponent. As I held her, I noted a familiar fragrance. "Is that lavender?" I asked.

She froze, puzzled. "What? Why?"

I remembered that lavender was her chosen poison for her rendezvouses with The Prince.

"That fragrance serves as a very loud reminder."

"Then perhaps you should refrain from sniffing my neck."

Taken aback, my grip loosened and she managed to break away from me. She adjusted herself in irritation and twisted from side to side.

"Troubles, Tennyson?"

"I cannot move in this damned corset, Holmes."

"Then might I suggest you remove it."

She paused, then placed her hands on her hips.

"You must always attempt to triumph by any means necessary."

"Then might I ask to borrow a shirt?"

I hadn't really been serious, but not to be outdone, I returned with a long, white, button down shirt. She snatched if from my hands, then slipped into her bedroom. She later emerged wearing her skirt, and now my shirt, with the sleeves rolled up to her elbows. Her appearance was downright comical.

"Now, we will be on equal ground," she nodded.

I raised my fists in the defensive position, and we fought on for perhaps half a quarter. Tennyson's form and swiftness had greatly improved due to the absence of a restraining corset, and she did manage to throw one punch rather harshly to my chest that left me slightly winded.

"I am impressed, Tennyson," I said with a cough. "But I was still being easy on you."

"Just admit you underestimated me."

I massaged my chest. "Do not become too self assured. Confidence is not to be confused with cockiness."

She moved her fingers to the top button of the blouse, and unfastened it. "You may have your shirt back now." My eyes must have widened for she laughed, then dropped her hands to her side. "*After* I change in my room."

I immediately ran to my journal and jotted down the date, along with my observation. 'If one behaves flirtatiously with a woman, but is subtle, she will respond in an equally flirtatious manner, as I have just witnessed'.

20th February 1888

Tennyson's first test as Mumford came quickly. A man's son had mysteriously disappeared at sea and he called upon me to investigate. The man, a Mr. Chester Kent, doubted the validity of what he was told by the first officer and claimed that he'd a father's intuition that something was amiss.

Mr. Kent was a conservatively dressed, heavier set man of his sixties, with thick, grayed mutton chops, and a thin, silver pince-nez clipped to his long narrow nose. He arrived with a cane and hobbled in with some effort. I gauged it was from a polo accident, some years back.

He was accompanied by a petite, doe-eyed female, with curly blonde hair, later identified as Miss Adriana Kent. She was not yet twenty, and her fashion sense had suffered from the absence of a mother figure at a very early age. Her Indian maid did her best with her limited knowledge of English dress, but Miss Kent wore far too much lace and frill for her barely five-foot frame. She reminded me of a pink rhododendron, and had been eyeing Tennyson's alter ego throughout the entire conversation.

"I was aware you had a partner Mr. Holmes, but have never heard of your friend Mumford here," Mr. Kent said, giving my mustachioed assistance a once over.

I had only seen Tennyson in her Mumford attire once before, but it just then struck me how much the brown wig, matching mustache, and tweed suit made her/him resemble my dear Dr. Watson. I tried not to smile.

"Mr. Mumford is a recent graduate from Cambridge and I have been teaching him my methods." I winked at Tennyson. "He shows great promise. You may speak as freely before him as you would before myself."

"Very well," Mr. Kent nodded. He removed his spectacles and placed them in his lap with a sigh. He coughed into his left hand, and took a deep breath. "My son, Michael, was always a bit finicky and perhaps a touch effeminate. In an effort to cure him of his wistful and soft nature, I had encouraged him to join Her Majesty's Navy. He reluctantly agreed, and was terribly unhappy from the start. Nothing was ever right. The entire world, or least the world within the Navy, was against him. I always knew him to be a rather odd boy, sensitive and self-righteous, with a touch of paranoia. Therefore, as it was remaining in line with his usual character, I mistakenly took his protests to be the usual objections he had to most everything in life." Mr. Kent shook his head sadly. "Sirs, I was horribly wrong."

He pulled a crumpled letter from his breast pocket, and carefully unfolded it. As the page was floppy, and more like fabric than paper, it was clear that it had been folded, and unfolded, numerous times. "This was his last letter before disappearing. Might I...read it aloud?"

I waved my hand, indicating he should press on.

"*Dearest father and Adriana,*" he began, but then paused. "My wife passed away some years ago, Mr. Holmes."

I closed my eyes to listen. "I had gathered that, please continue."

He nodded.

"*I am becoming concerned for my safety. The men are hard, judgmental and callous. They make a point to ridicule me, play horrid pranks, and criticize my every move. Recently, it has taken a turn for the worse. I have been called such appalling things, and threatened on several occasions. While at first I believed the threats to be empty, I no longer doubt their validity.*

One's time at sea is revered as being that which fosters lifelong friendships and comradery. However, I feel as though I have met my worst enemies. I have been trying to separate myself as best I can, but the continual injustices I have been blindly suffering from them are beyond endurance. The Number One, Ian Bloodworth, claims he will protect me, but I do not feel I can trust him. Human nature is truly at its most vile in this environment. Please, I beg of you, allow me to request a return home, for I trust they will grant it, and be glad to be rid of me.

Your loving son and brother- Michael."

"Did your son have a woman in his life?" Tennyson asked, in her lower pitched voice for Mumford, "a fiancée, wife, anything of the sort?"

"Sadly, no, he never expressed interest. He certainly had women calling, but he would just as soon read or spend time wandering about the gardens and riding his bone shaker," Mr. Kent shrugged. "He was a good lad, and smart too. I cannot believe that a simple sailing accident would be his demise. There's something not right there, Mr. Holmes, Mr. Mumford."

"So, they claimed it was a cruising accident," I said. "Did they not find the body?"

Mr. Kent took Adriana's hand, and sorrowfully shook his head. "He was never found. It has only been two days since I was informed."

I rubbed my chin thoughtfully, ruminating over the particulars of the case. I looked to Tennyson with a nod. "We will take your case, Mr. Kent."

"Thank you Mr. Holmes, Mr. Mumford!" Mr. Kent pulled a white handkerchief from his breast pocket, blew his nose, then returned the used hanky to its resting place. "I just want my son given fair dealings."

"What was the name of the vessel he was assigned to?"

"The HMS Dolphin. It was a sloop of war; colonial cruiser, and part of the Channel Fleet. They were cruising outside Edinburgh."

Mr. Kent rose to his feet, and I followed in kind.

"We shall do all we can," I shook his hand.

"I would be grateful," he said, then gathered his cane, and turned to exit.

His daughter pretended to drop something, and looked around on the floor for the phantom item as her father left our rooms. Once he was out of sight, she nodded as if she had found the invisible whatsit, and exclaimed, "Oh, here it is!" and stuffed the microscopic bit into her reticule.

She rose to her feet, and gingerly brushed back her hair as she approached Tennyson with a smile. "I... hope you do not find me forward sir, given the circumstances, but might I inquire as to whether there is a Mrs. Mumford?"

Tennyson folded her arms behind her, and cleared her throat. "There is not, at present."

Miss Kent radiated with excitement. "Oh truly?"

"However," Tennyson said curtly, "I am also not in the market for one. Good day, Miss Kent," she bowed stiffly, then turned and sat at the lab table in the corner. She coarsely flipped open my casebook, and feigned interest in the liquid contents of a retort.

The poor girl seemed crushed, and quickly dashed from the room slamming the door behind her.

I dropped to the sofa and chuckled. "Oh, I believe..." I breathed through my laughter, "I believe... you were rather harsh to her, James. The girl takes a fancy to you."

Tennyson jumped from the table and glared at me through her false mustache.

"That is hardly comical," she scolded. "Her brother has perished, and she is making courtship inquiries? Is there no respect for the dead? No sense of mourning? I do not think she has an ounce of intelligence buried anywhere in that ridiculous mass of fluff atop her neck!"

I laughed harder at her sudden explosion. "It appears you are desired regardless of which gender you assume!"

"Now then, the case?" she asked with a grumble, as she sat down.

"Ah yes, that little matter..." I inhaled. "Why ever did you ask if he had a wife or fiancé?"

"I have my theories."

I leaned forward, rested my elbows on my knees, and laced my fingers together with a smug expression. "Which are?"

"That he does not care for women's affections... but does so for men's," she pointed at me.

I had already formulated such a possibility on my own but she was in training, so needed to verbalize her assumptions in order to ensure their accuracy. "Explain?"

"He was being made fun of, called names...in a military setting, the most obvious reason for such behaviour, from what I understand, is that the man they ridicule, they are afraid of. Typically, because he cares for other men in a very 'unnatural way,' or has something equally disturbing about him. Mr. Kent said the boy was odd, and though he did not elaborate, I sensed that immediately."

It was now my responsibility to play devil's advocate, and challenge her observations. "From what physical evidence?"

"Well, none yet, but... I am quite sure I am correct."

"Very well, I shall now call you James Mumford, clairvoyant."

Tennyson rolled her eyes. "Then I shall simply say, it is a *possibility.*"

"Better."

"What is our first order of business?"

"Obviously," I rose up, "we must speak with this first officer, Ian Bloodworth. As Mr. Kent only recently received the news, I would speculate they are still on shore leave. We must work quickly," I grabbed my tweed ulster coat.

As I assumed, the ship was still in port at the Portsmouth Royal Naval Dockyard. Once granted passage by Commander Forrest, the ship's captain, he directed us towards his executive officer's cabins near the ship's stern.

Though he was engaged at the time, we managed an audience with Bloodworth later that afternoon. A seaman of eight years, with a stellar reputation, he was very much before the wind, and every bit a well-groomed, upstanding man of power. He was flaxen-haired, broad shouldered, and had an exceptional physique for his slightly shorter frame. His double-breasted jacket uniform, with a loop at the top of the sleeve stripes, indicated that he was a Lieutenant.

Though pleasant initially, when questioned about Michael Kent's disappearance he frowned, and walked towards the scuttle of his small, sterile cabin. "I had tried my best to shield him from the men," he folded his hands behind him, "but could only do so much."

"What was the reason for their animosity?" I questioned. "Surely all sub-lieutenants are subject to ridicule, but why was the boy so singled out?"

Bloodworth spun with a heavy sigh. "It is a shame to admit Mr. Holmes, but Sub-lieutenant Kent suffered from matters of the heart concerning our other lieutenant, Giles Thompson, who oversees the engineering operations of this vessel."

"Could you elaborate?"

"He was in *love* with Thompson. *That* was the issue."

I looked to Tennyson. She smiled, projecting, 'I told you so'. But had she been as aware as she thought, she would have seen my subtle smile back, 'I already knew.'

"Are you certain?" I approached him.

He walked over to his desk, and intently flipped through several pages on a clipboard. "Ask anyone from the wardroom to the lower deck! As Thompson is *not* of that sort, Sub-lieutenant Kent was rejected. I quite honestly believe it was a suicide," he looked up. "I told his father as much."

"He had mentioned that, yes."

"Sub-lieutenant Kent seemed troubled from his first day aboard, gentlemen; it surprised no one." Bloodworth looked to the clock on his wall. "Well now, is that the time?"

"May we speak to Lieutenant Thompson then?" Tennyson asked, as she stood from the folding chair by the door.

"You may try," Bloodworth said, as he unclasped a page from the clipboard, "but he is very upset about the whole business, and does not wish to discuss it."

"We shall be brief, but a conversation would be appreciated."

Bloodworth glanced over the page he was holding as he walked towards the door, then looked up. "I do understand wanting to help your client, Mr. Holmes, Mr. Mumford, but I'm afraid there is no mystery here to be solved," he quickly ushered us out of his cabin. "Now if you'll excuse me, I have matters to attend to." He walked down the narrow passageway then disappeared around the left corner. Clearly, we were to fend for ourselves in terms of locating Giles Thompson.

"I was right, wasn't I?" Tennyson whispered with a smile.

"Mumford, I must request that you follow my methods and keep your observations muted until we have returned to Baker Street. Even bulkheads have ears."

Thompson's cabin was just a few down from Bloodworth's, and to our good fortune he was present, however, Bloodworth had been correct in presuming that he would offer us no additional information. The youthful looking, dark-haired gentleman dourly bade us farewell, and stated he had much to do before they returned to sea tomorrow.

As we left, Tennyson pulled me aside and asked if she might have a chance alone. I conceded, and watched her slip back into Thompson's quarters and shut the door.

Once we returned to Baker Street, and she had removed her male attire, she relayed back the conversation she had with Thompson. He admitted to spending time with Kent, as he found him an amiable fellow, but when rumors of a very negative fashion began developing, Bloodworth warned him to pull away, as it could damage his reputation and chances for advancement. Panicked, he did as suggested. To explain the estrangement, Bloodworth concocted a story that Kent had made romantic advancements.

"This only caused the men to treat Kent worse," Tennyson said. "Thompson had advised him to put in for transfer to another ship, but then it became too late."

"Did *he* think Kent committed suicide?" I asked her.

She shook her head. "Not at all. In fact, he felt it was murder, but had no proof, nor did he know whom to suspect."

I leapt to my feet and paced the floor, puffing hard on my black pipe.

"Don't you want to know how I got him to speak?"

"We have the information we require," I waved her off, "and must meet with the crew immediately as they leave tomorrow afternoon. Early morning, Tennyson, your alter ego is again required."

21ˢᵗ February 1888

We managed access aboard the HMS Dolphin a second time, and relayed our desire to speak with the men to Commander Forrest,

235

who agreed. Lieutenant Bloodworth was not as understanding, nor as polite as he had been the previous day.

"This is pointless!" Bloodworth snapped. "Kent jumped overboard due to his rejection by Lieutenant Thompson."

"Would Thompson confirm that?" Tennyson asked.

"I gather you attempted to speak to him, yes? To no avail?"

"I did speak with him," Tennyson smiled. "Yesterday."

Bloodworth's face seemed troubled. "Oh?"

"But as you predicted, he did not wish to discuss details."

Bloodworth released the breath he had been unconsciously holding, and straightened his jacket. "Well, you *had* been warned."

"However," I said firmly, "I still desire a word with the crew, and I do have Commander Forrest's blessing."

"If you insist," Bloodworth turned to leave.

"And... individually."

Bloodworth spun on his heels with a frustrated huff. "Mr. Holmes, we haven't the time for that! As you know, we..."

"Yes, you have but a few hours. These are my methods sir, and as you claim this is pointless, it will indeed move quickly."

Bloodworth glowered contemptuously. "Very well, then you may use my cabin for your 'interviews'. I prefer my own chair."

"To elucidate Lieutenant, you are not to be present during our discussions."

Bloodworth's face turned red with rage. "These are *my* men! As they are my responsibility, I demand to be present!"

"Apologies, but I need an honest interview, and they are likely to be more truthful without their first officer on hand."

Bloodworth crossed his arms, then rapped his fingers across the stripe on his sleeve. "Then I will remain on deck. Carry on gentlemen."

As we began reviewing with the sailors in Bloodworth's generously-donated cabin, the overall feeling was that Sub-lieutenant Kent *had* suffered from paraesthesia, (or what psychiatrist Richard Von Krafft-Ebing had called, 'homosexuality' in his work *Psychopathia Sexualis*), but he never openly displayed the sexual inversion, or made advances on any of the men. They had only Lieutenant Bloodworth's report to go upon, concerning the said incident between him and Thompson. Some seemed uneasy, not entirely sure if it were true, but they also did not wish to voice doubt regarding their first officer.

When we were halfway through, Bloodworth suddenly barged in and ordered the current sailor in the room to leave. "I am afraid this little session is done for the day, gentlemen! You are out of time!"

"As you wish," I stood. "However, I do desire a quick word with just you."

The heated energy drained from his face. "Oh?"

"The men say you were the only one privy to the incident between Thompson and Kent, if in fact, anything did happen."

Bloodworth's anger returned. "Are you calling me a liar?!"

Lying like a rug. "I am simply trying to understand why you would inform the others, if Kent and Thompson said nothing, and no one else had observed it. Quite frankly, it was not yours to tell."

"It most certainly was," Bloodworth approached me. "Thompson is up for promotion; do you understand what that means? Do you even comprehend the amount of scrutiny one is placed under when being considered for a higher rank? You cannot allow *anything* to tarnish your reputation."

We were now standing face to face, or rather face to neck, as he was a good six inches shorter than I.

"I must ask you both to leave," he said opening the door, "as we are to set sail. Commander Forrest insists."

"We thank you for your time," Tennyson stepped between us with a bow. "You have been most helpful. Have you anything of Sub-lieutenant Kent's that we might give his father as remembrance?"

"I have already given... wait, there is actually. I forgot. A ring belonged to him." He extracted a gold ring from a small black velvet pouch inside one of his desk drawers. "This was found in his room. I am sure he would like it returned to his family. At least he had the decency to remove it before jumping." He dropped the ring into Tennyson's gloved palm.

22nd February 1888

We summoned Mr. Kent to our rooms the next day, and handed him the ring.

"I believe this belonged to your son?" I asked.

Mr. Kent's eyes popped. "Now, I am sure of it! This ring was from his mother. You would have had to pry it from his dead body before he would ever remove it!"

"Mr. Kent, I apologize that there is little I can do at the moment, for they have returned to sea, but we shall continue our investigation here in London."

"If you can find the person, I will wait as long as necessary."

"You have been most patient sir," I thanked him. "Oh, and where is your daughter this afternoon?"

Out of the corner of my eye, I noticed Tennyson stiffen. Mr. Kent was oblivious.

"Adriana had shopping plans with her aunt. I think she has been through enough lately."

"Agreed," Tennyson glared at me.

"Well, carry on gentlemen," Mr. Kent struggled to his feet, "and take as much time as necessary." He exited with a bit more hope than he had entered with.

I turned to Tennyson. "I was surprised Bloodworth did not suspect us of rummaging through his cabin before the interviews. He gave us that ring quite willingly."

"Why had he not given it to Mr. Kent when he first informed him of the death?"

"I speculate that he did not yet have it."

Tennyson removed her wig, and itched her head as she hummed. "Hmm, Bloodworth has a wife, correct?"

"Why, are you interested?"

She paused in fluffing her hair, and scrunched up her nose. "Did you not see the wedding ring on his finger?!"

"I noticed the ring yes, but it was a class ring from the naval college in Dartmouth." I raised an eyebrow. "Surely you noted the difference? There is nothing more untrustworthy than an obvious fact."

She groaned, then rested her wig on the table.

"Now then, evidently he has lost considerable body mass since obtaining it as the ring was turned upside down on his finger due to the weight of the stone, and being so loose on his finger, but none the less, it was *not* a wedding band. The blue gem had the insignia of the Royal Navy upon it."

"Oh."

"However, he most certainly is married, as his suit was newly pressed by a woman's iron and poorly prepared, therefore ruling out the possibility of any professional work being done. There was also a light dusting of a woman's facial powder on the shoulder of his jacket."

"Why would he not also wear his wedding band?"

240

"Could be for any number of reasons Tennyson, but not crucial to our investigation."

"If he attended the naval academy, wouldn't they have his current place of residence on file?"

"My dear, I must first ask you to resist the urge to guess, or jump too quickly to conclusions. The habit of doing so is most destructive to the logical faculty. But in following your train of thought, yes, Mrs. Bloodworth is our next quarry." I pulled my ulster coat from the rack, and threw her Mumford's black herringbone overcoat.

We made our way to the naval college, and were initially denied access to Bloodworth's records, given his rank. However, upon explaining the reason for our investigation they conceded, with the understanding that Bloodworth would be notified by mail of this, as was their policy. We hadn't much time now.

We arrived at Bloodworth's residence near Regent's Street and found his wife at home. She was younger than he, maybe six and twenty, but her eyes harbored a deep sadness. Her tiny sunken face was far too small for her head, and the dark circles under her eyes made her appear years older. Her auburn hair, severely pulled into a tight bun, was already showing signs of grey and her skin was dry and cracked. This woman was not well.

"May I help you, gentleman?" she timidly answered the door.

"Mrs. Bloodworth, I am afraid that we must ask you some questions," Tennyson said simply. "May we step inside?"

Mrs. Bloodworth gripped the skirts of her grey day dress, and stood frozen in the doorway. "Who are you, what do you want?!"

"I am Sherlock Holmes, and this is my associate, James Mumford." I stepped in. "We are here because of an incident that occurred on your husband's ship, and it is paramount that we speak with you."

She nodded uneasily and wrung her hands, then showed us inside. I noticed a lady's calling card in the card dish by the door, with the bottom right corner bent. This was important as a calling card bent in such a fashion signified a visit of condolence.

"He's not in any trouble is he?" she asked, as our footsteps echoed across the marble hallway and into the sitting room.

Tennyson's eyes locked with mine. I nodded. "As a matter of fact, he might be, as could his other Lieutenant, Giles Thompson," I said gravely.

Mrs. Bloodworth shook her head, and clasped her hands together. "Giles is a good man Mr. Holmes! Never a kinder man I knew! I know he's done nothing wrong!"

This was curious.

"Would you defend your husband so ardently?" Tennyson asked.

Just then the gothic grandfather clock against the wall chimed three times, and we lost Mrs. Bloodworth's attention to the pendulum, as she turned to watch it tick back and forth. As if in a trance, she said quietly, "my husband... is a troubled man."

242

The three of us sat down in the very immaculate living room. The French settee upon which Tennyson and I rested was carved in walnut, and upholstered with an olive-green velvet. The room was impeccably decorated in the style of Louis XVII, yet it lacked any warmth or comfort. The entire house in fact, seemed barren, and cold.

"A young boy was murdered, and we are questioning everyone on board, as well as their families. I do not know if your husband has mentioned this?" I asked.

She folded her hands in her lap. "Yes, he did. But oh, I swear it was not he!"

The bending of her arms caused her sleeve to expose a bruised left wrist. I gave Tennyson a sidelong glance.

"Interesting how everyone was led to believe it was suicide, including your husband," Tennyson stated.

Mrs. Bloodworth paused. "Oh dear me, I mean yes, he said that as well, I am sorry, I thought you meant..."

Tennyson jumped to her feet. "What are you hiding, Mrs. Bloodworth? Suicide and murder are two very different means of dying!"

I held up my palm as she was becoming too emotional, and Mrs. Bloodworth had already buried her face in her hands.

"My dear," I said to Mrs. Bloodworth, resting hand upon her shoulder, "I am certain this is difficult, but I need you to tell me exactly what your husband disclosed."

243

The frightened mouse put her hand over mine, and inhaled deeply. Tears fell from her eyes, and dripped onto the white lace shawl that covered her shoulders. I handed her my handkerchief.

Tennyson sat down and looked away. *Women...*

"He is not a bad man sir, he... he has problems with the drink... and I am certain that I am to blame."

I came round in front of her, and knelt down to be eye level. "Why would you say that?"

"At sea, I hear he is a fine, upstanding officer. Well respected and esteemed. But at home, well, he is just a different man."

"How so?"

"I married young, Mr. Holmes, and I do not think I am what he wanted. He was off to sea and I, well, with his family's standings, it would have been foolish not to marry him. We did not love each other, but in time perhaps, we hoped we could learn to do so." She sighed dejectedly, and rested my handkerchief on her lap. "I do not believe that ever happened for him."

"Is there someone else you feel he does wish to be with?" Tennyson asked calmly, as she looked at the floor.

"Oh no, sir," she violently shook her head. "He is always away. I don't know how he could have met anyone else."

I had to get her back on track, time was precious. "Your husband has a bit of a temper?"

"Indeed, especially when drinking... oh dear, if I say a word he'll kill me!" She sobbed into the already sodden cloth.

"Mrs. Bloodworth, I can protect you if you are concerned for your safety, but I can do nothing unless you tell me the reason."

"Do you swear it? Otherwise I am done for!"

I nodded.

Mrs. Bloodworth took a deep breath and blew her nose. "It...it was not intentional. My husband was drinking on deck one evening, and the young boy came to speak with him. He wished for a transfer because of what the men were saying, and it wasn't true. He put his confidence in Ian and asked if he believed the rumor, to which my husband said no, because he had made it up.

When Mr. Kent asked why, my husband admitted to fabricating the entire tale to push him away from Giles, so he would not lose his chance at promotion. Mr. Kent demanded that my husband come forward with his falsehood, and threatened to tell the men himself if he did not. It led to a bandy of words, then a tussle, and Ian accidentally knocked Kent over the railing. Upon running downstairs to review his condition, the young man was dead. He killed him, Mr. Holmes, he did not mean to!" She gripped the handkerchief, and wrung it around in her hands. "Oh that poor boy!"

"What would possess him to have as admitted as much? No offense Mrs. Bloodworth, but he does not strike me as one who is loose of tongue."

"He was terribly drunk the evening he related the story."

I nodded.

"Do you really think it was accidental?" Tennyson asked.

Mrs. Bloodworth shook her head, then again covered her face with the filthy, soaked through hanky.

"I need you to finish, Mrs. Bloodworth." I petted her head. "Please be strong."

She sighed. "Fearing the repercussions, he dragged the body to the weaponry room, sliced it into three bits, put the parts in a large sack, then threw the entire bag into the ship's furnace."

"And the boy's ring?" Tennyson questioned cautiously, as she came over to stand beside me.

Mrs. Bloodworth blinked in surprise. "How did you know about that?"

"Your husband gave it to us, claiming he found it in the boy's room. However, as he had not initially given it to Mr. Kent upon informing him of his son's death, it could only have been found more recently, most likely due to your husband's fear of being discovered during the investigation," I explained.

She nodded and sniffed. "Yes, he found it in the furnace as it had fallen off to the side and remained intact. He planned on sending it back to the Kents."

Not the brightest of men. Had he thrown it overboard, he would have removed the only piece of evidence as the duffle bag was clearly gone and the weapon, cleaned and replaced. Lucky for us, his conscience may have played a part in him preserving it.

"He will return March 14th for his parents' thirty-fifth anniversary, and his brother's graduation from the fencing academy," Mrs. Bloodworth said.

"Then we must know his every move as soon as you are aware of it," I said.

As we left Mrs. Bloodworth and turned towards the street, Tennyson bumped into a girl carrying several various-sized packages. It was Adriana Kent.

"Oh! Mr. Mumford, Mr. Holmes, how fortunate!" she greeted, as she flipped her blonde ringlets to the side. "Pardon me for running into you! I am awfully sorry."

"Afternoon, Miss Kent," we nodded in unison.

"Mr. Mumford, I..." She fumbled with her packages as she averted her eyes. "I would like to apologize, for my rather rash behaviour the other day."

"No harm done," Tennyson said.

Adriana's pink lips smiled as she gazed up at Tennyson. "Any luck about my brother?"

"I believe we are nearing the end, Miss Kent," I said. "We will be in touch soon, if I am not mistaken."

"Splendid. I shall let my father know. Oh thank you Mr. Holmes, Mr. Mumford!" She attempted to grasp her hands together, but it was a rather difficult feat with all her parcels.

Tennyson laughed at her. "Do not thank us now, as we have yet to solve the case."

"Oh, but I am sure you will!" Miss Kent nodded, "you are both so clever!"

She then quickly leaned into Tennyson, kissed her on the lips, and dashed away with a giggle.

The expression on Tennyson's face was priceless. I could not contain my laughter so snorted into my hand. Tennyson scowled, and wiped her mouth with the back of her hand to remove the pink lipstick. She adjusted her mustache that was now sagging slightly to the left, and blew her cab-whistle twice to summon a hansom cab. "I have had enough of Mumford for one day. Back to Baker Street."

16th March 1888

Lieutenant Thompson was notified of Kent's murder. Though shocked, he promised to say nothing until we had apprehended his colleague. Bloodworth planned on attending a banquet dinner March 16th for his brother's graduation, and that would be our time to act.

As planned, the guests left for the evening after the dinner party and only Bloodworth and his brother remained.

Before we stepped through the front doors of the building, I whispered to Tennyson.

"This Bloodworth character is a tiger, and his actions could become unpredictable and lethal if he senses he's been trapped. Though Lestrade and his men are outside waiting, you must be prepared..."

"I am ready for this, Holmes."

Once inside, we approached the Bloodworth brothers as they stood by the studio door, each dressed in a black sack suit and holding a glass of champagne. Lindsey Bloodworth bore a striking resemblance to his brother Ian, but was perhaps five years younger. He noticed us first, and nodded to Lieutenant Bloodworth.

"What are you doing here?!" Bloodworth scowled. "This is a private function!"

"So your wife said, but we have need to speak with you. We have solved the murder of your poor Sub-lieutenant Kent," I said. "May we have a moment?"

Bloodworth's face paled, yet he kept his temper even. "Oh?" He gestured for us to enter the studio then turned towards his brother. "Another time Lindsey."

The fencing studio was a large, rectangular space with shiny hardwood floors, and white walls that were lined with swords and helmets. Small cubbies were built into the back wall, and newly folded outfits and gloves sat neatly inside the small nooks. There was but one large window on the left side of the long room, where Lestrade and his men were poised, and waiting below for the signal to approach.

Bloodworth leaned against a white wooden table in front of the window, and rested down his glass. "Well?" he folded his arms, "let's have it then."

"Sub-lieutenant Kent was murdered," said I, "by Lieutenant Giles Thompson."

Bloodworth unfolded his arms. "What?"

"This afternoon we spoke to him, and he confessed. He claims your wife knew as well, and upon being pressured, her account matched his. He will not be going on to a promotion, he will be going to prison."

"That is impossible!" Bloodworth cried. "Kent committed suicide!"

"Apparently not, and Thompson must have informed your wife of the details, as she knew them quite well. Most brutal means to cover up the deed," I said.

Bloodworth began pacing the room like a wild animal. "My wife told you the details did she!? She never talks to Giles, not ever! So you are lying! When would she have spoken to him?"

"Your parents' anniversary dinner was the other night, was it not? And Rachel remained at home due to illness, am I wrong? I think that is explanation enough."

Bloodworth's eyes narrowed. "Giles would never dare come see her alone!"

I do not believe he trusted his own statement, for his tone was uncertain and broken.

"Perhaps he wished to confess to *someone*, and as you were not in, he told her?" Tennyson suggested.

"It was *not* Giles!"

I stood in front of him to interrupt his pacing. "Is he then taking the blame for another?"

"He wouldn't have!" Bloodworth panicked. "He cannot accept fault for something he did not do. I will not allow it!"

250

"Have you something to add that could clear him?" I asked.

"Though she did seem hesitant," Tennyson began, "your wife eventually pointed the finger. She appeared to harbor much animosity towards him..."

Bloodworth stomped his foot. "That is not true, she's in love with him!"

"She knew the specifics of the murder, including how Giles gave you Kent's ring after he found it in the furnace, which you then gave to us, as he assumed you would never suspect where or how he came upon it."

"He found it in the furnace?"

"The details are too gruesome to relate, we shall spare you that unpleasantness."

"He did *not* kill him!"

Bloodworth now possibly believed that Giles was taking the blame for him.

"If Giles is willing to admit culpability, knows the specifics of the railing accident..."

Bloodworth threw his champagne glass against the wall. "How dare she speak to Giles! How dare she! I'll kill her!"

"She expected this to be your reaction," Tennyson said, unfazed by his explosion, "do you care so little for your wife?"

"Why should I? She doesn't love me, she never did. She always wished she had married Giles! I told you, she's in love with him!"

"Her, or you?" Tennyson asked quietly.

Bloodworth laughed hysterically. "I beg your pardon?!"

Tennyson and I had gone over every aspect of the case in the three weeks before confronting Bloodworth. In that time, Tennyson had arrived at the case's solution without any coaxing or assistance on my part. As a reward for her successful resolution, I gave her permission to make the reveal when the time came. This would be her first experience in doing so and in handling the backlash from the guilty suspect, a skill she would have to learn.

"You married Rachel out of convenience," she began, "but never loved her. However, you could also never confess your true feelings for Giles as it would ruin you and your friendship. That is why Sub-lieutenant Kent's friendship with Giles made you jealous. While Kent was innocent of ever making advancements on Giles, as Giles had told us, you concocted a story to side the men against him, thus pushing them apart. Once you accomplished that, you made the mistake of admitting your deception to Kent. When he demanded you clear his name, and confess to creating the rumor, you killed him, and blamed it as a suicide. Thompson told us weeks ago that you threatened him with his promotion, if he did not side with you..."

Bloodworth ran from the table, and grabbed a sabre sword off the wall. He was hyperventilating, and his eyes were ablaze. "Giles has been a friend for years. I don't care what the little bitch told you, but that is a vulgar fabrication in which there is not a grain of truth! I admit I killed Kent, but it was an accident. I never meant to hurt the boy. I simply wanted him to... but what you are proposing, about my feelings for Giles, is monstrous. I will fight you to the death to defend my honour, if you dare continue with these mendacities."

Without looking to me for approval, Tennyson pulled a sword from one of the wall posts and held it at her side. "You deny them then?"

Bloodworth shot a venomous glance at Tennyson. "You should be made aware, Mr. Mumford, that I am an expert swordsman, so pursue this at your own peril."

Tennyson stepped closer to her opponent. "Then I am afraid this will be an unfair duel, as I am not. But if you will not confess willingly..."

Bloodworth laughed, and took up the defensive position. "Perhaps I will allow you the first attack then," he said, "to give you a sporting chance. En Garde!"

Tennyson nodded, but then lunged into him. She swept the sword from his hand with a quick press, and his weapon dropped to the ground. It echoed with a 'ping' as the bell guard hit the oak wood floorboards. Bloodworth glared at her contemptuously.

Tennyson swished her sword back and forth playfully. "I neglected to mention that I too, lie on occasion."

Careful Tennyson. This was not an exercise. It was a duel with a dangerous and desperate man, but she was not treating it as such.

Bloodworth snatched up his sword with a roar. They fought back and forth, Tennyson undeniably winning, but then Bloodworth surprised her and kicked her left kneecap which caused her to nearly lose her balance. As she attempted to steady herself, he cut her neatly across the chest, and pushed her into the table. She cried out, attempting to maintain as manly a yelp as she could muster, and leaned against the table for support. *Dear God!* I thought. Was she alright? I almost rushed to her side but could not risk him escaping. *Tennyson, I had warned you!*

Furious, I torn off my ulster, ripped a sword from the wall, and advanced on Bloodworth. "That was not a wise move, Lieutenant."

I fought him, perhaps the most violent and irrational I had even been in a duel, my emotions rather uncharacteristically ruling my actions. I cornered him against a wall and jabbed the point of the sword into his chest, leaving a visible indent in the fabric of his jacket.

"I should teach you a lesson for playing unfairly," I said grimly, "but there is no time. Drop your sword!"

He begrudgingly did so.

"Now on the floor!"

Bloodworth dropped to his knees and leaned his face against the floor as I roughly bound his arms behind him with Lestrade's handcuffs.

"I know I could hang for murder," he sighed, "and I accept that. But I beg of you, please do not disclose my feelings to Giles. I care not if he thinks me a murderer, but this would destroy him," Bloodworth pleaded. "Imagine if someone said Mumford there was in love with you?"

I looked over at Tennyson who shifted her gaze to the wall. He had no idea what he had just said.

"I will consider your request."

I turned back to Tennyson who was fading fast. Blood seeped through her jacket and onto her fingertips that were holding her stomach. When she noticed my stare she nodded, and moved towards the window to signal to Lestrade.

Moments later, Lestrade bustled in with his other officers. "Get that man to his feet!" he pointed at Bloodworth. "Has a long ride ahead o' him he does!" Lestrade folded his hands behind him. "So you nabbed 'em again, Holmes. I must say, you and Mr. Mumford here... Blimey!" he gasped, as he had just observed Tennyson's injury. "Is he going to be all right?"

"He's a bit wounded, so please move quickly as I must take Mumford to a doctor," I requested.

"No, no doctor, Holmes," Tennyson faked a smile. "It's not bad."

"Brave lad, but I fancy you had better listen to Mr. Holmes," Lestrade said. Tennyson glared at him reproachfully, possibly indicating he should mind his own business. "Then again, I have no horse in this race." Lestrade gathered the dejected Bloodworth off the floor, and rounded up his men.

Before they had exited, Tennyson suddenly collapsed on the ground. I ran over, lifted her in my arms, and carried her down to the carriage. Having laid her across the seat cushion, I shut the door. I took off my ulster and pressed it firmly against her chest. She whimpered slightly at the pressure, and blinked back tears. She was cold, and bleeding profusely.

I could not take her anywhere but home, still dressed as she was, so I gently carried her up the stairs of Baker Street and into the sitting room, then placed her on the sofa. My hands were red. I wiped them off on the white towel underneath the tea tray, already hearing Mrs. Hudson's rampage in my head.

Tennyson's eyes were closed, and her breathing, labored. I decided to summon Watson. Just as I reached the door, she moaned, and her eyes opened. "Where are you going?"

"Watson. You must be looked at."

She weakly shook her head as she tried to lean forward. "No, I am fine, really. It is not that awful."

"Then I shall fetch Mrs. Hudson."

"No, no she would faint."

"Then you must agree to have me look at you," I compromised. "Should I think it deserves more attention you will listen, understand?"

She nodded.

Once the jacket and waistcoat had been removed, I could see that her white shirt underneath was soaked through with blood.

"Dear God," I muttered. I lifted the edge of her shirt, then sighed. This would not be easy. "Tennyson, I am going to require you remove your shirt."

Tennyson's eyes flashed with terror.

"No time for modesty, I must see how deep your wound extends."

I carefully began to unbutton her shirt from the bottom up, and at the third red stained button, I could see where the cut ran up across her abdomen, and right beneath her bound left breast. The binder would also have to be removed. As I began unbuttoning her further, Tennyson began to tremble. Sensing her discomfort, I stopped.

"If you would rather Tennyson, you may finish removing things while I appropriate gauze and water."

"Please!" She nodded fiercely.

I went to the other room and fished around in the cabinet until my fingers finally wrapped around a roll of gauze with tape. I took the water basin, towel, and bottle of carbolic acid back to the sitting room, and placed it on the floor.

Tennyson's bloodied shirt was hung over the hearth by the fireplace, and she was lying on the sofa with a brown cashmere throw blanket covering the front of her. Her bowler hat, wig, and mustache were carelessly tossed to the floor next to her, and her eyes were closed.

I coughed. "Tennyson, I do need to see you..."

"Yes, I know." She sat up with some difficulty, but continued to hold the blanket over her chest.

I moved the accessories from the floor to the armchair and put the water basin directly below her as I dropped in the towel. I cleared my throat, indicating that she would now need to put the blanket aside.

I explained that she only need move it as far as necessary in order to clean the blood off her skin, and see the true depth of the cut.

I tore a strip of gauze from the roll, balled it up tightly, and dipped it into the acid. "Tennyson, this is going to sting. Horribly so. But I know you can cope." At least, I hoped she could.

Her eyes watched mine as I lightly patted the soaked gauze onto her wound to prevent infection and clean the skin. She sucked in air through her teeth, and pursed her lips together, holding in her breath. When I had finished, she released it with a slight sniffle.

Thankfully, the wound was not as devastatingly deep as I had feared. I grabbed the roll of gauze, and began unraveling it further. "You will have to sit up Tennyson and remove the blanket entirely, so that I may wrap this around your chest."

Tennyson gulped.

I thought for a moment on how best to make her the least uncomfortable. I told her that I would close my eyes, and she could move my hand to where her shoulder meets the top of her breast. Holding that starting point, I could bind it around her until she was decently covered.

I closed my eyes as promised, and heard the blanket drop. She guided my hand round her chest, and when she felt comfortable, she squeezed my fingers. "You may open them."

I did as instructed, then finished wrapping her to just below where the cut began, and taped the end. "Tight enough? Or perhaps too much so?"

She gazed at me with that expression of longing that I could not bear at times. "It hurts, but I will be fine."

"You should rest," I said, as I carefully scooped her up and bore her to her room, unable to look at her.

"Holmes?" she asked quietly.

"Yes, Tennyson?"

"I a... I... thank you," she mumbled.

"It is my duty to look out for you, as you are my... charge in a sense," I laughed, as I placed her in her bed. "Had I not warned you on the dangers of being too confident?"

She drew her lips into a half smile. "Duly noted."

Once she was tucked in, I sat down next to her. "Do you need anything?"

She placed her hand over mine. "No, thank you."

I slid my hand away from hers then rose up quickly. "Should your mind change, I'll be in the sitting room."

"Holmes?"

"Yes?"

"I am... glad you were there. Thank you."

"It was my fault you were put in such a position from the start," I said carelessly, "you should be cursing me, not thanking me."

"We are all capable of making our own decisions, and you cannot blame yourself for another's actions. Is that not what you told me?" She closed her eyes. "Then do not blame yourself for mine."

CHAPTER 22

PARIS

23rd March 1888

After our last exploit, to ensure Tennyson had adequate time to heal, I sent her to her father's for a week of respite. What did I know of caring for a woman? Mrs. Hudson also took some time away to tend to her cousin, and brought in the stuffy Mrs. Turner to oversee things in her absence. Admittedly, I missed Tennyson. I was grateful for Watson's company during a case that arose whilst Tennyson was immobilized, but I believe her absence had me distracted, as I was unfocused, and the result was... well, it was not one of my finer moments. As the case involves international royalty, I shall refrain from disclosing the details for now, but it was yet another learned lesson in not trusting women.

I can only imagine Tennyson's smugness once I relate the details, and I am indeed quite certain that she, and this American woman, Mrs. Irene Norton, would have got on splendidly in different circumstances. So very similar are they in their bad decision-making, and stubbornness.

26th March 1888

I had only recently decided to incorporate Tennyson as a necessary accessory for my next international case, when one arose.

This particular assignment brought us to Paris, France, a city and country I very much enjoy visiting, but had not had the pleasure of travelling to in quite some time. It concerned a note that had been delivered to the French police, speculating that an assassination attempt was to be made upon the French President, Marie Francois Sadi Carnot. I was enlisted to investigate by a colleague of mine, Francois Le Villard, and my presence was required immediately. I agreed, but only under the condition that Tennyson would accompany me. They reluctantly accepted.

"I do so love French!" Tennyson had said once I'd informed her of the case. "The language and the people are the most beautiful, and romantic in the world."

"Unless of course they are trying to kill you," I reminded her.

27th March 1888

Tennyson said she spoke decent French but after observing her for several hours, I could attest that she had been far too modest in the evaluation of her competency. We checked into our hotel rooms then hopped a carriage to the police station. Upon meeting with Le Villard, it was explained that his fellow officers took the note to be nothing more than a hoax, but as it regarded the President, he refused to take it lightly. Though skeptical of my bringing a woman along, his reservations magically melted the moment he met Tennyson. With her bluebell and silver checkered dress, along with her white crocheted gloves, La Villard likened her to an angel. She certainly had a way with men.

In reading over the letter, I could think of only one man who would send such a note, though it was not written in his hand. It appeared to be a trap, and one specifically meant for me. I now wished that I had not taken Tennyson along, as this was proving to be a far more dangerous trip than I imagined.

Le Villard was positive that the threat involved someone within the loyalist group of Georges Ernest Boulanger, a vehemently political man who had been threatening to overtake the Republic with a military dictatorship. Though logical in theory due to circumstantial evidence, it was far too obvious an answer to have been correct, for just such an assumption, the author had been banking on.

Once at our hotel, I explained to Tennyson that I surmised this was the work of Professor Moriarty, an unscrupulous man whom I'd been playing cat and mouse with for some years. The threat, whether real or not, was created purely to lure me to Paris. Her life could be in very real jeopardy.

As I expected, she refused my offer to send her back to London, but secretly, I was grateful.

After several days of investigation, we concluded that the threat was valid, and was being headed up by one of Moriarty's associates, Mr. Nigel Breen. The attack was to commence on March the 30th, before midnight.

29th March 1888

The day before the assault, a type-written letter arrived at the hotel's front desk. It was from Mr. Breen. He professed his innocence, and claimed that he was forced into the plot against his will. In return for his amnesty, he promised to reveal the plot's details for the following evening.

As my presence was requested at his personal residency, there was no question it was a trap. I responded with acceptance upon the condition that my partner, Tennyson, could accompany me. A reply was left several hours later, agreeing to my terms.

About an hour later, Tennyson and I went for a walk by the river's embankment to discuss the particulars of the case. I turned to observe a flock of pigeons, twisted my head to say something clever to her, but then found her missing. I panicked. In a horde so thick and hurried, how would I find her? Had Breen or another of Moriarty's men spirited her away?

My cardiac pulsation was significantly higher than the average seventy beats per minute.

I called out her name, and received no response. I began to move quickly through the sea of strangers, the lump in my throat growing larger. Just as I was to call out again, I found her in an alleyway, talking to a street vendor selling paintings. My worry turned to anger. "Tennyson, there you are!" I said, slightly winded.

"There I am what?"

I was in no mood for banter. "I thought I lost you."

263

She removed a gilded jade compact from her bag, and inspected her makeup in the small round mirror. "Well, now you found me. Besides, I have been watching my back," she said, pointing to the mirror in her compact and shifting it to view the people walking behind her. "Why, were you worried?" She snapped the lid closed.

"No, simply annoyed," I lied, "for this evening's events will require careful mapping and strategy, so we must return to the hotel and review our strategy."

As we sat on the purple chaise lounge in my hotel room reviewing our roles, Tennyson suddenly paused, then absent-mindedly began to toy with the already loose velvet button on the back cushion of the lounge.

"What is it Tennyson?"

"This is not right," she sat forward. "See here, it does not make sense to have us both go. If you indeed suspect him to be in league with Moriarty, I should notify the police, and wait with them until the right moment. Having us both in harm's way seems utterly ludicrous."

"While I am not denying you've made considerable progress in the art of detection, you are still inexperienced, so I ask that you trust me."

"But Holmes, you cannot gainsay my point! I speculate that..."

"If you are so convinced that yours is the proper method, then I will step down." I leaned back on the lounge, and closed my eyes. "Very well then, this is your ship now, Captain, and I will be your skipper."

264

"Holmes please, I did not mean..."

"No no, I relinquish my authority; the steering wheel is yours. If you are indeed successful, then bravo, Madam. Otherwise, you are never to question my judgment or advice again."

"Well I... mmm... yes but... Holmes, I am sorry if I upset you..."

"Tut! And not a bit!" I grabbed my pipe and tobacco from my suitcase, then stuffed it partway. "This is your chance to utilize what I've taught you, and validate my abilities as a teacher."

I stepped into my carpet slippers near the window, wandered to the balcony door, then pushed it open. It was quite cold outside, but I had already committed to travelling outdoors. I pulled a match from my pocket, struck it against the bowl, then lightly puffed into the mouthpiece. Once I was certain it had caught, I nodded back to her. "I will be on the balcony, and when you have properly formulated our plan, relate it back to me." I hoped it would be soon, as I was finding it difficult to refrain from shivering.

As I slowly closed the balcony door, I heard her mutter something about jimsonweed and my morning tea, under her breath. She amused me to no end.

Of course my initial proposition was flawed, very much so. This was my chance to offer her a case in which she alone could take credit for. As she would not have accepted it outright, I needed her to instigate the coup.

Should she plan our strategy successfully, I will have further details to disclose on our adventures tomorrow. Should she not, then this could potentially be my final entry.

30ᵗʰ March 1888

Yesterday evening we proceeded with Tennyson's plan, where I would appear to send her back to London on the five o'clock boat, claiming I wished to handle the case alone. I voiced my presumed actions loudly for anyone who wished to hear, and from the docks headed to Breen's.

In the meantime, Tennyson was to change costumes, disembark from the boat, notify the police and Le Villard, and wait until the agreed-upon time for her to intervene. Simple enough really, and as I knew I was stepping headfirst into a trap, I was prepared. Or, so I thought.

Upon arrival at the Breen residence on the outskirts of the city, I called once for Breen through the open front door, then stepped inside. I appeared to close it behind me, but left a small chuck of wood lodged in the doorjamb, to keep it propped.

A light burned on the second floor. I removed my Webley revolver from inside my coat pocket, and cautiously stepped up the creaking staircase. A low, dull hissing sound suddenly filled my ears, and I smelled a unique and indistinguishable odour. Realizing it was some type of gas, I pretended to collapse on the floor, but tucked my nose inside my coat to refrain from breathing in as much of the contaminated air as possible. Two men approached me. One removed my gun, and I heard it drop onto a table. The other tied my hands behind me. They lifted me up, dropped me in a carriage, and we travelled several blocks until we reached the waterfront. Three lefts, one right, and another two lefts.

266

When I 'awoke', I was by the docks of the Seine atop a stack of rotting crates, and Mr. Breen stood by me with the smile of The Cheshire Cat. His gangly body, elongated face, and brown beady eyes gave him the appearance of a hairless weasel in a man's brown sack suit and bowler.

Unfortunately, Tennyson would not be able to find me here, so it would now be up to me to handle the situation. As long as she was safe...

"Did you enjoy my little perfume?" Breen asked as he adjusted his thin, brass-rimmed glasses, "I wished to have one last chat with you before I gave the final word for the assault, therefore I made this batch less potent. I presume you didn't think I saw through your little charade of announcing your plans to send your partner away, now did you? Nor did you suppose we had someone following her, and watched her hop off the boat in disguise either, aye? Though a convincing change in persona, sadly, her travel bag gave her away. Surprised, really," he shook his head with a laugh, "that you had not the foresight for such a minor detail."

Now I was concerned. Had they taken her? Was she alright? I struggled with my bound hands to see how loose the rope was. Not terribly.

"Why the stone face? Expecting to be saved, Holmes? Unlikely, for you are quite restrained at the moment and no one knows where you are. And don't expect that pathetic female partner of yours to find you either." *Ah, so she is safe. That changes things.* "Now, the problem is, Sherlock, may I call you Sherlock? On one hand, the professor would love to have you on our side; on the other, you cannot be trusted to turn. No matter," he shrugged, "as the master is not entirely ruthless, this should be quick, tidy, and relatively painless."

A man came up behind me and lifted me to my feet. I estimated he weighed roughly fifteen stone, was not terribly coordinated, and I could easily get the upper hand. Tripping his leg I could knock him to the ground, dive at Breen, knock him off-balance, drop to the floor, and loop my arms around my legs to the front of me. This could all be accomplished in a matter of moments, as soon as I felt the timing was right.

Breen pulled a pistol from the holster at his side. "You have been a nuisance for years Holmes, and it's time your career was at its end." He reset the trigger, and aimed the muzzle at my chest. "I believe this type of drama is called a tragedy, is it not?" Breen removed his hat, revealing a head of short, prickly grey hair, and placed it over his heart in a mock gesture of sorrow. "Therefore I shall weep for our fallen hero."

I wished he'd get on with it.

As he twitched his finger to pull the trigger, and I prepared to trip my unsuspecting captor, a shot was fired from around the corner, and lodged a bullet in the base of Breen's thumb. He hunched over with a scream and dropped the gun, then watched in horror as it slipped through the slats of the docks and into the waters below. I turned to see Tennyson, standing tall, with my Webley revolver aimed at his head.

This altered my plans quite a bit, as Tennyson's life could now be in danger. Blast it woman!

Breen nodded to his cohort. "Alain!"

Tennyson quickly jerked her head in the direction of Breen's companion who had slid a pistol from his grease-stained coat pocket. He fired at a stack of crates directly behind her, and they exploded in every direction. She dove to the ground, but not before firing off a round herself, hitting the man in his right foot. His gun fell from his hand and he howled in pain as he withered down to his knees.

"Holmes, the gun!" Tennyson coughed, as she rolled across the dock to avoid the falling debris of wood and dust.

I fell backwards to the ground, swung my arms around my legs to the front, then reached my tied hands out to grab the fallen firearm.

As my head was tucked down, I heard another shot ring out. Jerking up in a panic I was relived to see that the shot had come from Tennyson as her revolver was smoking, and Breen was oozing blood from his shoulder. He screeched like a cat on hot bricks.

I was puzzled, as Tennyson had been instructed not to fire unless she'd been in danger. As if reading my mind, the soot covered woman pointed to her left where a jackknife was lying on the ground next to Breen. It had obviously been in his hand only moments before.

Tennyson jumped to her feet, picked up the jackknife, then approached me with the blade. She sawed through the rope around my wrists, then tossed the remnants aside.

"Pretty good, Tennyson," I applauded. "Pretty damn good!"

"All in a day's work," she beamed, then dusted the black from her purple bustle dress. Her face, covered in flecks of ash, gave her smile a menacing yet playful quality.

269

I heard the warning bells of the French metropolitan police and within moments, five men were involved with the handcuffing, and escorting, of Breen and his companion to the carriage.

"Might I have the pleasure of your Christian name, Miss Tennyson?" Breen asked, as he paused in front of her. "It is only fair I know my opponent."

I stepped between then. "You may not."

Tennyson moved to the side in order to face him. "Scarlett, the pathetic female partner."

"We underestimated you," he said with a hiss, "that is clear."

Breen was then pushed in the back by one of the officer's guns and led towards the carriage.

"Till we meet again, Scarlett Tennyson," he called back, "which shall not be soon enough."

Francois Le Villard strolled over to us with a grin, and outstretched his hand. "Thank you much again as always, Monsieur Holmes," he shook my hand, "And to you Madame *Scarlett* Tennyson." He swept her hand up for a kiss. "We are much grateful to your help also."

"Till next time?" I asked, as I shook out my cap and blew off the dirt.

"Oui," he nodded, then with a whisper he grinned, "And, mon dieu what a woman Monsieur Holmes! We hope to see her again as well!"

Indeed.

"You surprised me, Tennyson," I turned to her, "and, possibly saved my life." The last sentence was a stretch, but she had earned it.

"You seemed to have things under control," she handed me my gun, "but why take chances?" It was still warm.

"How *did* you find me?"

"Quite simple, really," said she with a flourish, brushing back loose strands of hair from her face. "When I arrived at the Breen residence and saw your revolver lying on the desk, I knew things had gone awry. I noticed a scrap of burned paper in the fireplace reading *'he will expect it. End it at the docks where...'* then I discovered a package from the Paris docks labeled 'East 6'. As there were several such empty packages in the dustbin, I assumed it might be a locality of frequent usage. I put the two together, and reached the proper conclusion."

I wiped some of the dirt from her face with my fingers in order to see the red blush of triumph. "Clever girl."

"I learned from the best," she blushed a brighter red. "Observation, deduction, and knowledge. I was only following your methods."

"Now physically, however did you mange to roll so effortlessly across the dock? That was quite the feat."

She cupped her hand, looked around, then whispered, "I'm not wearing a corset."

I chuckled and shook my head. "By any means necessary," I said, remembering one of our conversations. "Bravo on your first case, my dear. I believe we should celebrate with a drink?"

271

"Wine at Café De La Paix in the Grand Hotel," she decided. "I would like to view the Opera Garnier from the inside terrace."

I took her arm in mine but felt her shiver at my touch, so removed my ulster to offer her.

"Holmes really, I am fine," she stepped back.

"No you are not." I wrapped it around her then buttoned the top clasp. "I warned you to bring warmer attire. Now isn't that better?"

She had those diamonds in her eyes again that were becoming more and more prevalent.

"Yes, thank you."

Her adoration at times was quite flattering. "You are welcome," I said, then kissed her on the lips.

Tennyson breathed deeply, and her eyes flickered.

"Is there something the matter?"

"Why... did you do that?"

"I thought your lips might be cold as well," I said simply. "They are not." Though it had been purely in jest, as an afterthought, it occurred to me that perhaps my previous action was somewhat inappropriate, even between friends. I shrugged it off as I turned away.

"And... if they were?" she pressed.

"I would have kissed you longer," I responded without thinking. I paused with a frown. *That was not what I had meant to say.*

"Oh."

After several rounds of drinks, we returned to our hotel, and she suggested a quick nightcap in my room before bed. Happily drunk, Tennyson flung open the bay window of my room with a merry sigh, and stepped out onto the balcony.

"It is such a clear night," she gazed into the sky. "How awfully lovely. You can see positively everything. Cassiopeia, Hydra, Ursa Major, Draco, even Orion is still visible..."

"You see all those fellows up there?" I stood beside her. "A bit crowded I'd say."

She stared at me in shock. "Are you not familiar with them?"

"I have little use for astronomy in my occupation, therefore, it is wasteful to invest any energy into it."

"Must everything in life have a purpose? Why cannot something exist, simply for the sake of beauty, or contrast, or because it is pleasant? There is a point where practicality should evaporate, and you can enjoy something for being what it is, and nothing more."

"Everything *must* have a point Tennyson, else it is a squandering of time and a misuse of logical resources."

"I truly pity the person who cannot enjoy something unless he feels it will benefit him in some way," said she angrily, "if you will excuse me, I shall retire to my room." She stepped through the French doors back into the room, then exited to her chamber across the hallway.

As I watched her leave, I suddenly realized how important she had become to me. Not just as a partner with perfect aim, but as a companion I very much enjoyed spending time with. I admit to feeling a touch of remorse that I cannot provide for her what she so desperately seems to desire from me outside of being a mentor. I am simply not capable. And though at times I can sense the disappointment in her voice, especially tonight, I truly hope that she will one day find happiness with someone. I also pray that in some small way, I will still be included in her life when she does so.

31ˢᵗ March 1888

The last day of our trip we decided to stroll down the trellis by the Seine to view the various shops and street vendors for which the city is famous.

As we made our way along the pavement, a generously proportioned man of the Orient stepped in front of us.

"Madame! Your beauty must be captured!" he kissed his fingers to his lips. "Come, I take photograph!"

"Oh no, I could not..." Tennyson protested as he took her hand and pulled her towards building with a hanging sign that read, 'Horace Soleil, Atelier de Photographies'

Out of the corner of my eye I swore that I saw The Prince leisurely ambling about just a few streets away. I wasn't entirely certain it was he, yet I knew he typically ventured to France during the springtime so it would not be out of the realm of possibility. I needed to remove her from sight, and quickly.

"Gratuit! Come!"

"Go on," I urged her inside. "I'll return momentarily."

"Where are *you* going?"

"I shan't be long." I tapped her on the nose. "Indulge yourself; how often do you travel to Paris?"

As I stepped outside I sighed with relief as His Royal Highness had apparently disappeared. I wandered in and out of several shops before returning to the studio, and when I stepped through the door, I observed Tennyson standing in front of a colourful countryside backdrop, with a large camera set up about thirty feet away from her. It resembled an accordion positioned atop three long wooden legs with a black curtain draped over it. The thick man was hiding underneath, and was instructing her in French on where to stand and how to hold her hands. I saw a flash, then the man crawled out from under the cloth.

"Now one with Monsieur," he exclaimed, as he pushed me next to her.

"I do not photograph well," I stepped away.

"Oh please Holmes," Tennyson begged.

I sighed and stood beside her, then folded my hands in front of me. Shortly thereafter, there was another flash.

"I shall have in two days time," the Frenchman said.

I explained that we were bound for London that evening, so gave him my card to have the photographs mailed to us, and paid the shipping fee in advance. 'Gratuit' indeed.

On the boat ride home we had been seated in the lower deck when Tennyson suddenly rose from her chair, and headed upstairs. I waited a moment before following her.

She was standing by the bow, holding onto the railing, her calico skirt fluttering in the wind like a tormented ship sail. I pulled my gold cigarette case from my pocket, lifted a stick, then stepped beside her as I pulled a match and struck it across the rail. "Windy, isn't it?" I asked, as I cupped my hands round the match and lit the cigarette.

Her face was white, and her lips, a subtle shade of blue. I felt her cheek with the backside of my hand. It was frigid. "You should come inside."

She glanced over at my cigarette. "Might I have one?"

I laughed as I pocketed the gold cigarette case. "As Bohemian and modern as you are my dear, I do not think that would be proper."

"It is truly a man's world," she sighed in frustration, then turned back to the water. "I will come inside in a moment."

"Suit yourself." I took several more puffs on the fag, then deposited it over the railing and turned to head indoors.

"Holmes?" she called.

"Yes?" I turned back.

"Never mind," she stared at the ground, "you... wouldn't understand."

"I might."

She bit her lower lip. "Have you ever loved something so much that you wished you could preserve it in time, exactly as is, and return to that moment whenever you please?"

"No," I shook my head, "I am afraid not. One must never linger in the past, but look ahead to the future. However, what is it that *you* are so fiercely passionate about?"

She stared at the door. "Then I suppose everything runs its course, and all things change in time," she said, ignoring my question.

"How so?"

"If I am indeed to pursue my own practice," she looked at me, "my name will become known. I appreciate your concern, but you need not trouble yourself with shielding me."

"I was wary of exposing your identity to one of Moriarty's loyalists. That is all. Now, *what* changes in time?"

Her eyes were glass. "My father suggested that I leave Baker Street. He said it is far too dangerous for me to be living with you."

I sighed, well aware of what had caused her father to react so. "What was your response?"

She turned back to the ocean. I could have questioned her further but perhaps I did not desire to know the answer. Tennyson was learning quickly, and her self-assurance was rising. Though proud of her, this newfound independence could speed her departure from Baker Street, as she had indicated. This might be a subtle hint that such a time, was soon approaching.

I was tempted to feign indifference, and tell her that her father was probably right. My prediction was that she would then beg to stay on longer, and insist she had more still to learn. But instead, I said nothing.

~ ~

Jonathan looked up from the journal to the clock on the wall. He had twenty minutes until his English Literature class. He quickly closed the journal, slid it under his bed, and grabbed a hard bread roll and brown pear from his desk.

So Moriarty's men did know my mother's name... he thought, as he wrapped the roll and fruit in a red cloth napkin then shoved it in his satchel. *I wonder... does Nigel Breen come back for revenge?*

As he skipped out the door towards King's Court, he felt light, and gay. He was beginning to think that perhaps Holmes really *did* love his mother. He wondered how they had been together, and how they might have lived as a family if only...

He was suddenly jolted from his reverie when something warm and wet land on his hand. He sniffed, and wiped his eyes before reaching the classroom.

CHAPTER 23

IT WAS JUST AN EXPERIMENT

Upon returning from class, Jonathan remembered that he was due to pick up his photograph from Edith, so dashed over to the admissions office to meet her, and ask about the gardens.

Edith greeted him with a handshake, and gave him a brown bag with the thick photograph inside.

"Miss Leahy, I have another question," Jonathan said, hugging the bag to his chest, "was my mother much of a gardener back then?"

If she said yes, he would chance a trip to the Newnham gardens to see if there were any bean plants that might have served as an appropriate burial site for a box of letters between 'Jack' and 'Bean'.

"Oh, she was," Edith said.

Jonathan smiled triumphantly. "Did she ever tend the gardens here at Newnham?"

"She did, but unfortunately, the small garden that we had kept was completely renovated in '92. Anything that existed back then is long gone."

Jonathan felt a sharp pain in the pit of his stomach. IF the box had been buried there, it most certainly was gone, and any hopes of finding it were completely futile. This could possibly be the end of his mission, but he needed more clues to be certain.

As there was still time before his phone call with Abigail, he quickly returned to his room and continued reading, hoping to find anything that would rule out the garden as a possible hiding place.

~ ~

6ᵗʰ April 1888 (Tennyson's Birthday)

Shortly after a late breakfast and my pipe, I asked Tennyson to please hand me my violin. As she stepped over to the corner of the sitting room to retrieve it she squeaked, noticing the small, pink, wrapped box behind the violin's case.

"Happy birthday Tennyson!" I laughed, as I had purposefully not mentioned it until now.

She picked up the package and began to unwrap it. As the paper crinkled to the ground, she lifted up the box's lid, and gasped. "Oh my, it is lovely Holmes," she murmured, as she held up the intricate silver locket with a gold dove embossed on the front.

"There was a reason I left you in that photo studio in Paris," I winked, "May I?"

Tennyson nodded and I moved behind her, unclasped the claw, and raised the necklace over her head. As my hands moved from the front of her shoulders to her neck, I deliberately brushed against it as I fastened it closed. I felt her quiver at my touch. I knew precisely what I was about, and my prediction of her response had been flawless. At that moment, I knew there was indeed a way to control and manipulate women. What a find I had uncovered! All the loggings of behaviour, emotions, and responses I had done over the past few months were conclusive. If you offer women attention, with the proper amount of subtlety and interest, they respond favourably. But there is a mixture and balance that must be reached in order for it to be successful. As I had observed her with other men who did not meet the required balance of attention, it was clear that over eager suitors would fail.

Gloating over my own success, I leaned in and whispered, "perfect," then took her by the shoulders and energetically spun her around. "It looks absolutely wonderful on you," I beamed, then moved in closer to her. "Oh, and there is one more thing..."

She closed her eyes and inhaled.

I lifted the locket from her neck and said, "I took the liberty of having it inscribed for you."

"Oh," she breathed out, opening her eyes in embarrassment, "what does it say?"

"S.T., avec affection, S. H."

"Is it, actually written in French?" she asked, pained.

"Oui, Madame," I nodded, as I released the locket and pulled back.

She took a deep breath. "I suddenly do not feel so well," she said with some difficulty, "I must go."

Before she could leave I stopped her, and put a hand on her shoulder. "Tennyson, are you quite alright?"

She seemed pained by my touch, and violently broke away from me. "I have a headache, please!"

"Tennyson?"

She halted immediately. "Yes?"

Her eyes seemed searching, searching for something I could not give her. I sighed.

"Yes, Holmes?"

"Bon anniversaire."

"Merci." She picked up the locket, and held it in her palm. "It is beautiful. You really shouldn't have." She quickly dashed from the room, into her bedroom, and closed the door. I could hear her sobbing. I was taking this too far. It felt malicious, and bordered on cruelty.

A few moments later, Tennyson emerged from her room and stormed towards the door.

"Where are you going Tennyson? I thought you had a headache?"

"I wish to see Miss Whalley. Good day."

"If you haven't made arrangements already," I chased after her, "I should like to take you to dinner this evening..."

She paused in the doorway, then dug her fingernails into both sides of the doorframe. "I intended to spend the evening with my father, Holmes." She turned her head towards me and tears were dripping down her cheeks. "And truly? You've done quite enough already, thank you." She slammed the door and flew down the stairs, then exited the building.

I had hurt her, and felt terrible. I never intended to cause her pain. Deal or not with my brother, I will have to discontinue the experiment and destroy my work. It seemed harmless at the onset, but now, that was no longer true. She *is* a human being after all, and not a lab rat that can be discarded after the experimentation is over.

~ ~

Jonathan threw down the journal.

"I take it back! I take it all back! He never loved her, not ever! Could he be so cruel? This explains Celeste's tirade of abuse about her birthday!"

He knew that Holmes wasn't purposefully trying to hurt his mother, but it made him angry, and he was back to hating him.

He needed an escape, so left campus to head into town. As he wandered through the snow-covered streets with his hands in his pockets, a small terrier happily jumped in and out of snowdrifts, while a small child frantically chased after it.

Couples walked by arm in arm, their cheeks rosy and their eyes full of affection. An old, weather-beaten man with skin like a dried-up fig sat on a front stoop and drank something from a small tin cup. His faded eyes watched Jonathan curiously. *Holmes?* Jonathan shook his head, and continued walking. *Is this even worth pursuing anymore?*

A little boy, possibly six years of age, with his black wool coat covered in clumps of ice, happily ran to his mother and laughed as she scooped him up in a warm knitted shawl. She first scolded him for running off, but then hugged him tightly, and kissed his forehead.

Jonathan felt sick.

People shuffled quickly down the pavements as the wind increased and the air temperature dropped. He was becoming more and more alone. He spied a man with a lantern pole hurrying down the cobblestone streets, lighting the lampposts above him. Jonathan paused, and struggled out his pocket watch to check the time. It was a quarter to seven. Damn, he was going to be late.

He dashed back up the hill and ran to the phone box near Master's Lodge. As he waited for Abigail's call, he rubbed his hands together, and shivered. He was colder than he thought.

His stomach growled, and his teeth chattered. He nervously chewed on a loose thread on his mitten until the phone rang, but as he grabbed for the receiver, he fumbled it and it dropped from his hand. Cursing the phone, he ripped off his mitten and managed the receiver to his ear.

"Hello, Abigail?"

"Hello Jonathan!" Abigail sang on the other end. "Sorry I'm late. What you so upset for?"

Jonathan leaned his forehead against the cold glass of the phone box. "Sherlock Holmes is an ass."

"Now what did he do?"

Jonathan stood up straight and rubbed his forehead, the cold window was giving him a headache. "I simply do not understand how he ended up with my mother. He never really loved her. He is completely heartless, or loveless, or whatever the term is. He does not know *how* to love someone; he said so himself."

"Why did they marry then?"

Jonathan played with the earpiece cord, swinging it back and forth. "I don't know... perhaps he pitied her."

"That's very sad Jonathan. Everyone should be able to love. I fancy life would be very empty without it..."

Jonathan kicked the base of the booth. "I cannot read any more. Celeste was right, I may as well be done with it." He drew a heart in the condensation on the glass with his finger, then put an 'x' through it.

"The truth can be painful, but don't you want to know either way?"

"No! For it will make me despise her as well for having so little self respect if he did not! She was brilliant and beautiful, Abby. Everyone wanted her. Yet she went with a cold, emotionless automaton. And how do I fall into this? Was I a mistake? So when my mother was murdered, it was the perfect opportunity to be rid of me as well?" he erased the heart entirely with his palm, then slumped down against the wall.

"You need to finish the notes Jonathan."

He picked up a small stone on the ground, and rolled it between his fingers. "You think I should?"

"Look, why would Holmes be looking for you, if he did not care?"

"Maybe he fears I will discover the truth; find the box, solve the mystery, and prove him a fraud. What if the whole idea of me being in danger is a ruse to dissuade me?" Jonathan threw down the stone, the paused. "Do you really think he cares?"

"I do. If I am wrong, you need never listen to me again."

Jonathan skidded up the side of the glass. "Well, if it gets worse your fate has yet to be determined."

"I'll take that chance," she laughed. "Finish it. Any other news?"

"Just that if the bloody box did exist, it's probably long gone. I thought it would have been buried in the garden, but they remodeled it in '92."

"Do you know for fact she *buried* it?"

"Well, no."

"Then do not give up. Maybe it's in her old college somewhere?"

"Newnham is so heavily guarded with porters, I couldn't possibly sneak inside."

"You'll find a way. Now chin up!"

Jonathan frowned as he hung up the phone, but knew she was right.

He left his coat on once through the door, as his room was freezing. He kicked the snow off his boots before placing them next to the entranceway and noticed that his left sock had a hole in the big toe. Where was a woman to darn it when he needed one? He turned the deadbolt lock, then threw a blanket over his shoulders and dragged out Holmes' journal.

~ ~

7th April 1888

I visited my brother at his office at the Diogenes Club this afternoon to inform him of my decision.

"I am afraid that I must discontinue my experiment," I told him, expecting him to gloat, and believe that I had actually failed in proving my theory.

Mycroft eased into the back of his desk chair. "Ah, so you began to test your hypothesis about controlling emotions and found that it cannot be done," he smiled. "Did I not explain to you, my brother, that neither people nor emotions can be predicted or controlled?" He gestured for me to sit, but then grinned, "any more than *you* can be predicted, and controlled?"

I wrung my hands around the rim of my bowler feeling foolish, as I often did with my brother. "Are you insinuating that I am not a person?" I tried an attempt at humor as I sat.

"You are quoted as being more of a machine than anything else Sherlock, but as I have experienced you angry as a child, I know better."

"It was not a matter of 'failing' Mycroft, more that I could see I was causing her pain, and experienced guilt for hurting her."

"So, you felt compelled to desist as it was going too far."

I grew impatient for this conversation to end, so shifted uncomfortably in the chair. "Technically, yes."

"Sherlock, I will ask you this, though I already know the answer," he rose from his seat, "do you love her?"

I jumped up angrily, and threw on my bowler. "No, I do not," I said coldly. "And perhaps the sooner she leaves Baker Street, the better."

"You can lie to yourself, but you cannot lie to me," he said glibly, as he sat back down, "you are not as indifferent to women as you would like to believe."

"This is absolute bosh!" I cursed. "You may sit there and make nonsensical conjectures till your voice withers away, but as you've never so much as had tea with a woman, you have no authority on the subject!"

Mycroft grinned, amused at something. "When you come to terms with your feelings... *I'll* be expecting an apology. Remember, I am never wrong."

"Good night, Mycroft." I bowed curtly, then turned to leave. "Smug-faced pedant."

I stomped from his office, enraged. Perhaps he had been correct about Tennyson, but *I* did not love, I could not. I would forgive such a comment from Watson, or someone who knew me less, but Mycroft? Clearly he mistook my empathy for Tennyson as actual feeling. Did he not know me? Had I not been his brother for over thirty years? Should I ask him if *he* was really a woman?! My skin burned, and I desired to crush something. Yes Mycroft, you are wrong at last!

11ᵗʰ April 1888

Tennyson and I had recently lost a case about a man who was wanted for murder. As he had been on the run, and ultimately drowned in the East River, the matter was closed without much resolution, a hard finale for me to stomach. I admit I was difficult to live with during this time, as I squirreled away in my room and ruminated over the unnerving aspects of the case. Tennyson stood me with the patience of a saint.

It had been positively pouring today, and Tennyson was off collecting a novel she had wanted from Hatchard's bookshop in Piccadilly. She had been gone some time, and just as I was debating becoming worried, she suddenly rushed through the doorway dripping wet, and bursting with news.

"Holmes!" She attempted to catch her breath. "I ran all the way from the Strand in central London to tell you!" She removed her black-feathered hat, wrapped its train around the brim, then set it down on the sofa. "You'll never suppose whom I saw!"

"Oh?"

She tightly wrung out her black skirt. "Death has clearly not become him, for he has returned to the world of the living."

"You know I despise guessing games."

"Jasper Wilson is alive!" she said excitedly, brushing wet strands of hair from her face. "I was passing by Somerset House, and in my peripheral vision, someone appeared familiar. As implausible as it seemed, I've learned to never accept death as a reason to rule out a possible suspect. When he turned his head, I observed the identifiable scarred left nostril and cheek and knew it to be he! I dogged him until he landed at The Tottenham on Oxford St., then observed him single out a man at the bar. Overhearing their conversation, Wilson plans on being in town a fortnight before heading to America; New York specifically. He's staying at the Bristol under the alias of Elbert Gorey. Case re-opened!"

"I'll alert Lestrade immediately," I jumped up. "Well done, my dear!"

Tennyson sneezed. "Thank you, but I must change immediately, for I am positively soaked through."

She struggled to remove her sodden, black-beaded wool jacket, and huffed in exasperation.

I laughed. "Need a hand?"

"Two, preferably," she nodded.

I took one coat arm, then the other, and with some effort, was able to peel it from her body. I moved behind her and without thinking, unbuttoned the top clasp of her dress. Before I could reach the next hook, Tennyson spun around and snatched my wrist.

"I can handle the rest myself, Holmes," she said icily, as she pushed me away.

"I am sorry. Of course you can," I gulped, as I stood with her coat draped over my arm. Why had I done that?!

She banged into her bedroom and slammed the door. I dropped her coat to the ground and threw off my dressing gown. Popping on my billycock and ulster, I dashed out to send on a wire to Inspector Lestrade at Scotland Yard. He had to be informed of this immediately.

As I sloshed through the street, rain pelting on my shoulders, I shook my head and tried to deliberate why I had acted without thought just then. What would possess me to begin undressing her further than that which she requested?

290

When I returned, I studied her jacket on the floor where I had left it then picked it up and hung it over the fire guard by the hearth. Rather than analyze my previous motives further, I decided I would take my mind elsewhere.

I lightly tapped the syringe with my index finger, and had just rolled up my sleeve, when Tennyson walked past my bedroom door then stopped and stared. In my haste, I had left it open. She was dressed in the red satin walking dress she had worn on the first day of her arrival.

"What are you about to do, Holmes?"

I reached for the doorknob, but she caught her hand between the doorframe and the wooden panel, before I could close it.

"Why must you?"

"Must is not the correct auxiliary verb Tennyson, it is more that I would 'like', and 'desire to'. Now if you'll excuse me..." I again attempted to close the door, but she held firm.

"Have you any idea what it does to a person, Holmes? I am certain you've heard how opium destroyed the journalist Thomas De Quincy, and *your* chosen vice is far more potent. A mind like yours should not be wasted by..."

"Let me be, Tennyson."

"Why not simply go for a walk or read if you are under-stimulated?"

I felt my temperature rising as I shoved her from the room. "Because it produces immediate gratification."

291

Tennyson then surprised me and grabbed the syringe from my hand and held it behind her. "No, Holmes," she shook her head.

She turned to leave, but then I reached around her waist from behind, and pulled her towards me as I stretched out my hand for the syringe. She curled forward, clutching it tightly between her hands, and struggled to break free. We battled briefly as I attempted to pry it her fingers, but I'd soon had quite enough, so violently spun her around and shouted, "I *need* it dammit!"

Tennyson froze. She pushed herself away, then thrust the syringe into my hand. "Do what you like then. Though should you overindulge, become comatose, and consequently die, I will do nothing," she said, her eyes red. "And, I won't care." She then stormed out the door and headed downstairs, presumably to speak with Mrs. Hudson about what a monster I was.

I examined the syringe in my hand, then angrily threw it to the floor. I shifted my gaze to the window and watched as rain drops trickled down the glass like tears. Would she really not care?

CHAPTER 24

HOW THE MIGHTY HAVE FALLEN

13th April 1888

It was the Friday evening I had purchased tickets to take Tennyson to see La Traviata with the Watsons. I was attending somewhat reluctantly, as I didn't relish wasting a free evening with Mary Watson, however, as this was my Christmas gift to Tennyson, I was going for her sake. With any luck, Mrs. Watson and her mouth would seat on the far right of me so I would not be subjected to her incessant chatter. While the gods smiled upon me in terms of seat placement to avoid any distractions from the gregarious Mary Watson, I was, nonetheless, quite distracted. That is not to say that the performances were lacking, the cast was certainly skilled, but I found myself watching Tennyson, more so than the actual opera, for the bulk of the evening.

At the end of Act III, tears streamed down Tennyson's face as the female lead died in her lover's arms. I instinctively reached out to hold her but caught myself, yet again, questioning the reason behind my actions.

My emotions were decidedly muddled. The lines between them seemed crossed, and undefined. There was a throbbing pain in my head and chest, and I felt nauseous. I was experiencing... something, something I could not articulate. What was happening to me? Was I ill?

After the performance, as we awaited our carriages in the slight rain, Watson approached me. He no doubt wished to discuss the night's production, but I was in no mood for him. The majority of what he blathered on about I only partially heard, but his final sentence caught my complete attention.

"...and Miss Tennyson looks particularly lovely this evening, doesn't she Holmes?"

My guard went up. "Why would you say that?" I snapped.

"Well, doesn't she?" he asked, slightly startled by my reaction.

"I... yes, the... well..." I began stumbling over my words as I noticed Tennyson gracefully descend the steps of the opera house in her aquamarine, sequined evening gown. "She does at that," I managed, taking a deep breath. I was mildly aware that there was some link to my emotional state and Tennyson but just how so, I still wasn't sure. I then realized that something fascinated me about the way she moved, much like a dancer-- very lithe, agile, and elegant.

As Mary Watson was too busy chattering on to watch where she was going, she accidentally stepped on Tennyson's dress train as they neared the bottom step. Tennyson would have fallen forward if I hadn't dashed over in time, and caught her in my arms.

I held her briefly, feeling frozen in time on those steps, my head hurting worse. That slight hint of green in Tennyson's eyes seemed to sparkle as she said, "Thank you Holmes," snapping me out of my reverie. My chest was tight, as if in a vice.

After Mary had apologized, and the Watsons thankfully left, Tennyson and I entered the next available carriage. I attempted to breathe normally, but I felt as if my pharynx was constricted.

"That was a lovely production, wasn't it Holmes?" Tennyson asked with a smile.

"Yes, indeed."

"Thank you again for taking me, it is my favorite opera actually."

I wanted to jump from the carriage as I felt suffocated. The knot in my stomach and the pain in my chest was increasing by the moment. I had no desire for a conversation.

Sensing my discomfort, Tennyson leaned forward and put a blue-gloved hand on my knee then asked, "Are you well Holmes?"

Her touch felt like fire. Why did it pain me so? "Yes, quite," I said, as I shifted my knee away from her, and pulled my opera cloak over my leg. "I am weary from the week's excursions."

Once we arrived to Baker Street, I swiftly headed upstairs without holding the door, then carelessly threw off my bell topper and cloak, and headed to my bedroom.

"Holmes, do you still wish for me to fetch that manuscript tomorrow?" Tennyson followed behind me. "I could head out straight away once we've..."

I turned to face her with a fierce look.

She halted in surprise. "What?"

"We shall discuss in the morning. Now if you please, I would like to be left alone."

"Holmes, what in heaven's name is wrong? Have I done something?"

"There are limits to my patience *Miss* Tennyson. I am not well, and need rest. Good night," I closed my door.

"I apparently do nothing but agitate him as of late," I heard her sigh on the other side.

I frowned. I was not angry with her. I... in truth did not know what was wrong with me. I should not have been so short with her. I sat on the bed and clasped my hands between my knees. *Good God, what is the matter with you Holmes!?* I made a fist and punched the pillow. Am I slowly losing my mind? Catching a fever, an illness? Regardless of how detrimental, my mind needed to be cleared, as I could bear no more. I hurriedly gave myself a barely diluted injection of cocaine, not caring the consequences, and leaned back as I waited for the drug to take effect.

As I slipped into a restful, euphoric state, it suddenly occurred to me what my troubled mind was fighting against. Why I felt so ill, why I was behaving in such an uncharacteristic manner with Tennyson, and why... her mere touch had affected me so in the carriage.

"I am in love with her."

This was no longer a game. It had been wrong, horribly wrong of me to have experimented on her, and now, as punishment, I developed feelings for her. Mycroft was right. Emotions were not predictable or cyclical, and they most certainly were not controllable, as I could now attest. The great Sherlock Holmes has fallen, felled by a woman, and I've never been more incensed with myself.

I remember squeezing my eyes shut, feeling quite pained, as a myriad of images and fantasies swirled through my addled brain. I then fell into a deep, and frightful sleep.

I awakened the next morning to Tennyson shaking me, begging me to open my eyes, her voice filled with terror.

Her hair was down, and she was still in her nightdress. She had been crying, as tear trails stained her red cheeks. I turned my head and noticed that I was lying on the floor in the sitting room. It was dark outside, and the clock's hands were at three and twenty. I was thoroughly confused.

When she noticed my eyes were open, she hugged me tightly. "Thank heavens you are all right!" she cried, her long hair brushing against my neck. It tickled, so I laughed, which caused her to quickly pull away. "Sorry, I... was carried away."

I would have very much enjoyed her holding me longer. I suddenly felt dizzy. "Whatever happened?"

"I was preparing for bed when I heard a loud crash, and came running out to find you on the carpet unconscious. You overdosed, didn't you?"

I honestly didn't remember leaving my bedroom that night. I noted the cleaned up broken glass piled neatly in the dustpan by the fireplace, and wondered what on earth I had been about? Everything was foggy. I felt lightheaded as I tried to sit up so thought better, and rested back down.

"Were you bored last night? Unhappy? I thought you only resorted to your vice in order to escape monotony, or dullness? You did seem distracted last night, but had you disliked the opera that severely?" she asked, perhaps a touch hurt.

I sighed. I could not tell her the reason. "I also indulge when I am frustrated, or anticipate the potential of becoming too emotional."

"Then what prompted it?"

"Tennyson, I do not wish to inform you of every thought, every observation, that passes through my mind. Sometimes, my contemplations become too much to bear, and it is simply better to avoid them."

She sighed. "Well, please *do* be more careful. I thought I'd be contacting the morgue this morning."

"You cannot get rid of me that easily," I grinned. "Ah, so you *do* care after all."

She gazed at me curiously. She truly was beautiful, the way her eyes would shine, and her nose scrunch up when she was angry.

She must have noticed me staring at her, for she impatiently asked, "What?!"

"I liked your dress," I mused.

"I beg your pardon?"

"Last night, I liked your dress. It was quite lovely, as were you. Venus herself would have been jealous."

Tennyson cocked her head, perplexed. "Yes well, may I help you to your room?"

I closed my eyes. "No no, I am quite content just lying here."

"We should move you to the sofa, at least."

I thought for a moment, genuinely unsure. "That *would* be better, wouldn't it?"

"Yes, it would," she laughed. "Come then." She took my arms, and helped me to my feet. I felt made of rubber, and could barely stand. Detecting this, she put her arm around my waist, and assisted me to the sofa. I sat down and must have pulled her with me, for she fell over onto to my lap. She paused, looking into my eyes. I wanted to kiss her. I either ran my fingers through her hair, or perhaps I *did* try to kiss her, I cannot be certain at this point, but she turned her head, and quickly shifted off my knees to the sofa cushion.

"Tennyson?" I tugged on her left hand, feeling rather childlike. "Thank you for looking out for me. No one's.... ever really done that."

"You are your own menace at times. One cannot help but care for someone like that."

Our hands were still touching. I squeezed hers. "Care, Tennyson? In what sense?" If she admitted to loving me, I decided I would kiss her.

She pulled her hand away. "You are very immature at times, like a little boy. I suppose all women have that motherly instinct where they wish to nurture those who need it most," she rose up. "But as I see you are in fine shape now, I will return to bed."

I leaned back on the sofa, and stretched out across it. "Well I would certainly trust my life in your hands."

She walked up towards her room, then paused by the doorway. "Then you are too trusting for your own good."

"Tennyson?"

299

She folded her arms and leaned against the doorframe. "Yes, Holmes?" she sleepily blinked at me.

I gulped. "I am... glad you are here."

She saluted me, then closed the door.

Dear God, was I right? If I expressed any outright romantic interest she would no longer care for me? Or had her affections already moved on? In either case, I was now in a very awkward position. Could love be so filled with irony?

All my life I had vehemently abstained from any type of passion or romance, as I never wanted to endure the type of emotional anguish I was currently experiencing, but now, I had allowed myself to be vulnerable.

I moved to the bookcase and pulled a thin, brown paper bag from atop several books on the bottom shelf. Inside, was the photograph of Tennyson from Paris. I slipped it out, and rubbed my finger along her outline.

Perhaps these thoughts will fade? Merely an amourette? Though I love her, I truly believe this is only a temporary character flaw. Once I return to my senses, things will be as they were. I simply... need time. Or, am I willing myself to believe it, only to better prepare for her eventual departure?

CHAPTER 25

"PLEASE DO NOT LEAVE"

4th August 1888

Tennyson never spoke of her family, save for the occasional reference to her father who lived in Cavendish Square. Thus being the case, I gathered there wasn't a particularly close connection between them. You can imagine my surprise when I handed her a letter one day, and she spontaneously burst into tears upon opening it. It was about her father. He was deathly ill, and hadn't much time left.

I accompanied her to St. George's Hospital where I met her father, Alexander Tennyson, for the first and last time. Whilst Tennyson was roaming the hallways in search of a glass of water, in his delusional state, her father had begged me to please care for his little girl. I promised him that I would, and he passed away just after we had shaken hands, sealing the deal. I mentioned nothing of this to Tennyson.

5th August 1888

The day after her father passed, Tennyson was quiet. For the first time in our acquaintance, she attended the afternoon service at her father's church in Cavendish Square.

Upon her return, she stated that she wished to visit Celeste that evening as she had known her father, and could be a valuable support. When I inquired as to whether I could escort her for safety reasons, she very firmly said no. Apprehensive about her fragile state, I donned my long grey travelling cloak and cloth cap, then followed after her.

Strangely, she was headed towards Whitechapel, not Westminster. I was certainly glad that I had dogged her now. Why would she travel to one of the most wretched hovels of the East End? When she reached George Yard Buildings, to my surprise, and more aptly my devastation, I discovered the reason. She had come to meet with The Prince, yet again. His corpulent figure was unmistakable.

My heart sank. I hid in the gas lamp's shadows by the main gate's archway, and strained to hear their conversation.

"You decided to show, I see," The Prince said bitterly. "As I assumed you would not, I had a secondary plan in mind, hence the location."

"Ginger Beer and cards I'd imagine? Or is it the Royal Cambridge Music Hall this time? Contrary to its title, it is not terribly fitting for royalty, Jack..." Tennyson smiled.

Why does she call him Jack?

"I have not seen you since New Year's Eve," he folded his arms and turned to the side, "I was about to give up on you."

She pressed his arm. "I am sorry I gave you doubt. If you can forgive me..."

He grabbed her hand, and kissed it fiercely. "I have been out of my mind yearning for you! Why have you not shown the last few times? Do I no longer interest you? Have you someone else now, and this is your final farewell?"

Tennyson laughed. "Yes, I am presently involved with Emperor Alexander III of Russia. No, that was not the reason. My father has been ill..." her voice faded to a whisper. "He... passed away yesterday."

His Royal Highness, or 'Jack', calmed slightly at this, and took her hands. "I am sorry for your father, but wounded you stayed away. Has Holmes kept you so busy? It pains me to imagine you as a working woman. You should be attending lavish parties, and having tea with duchesses..." he took her in his arms, "and... be sitting by my side." The Prince then kissed her lips, a long lingering kiss that made my stomach turn. I felt a sickening sensation in my gut and truly thought I would vomit. I had to look away, for it was extremely painful to see her with him.

"I have missed those lovely lips of yours," he said flirtatiously. "And I forgive you my loved one, for I could never stay angry with you for long."

"Thank you. Sometimes, we become so lost in our work, that we lose sight of those who truly care about us. I realized that when my father passed, and I felt alone. I took him for granted, and will not make that same mistake with others in my life. I came here tonight because I needed to be with someone who loves me."

If only you knew Scarlett, if only you knew.

The Prince wrapped his arms around her, and kissed her on the cheek. "My loyalty to you is, I hope, a thing you never think of doubting!"

"And, there was another reason..." she pulled away.

"Oh?"

303

"I am so sorry Jack, but I was forbidden to see you!"

"Forbidden! By Holmes? Whatever for?" The Prince grabbed her by the shoulders, and shook her harshly. "How does he know about us?"

"I swear I have said nothing! He's Sherlock Holmes! I tried my best to keep you a secret!"

"Good God Scarlett! This is unacceptable!" The Prince paced angrily. "Has he told anyone else? Does he know you came here tonight?"

"No! I told him I was to see Celeste. We are safe, I promise."

He whipped his head around for a quick visual search, so I leaned further into the archway, away from view.

"He did not seem suspicious," Tennyson assured him, "normally I can tell."

"You can tell," The Prince narrowed his eyes. "You are far too close to him than is good, or will be tolerated. Now pray tell, what reason did he give for not seeing me?" Then seeming concerned, he asked, "He is not jealous, is he?"

"Of course not!" she laughed. "Holmes has no interest in women, you know that!"

I had to smile at the irony.

"He was spouting out about politics, and being in danger, and other such nonsense, but I did not believe a word."

The Prince caressed her cheek. "Then why not come?"

"There are other issues Jack, the same ones since Cambridge. I also, well... did not care to make him angry."

The Prince threw his hands in the air, and slammed them down to his side. "Did not care to make him angry? What of me? *I* was angry! Scarlett, what power does this man have over you? What do his feelings matter? As if he has ever considered yours. Or... has that changed..."

"Jack, what if he were to reveal us if I disobeyed him?"

"What is he, your master? How tightly is his leash wound around you?"

I was considerably offended by that comment.

"You sound like Celeste! She has been badgering me to leave for months! I have nowhere to go, especially now. Truly, you are being most unkind!"

Celeste had been telling her to leave? Why? Miss Whalley and I had never seen eye-to-eye, that was undeniable, but she must positively loathe me to be advising her so. What had I done?!

"Stay with Celeste then! She is your dearest friend, is she not?"

"Though I love her dearly, I could not live with her. We are far too different."

"That settles it," he nodded. "I never approved of you living there from the start. A single woman should not be living with a single man, unless they have other intentions. He should have known better. Well no more, not if I have my way, and I usually do! You will leave Baker Street, and come with me. I insist upon it! I cannot stand to have you with that man any longer. He is poisonous, a cold, passionless trout. He treats you without respect or dignity, mocks your interests, and quite obviously ignores the very fact that you are a woman, and deserve to be handled with care, and delicacy."

My God, what has she been saying about me?

"You cannot blame Holmes," Tennyson said quietly. "That is his nature."

"That does not excuse his behaviour. He is not worthy of being in your presence."

"What are you proposing?"

He again embraced her. "Come and live with me darling, if you would. It is where you belong. I could give you everything you ever dreamed of. What could Holmes possibly offer? *I* can offer you love, wealth, and a world of pleasure."

This sentence cut me to the core. Perhaps he was right? Why be with me? How could I compete? He was a Prince, he was romantic, he knew how to handle a woman and he more than likely *could* give her whatever she wanted. No, be reasonable Holmes. She would be a confined and trapped woman, a mistress to a Prince. I felt certain she was destined for so much more, and selfishly, I could not imagine my life without her.

"The Palace? Are you out of your mind?" she asked.

"No, Malborough House, and then to Sandringham in Norfolk. You'll be safe and left alone there. Then, when the time is right, we will be together."

306

Malborough House?   With his circle of racy, pleasure- loving friends of the Malborough House Set? That would never suit her in the least!

"But what of your family?   How would it suddenly be acceptable? There will never be a *right* time, your Highness..."

"Shhh! Remember it is Jack, as it must always be when we are not entirely secure. It will be handled. Pack your belongings tonight. I will cancel our arrangements for the evening."

"What if I leave and Holmes creates a scandal?"

The Prince laughed maliciously. "Do you fancy he would? It is his word against mine. Whom do you think the public will believe? Me, or a man who has been living with an unmarried woman, and is creating stories out of jealousy? He is far too concerned for his reputation than to risk my wrath." *The wrath of the Royal Family. I am certain the papers would love to hear that comment.* "Now, will you leave in the morning as I ask?"

I watched her carefully, but it was too dark to read her face. Would she settle for someone she did not love? Or had her affections returned to him?

She answered by nodding her head.

I closed my eyes. I felt as if my heart was being squeezed through a laundry mangle. I had lost her.

"Good! I shall plan for everything. What time does Holmes arise?"

"After eight. He has his morning pipe, then breakfast, then another pipe."

"Then leave before then, at seven."

"But what if he rises earlier than usual? Or notices my packing?"

The Prince paused for a moment, thinking. I am certain it was a considerable strain for him.

"Claim you are heading to Cavendish Square to settle matters concerning your father's estate. I will have a carriage waiting for you near the newly built Law Courts on the Strand, before it becomes Fleet Street. They will take you Pall Mall. There's an entrance to Malborough House near The Beaconsfield Club and I will be waiting there for your arrival, which will not be soon enough." He kissed her. "Oh, how I love you!"

"I love you as well," she said half-heartedly.

Ah! I thought. *Perhaps all is not lost.*

I wandered the streets for an hour before returning home, running things over in my mind. As I carefully walked up the stairs and through the front door, I tiptoed up to her bedroom and creaked open the door.

An open suitcase lay on her bed, and the photograph of us from Paris had been tossed into the dustbin.

"My dear, whatever are you about?"

Startled, Tennyson whirled around and in doing so, accidentally caught her Nile green skirt on a wooden splinter from the bed frame.

"Does the term 'knocking' mean nothing to you?" she huffed, as she yanked the fabric free, causing it to tear.

I removed my cap, and threw it on the bedpost. "I take it your visit to Miss Whalley was enlightening?"

She crossed her arms.

"Now where are you going?"

"I believe the answer to either of those questions is none of your affair, sir," she continued to pack, but with a quickened pace. "And where are your manners? Didn't your mother ever teach you that barging in on someone is disrespectful, and furthermore, rude?" She rustled to her closet, and pulled out her black velvet opera cloak and hatbox.

"My mother died when I was very young, and 'none of my affair'? As you live with me, I am within my rights to question your apparent travel plans."

She slammed the hatbox on the bed and continued to pack.

"You wouldn't be off to see whom I strictly prohibited you from seeing, now would you?"

"Refresh my memory, as I can't quite seem to remember."

"Oh, I believe you can. I will grant you one minute's time to desist in the harried gathering of your possessions and come to your senses."

She leaned on the hatbox, and glared at me. "You think you can tell me what to do?"

"As a matter of fact, yes. Quite frankly, I could completely control you if I so desired."

She reached around her neck, unclasped the locket I had given her, then poignantly dropped it on the dresser. "Is that so?"

It pained me see a gift that I had so carefully selected for her discarded so ruthlessly, but it was of the utmost importance that I appear detached. "You forget that I know secrets of yours. You also could not manage without me so therefore, must do as I command."

Her eyes blazed a bright green, and her rouged cheeks flushed redder. "I, my dear Holmes, am at no one's command!"

"As a mistress to a Prince, you most certainly would be."

She snatched up her jewellery box and placed it in the suitcase, purposefully leaving her locket behind. "Trying to frighten me, are you?" She slid her hand across the dresser, knocking the locket into the dustbin. "*Highly original tactic.*"

"I am opening your eyes to what your world will become. It will not be the fantasy dream life you are painting for yourself."

"I will always come and go as it suits me, and as I please." She kneeled down on one knee to grab at a silk stocking beneath my foot. "And, if you please..." she said, tapping her index finger on my boot, indicating that I should step aside.

I kept my foot where it was. "Tennyson, I would like you to listen."

She again pulled at the stocking. "And I should like you to move!"

310

"Very well, if you will not listen willingly, then I shall have to force you." I grabbed her by the forearms and with some opposition, lifted her to her feet. I held her tightly, taking the chance that I might still have some power of persuasion with her, then kissed her. She initially clawed at me in protest, but then melted into my arms. She still had feelings for me, I would win this battle.

"Now then," I tenderly brushed her cheek, "you were saying something about being under no one's command?"

"I... um... yes..." she seemed in a daze. She then pursed her lips, narrowed her eyes, and slapped me across the face.

Fueled by her fury and the sting in my cheek, I gripped her by the shoulders and kissed her again. This time longer, harder, and more ardently. It was all I could do to keep from exposing how I truly felt, from telling her how much I loved her. The euphoric rush was virtually overwhelming, but it still must seem like a game.

When I released her, she collapsed in a heap to the floor. Her defeated eyes longingly searched mine, hoping, perhaps praying, that she could see even a flicker of feeling.

Not yet, I thought.

Unable to detect anything beyond impassivity, she hung her head.

With her attention directed to the floor, I took a moment to rub my cheek. That had certainly smarted. "You do not love him, Tennyson."

"Though you observe much," she shifted her gaze to me, "you do not know everything."

311

"I knew that the best way to acquire your attention was to kiss you, that was knowledge enough."

"I was surprised!" she stood. "Had you knocked me over the head, I would have behaved just the same!"

"Not so, for remember that Friday evening in February where you drank entirely too much?"

Tennyson's brow furrowed, and her eyes darted from side to side as she searched through her memory.

"Well, I kissed you that night, and you had the same reaction."

Tennyson turned her back, and leaned her hands on the wall for support. This appeared to be troubling news to her. "Why would you do that...?"

"I was merely curious as to your response," I shrugged, as if referring to a chemical reaction and not an emotional one.

She closed her eyes, and breathed in softly with a slight laugh. "An experiment." She turned her head, and glared at me. "*I* was an experiment. What do you want Holmes? What are you waiting for? That I confess I am madly in love with you, so you can further ridicule me and point out the fallacies of being emotional and affected?"

"All I am asking... is for you to stay."

She pushed away from the wall. "Why? You can easily get another lodger, and one that would *help* you financially, not drain you." She swiped a blue knitted scarf off the bed and proceeded to carefully fold it into squares.

I walked over and slammed her suitcase shut, which caused her to jump. "Yes, but one who would not be you. Now what are you running away from?"

She re-opened the suitcase, and threw in the scarf. "I am not running away."

I again closed it. "Then why are you leaving?"

She reached for the suitcase's handle, but I grabbed her wrist and held it back. She tried to break free, but my grip was too strong for her. "I want to be with someone who loves and respects me, is that so wrong?"

I released her, but my eyes dared her to continue packing. "Despite my opinion of His Royal Highness if you do not love him in return, then it *is* wrong. And no one here loves or respects you? Is this your assessment, or Celeste's?"

She folded her arms over her chest. "Mrs. Hudson aside, no, no one does. And why are you bringing Celeste into this?"

"Did she not tell you to leave?"

She frowned. "Why would you say that?"

I sighed. "You saw her this evening, correct? Then is she, or is she not, the reason you have decided to depart?"

Tennyson brushed her hair behind her ears.

"I thought not. What would people say if they knew you were involved with The Prince?"

"I did not say I saw The Prince..."

"You don't have to, I *know!*" I shouted, angrily knocking her suitcase from the bed, "you cannot be with The Prince for he does not know how to love you...!" I paused, then took in a deep breath. I was becoming careless, and letting my emotions show.

Tennyson backed up in alarm, her eyes wide. "What?"

I adjusted my tie, and cleared my throat. "He lives in a whirl of amusements. His fancies come and go."

She picked up her suitcase, and began to collect the loose articles of clothing that had spilled out onto the floor. "Who is to say I could not be the one to change him? How do you know?" she asked, carefully placing the undergarments, stockings, and brushes back inside the suitcase, then resting it on her dresser.

"I do *not* know, but I can make a fairly accurate prediction, based on previous behaviour. My opinion of His Royal Highness and his companions is this. The difference between the common folk, and men of that nature, is similar to that of a photograph, versus an impressionistic painting. One reproduces with pitiless fidelity, though the focus may be distorted, and the other represents whatever erratic, colourful fancy one chooses to see. Between the two, it is their preference to focus on the meaningless collection of splatters, as they can interpret it as something pleasant, whereas a true slice of reality that cannot be misconstrued, they tend to avoid like the plague."

Tennyson slide open a dresser drawer, snatched out several pairs of gloves, then slammed it shut.

314

"Do you truly believe he would give up everything for you? He loves the idea of you, like he loves the idea of high art, though he barely understands it."

"The great pontificator saves us all, yet again," she said snidely as she tucked the gloves into her suitcase.

"I am saving your reputation, which would be blackened, consorting with royalty. How fortunate do you believe Miss Lilly Langtry to be these days?"

"She, was a married woman," Tennyson hissed as she moved to the mantelpiece and gathered up writing utensils and paper to the left of the clock. "What, do you plan to tell all of London?!"

"I am not saying I wouldn't, let us reason it that way."

Tennyson kicked over the dustbin. "It is your word against his, and the people adore him."

"As valueless as popularity is."

With a huff, she threw the contents of the desk drawer into a long box, then knelt down to reach for her white satin slippers underneath the bed. I slid them away from her with my foot.

"You also cannot discount the physical evidence, such as the *billets-doux* he has given you."

She froze. "What?"

"I have confiscated several such love notes, enough to easily incriminate him. I am surprised you failed to notice them missing."

Tennyson lunged across the floor, grabbed hold of a slipper, then fiercely threw it at my head, which I somehow dodged. "Not only do you spy on me, you rifle through my belongings?!"

"At the time of securing them, you had only recently..."

She grabbed up the other to throw, but as I anticipated the attack, I managed to duck, and the slipper hit the wall.

"You blackguard!" she screamed. "Then you never trusted me!" She paused, then hugged her elbows into her waist.

I took her slippers from the floor, and tucked them back underneath the bed. "Then, we are quite clear you are staying?"

She looked me hard in the eyes. "I saved your life once, does that mean nothing to you?"

"And I saved yours, so we are even," I said coldly.

Tennyson began to unpack her suitcase, but then rested her palms atop the dresser and sighed heavily. "Why do you do this?"

"Do what, pray tell?" I was admittedly finding some perverse pleasure in her discomfort.

"You taunt me, torment me with false affection in order to keep me a prisoner trapped in your world, and then treat me however you wish. I in turn, am expected to endure it, in hopes that I will please you enough to... to..."

"To what, Tennyson?"

"I am your slave Holmes, yet I mean nothing to you!" she spun around.

I stepped over and took her by the arms. "That is not true, you have become a rather necessary ally, and I quite enjoy our professional partnership. Now stop all this nonsense."

"But... that is all, isn't it?" she asked sadly, as she pulled away.

I lifted her chin to look at me. "My dear woman, what is it *you* want?"

She shook her head and turned away.

"There is nothing you wish to say to me?"

"No."

"Be certain, for there are limited windows of opportunity in life to embrace and disclose what you typically feel you cannot," I touched my fingertips to her shoulders. "One rarely gets a second chance to do so."

She slowly faced me, swallowed, but then exhaled loudly and covered her face with her hands.

"In that case, we have nothing further to discuss, and I bid you goodnight."

I attempted to leave, but before I could reach the door, she seized my arm. "Holmes, wait?"

"Yes?"

"I don't quite know how to, um... well it is all very complicated..." she muttered as she absently began to rub her index finger along my jacket's lapels.

I brushed aside a loose strand of hair from her face, and tucked it behind her ear. "Then simplify it, as I've taught you."

She looked at me with a sigh, then pushed away. "You are an emotionally-detached, analytical machine. Far too logical to even remotely comprehend..."

I put a finger to her lips. "Try me."

She twisted her back to me. "It does not matter how I feel."

I spun her shoulders to face me. "It matters, continue."

She took a deep breath, then moved to her vanity, the small, low seated teak accessory she had crammed between the mantle and the closet, and began to play with her make-up accessories, lining them up against the oval mirror. "There is something that happens to me when I am near you, something... I feel..."

"And?" I asked her reflection.

She took up a cotton puff and nervously began twisting it between her fingers, averted my gaze. "As long as I am with you, the location or subject matter is inconsequential." She replaced the puff, then scooped up her opera cape on the bed. "Even... if you are cross with me and would rather toss me out of the window than continue our discussion, I somehow find your angry passion... alluring." She quickly returned the cape to the closet, keeping her back to me.

"Alluring?" I smiled, "an odd adjective choice, but continue."

"And," she turned, "I tolerate far more from you than I should," she said, crossing her arms in earnest and approaching me. "You are selfish, ungrateful, self-righteous, play your silly violin whenever it strikes

318

your fancy, smoke incessantly, indulge in addictions most un-becoming and destructive, hate my only friend, set off firearms in the apartment, and your methods of detection are *most* unorthodox."

I rubbed my neck. I suppose that *is* a rather long list of negatives.

"You forget punctual and financially generous."

"You are also obstinate as a mule, and while you claim we 'work well together,' you harbor this intense hatred and distrust of women for what reason, I have never fully understood."

"Tennyson, if you would..."

"This was only to be a temporary situation until I had learned enough, and I feel I have!"

"Then... you no longer need me?"

She closed her eyes. "With my father gone, I realize how short one's life can be. Far too many years are wasted that you can never retrieve. If I leave now with The Prince, or later on my own, I *will* be leaving. What care the reason?"

"He is not whom you want to be with, that is why."

"Why should that matter?"

How absurd this entire conversation is. "For perhaps the person you want to be with, also wishes to be with you." I took her hand. "Please don't leave."

"I thought you had established I *could* not, even if I choose!" she exploded, breaking away. "You are being most contradictory!"

319

I held up my hands in surrender. "Steady there Tennyson, I honestly cannot force you to do, or not do anything. Do you truly find me so controlling?"

She plopped down on the bed, and crossed her legs.

I sat next to her. "What would my reason need be, for you to remain?"

"I am not Watson, and would prefer to not be ignored as such. The postman gets more of a response than I and at times I feel invisible, that I am the furthest thing from your mind or care."

"Then I have hidden myself well." I took her by the hands, and pulled her to her feet. "My dear, allow me to clarify. I do in fact care who you are with and why you are with them, because *Scarlett,* I... I love you." It was more nerve-wracking to say those words to her than I had anticipated.

Her jaw dropped and she wobbled on her feet. "What did you say?"

I thought she would faint, so drew her into me to prevent her from falling. "You heard me. Scarlett darling, I love you," I managed with more confidence. I leaned in to kiss her.

She shook her head, and broke away.

"I do not know as I can say this again Scarlett, so hear me now."

She lifted an eyebrow. "How can I trust you? Are you not saying this to keep me from The Prince and 'save' my reputation? Or so that you may continue to dangle me like a worm on a hook?"

"You are much too lovely to be pierced by a sharp metal object."

320

I explained to her the progression of things. How the passion was not always there, but grew over time. I admitted to the deal with my brother and when I confessed that I had loved her since the night at the opera, she questioned why I had waited to tell her. I finally opened myself to vulnerability and expressed my fears of falling out of her favour once she possessed me. Perhaps I would be a horrid lover, and companion? I apologized for not telling her sooner, but now that she was aware of my feelings, she could make an informed decision.

"I am staying," she hugged me tightly, but then searched my face. "Tell me, is there truly love behind that cold mask you wear so well?"

"Months ago, when your father said you should leave, what had you returned with?"

"To take a long walk off a short pier," Scarlett grinned, "but that was then. More recently, I've felt so heartbroken and alone, Holmes. That was my reason for leaving, nothing more."

"I promise that you won't be," I stared into her eyes, "ever."

"How I love you, Sherlock Holmes," she whispered.

"Oh Scarlett, how I have wanted you," I let slip. I backed up, mortified. "I should not have admitted as much. This... heightened sense of emotion is still fairly unfamiliar to me, as are these... sensations, and how to control them."

"Well!" she laughed, "though, did you not tell me feelings *cannot* be controlled?"

"Yes--"

She pushed me onto the bed, sat on my lap, and began to unbutton my jacket. "Then do not try," she said in low voice.

I gulped. Were we moving too fast? Should I be more respectful? I had not anticipated this aggression from her. She grabbed my tie, pulled me into her, and kissed my lips. Wrapping her other arm around my shoulder, she leaned into my chest. Her intensions were clear, but I knew any advances on my part were unfitting. Such intimacies took trust, and time, so I would not allow things to be rushed, I would not... oh, damn time!

I slowly lifted her skirt, and rubbed my hand along her stockinged leg. "Why Miss Scarlett Tennyson, are you attempting to seduce me?" I said, all too willing to play along, and putting any thoughts of being a gentleman aside.

She tossed off my jacket, and began to unbutton my shirt. "Only if I am succeeding," she whispered. "If you want me, you may have me."

I swung her around, pressed her down on the bed, and kissed her neck as I slowly moved my hand down to her chest.

"Oh Sherlock," she moaned.

Hearing my name with such an impassioned inflection only motivated me further. Soon, layers of skirts, silk stockings, lace undergarments, and various other articles of clothing quickly flew to the floor. I was attempting to be tender, but the exhilaration of anticipation made it difficult to focus. In my mind, I wasn't undressing her fast enough.

I then paused, suddenly anxious, as no action is without consequences, and particularly, such intimacies as these. She assured me that now was never a more opportune time, so I threw all reservations aside, and decided to not give it another thought. I had never wanted anything more, and could not have stopped myself had I wished.

Our interactions became more heated and hurried...and then, the defining moment. The one I had eagerly awaited but not expected so soon. She reached out, turned the lantern's light to a low dim, and closed her eyes as our bodies intertwined and became one.

For the first time in my life I felt euphoric without the aid of medicinal drugs. And what a feeling! I shall remember that night, and her, for as long as I live.

~ ~

Jonathan banged the journal shut. "That is enough!" he groaned, as he rubbed his hand down his face. "I could have done without the last page. Mum, really!" He shoved the journal under his bed, feeling dirty.

He needed to clear his mind, so stepped outside for a walk in the snow-covered courtyard. As he passed King's Chapel, he spotted a group of other students rollicking across the snow like a bunch of playful puppies, pushing and pawing at each other as they laughed.

One of the boys in a thick beaver fur coat noticed Jonathan, and paused.

"Hello, are you not attending the social?"

"The what?"

"The quarterly dance with the girls. Only time we are ever permitted to fraternize with them."

Jonathan shifted his feet in the powdery ice crystals beneath his boots. Though a university freshman in name, he *was* just thirteen, and hadn't really any interest in girls.

"Come on, just for a bit!" said Gabriel Adams, who had just run up behind the other boys. "Every girl on campus will be there!"

"*Every* girl?" Jonathan asked, now with a thought. "So the residence halls will be completely empty then?"

"Oh I would assume so!"

"The porters would not be left behind?"

"Their only purpose is to provide security for the female students. I would imagine they go wherever the women go. It would be a sad evening indeed to be guarding an empty building... Ah ha!" Gabriel winked with a smile, "I see where you are thinking now..."

Jonathan gulped. *You do?*

"Yes," Gabriel added as if reading his mind. "The women will be guarded, *even* at the dance. Sorry old chap."

Jonathan looked up at the full moon, then surveyed the courtyard. The moonlight reflecting off the white landscape would provide the most natural form of illumination to clearly see where he was going, if he were to sneak over to Newnham, and, there would be no one there for the duration of the dance. What better time to break in and hunt for the Trinket box than now! It was practically an invitation! Searching outside had proved to be pointless, but if he could find his mother's old room... was it Number 29 North Hall, Celeste had said?

'You will find a way,' Abigail had told him, and now, he possibly had.

"I am sorry Gabriel, I'm afraid I have to get back to some important work. But you fellows go along."

CHAPTER 26

NEWNHAM SOUTH HALL

The main hall of residency at Newnham, North Hall, was deserted. The lights were out and the building loomed like a giant monster, threatening to consume Jonathan alive if he dared to enter. He steeled himself and adjusted the black silk trouser stocking he had thrown over his head, so that he could better see through the holes he had made for his eyes.

The doors would most certainly be locked, so his only hope was finding a window that might have been opened a crack or left unlatched. The moon guided him as he circled the building... searching.

Luckily, one window on the ground floor was unlocked. He peered through the ice-frosted glass to verify that the room was indeed empty, and saw that a wooden chair had been pushed up against the windowsill. Odd. He quickly scanned the area, and seeing nothing but snowflakes moving in the night air, he pulled a knife from his satchel that he had snaked from the dining hall, and wedged it between the windowpanes. As he attempted to pull it open, the hinges creaked loudly. He paused, and listened.

He then heard snow dropping behind him, and spun around in alarm.

No one was there.

A bohemian waxwing had landed on a thin tree branch, and a lump of newly fallen snow now rested in a pile beneath it. The small bird's movement must have loosened the snow on the branch, and caused it to fall. Jonathan breathed in, then exhaled, relieved. Sensing it was now or never, he quickly crawled in through the window and stepped down using the conveniently placed chair as a stepladder.

Once inside, he pulled a candle and a match from his satchel, then struck the match against the wall, causing it to ignite. The girl's room he was standing in overflowed with lace, photographs, and knickknacks. There was a small wooden desk to the left, a single bed with an iron bed frame and white lace coverlet on the right, and several prints hanging on the floral papered walls.

The candlelight cast dark shadows across the bed sheets and pillows, like lurking demons, watching his every move. He'd never felt more uncomfortable. If his mother had known where he was and what he'd done...

But steady on...

He never knew his mother, and that was the entire reason he was here.

Keep things in perspective Jonathan.

He moved outside the room, and noted the number on the door. 20. He was closer than he thought, and 29 would certainly be on the ground floor. He crept along a long corridor that stretched out to eternity as the numbers slowly went up. 21, 22, 23... He stepped inside a suite, which was a sitting or lounge area bordered by several rooms, and paused in front of door Number 29. With a gulp, he turned the handle, and found that it was locked.

No! He tried the other doors in the suite, and all of them opened, except 29. How would he get it unlocked? He peered at his reflection in a large, rectangular gold mirror that hung above an ornate fireplace of wrought iron and white wood, and sighed. With his stockinged head and all black wardrobe, he looked like an East Asian mercenary.

He wondered if this was equally as much a waste of time as the gardens had been until he looked down and paused. Between the iron and wood of the fireplace were several panels of white and grey tiles with flowers and leaves painted on them. He ran his finger over one of them and muttered *Vicia fabaVicia* in Latin.

As his foster father Francis Eaton had been a botanist, Jonthan recognized the leaves as belonging to a broad bean plant. *Bean.* Could it be? He began feeling around the mantle for anything that seemed out of sorts, and studied the tiles until he found one that had part of the sealing broken at the bottom left side of the fireplace.

He pulled a safety pin from his satchel and jabbed it between the two bottom tiles. Just as he suspected, the one closest to the floor was loose. With some prying, he was able to remove the tile and found a wooden board behind it.

He pushed on the board and with some effort, was able to remove it. Behind it, was a small, hollowed out space, and inside, sat a rectangular dark wooden box with a bird motif carved on the top.

'She never attended any of the dances, always preferred to stay in the residence hall' Jonathan remembered Edith saying. That must have been when she carefully took the time to create such a well-hidden spot for her precious box, when the rest of the women were gone for a good several hours.

328

He gleefully pulled out the box, replaced the wooden board and tile, and then held up his treasure to the mirror, as if his reflection would congratulate him on a job well done.

Even Holmes never found you, Jonathan thought smugly, *because he didn't know where to look.*

He attempted to open it, but found it locked. There was a tiny keyhole in the front that would apparently require a key or, a very effective tool to jimmy the lock. He would have to wait until he could sneak into the workshop during business hours on Monday to find the proper instrument to break into it. With his mission complete, he stuffed the box in his satchel, ran down the long hallway to room 20, then crawled back out of the window and exited into the courtyard.

He heard laughter and footsteps approaching, so hid behind a snow dusted fountain in the garden until he saw a girl dragging a male student by the hand towards the window that Jonathan had just been through. The girl looked around, pushed open the window, then with a giggle, she crawled in and gestured for the boy to follow her. Ha! So that was the reason for the chair!

Once the window was closed, Jonathan cautiously snaked through the compound then broke into a run as he passed Newnham's boundaries, hurrying off to his room. As Watson would have written, the game was afoot!

Now more determined than ever to finish the journal before opening the box, Jonathan flipped it open and thumbed through the next few pages, praying they would be devoid of intimacy. Finding them free of anything inappropriate, he settled down to read.

~ ~

6ᵗʰ August 1888

I was awakened by the front door thumping open and someone bustling about in the sitting room, banging around saucers and teacups. Mrs. Hudson. There was a sweet flowery scent as well as an entirely unfamiliar one that lingered in the bedroom. As my mind played back the previous evening, I was able to identify the odour. Lavender and sex. I felt a heavy weight upon my chest, and opened my eyes to find myself in Scarlett's room, with a slumbering, naked Scarlett pressed against my body, her head resting on my torso.

"Miss Tennyson, breakfast!" Mrs. Hudson knocked.

Dear God!

Scarlett awoke with a start, and looked at me in panic. "Holmes?"

"Answer her, quickly," I whispered.

"Just a moment, Mrs. Hudson, I slept in. I will be out presently!" She jumped out of bed, and searched around for her dressing gown.

Mrs. Hudson then knocked on my bedroom door, and announced the same. When I did not answer, I heard my door open and Mrs. Hudson huff, "Out again, eh?"

"Holmes? What do we do?" Scarlett asked, now wrapped in her emerald dressing gown.

I sighed. This would have to be her choice. "Scarlett, the decision is yours. However you are most comfortable."

"What do *you* want me to say, Holmes?"

"Sherlock," I corrected her, "your choice will be mine."

She nodded, stood, and grabbed her brush from the vanity. "I am not ashamed if you are not," she said, running it through her hair.

"How could I be!?"

"Very well then," she fluffed her hair, "so be it." She opened the door with a cheerful, "Good morning Mrs. Hudson!" then closed it behind her.

"Good morning Scarlett," I heard Mrs. Hudson say, "have you any idea of Mr. Holmes' whereabouts?"

"Well, I..."

It would be up to me to make the reveal, so I threw on my clothes from the previous night and attempted to look as presentable as possible before I stepped into whatever consequences awaited me. "Good morning, Mrs. Hudson," I greeted, as I flung open the bedroom door and leaned against the doorframe.

Mrs. Hudson blinked her eyes in astonishment. "Now just what are you doing in Miss Tennyson's room then?"

Did she really require an explanation? I looked to Scarlett, who nodded. Damn.

"I--" I swallowed, "I was with her last night." My nervousness actually caused my voice to crack mid-sentence.

I thought Mrs. Hudson would die where she stood, the look on her face...

"Oh my, oh my! Dear me!"

Scarlett put a hand on her shoulder. "Are you all right?"

Mrs. Hudson snapped her head towards me. "You mean to say that you and Miss Tennyson...?"

I nodded sheepishly.

Her shock then shifted to amusement and she clapped her hands with a laugh. "Well, it is about bloody time!"

Scarlett and I looked at each other, puzzled.

"I have seen how you two are for months! Both always eyin' each other, when the other wasn't lookin', it was downright childish! Glad you came to your senses. If you love each other, you should be together. That is the end of it!"

"I do love him," Scarlett admitted shyly, an unusual temperament for her.

"And you, sir?" Mrs. Hudson pointed, glaring at me through slit eyes. "What have you to say for yourself?" She simply had to hear the words she never dreamed I would say.

"I love her. Does that meet with your approval?"

She threw her arms around me. "Oh, Mr. Holmes! I never thought I'd see the day! I knew you would be good for him," Mrs. Hudson winked to Scarlett, as she patted her arm. "Just the thing you needed, Mr. Holmes."

I had truly been set up, but at this junction, I wasn't about to complain.

Mrs. Hudson circled her arms around us, and hugged tightly. "I could not be happier for you two. It does my heart good!"

Scarlett cleared her throat. "You... brought breakfast?"

She grinned. "Oh! Yes I did! I am sure you two have worked up quite the appetite."

Scarlett and I looked at each other, embarrassed.

"Eat up then!"

She pushed us towards the tray, which held two plates of eggs, sausage, crumpets, and a large pot of tea. For the first time since I could remember, I actually had a stomach for food.

Mrs. Hudson then stared me square in the eye and warned, "You realize you must marry her now, don't you?"

My hunger suddenly vanished, and the smell of cooked food made me nauseous.

"I will leave you to it," Mrs. Hudson said as she squeezed Scarlett's hand, then exited through the door. I heard her whistling as she descended the staircase.

Scarlett coughed, and picked up the teapot. "Tea then paper?" she asked, gesturing to the teacups on the table.

I gently removed the pot from her hand, placed it down, then took her hands in mine as I shook my head. "As today is Bank Holiday,

I propose we forgo work, and spend the entire day enjoying each other's company. Have we an accord?"

She nodded with a laugh.

"Je t'aime," I held her. "I never thought those words would leave my lips, not for anyone."

CHAPTER 27

A ROYAL PAIN

29ᵗʰ August 1888

I accompanied Scarlett to the London Symphony in Covent Garden this evening. I had purchased a dress for her for the occasion, a cream-coloured taffeta ball gown with several different layers of satin and silk, and two splendid gold and diamond brooches stitched within the bodice. Though it was quite the production lacing up a woman's corset for the first time, it was every bit worth the effort.

As Scarlett and I wandered up the steps of the theatre, I noticed a procession of footmen filing out from a carriage on the street below. It was the *royal* carriage. I urged Scarlett to move quicker towards the door but we became trapped as a glamorous crowd standing outside the entranceway was blocking us.

In a moment's time, The Prince, followed by his large entourage of servants, had made his way up to the entrance. He noticed us immediately, and glared contemptuously as he passed by. Thankfully, any discussion was avoided.

During intermission, we strolled through the lobby sipping champagne, discussing the program thus far. As everything is at The Prince's disposal in the hallway behind his balcony box, he never leaves his chair. Therefore, I knew we were free to drift as we pleased. To my disappointment, His Royal Highness changed his habits. Dressed with a dazzle of orders pinned to his chest, he came waltzing around the corner with a cigar dangling from his lips. He paused briefly for a casual 'hello' and 'how are you?' to several persons, but his destination and quarry were clear. He was headed for Scarlett.

I opted to let her handle this alone, as this was between them.

He took the cigar from his mouth, gently lifted her white-gloved hand, and kissed her fingers. "Good evening Miss," he greeted, as if she were a stranger, looking at her with a caressing glance, and absorbed expression.

She lowered her eyes, and curtsied. "Your Royal Highness."

"That, my dear, is a very pretty dress. It shapes you perfectly. Wherever did you find such an attractive piece?"

She said nothing, and still avoided eye contact.

The Prince lifted her chin with his forefinger. "No need for formalities, Miss...?"

"Tennyson," she said quietly.

This was intolerable. I should have stayed by her side.

"Have you a Christian name, Miss Tennyson?" he smirked knowingly.

She faked a smile. "Scarlett, sir."

"Scarlett, what a deliciously lovely name, though shouldn't you be dressed in red this evening?"

I could feel my heart racing as my blood boiled. Scarlett stood perfectly still. She was handling this far better than I.

Receiving no response, The Prince tried another tactic. "Where did you purchase so fine a garment?"

Scarlett looked at me, a hint of fear in her eyes as if asking, 'do I tell him?' I shook my head and she responded with, "I am... not sure, it was a present."

His face shifted into a sour expression. "Oh? From whom?"

She gulped down the rest of her champagne. "From... umm... my suite-mate." She looked away.

His Royal Highness' pale, blue-grey eyes turned steely, and his celebrated affability evaporated. He straightened up and took a deep inhale from his cigar. "So I see," he hissed, smoke pouring from between his grit teeth, "I hope he provides you with more than just *presents.*"

Scarlett clutched the empty champagne glass between her hands. "Indeed."

The Prince snatched up the glass, placed it on a table, then pulled a folded note from his pocket, and discreetly slid it across her gloved palm. "If you would not mind asking where it was purchased, I would very much like to see you about it, Miss Scarlett Tennyson," he said quietly, taking another drag on his cigar. As smoke curled around his lips, his grin reminded me of a gargoyle, or some sort of demon from Hell.

Scarlett crinkled the note in her fist, then curtsied. "Yes, sir." As she turned to leave he grabbed her arm, whispered something in her ear, then tenderly brushed her hair with the backside of his hand. "You are too kind," she struggled away from him, then fluttered into the ladies powder room. What had he said to her?

337

The Prince followed her with his eyes then turned, and noticed me. He sauntered over with a smug expression, and crossed his arms over his barrel chest.

"Well well, aren't you Sherlock Holmes? The *great* detective? Or did you change your name to Giacomo Casanova?"

"That is correct, Your Royal Highness," I said cordially. "Though I would hardly categorize my abilities as being great."

"Neither would I, actually," he said coldly. "I have heard much about you. You and your little exploits or adventures, or whatever they are called. A novel about you was recently published, correct?"

"Yes, and I am quite sure you would find the title most intriguing," I nodded, wondering if he'd actually seen it. Surely he would have more to say had he known the title to be, *A Study in Scarlet.*

He sniffed indignantly. "Cannot say as I have read it. I think I'd find it dull."

He had not. I finished my champagne, and placed the glass on one of the high, red-clothed tables in the lobby. I was ready for him. "Forgive me if I am mistaken, but I hear you have an aversion to the written word, regardless of the content."

He had certainly not expected such a response from me, as his eyes went wide. I was perhaps overstepping my bounds by insulting him, but my emotions were ruling my tongue.

The Prince sucked on his cigar, then blew smoke in my direction, so I had to take a step to the side to avoid it. "So, you keep our streets secure from vermin and murders, do you?"

"That is part of the nature of my profession, yes."

"Then you'd best get to it, eh? Seeing as how one of your more recent villains has newly escaped?"

He was of course referring to Nigel Breen, who had only but yesterday escaped from the French police by the aid of an unknown saviour. I blamed The Professor.

"He is not one to be trifled with, I understand."

"He is certainly someone I can handle," I said back.

"Perhaps it would be most sensible to return to your *singular* work, least any further damage is wrought," he said with a hiss. "You should not be so cavalier with such a powerful man."

Laced with a double meaning, I didn't know he had it in him. "Forgive me, but even detectives and men of the law may deviate from the professional on occasion, and enjoy the finer things in life. Though perhaps I should resort to wearing a mask, thus freeing myself to say, or do, whatever I please, without the fear of being summoned to my responsibilities. Works well enough for others."

The Prince stiffened. "So it has a sense of humor, does it? Normally men of your kind are stuffy, and boring."

I folded my hands behind me, and smiled. "Then I am quite relieved I have not 'bored' you. Admittedly I am surprised to see you here as I understood you preferred the more lively and exciting scene of the music halls and opium dens."

The Prince sniffed and rubbed his nose with his forefinger. "I don't believe you would know exciting and lively if it hit you on the head."

"*She* would disagree with you, very much so." I might have said too much, but could not pass up such a golden opportunity to retaliate. The Prince scowled, and tossed his cigar into the nearby dustbin. Touché.

"Keep up the good work then," he said, "I am certain we will meet again."

"I rejoice to think so!"

The Prince held out a hand. "I should like to shake the hand of man whom so many *deeply* admire."

I imitated him. "As Your Royal Highness pleases."

He grabbed my hand fiercely.

"She is, and will always be, mine! Enjoy her while you can, for if you feel you can keep her, you have never been more wrong."

"I believe you are referring to something you never owned in the first place... sir."

He released my hand with grin. "Mark my words Holmes, you cannot win. You are not even half the man I am." The Prince turned, and marched around the corner. He was correct in that I was not half the man he was, I might have been a third the physical specimen for he was not so much a man, but a whale. It was in this ridiculing, and rather gratifying moment that Scarlett returned.

"Why the smirk, Holmes?" she asked, her face newly refreshed. I could see she had been crying, as her cheeks and nose were still slightly red.

"His Royal Highness and I had a nice chat. We got on famously."

She took the folded-up letter he had given her, and tossed it into the dustbin. "He is an immature child and a bully. I will have nothing more to do with him or his flippant pursuits!"

She took my hand and pulled me towards the theatre and back to our seats.

"What *was* that, Scarlett?"

"He wishes to see me for a private meeting at Malbourgh House tomorrow. He is an even bigger buffoon than I imagined, if he thought I'd come!"

"Not even to officially end it?"

Scarlett halted in the aisle, and turned towards me. "My feelings towards him have changed, that is obvious, and based on his behaviour this evening, seeing him will accomplish nothing." We continued on to our seats, and sat down. "Besides, I do not trust him and would not be in favour of being alone with such a person."

"Though hardly a decent man, he *is* royalty and deserves the courtesy of a proper rejection. If you convey nothing, he will be angry, as this is twice now you have slighted him. Royals are accustomed to getting what they want, and he will not take this lightly."

"I will be forgot by tomorrow morning," she waved off my worries. "He could have any woman he wants, as he always told me."

"Yes, but sometimes people want more what they cannot have."

She picked her program off the floor, and scanned through the second page. "You mustn't be so grim Holmes. Have faith that it is better to leave things as they are." She gasped, and pointed to the third column of printed words. "Look, Mendelssohn is next!"

I laced my fingers together to serve as a cradle for my chin, and closed my eyes as beautiful music suddenly filled the air. Despite the charming, melodic tune, I felt ill at ease.

~ ~

Jonathan pulled out his notes from the Ripper files and quickly sifted through them. He did not see anything that matched The Prince. Perhaps he *was* wrong? This new information about Nigel Breen having escaped opened up another door. Did The Prince *hire* someone to have his mother murdered? Could it have been Nigel Breen? His head hurt from thinking too hard. Based on these new facts, he would have to ask Abigail for something sooner than planned, so wired her to speak on Monday. He looked over at the trinket box. Would that have the answers?

Early Monday morning, Jonathan awoke from a frightful nightmare, drenched in sweat. He gasped, leapt out of bed, and ran to the door to be sure it was secure. Finding it was locked, he filled his lungs with air, then turned on the lamp. He ripped off his shirt that was clinging to him and threw it the floor. Dropping backwards onto his bed he closed his eyes, breathed in, and tried to shake the sickening feeling he had in his gut.

In the dream, he was back in Hoxton, though it wasn't really the Hoxton he had known... *He was walking down a seedy alleyway in the dead of night, and came upon a purple velvet curtain, draped across one of the walls. It was covering a large door. Curious, he yanked it aside, and saw the mutilated bodies of the women from Jack the Ripper's Scotland Yard file. They stood motionless in the doorway, stripped of their clothes, and sewn back together. Jack's last victim, Mary Kelly, the most mangled and torn apart of all of them, lay in pieces along the wall.*

Repulsed, Jonathan moved to yank the curtain back in place, but then the women's dead eyes suddenly snapped open.

Jonathan jumped backwards, but lost his balance and fell to the ground.

"Let it be boy, or you will be his next!" the women all hissed in unison, as their tongues morphed into the forked form of a snake's. Their bodies then collapsed on the ground and the elaborate medical stitches that had sewn them back together, suddenly together came undone. Fresh dark red blood gushed from their wounds and oozed across the cobblestone towards Jonathan.

Jonathan frantically scrambled backwards to avoid the sea of blood that was descending upon him as maniacal laughter echoed through the air. As he whipped his head around to search for the source, he gasped as a large shining knife came slashing down towards him. "No!" he screamed, holding his hand up to his face.

He must have screamed aloud for his throat was scratchy and dry when he was jolted awake. He took a sip from the glass of water on his bedside, then slid out Holmes' journal.

"Something is pushing me to hurry," he gulped as he looked at the trinket box sitting innocently on his desk, then flipped open the journal. "Tell me Holmes, who was it?!"

CHAPTER 28

CHANGES

7ᵗʰ September 1888

The night after the Symphony I began having bizarre dreams and sensations of anxiety. These dreams then turned to nightmares, and as their frequency increased, I began to thoroughly dread the night. All things considered, life could not be more ideal, so why the paranoia? Though my abstinence from cocaine (upon Scarlett's request) had certainly created its share of adverse side effects, I could not blame the drug's powers for my restlessness.

Upon further analysis, I found the cause of my distress was fear, and more specifically, a fear of the future. The Prince's parting words had haunted me and I wondered, could he in fact, ever steal her away from me? The thought seemed improbable but none-the-less, how could I be certain?

My imagination played out such a scenario as Scarlett and I dined at Simpson's on the Strand this evening, to the point where I was too distracted to even take notice of our meal, and barely touched my plate of turbot and quail. The brandy I normally enjoy seemed tasteless and metallic in my mouth, and the cherry tart could have been made of yew for as much mind as I paid it. Scarlett noticed, but thankfully, was too accustomed to my irregular eating habits to comment.

After dinner I hailed a cab, spoke discreetly with the driver, then helped Scarlett into the hansom carriage. As we turned south down Whitehall, as opposed to north to Baker Street, Scarlett questioned as to where we were headed. I asked her to trust me.

When we finally arrived at our destination, which was the Palace of Westminster, I produced a small key from my pocket.

"I have something I'd like to show you," I whispered, as I unlocked a door.

Without questioning me, she allowed me to take her up the sixteen flights of stairs to the tower, to Big Ben's belfry. As she marvelled at the beautiful view of the city and River Thames through the tall slender gothic windows, I took a deep breath, and wiped the sweat from my shaking palms onto my jacket. Was I entirely certain about this? What I was about to do, I could never take back, and there would be no returning to how things were. It could change my life forever. I reached inside my coat's breast pocket, and nervously pulled out my cigarette case.

"Care for a smoke?" I asked Scarlett.

She gave me a wry smile. "It is unfair to tease, Sherlock."

"No, no, I am quite serious," I said, as I held it out to her.

She paused with a puzzled expression, then approached me and held out her hand. "Very well then," she laughed, "you are truly attempting to corrupt me, are you not?"

"No, rather the opposite." I flipped open the lid to reveal a folded-up piece of black velvet, neatly tucked inside. "That, is for you," I gestured for her to take it. "Open it carefully, please."

As she gently unwrapped the cloth, she gasped.

"My God," she said, as she stared at the finely decorated ring that now rested in the palm of her hand. There were three diamonds in the center surrounded by rubies that were arranged in an oval shape across the gold band.

I dropped to one knee, took her hand, and gripped it tightly. "My dear Scarlett, you have changed my life and my world forever. My reality would be a very empty, incomplete, and intolerable place without you... I..." My words were running together, and I was speaking too quickly. I had to breathe. "I... promised your father I would care for you and plan to see to it, if you will permit me." I took a deep breath and looked into her sparkling eyes. "Miss Scarlett Tennyson, I should like to make an honest woman of you, so therefore... will you marry me?"

Though I had rehearsed my speech a dozen times over, I had forgot to say almost everything I had previously scripted. It felt rushed and cliché, anything but what I wanted.

Scarlett inhaled deeply and looked away.

My heart sank, I had failed. I released her hand, rose to my feet, then looked out onto the river, attempting to mask my hurt. "Perhaps, I was wrong in the timing--" I covered, hoping that was the reason, and not that my speech had been less that impressive.

"Yes," Scarlett said, with a sniff.

Was she crying? Had I been that awful? I turned to face her and found her smiling, with tears streaming down her checks.

"Yes Sherlock Holmes, I will marry you!" she cried, flinging her arms around me, now wearing the ring on her finger. "Whatever happened to the man who once said, 'I should never marry myself, lest I bias my judgment'? Can that truly be the same person I see before me?"

I kissed her, incredibly relieved. "I believe that marriage serves a valuable purpose by defining committed monogamist relationships."

"Yes, it is the same person," she grinned, wiping her eyes. "And *now*, may I have a cigarette?"

When we reached the bottom of the stairwell, I scooped her up and carried her to the cab that I requested wait for us.

For certain, no one can take her from me now.

9ᵗʰ September 1888

A letter arrived from the palace today whilst Scarlett was out. Though not addressed to me, I nonetheless felt compelled to open it. As I tore through the thick, gold-lined envelope, it began:

"My fair Scarlett..."

It was from The Prince. I angrily skimmed through the note, wondering what in the world he wished to say to her. It expressed his concern, his affection, and his burning desire to see her. It ended with...

"Now my loved one, I bring these lines to a close, as I must dress for breakfast. God bless you, my own adored little Scarlett.

-Forever Yours, Your Only Love."

How dare he send her such a greeting?! I took it upon myself to tear up the poisonous letter, and burn it in the fireplace. What purpose would it serve to give it to her now?

~ ~

Jonathan grabbed his pocket watch from the bedside locker and checked the time. He had a half hour until class. He groggily crawled out of bed, shoved the trinket box underneath it, and proceeded to dress for the day.

As he was crossing back from class that evening, Gabriel Adams came running excitedly towards him. Jonathan rolled his eyes, assuming Gabriel wanted something.

"Holmes, I have the most amazing news!" Gabriel spouted, out of breath.

"You've learned to spin straw into gold?"

Gabriel gave him a look. "See here, there is something you positively must see! Are you busy?"

No, but only if you stop calling me Holmes! Jonathan thought as he looked at the clock tower. It was a quarter past six. "If it is not too time consuming yes, as I have a telephone meeting."

"Won't be long at all, I promise. Whom are you ringing up?"

Jonathan froze. What should he tell him? "A... a friend from back home."

"Now, where are you from, Jonathan? We never really talk about *your* background. I just prattle off about mine!"

"I've... moved around a bit. Not really sure where I consider home." It wasn't a lie.

"Where do your parents live?"

If Gabriel was indeed someone he could trust, Jonathan would have to be honest with him eventually, but for now, he was still a newer friend. It was best to keep details to a minimum, as he was closing in on what he had come here for. "My mother died, and my father... lives near Regent's Park, and the Baker Street underground in London." That was close enough.

Gabriel grinned. "221 B Baker Street, correct? Sorry, just having a game. I would place a bet you were related if I did not know better."

Jonathan snorted.

"Oh, but it is not as if you look like him." Gabriel then gave Jonathan a once over, and squinted his eyes. "Well, not too much so, now come! You of all people will appreciate this, Holmes!"

Jonathan smiled. "Lead the way then, Watson."

"Oh blast, Hopkins then!"

Inside Gabriel's apartment, there was a large purple blanket covering over an oddly shaped object. Jonathan had a flashback to his nightmare but shook his head, knowing that for certain, mangled bodies wasn't what lied beneath.

"Ready, Hopkins?" Gabriel asked gleefully.

He *was* absolutely sure it was bodies, wasn't he?

Gabriel threw off the blanket to reveal a strange looking two-seated bicycle. "Ta da! It is one of those 'motorcycles' they made in Germany! Hildebrand & Wolfmüller. It's a '97. Was rather cheap as they claimed it was broken but I am sure I can find a way to fix it. They modified the seat saddle so it accommodates two. Perhaps myself and a lady," Gabriel rubbed his hands together.

Jonathan squatted down for a closer look at the bike. "How did you manage it in here?" he asked, "it must be heavy."

"No so. It's about seven stone. I hear it can move twenty-eight miles per hour! Outrun a carriage any day! Size it up for me, would you, Holmes? Er... Hopkins?" Gabriel asked, leaning over with his palms on his thighs.

Jonathan tapped the steel tubular frame with his knuckles. "It apparently has a hollow frame and a surface carburetor," he said, as slid his hand over the contraption attached to the rear wheel, "at least, I believe that is what it's called?" His eyes moved over the small steel rods in the middle of the bike, as he formulated a theory on how they generated motion. "It appears to be driven by these connecting rods, or wands." He pointed at the large engine tank over the rear wheel. "This engine looks like it holds some type of fluid, water perhaps?"

Gabriel shrugged. "Perhaps, but how would you start it?"

"I have reason to believe that all you must do is refill these pistons with water. The water would then move from the pistons into this engine, and generate the energy necessary to move the bike. The power is delivered to the rear wheel here," Jonathan pointed, "via pushrods that are linked the engine's pistons. Do you see?"

A puzzled Gabriel shook his head.

"Well, the pushrods then return by the force generated from these two large rubber straps on either side of the bike, like a steam locomotive really."

"Come again?"

"You've been on a train haven't you?" Jonathan laughed. "The pistons push water up into the cooler and give the engine the ability to run. Refill this compartment, and it should work splendidly, unless there is internal damage."

Gabriel blinked. "Suppose that's all there is to it?"

Jonathan shrugged. "Possibly?"

"Let's do as you suggested to determine what's wrong!"

Gabriel grabbed a jug, filled it with water, then handed it to Jonathan. Jonathan then opened the engine's compartment, poured in the water, and closed down the lid. Gabriel stood back, admired it, then frowned. "How's it start?"

Damned if I know! Jonathan sighed. It was obvious that Gabriel wanted to show him his new toy, because he thought Jonathan could fix it. He gave the bike a once-over, and his eyes landed on the ignition. He twisted and held it, then the bike roared to life.

"That is brilliant Jonathan! However do you think of these things? Now, what seems to be amiss?"

The boys inspected the bike, but it appeared to be working well enough as far as they could tell.

"Bloody liars," Gabriel snorted, "functions just fine. You want to take it for a go?"

Jonathan looked at his pocket watch. Five minutes to seven. "Terribly sorry, but I have my telephone meeting."

352

"Ah yes, another time," Gabriel shrugged. "Oh, and don't be up too late tonight, got a lot to cover tomorrow. Could you meet at the lab at six o'clock?"

Jonathan groaned.

"Now, I know your classes don't begin until two, but I truly need your help on this one. I will give you handsome extra if you would."

Jonathan sighed. "Be there at six." He glanced across the room and noticed a wooden easel with an unfinished painted canvas propped up, depicting a Renaissance scene. "Been artworking I see. Shakespeare?" he asked, pointing to the man in the foppish hat and pantaloons in the portrait.

"No, Wallis, a chap I met at the Arts Club in Chelsea. Brilliant playactor. Loved his Cassius in Othello, so was inspired to do a bit from the performance. Don't tell the chaps though, I'd never hear the end of it."

While he waited for Abigail's call, Jonathan shook his head with a smile as he thought about his funny friend. How fortunate he had been, that cold winter's night, to have run into someone who was now such an important part of his life. As annoying as Gabriel could be at times, Jonathan was grateful for his friendship.

The phone rang. "Hello, Abby?"

"Hi Johnny."

"Apologies for moving up our conversation, but I need to ask you to search for something."

353

"What am I to look for?"

"Any files on Prince Albert Victor, James Moriarty, Nigel Breen, or Jack the Ripper. If there is one for each, then all five please."

"That would be a lot to take without Mycroft noticing. Why?"

"I.... cannot explain now, as I am not sure. But if those files exist, I *must* have them. Any news?"

"No, and hours are longer than normal."

Abigail seemed gloomy, and not her usual self.

"Mycroft is not overworking you, is he?"

"Oh no!" her voice perked up. "I am fine, truly. Just.... his housekeeper has been ill, and I have been taking care of everything. Lot of work it is. You are all right up there?"

"I am managing, yes. Abby, I found the box!"

"By the crown jewels, that's wonderful news! What was inside?!"

"It's locked, so I'll need to borrow some tools from the workshop to break it open."

"Well do let me know! I am sorry to be short, but must go. I will try to find your files for you."

"When this is over Abigail, I promise to do something special for you for all your help."

"Hmm... I might have a suggestion, but we will talk more next week. Mondays are difficult to get away. Good bye, Mr. Hopkins." She hung up the phone.

Jonathan sighed. "Good bye, Miss Hopkins," he said into the dead receiver. He missed her more than he was willing to admit.

The workshop was already closed when he arrived, so he returned to his room and continued Holmes' journal. He was secretly hoping to finish it before opening the box because now that he had it, something about opening it made him uneasy...

~ ~

29th September 1888

The day Miss Scarlett Tennyson became Mrs. Sherlock Holmes. A name I never thought I'd hear. A year ago, had anyone claimed that I would not only be intimate with a woman, but marry her within a few months' time, I would have demanded that he commit himself to the nearest asylum and thrown away the key, but here I stand, the 'great' Sherlock Holmes, a husband to a wife.

It was a perfect autumn day with golden leaves underfoot, and that soft low light that comes at this time of year, with the sun shining on old bricks and stone like a visit from heaven.

When the pastor pronounced our new titles, I felt as though I were stepping into an alternate reality for in some ways, I am *not* Sherlock Holmes. I have emerged from some dark place and only now, seen the light on the other side of life. I will never be the same, nor would I wish to be.

8th November 1888

The past few days, Scarlett has been awakening with unusual nausea, tenderness, and the complaint that her chest hurt. When she fainted on the street curb this morning, I demanded that she seek a professional opinion on her condition, which brought us to Watson's practice in Paddington. He was alone with her only briefly, then emerged with a puzzled expression.

"Yes?" I asked nervously.

"Scarlett is with child."

I could not speak.

"Holmes?"

"Is... is.... she all right?" I finally managed. "May I see her?"

Watson nodded his head. "I would *demand* that you do."

I found my wife curled tightly in a ball on the chair when I entered the small room.

"You have heard then?" she sniffed despondently, refusing to look at me.

I placed a hand on her shoulder. "Yes. And I know your thoughts."

"Then you agree with me?" she looked up.

"No, I do not."

"It will ruin positively everything! I refuse to go through with this, and you should support my decision!"

"Certain things in life you cannot plan, nor predict. We will manage, I promise."

"This will make our lives very different Sherlock, and complicated in every way. Are you prepared for that?"

I nodded, though how could I possibly be prepared for something I knew absolutely nothing about? "Names?" I changed the subject, "if a boy, why not Jonathan, after the doctor who discovered him?"

She nodded.

"And girl?"

"Celeste," she grinned.

Dear God, I do hope I know what I am doing.

4th March 1889

Watson has again become my full-time partner and casework chronicler whilst Scarlett is immobilized and removed from duty, at least until the birth, and then, for several months after. Being positively bored and frustrated with the lying-in process, she has taken up writing her own journal and shares them with me when she is of the mood. While she is a phenomenal painter with words, her thinking is a bit too modern for her own good, and I have advised her to keep her scribblings between us, and us only. My dear woman, some things are best left off paper!

17th July 1889

This morning I was awakened by Scarlett screaming and found her leaning against the bed frame, tears streaming down her cheeks.

It was time.

I sprang from the bed, hurriedly changed from my nightclothes, and fought to dress myself as quickly as possible, my fingers tripping over buttons, and my arm struggling to wriggle through my inside out sleeve. I forwent lacing up my shoes, and dashed out to send a wire to her doctor.

As Watson had recently stepped down as her physician due to time constraints, he had recommended Dr. Daniels to replace him. It had bothered me that Watson abandoned us not a month before Scarlett's due date, but my assumption was that Scarlett and he were not getting on, and he did not wish for personal squabbles to affect him professionally. She had always found Mary Watson to be rather airy-fairy, and was quite vocal in her opinions. In her emotional state, she could have said any number of things to anger him, and degrading Mary I would predict, was likely to be at the top of that list. I was saddened, but understood.

Dr. Daniels arrived quickly, followed by a midwife. I had not been informed that a midwife was to be present, but I assumed Scarlett had requested one during her consultation. I was instructed to leave so settled for a whiskey, or several rather at The Criterion, and impatiently waited the several hours before returning home. How I wish I had my cocaine!

Just as I walked back up the stairs, now slightly inebriated, I heard a blood-curdling scream, and raced through the door. The bedroom door was closed, so I banged on it loudly. The midwife poked her head out.

"You may not come in," she said sternly, then slammed the door.

I heard another scream. Had he not given her chloroform!? We had agreed that she may use the chloroform inhaler as an anesthetic for the birth, for if Queen Victoria believed in it, so did Scarlett. As I was not one to refuse her anything at this point, I had agreed. From her screams, I feared he had not administered it soon enough.

I banged on the door then heard a baby cry. I stopped, stunned. It was not a familiar sound to hear in my own rooms. I moved to turn the doorknob, but then Dr. Daniels flung open the door, and greeted me with an outstretched hand.

"You have a healthy little boy, Mr. Holmes," he shook my hand, "congratulations."

"A son?" I said stupidly, still in shock.

"Yes, a son. Come and meet him," Dr. Daniel's ushered me in.

As I approached the bedside a blanketed lump rested in Scarlett's arms. My heart skipped a beat. That was *my* son, *my* boy. My emotions were overwhelming me. I felt dizzy.

Scarlett was weak and exhausted, but had a warm glow about her.

"Sherlock, you are a father," she said softly.

"I am a father," I echoed her, unable to believe what I had just said. "Jonathan, then?" I petted her head. She sighed uncomfortably, and turned her head away. "Have you changed your mind?"

She paused as if to say some more, buy then shook her head. "No, Jonathan... is fine. But Alexander should be his middle name, after his grandfather."

I nodded as I stroked my new son's tiny head. "Welcome to the Holmes family, Jonathan Alexander."

~ ~

"My mother never told him," Jonathan closed the journal. "To think I was named after that man..." He tried to avoid focusing *too* much on Holmes' excited reaction, for he still didn't know what happened after his mother's death. Somewhere, somehow, those feelings of joy and pride had vanished. Otherwise, why would he have given Jonathan away? He curled up on his comforter, and blew out the light.

CHAPTER 29

THE END OF THE HOLMES FAMILY

With some difficulty, Jonathan managed to meet Gabriel at the appointed time the next morning. He remained at the lab for several hours, then promptly returned to his room, and napped until after lunch. Half the day gone.

He was grabbing his books for Classics class, when he heard a knock on his door. A tall, blonde youthful looking messenger stood in the doorway, holding a letter of some sort.

"Urgent delivery, for Mr. Hopkins," the messenger said, handing him the letter, "will you sign please?"

Jonathan signed the slip for the letter, thanked the boy, then closed his door. He ripped open the telegram in a panic. It was from Abby.

"Found one on J the R will call tonight normal time Ab"

Jonathan exhaled with relief. He stuffed the note in his pocket, snatched up his books, then galloped off to class.

"I found one you wanted," Abigail voiced over the phone that night, "but nothing on Prince Albert Victor, Moriarty, or Nigel Breen."

"Why did you not use ciphers in your message?"

"I did not have time, Jonathan! I wanted to get the message to you as soon as possible."

"Could I acquire it when next in London then?"

"Possibly, but I was not able to take it. Mycroft returned from Whitehall early, so had to close up the cabinet and leave."

"Oh." Jonathan was puzzled. "Then, why the urgency of the call?"

"I... wanted to let you know, and... just needed to hear your voice."

There was a moment of silence on both ends of the phone.

Jonathan rubbed his neck. "No one saw you, correct? And you did not leave anything disturbed?"

"I left rather hurriedly, but think I was careful."

Jonathan bit his lip while he waited for her to say something more. Nothing.

"Anything... else? I am to meet my friend at the lab this evening," he lied. "So if there's nothing more to—"

"Friend?" Abigail asked concerned. "How do you know them?"

"Oh, bumped into him one night, quite literally in fact," Jonathan laughed. "He's a senior, Natural Sciences student."

"Ah... *him*," Abigail breathed out.

Jonathan was confused. "Did I mention him before? Gabriel Adams? I don't recollect ever..."

"Oh no, just... I am glad you have a friend."

"But you Abby, are my *best* friend. I would be utterly lost without you."

Abigail was again quiet.

"Are you still there?"

"I should go," she said quickly. "I have an appointment this evening, and Mr. Esher don't like me to be late. Till next week, good night Jonathan."

"Good night." Jonathan hung up the phone, and stared at the receiver. He had never lied to her to get out of a discussion before. What just happened? And who was Mr. Esher? Was he a friend, an interested man, or...he shuddered to think, a 'customer?' No, absolutely not!

He retired to his room, deciding to escape through Holmes' journal. That at least, had been positive lately.

~ ~

10th September 1889

Scarlett received another letter today. As it had been over a year since our last encounter with The Prince I had relegated him to the furthest corner of my mind, but this correspondence, unlike the other, was devoid of warmth. Instead, it was blistering, threatening in nature. He was angry, resentful, and claimed I was unworthy of her affections.

The fate of Mary Vetsea at the hands of Crown Prince Rudolf in the beginning of the year came to mind as I read through the pages. I was worried, frightened by his latest inflammatory threat. He demanded to see her, and felt that he was owed an explanation, at the very least. Scarlett shrugged it off, saying that more than likely he had heard or saw something recently that reminded him of her. His obsession would fade within the week.

I believe it was Reynold's Newspaper that had once said of The Prince, '*such a man should not only be expelled from decent society, but is utterly unfit and unworthy to rule over this country.*'

Such a man is unworthy of virtually everything...

~ ~

A page had been torn out after this entry, as the jagged remains still lingered in the binding of the journal. *Odd.* There was one entry left. Jonathan looked at the date and felt his stomach turn as he held his breath. It was February 15th, 1891, the day after his mother died. He quickly flipped back to the previous page, too terrified to read it. He breathed out and sighed, then slowly turned the page as his eyes began to well up. He needed to know what was on that page, even if it destroyed him.

~ ~

15th February 1891

No matter how I stoke the fire, add more wood, or move closer to the flames in the fireplace, I cannot keep warm, for the fire inside me has extinguished, and the light has been blown out. I feel as though I have lost all will to exist. Sleeping, eating, and breathing seems to require more effort than I have the resources for.

364

Last night, my world ended abruptly. In less than an hour's absence, I returned to our rooms to find my wife dead. Or is she? Is there any possibility that this is only a hellish nightmare, which I will soon awaken from and run into my wife's arms and kiss her and thank the gods that she's alive? No, for every inch of these rooms are empty, barren, and sombre reminder of the reality I've been catapulted into against my will and without my consent. She taught me to love, gave me a reason for existing, but was stolen from me by a person who was consumed by jealousy and hatred of my presence in her life. If ever I needed further justification to bring a murderer to justice, and by any means necessary, this would be the penultimate.

I will chance my life, reputation, and credibility to see this demon convicted, and shall not rest until either of us is expired, and it is finally finished between us.

Our son is lost to me. I am completely devoid and depleted of any true emotional affection or care, and do not know if such feelings can ever resurface. I am in no form to be a capable and stable parent, so I must leave him. It is better he be cared for in a more fitting manner by someone else for the time being, than to be saddled with my unpredictable schedule, style of life, and destructive vices as I predict I will eventually and inevitably slip back into them. This is best for him. Dear Jonathan please forgive me. Perhaps, one day, I can return for you."

~ ~

The words, "Though death would be a welcome release..." had been written after the last sentence, then crossed out.

Jonathan dropped the journal to the floor, and leaned against the wall. He blew air through his mouth and closed his eyes, trying not

365

to cry. He was angry. He felt unloved, unwanted, and saw how his very existence must had served as a reminder of the woman Holmes had loved and lost, which is why he sent Jonathan away. He couldn't handle the pain.

Jonathan wiped the tears from his eyes, and opened the desk drawer that had held the faded envelope. Picking up the packet, he violently snatched up the journal, threw the book back inside, then slammed it into the drawer, causing one of the envelope's edges to rip as it caught in the crease. "I never want to see that damn book again."

He retrieved the trinket box from under his bed, then rubbed his fingers along the top, feeling the smooth carved wood underneath his fingertips. "Does it really matter who you were?"

PART III: FINDING JACK

CHAPTER 30

RIPPER TIME LINE

The next few weeks Jonathan didn't care about anything. He ate little, over slept, and was behind in his schoolwork. He neglected Gabriel, and barely said two words to anyone.

On his last call with Abigail she implored him to return to London for a visit so he agreed to come down the week of the thirteenth of February.

As Jonathan's train was to arrive in the early afternoon and Abigail was still working, she asked him to meet her in Kensington Gardens for lunch to give him her key. As he trudged through the park in the thin dusting of snow, he spotted her sitting on a green park bench with a picnic basket. He smiled, for the first time in weeks. He crept around her from behind, then plopped down next to her on the bench. "Hello Miss, this spot taken?"

Abigail gasped, then looked over and giggled. "Glad to see you smile, sunshine," she handed him the basket.

He examined it confused. "Thought we were going out for lunch? It's freezing out here!"

"Look *inside*," she pointed. "It's what you wanted."

Jonathan perked up. "The Ripper files?"

Abigail nodded and blew on her mittened hands as she rubbed then together. "I wanted to surprise you. You needed to cheer up a bit but I didn't want to give this to you where someone could see it."

He hugged her. "You are wonderful Abby!"

She rested her head on his shoulder. "I am not either," she whispered. "Though, I should get this one back sooner than later, as Mycroft is becoming suspicious. There's a... there's an envelope in there too, with some money for you..." she swallowed.

"Abigail, please. I don't..."

"Take it Jonathan!" she practically shouted.

Jonathan put a hand on her shoulder. "I will then, now calm down. I was not trying to offend you, is anything wrong?"

Abigail took a deep breath, looked at the ground, but then shook her head.

"My friend at school is paying me to help him with his research. You should save your money, buy a warmer pair of mittens," he squeezed her hands. "Mycroft is obviously impressed with you, else he would not have given you a raise. Maybe you could invest in..."

"Just never mind then."

"Are you all right?"

Abigail sniffed with a shiver. "Sure enough I am."

He opened the folder a crack, then peered at the pages inside. "Any notes of importance in it?"

"I did not want to disturb anything, so haven't looked. What did you find in the trinket box?"

"I... have not opened it yet."

"What!? Whyever not? I thought that was why you wanted the folder? What are you waiting for?"

"Well, I... I felt guilty opening it, but perhaps what I need will be in this folder."

"Guilty? That was the entire reason you went to Cambridge!"

"Not the entire, didn't you say I needed to get away from Holmes, and also that an education would be good for me?"

"Yes but... you had no trouble reading an entire 'diary' of your father's, but won't open your mother's box with letters she didn't even write?"

"It is silly, I know. I promise to open it when I get back."

Abigail rolled her eyes and pointed to the folder. "What are you hoping to find in there?"

Jonathan closed the folder, then slipped it back under the white cloth in the picnic basket.

"I will let you know on our next call, if I do in fact, discover anything."

Abby stared at him blankly. "You are not going to tell me?!"

"I should not disclose anything to anyone, least I get them too involved."

371

"But, I am involved!"

"The temptation to form premature theories upon insufficient data can be dangerous, so to protect you..."

Abigail's cheeks flushed a bright red. "I do so much for you Jonathan because I... I wish you would trust me for once!"

Abigail was in an odd temperament today, and he was taken aback by her anger. "It has nothing to do with trust, Ab. If I learned anything from Watson's narratives, Holmes always said that results should be given conclusively, not in stages. I do not want to say anything until I am sure, for the consequences of my being correct could be disastrous."

Abigail rose to leave, then curled her fists at her side. "Well then, good luck, Mr. Holmes!"

Jonathan grabbed her by the arm, and pulled her back down. "Abigail, listen to me. You are already in over your head! I promise to tell you everything when I know," he whispered. "And call me anything in the world if you are angry, but *please* not Holmes. It is bad enough when Gabriel does it."

Abigail ripped her arm away. "Well enjoy the rest of your day Jonathan... whatever your name is."

"If we are addressing names," Jonathan pounced, standing up to face her, "then who is Mr. Esher, AMBER!?"

Abigail gaped at him. "I don't see as that's any of your business!"

"As you let slip the name, I feel justified in requesting further information. If he is responsible in any way for your current shift in mood, cool temperament..."

"You never ask me anything about myself! Not where I came from, whether I liked my parents, what my favorite colour is, and *now*, you want to care? When it's something that interests *you*!? Always have to try and pick everything and everyone apart if you see fit to do so, don't you? You are more like your father than you'd like to admit!" she stormed off down the pathway.

Jonathan started after her, too enraged to comment, but then he paused, snatched up the picnic basket, and marched away in the opposite direction. He came upon a branch in the middle of the pavement and picked it up, then threw it across the frozen pond nearby.

"Bah! Women!" he stewed with a grunt. He turned his head to look back at her, but she was already far along down the pathway. "Oh, the hell with her!" he snarled, as he headed back towards the train station. He would *not* be staying in London after all.

As he turned down the hallway and entered his room back at Master's Lodge, Jonathan angrily threw the picnic basket against the wall, and kicked the door closed. He pushed in the light switch, then sighed as he stooped over to pick up the Ripper file that had fallen out of the basket. He dropped it on his desk, flipped it open, then paused. It was written in a different hand than Holmes' or Watson's so it must be Mycroft's.

~ ~

When I observed my brother's recent obsession with every movement of the monarchy I cornered him into a confession. He admitted to confronting Scarlett on a relationship with 'His Royal Highness' long ago, and he had told her to end it. 'His Royal Highness' could be none other than Albert Victor Christian Edward, or Eddy, as he was nicknamed, as I am aware that he attended Cambridge the same years as Sherlock's wife. I could not believe he had kept this from me.

He refused to confirm my theory, but expressed his need for a safe place for Jonathan. I gave him the name of a dear friend from Cambridge who had two children of his own and had wished for a third with no success. Jonathan would be loved, cared for, and kept under cover. Sherlock agreed.

It was not until my brother's recent presumed departure from life that he revealed His Royal Highness was also the infamous Jack the Ripper. I was aghast. "Are you certain?" I had asked him, during one of our few correspondences. His response was the below timeline, though what I am to do with this information remains a conundrum. I will file it away in the hopes that none of it shall ever surface, not even in the centuries to come.

~ ~

A loud knock echoed on Jonathan's door. He rolled his eyes, closed the file, and threw it in a drawer.

Gabriel was standing in the hallway.

"Haven't seen you in ages!" Gabriel greeted. "Come, let us have a drink at The Eagle and you can enlighten me as to your reason for being so mysteriously absent as of late."

Jonathan couldn't tell him the real reason but agreed, knowing that Gabriel would quickly lose interest if Jonathan changed the subject to something about *Gabriel*.

While sipping ale, and munching on fish and chips at a small round table in the corner of The Eagle Pub, Gabriel asked if Jonathan would like to accompany him and few other students to France for a long weekend. They planned on assessing medical schools, such as the Sorbonne, and hospital residencies within the country. They were to leave that Thursday and return Saturday night. Jonathan explained he couldn't afford to do so and besides, he was only a freshman. Gabriel said he would pay his way, as he needed a break as his schoolwork was apparently bogging him down. Jonathan consented so wrote Abigail for her number, as he could not be sure of his exact whereabouts for Wednesday, that is, if she even wanted to talk to him. She wrote back and after decoding her response, he found that it read,

"Have a pleasant time Johnny. Here is where to reach me Wednesday..."

Whilst in Paris, Jonathan almost forgot to call Abigail that Wednesday evening as the boys had been drinking and talking all afternoon and he'd lost track of the time. He stumbled to a phone box, and dialed the number on the scrap of paper in his hand.

"Hello?" he heard Abigail on the other line.

"Bonjour!" he sang happily. "Comment allez-vous?"

"I don't know French, Jonathan. Having a nice time? And did you look at that file I gave you yet?"

"What-that? Oh, no..." Jonathan was slurring his words.

"You are three sheets to the wind, aren't you?!"

"No," he lied with a grin, then began to laugh.

"Dammit, Jonathan you are thirteen! I cannot say as I like your new friends!"

"They don't know I am!"

"Ohhhh! Just...ring me when you are sober!" The phone hung up.

The rest of the evening became a blur, so he decided to avoid alcohol for the remainder of the trip. When they returned Saturday afternoon, Jonathan completed his schoolwork for the coming week then remembered his brief conversation with Abigail. He cringed, and decided to wire her a telegram. First to apologize, and also to ask if he could stay over Wednesday night instead of having their phone conversation so he could return the Ripper file to her. After sending the message, he returned to his room and continued reading Mycroft's letter.

The next page was written in Sherlock's hand.

"Hello, what's this?"

~ ~

My brother, I would like for you to examine the following facts if you are still unconvinced, and meditate on your conclusion. You know

I am never one for speculation without evidence, so I present to you a theoretical timeline to explain, and weave together various and sundry events. This timeline, coupled with the last few letters I had found from Jack to Scarlett serve as rather damning evidence. In the letters he had threatened her, and blamed her as the reason for his misdeeds. The poor woman must have been terrified, but why had she never told me? I cannot know what her thinking was, though I certainly pray she had not concealed these in order to keep me from worrying or attacking him myself to defend her. Add in that the Ripper was clearly left-handed, as is His Royal Highness, then you have all the information needed to prove his guilt.

As I have researched, these dates are in keeping with The Prince's typical travel patterns, thereby verifying that he was in London at all the appointed times, and able to commit all of the murders. Summers are spent in London, October in Scotland, late November through February at Sandringham, and March in Paris. You will see how the dates below fall within that normal precedent. Therefore, there is no excuse, nor alibi of travel.

5th **August 1888**- Scarlett plans to leave Baker St. to run off with The Prince (otherwise known as 'Jack,') but instead, she professes her love for me, and stays. Nothing is communicated to him of the change in plans.

6th **August 1888**- Martha Taubaurn murdered in George Yard Buildings. Assuming 'Jack' did not take kindly to being so quickly discarded, he slips into mania and keeps their pet name of 'Jack', but adds on 'the Ripper', to his fictitious title. Martha was murdered in the exact location where Scarlett had last met with The Prince and to note,

377

was wearing a green skirt, the very same shade of green that Scarlett had been wearing the night before.

29ᵗʰ August 1888 – Scarlett & I have a run in with The Prince at the symphony. He gives her a letter, asking her to meet with him the next evening. She declines the invitation but again, communicates nothing, simply does not show. This was the first I began to worry about a possible backlash of jealousy.

31ˢᵗ August 1888- Polly Nichols' body found that morning in Bucks Row, not far from the first murder.

7ᵗʰ September 1888 - I propose to Scarlett. Though alone, I can only imagine the hansom cab driver I had requisitioned alerted him. He must have allies everywhere, Mycroft! How did I not see!?

8ᵗʰ September 1888 - Annie Chapman killed at 29 Hanbury Street, only hours later. 29 was Scarlett's college room number.

I had remembered the name, and appearance of our cab driver from that night and attempted to locate him, only to find that he had died in a suspicious carriage accident not days after our encounter with him. Most telling, is it not?

29ᵗʰ September 1888 - Scarlett becomes Mrs. Sherlock Holmes at St. Mary-Le-Strand Church in Westminster.

30ᵗʰ September 1888 - Double murder night for the Ripper. Catherine Eddows, wearing a green skirt, and Elizabeth Stride, with a red rose pinned to her dress.

*Jack sends his first letter to Scarlett, admitting that he was the Ripper, and that her refusal of him had brought him to such lengths. He details the murders to this point most perfectly as proof, and claims that the red rose he left will be the first of many unless she does as he asks.

I found this letter and the others, buried between the folds of a corset in her dresser. She knew Mycroft, she knew he would come for her, but told me nothing. Am I so perplexed by women that I could not sense this?

8ᵗʰ November 1888 - Scarlett is found to be pregnant. In The Prince's next letter to her, he reminded her how he had once conveyed his desire and hope that they would have children together, and how she claimed she never wished for any. He related how infuriated he was to learn that she had lied to him.

8ᵗʰ November (Thursday night) 1888 - Mary Kelly murdered. He removed her abdomen, breasts, and generally mutilated her body in any area that might have been related to child birth and child rearing. She was found 9ᵗʰ Nov., Friday morning, which, interestingly enough, is also His Royal Highness' birthday.

4ᵗʰ June 1889 – Remnants of Scarlett's ex-college friend, Elizabeth Jackson are found washed up near the River Thames. Coincidence? I paid it no mind then, and I curse myself for my sheer stupidity!

17th July 1889 - Jonathan born.

17th July 1889 - Alice McKenzie killed in Castle Alley and according to the inquest, possibly by someone she met at the Royal Cambridge Music Hall, a location The Prince was known to frequent quite regularly.

10th September 1889 - Scarlett receives another note from The Prince, a short threatening request to speak with her that evening by the Thames Embankment. This was the only one she had shared with me, as I had been present when it arrived.

10th September 1889 - Pinchin St. torso discovered under a railway arch, but notably, the woman had not been dissected at that location. The murder was committed near the river, due to the large amount of salt water present in the lungs. The Yard categories this as part of the 'Whitehall Mysteries' and not the Ripper's doings at all. What failures at detection are they!

13th February 1891 - Frances Coles murdered in Swallow Gardens. A black hat was placed beside her body. In the very last letter from The Prince to Scarlett, he mentioned that he would leave her a message, his *final* message, with his *last* victim, under a hat beside her body.

Whether or not she ever found that note, I will never know, but the records and inventory from Scotland Yard on the Ripper case made no mention of a note or message, so perhaps... it never existed, or perhaps... it had been removed? I had been out to retrieve Jonathan at the time, so cannot say with certainty either way.

13ᵗʰ February 1891 - Scarlett killed before midnight, the completion of his oeuvre.

The murders then stop. He is done. He finally went after the one he wanted, but could not have, to ensure that no one else ever could either.

I believe we had been followed since the night of 5ᵗʰ Aug 1888, and any event, or element in our relationship that displeased him, led him to kill another innocent woman. Dammit Mycroft, if I am allegedly the greatest detective that ever lived, how could I have been so blind? Had I but known, I might have saved her life. If only she knew I could have protected her, and if only I had told her certain things sooner...

With The Prince hell-bent on continuing his revenge, it was of the utmost import that I vanish and find a safe place for Jonathan; somewhere that his past and his ties to me could be well hidden. I hope to someday have my son's forgiveness, if he ever learns of me. I only tried to do what was best.

My brother, I must ask you to carry on with keeping my location a secret. Also, please continue to maintain my rooms, assets, possessions, and finances as you have been doing so well. I am entrusting you with a sealed package, containing notes of a very personal nature that I shall send shortly. However, I must request that should I ever perish, destroy it. It cannot ever fall into the wrong hands, for the consequences would be catastrophic.

381

Thank you for your guidance, support, and love, always. I cannot think as I have ever professed as much.

Your younger, and naive brother,

Sherlock

~ ~

Jonathan closed the file. Holmes had the notes?! He had the proof? Letters where Jack admitted to being the Ripper? Why did he not turn The Prince over to the authorities!? He looked over at the letter box, took the dining hall knife from his plate from lunch, and plunged it into the keyhole, no longer caring about finding a proper tool, but wanting to break it open. He wriggled the knife around until he broke the seal, then popped the box's lid.

Inside, were several pieces of jewellery; a ruby ring, jade and gold dew drop clip on earrings, and a gold bracelet with the inscription 'from Jack to Bean'. There were multiple letters and pieces of paper folded over and tightly packed inside. Some pages were letters from her father, whilst others were thin scraps of paper folded over three times with a different drawing on each section to create an odd-looking creature. It appeared to be some sort of game where someone drew the feet, someone else the middle, and perhaps someone else the head. The letters at the very bottom... were from Jack.

Jonathan opened one, and began to read...

'My fair Bean, I received your latest note and I assure you that you too, are missed. It brings me much joy to know I have your love and affection, and above all, your loyalty to me, without which, I would be most displeased my dear one. I must always protect my rare red rose from the weeds and the vermin of the gardens, must I not? Do not

382

apologize for your candour, and I swear to you that I pledge my heart to my one and only. Fear not, for I will remove anyone who attempts to come between us and take you away from me. That is my power and my promise to you. One day, we will be together, for I deserve you and have earned you, and none should be allowed to have you but me, my princess. I say that fondly, and only for you to understand the hold and control you have over me. I am YOUR Prince, for you are unlike any other...'

Jonathan stopped reading and unfolded another letter. The more he read, the more he realized that although this man clearly loved his mother, he was rather insane with his jealousy, and paranoid in his fear of losing her.

While flattering on one hand, it must have terrified his mother to be in a relationship with someone who seemed so volatile, and teetered on the brink of destructive behaviour. She must have sensed his possessiveness, which is why she kept the letters, perhaps to protect herself. But why hide it at Cambridge? So that her father or Holmes would never find out? And why had she continued seeing him after college? Out of fear for her life if she did not?

Jonathan stopped reading and closed the box. This, along with the file, had everything he was looking for! It was the final piece to the puzzle. This proved The Prince killed his mother, *and* was Jack the Ripper! And apparently, Holmes also had specific letters where Jack confessed as much!

He smacked his head with his palm. "If Mycroft was the only one who knew Holmes still lived, he must certainly know that I am tracking everyone. *That* is why Abigail needed the file back! Holmes knew I had found Celeste, meaning Watson's notes were discovered missing. Oh good God, what if Holmes tried to retrieve his journal in an effort to stop me, and it was not there!? Abigail could be in a great deal of trouble!"

CHAPTER 31

THE PHONE CONVERSATION

For the next two days, Jonathan received no responses from Abigail. He was anxious and concerned, but would not venture to London, not yet.

When Wednesday arrived, he rushed for their weekly phone conversation, and prayed she would be there. The fear that she would not, was resting forefront in his mind. He sat by the phone and waited, anxiously. It was five minutes after seven now. Was she all right? Had anything happened? He *hoped* that she hadn't written due to being angry, and not because of any danger she might be in. But, would she even ring up then?

The phone rang.

Jonathan jumped onto the receiver. "Hello, hello, Abigail?"

"Jonathan?" Abigail's voice was quiet.

"Abby, oh thank goodness you are there! I have the most amazing news!"

"Oh?"

"First though, I am terribly sorry about last week in Paris. It will not happen again. It was immature, and foolish of me. You are too important to risk upsetting, so I will be more conscientious in the future. Did you happen to get my telegram?"

"Yes Jonathan, go on," she said flatly.

385

Jonathan had a strange feeling in his gut, but tried to ignore it. "Based on the file you gave me, with notes from both Sherlock and Mycroft on the Ripper, everything matches up. The dates and times of the murders, life events of my parents, it all corresponds! I can tell you Abigail, finally! My mother was involved with The Prince in college. Her secret name for him was 'Jack', and his for her was 'Bean'. The letters in my mother's box confirm his identity, and his correspondences to her were definitely from the mind of an unwell and slightly psychotic man, one who was deeply obsessed with her and jealous of anyone else.

Even though she had been afraid of him, she had planned on leaving Baker Street, but ultimately, remained with Holmes. The Prince went berserk and created the alternate identity of 'Jack the Ripper'. He followed my parents throughout their relationship, killing women to unleash his frustration concerning different monumental points in their lives! He even confessed as much to my mother in several letters before she died. She knew Ab! She knew who he was!"

"Why did she not tell anyone?"

"Perhaps she was afraid of what it would do to the country? Perhaps she worried that he would do something to Holmes or me? But ultimately, realizing he could never have her, he killed her. The murders then stopped. It is all here. It all makes perfect sense!

"So you see, with your help and support I now understand what happened. This can end; it is over. We will turn this information over to the authorities, the Royal Family will be forced to confess to covering their sins, and I will be free from the uncertainty and anxiety that has plagued me my entire life. We have them, Abigail! We have them by the throat!"

There was silence on the other end.

386

"Abigail?"

"Yes, I am here." She sounded pained.

"Are you, all right? You are not in any kind of difficulty, are you?"

"No, I am not. Not at all."

"Are you still upset with me?"

Abigail laughed lightly. "No Jonathan, I could not be. I am... very glad you have told me all this. I have to go now. Please, be careful. You are my best friend. The bible quote of the week comes from the Archangel Gabriel..." She paused, then spoke slowly, "Though feeling blameless, spending accountable hours amidst men shaming God, implies belief in condoning swine," she again paused. "Be sure to note that in your journal. Good bye, Jonathan."

The line went silent as Jonathan heard a 'click'.

She had hung up.

Jonathan held the phone's receiver in his hand. "Archangel Gabriel? What the deuce was she babbling about? Biblical quote? She knows I am not religious. Something *is* wrong. I will go to London, tomorrow. Do not worry Abby, I am coming!"

CHAPTER 32

TIME IS UP

The next morning Jonathan awoke later than he wished, then gathered his things for travelling to London. As he headed towards King's Court, he noticed a cluster of students and professors in a circle by the gateway, at the end of the long avenue of lime trees. As stepped closer, they were chattering wildly. He peered around them to see what the fuss was all about, and his body went numb.

Abigail, was lying propped up against the gateway like a ragdoll. Her throat was slit, and a deerstalker cap sat neatly on the ground next to her. Written in blood on the brick wall behind her was...

"Give up the case Holmes, else I'll have YOU by the throat. -- JACK.*"*

Just as Jonathan was about to turn and run, Gabriel came up beside him and gasped, "My God! The poor girl! I wonder if she was a student here, Holmes?"

As Gabriel gave Jonathan a look, Jonathan struggled to see Gabriel clearly through the pools of water that were forming in his eyes.

Gabriel's face softened. "You knew her, didn't you?"

Jonathan remained still.

Gabriel put a hand on Jonathan's shoulder. "Who was she?" He then squinted at the wall. 'Give up the case, *Holmes?*' His eyes went wide with a sudden realization as Jonathan shrugged off his hand then dashed away.

Jonathan screamed as he threw his pack on the floor and paced his room. "Who knew? Who the hell knew our *exact* last conversation? Why would she tell anyone...? Why..." he paused, and closed his eyes. "Bloody hell. How did I not see?"

He jumped into his desk chair, and wrote out Abigail's last words. '*Though feeling blameless, spending accountable hours amidst men shaming God implies belief in condoning swine*'. Circling the second letter of each word per their cryptic code, he found that it read, 'help, come home now.' He had completely missed her message. Now, the only person in the world whom he trusted was gone, and because of him. He was no different than Holmes, just as Abigail had said, for now *he* had let the only person he cared about die, by being blind. They were not so very dissimilar after all.

"I am so sorry, Abigail," he sobbed, as he dropped to his knees and cried into his bed sheets. His life felt meaningless now. No one to talk to, no one to share his findings or daily dealings with, and no one who cared about him. Celeste had been right. He should have let it go. Not knowing how else to cope, he went to The Eagle and drank pint after pint until he was quite intoxicated. He staggered back to his room and collapsed, drunk as blazes.

He was awakened sometime later by a voice calling his name.

"Jonathan, Jonathan, wake up."

He angrily rolled over to see who was bothering him. There was no one there. Jonathan blinked his eyes. His vision was still a bit blurry. "Who is there? What do you want!?" He turned to face the door, and saw the pale image of a woman standing in the doorway. Jonathan pulled the sheets tighter around himself and rolled over. He must still be drunk.

"Jonathan, you cannot give up," the woman said with a crystal voice.

Jonathan turned back around then sat up and rubbed his eyes. From how it looked, Scarlett Holmes was hovering in the doorframe. She was so beautiful, like an angel, just as Dr. Watson had described.

"It cannot be," he murmured, throwing off the sheets and swinging his legs over the side of the bed. "Mum? You really there?"

The apparition drifted towards him, then stopped near his bedside. "You have come too far, son."

"It is over, Mum, everything is over. Abigail is gone, *I* have been discovered, and I am completely alone. What am I to do?"

Scarlett's ghost shook her head. "No, it is not. If you give up now then that poor girl died for nothing. She sacrificed herself because she believed in you, now *you* must believe in you. Finish this, Jonathan."

"But how!?"

Scarlett smiled, sat down next to him, and ran her translucent fingers through his hair. "You are a bright boy, like your father, you will find a way."

"I have *no one,* mother!"

She frowned, then wrapped her arms around his shoulders. Her touch was frigid, so he leaned back with a shiver.

"You have family still, Jonathan. Use them."

"But you are gone!"

She rested her hands atop his and sighed. It was like an arctic chill against his fingers, but he did not pull away. "You have a father who loves you."

Jonathan looked away. "I do not believe that he does."

Scarlett turned his chin towards her, and stared him in the eyes. "You were born out of love, and that love did not die with me. He needs you Jonathan, as much as you need him. He has been just as lonely."

Jonathan tried to hug her, but his hands only passed through filmy air. "Then why did he leave? Why not come back for me?"

She took his face in her hands and smiled. "My stubborn boy, he has been trying to tell you."

His cheeks felt frozen. "I need you mum. I don't want to see him."

Scarlett's ghost rose from the bed. "Go to your uncle, then. I am always with you, but *you* have to see this through."

"What can I possibly do?"

"You are your father's son!" she laughed lightly. "You can do anything." Her spirit receded backwards and began to fade from vision. "You *will* find a way."

"Don't go, please don't go. You cannot leave me again. I love you!" Jonathan closed his eyes then opened them, only to find himself on the floor of his room and Holmes' journal wrapped tightly in his arms.

His mother was right. He had to finish this. For her, and for Abby.

He grabbed a few articles of clothing, then packed the handgun he had stolen from Francis Eaton. He never expected to need it, but now, he might.

As he walked through the front door to the outside, it began to pour. He pulled his white collar high around his neck, and began to sprint down the walkway when Gabriel stepped through the gates with an open umbrella. Jonathan had never been happier to see him.

"Where are you going?" Gabriel asked, as he held the umbrella over both of them. "Are you all right?"

"I did know that girl, very well in fact."

"I know."

"Gabriel," Jonathan looked at the ground, "I have a confession to make. You were right all along. I am in fact, Sherlock Holmes' son. I am so sorry to have lied to you. This was all my fault."

"Then that message *was* meant for you," Gabriel said. "I... somehow guessed, son of Sherlock, you *are* the Holmes they were warning."

Jonathan nodded. "I did not want anyone knowing. Perhaps one day, you will understand why—"

Gabriel solemnly shook his head, and put a finger to his lips. "I will not say a word, nor will I ask for an explanation."

In that moment, an unspoken pact for lifelong friendship seemed to form between the two boys. Jonathan knew that he could, and would always be able to, trust Gabriel completely. "I have to go, back to London. There is something I must do."

"Are you also in danger?"

"Most likely, yes."

"Well Jonathan, whatever troubles or mess you might be in, I shall be of assistance. I will *be* your Watson."

Jonathan smiled, touched. "I appreciate that, but I'll be fine."

Gabriel lifted an eyebrow. "Are you certain?"

Jonathan nodded.

Gabriel held out a hand for him to shake, but instead, Jonathan hugged him close and whispered, "You are my best friend, Adams. I value you more than you know."

"Never had a best friend before," Gabriel beamed hugging him back. "Here," he said, handing Jonathan his umbrella, "you need this more than I." He reached inside his coat pocket, and handed Jonathan a pound note. "This could be useful also. I am here if you need me."

Jonathan waited on Hills Street for a carriage to take him to the Cambridge railway station. When one finally pulled up he went to hop in, but then stopped. A growler carriage had wheeled up directly behind his, with several men waiting inside. One man jumped to the curb to light a cigarette, and glowered at Jonathan through his black handlebar mustache.

As Jonathan's brain was already working on a heightened sense of caution, he reasoned that he was over-thinking this, so climbed inside, deciding to ignore his instincts. "Cambridge Railway Station, please," he told the driver.

He folded his umbrella, placed it to the side, then leaned back into the leather cushioned seat and closed his eyes. His mind drifted to thoughts of Abigail. His last visit with her had ended in anger, and with fighting words. He wished he could take it all back. Now, he would never again see her smile, or hear her laughter, or play the piano with her sitting beside him, swinging her legs in rhythm with the music. And what legs she had... Just as he was picturing her, his eyes snapped open as he heard his carriage *and* the one behind him, start off simultaneously. He peered out the window.

The mustachioed man from the pavement sneered, then drew his finger across his throat and made a cutting sound like a knife. Jonathan pressed himself further into the cushion. *Oh hell.* As they continued on he noticed that they were heading in the wrong direction.

Northeast. "Towards Norfolk," Jonathan realized. "Sandring-ham. Someone of the crown wants to make damned sure I don't let out The Prince's dark secret. Is it Prince George, protecting his brother? Or their father, the King, protecting his son? Do they plan to kill me as well? I doubt I am being invited up for tea."

He had only moments to formulate a plan on how he'd escape. Soon, they would be travelling over a bridge with a short enough drop that he could easily open the carriage door and jump out. Also, not far from the bridge was a river, so if he managed to land safely, he could dive into the water, and follow it to where it crossed the train tracks in Birmingham. As frigid as the waters would be this time of year, he'd rather risk drowning or dying of hypothermia in the river than being ripped apart by hired mercenaries.

He opened his satchel, pulled out the gun, then stuffed it in his trousers as he waited for the right moment to leap from the carriage.

As they crossed over the bridge, Jonathan opened his umbrella to break the fall, counted to ten, then flung open the carriage door and leapt out. He dove to the ground, covered by the umbrella, then tossed it aside and rolled away from the carriage.

The bridge was wider than he remembered. He was a good twenty paces from the edge. His carriage stopped, as well as the second one, and three men jumped out.

Jonathan sprang up to run, but the rain soaked bridge was slick and he slipped backwards, landing on his hip. He winced in pain, but quickly pulled himself up and rushed towards the edge, only to be cut off by a scraggly looking young man in a thick blue pea coat.

The man crossed his arms. "Going somewhere, Mr. Holmes?"

"My name-- is not Holmes!"

Jonathan whirled around to see the other two men now behind him.

"Nowhere to go, is there?" said a short, stout Lascar with a thick Indian accent. "Think you had better come with us, as someone wishes to see you."

Jonathan pulled out his pistol, and aimed it at the two men. "Tell them I politely decline their invitation."

The other of the two men in front of him, an older man with a thick neck and exaggerated lips, pounced in front of Jonathan and eyed his gun with interest. "Nice gun there, looks American, what make might that be?" he asked.

Jonathan was suddenly hit from behind with the blunt edge of a knife, and dropped to his knees. The two men advanced. Having but a moment to react, Jonathan thrust his right hand behind him, and fired. He heard a scream, then the *ping* of a knife as it hit the ground. Pea coat grabbed at his bleeding leg where Jonathan had shot him, and howled like a dying animal. Jonathan crawled in the direction of the knife, snatched it up, and pointed both weapons back at the other two men.

"I don't care what the master says!" the injured man spat, "he's not getting him alive!" He looked over at the Lascar. "Grab him, Nabil!"

"Careful Benny!" thick-lips warned. "It will be our necks if anything happens to him! You know what he said..."

"I don't care how badly His Majesty—"

"His Majesty!?" Jonathan repeated. *He is protecting his son.* Stunned by this news, Jonathan wasn't prepared for Nabil diving at him and he was knocked to the ground, losing the knife in the process. The two became entangled in deadly struggle for the gun, kicking and tumbling on the wet cold ground. Nabil punched Jonathan in the stomach then went for his throat, but by putting more energy into his left hand to strangle him, his right hand weakened, and Jonathan was able to yank the gun away.

Benny kicked the knife towards Nabil with his good leg, then limped over to the second carriage, and leaned against it. "Kill him! Just kill him, Nabil!"

Nabil rolled over, straining for the knife, but before he could attack, Jonathan aimed the gun at his head. "So help me, I will kill *you* if you move another inch!" Nabil backed away. "Now drop the knife."

Nabil let it fall to the ground.

Jonathan scrambled to his feet, scooped up the knife, then pointed his gun at the two men still standing. "The King sent you, did he..."

He heard the distinctive *click* of a shotgun behind him, so spun around to face the sound's source, and reflexively fired. He was stunned to see that he had actually hit the second coachman in the chest. The man fell over the side of the carriage, and his gun with him.

Jonathan turned towards the first driver. "Have you any fancy ideas as well?"

Had he really just killed someone?!

The cab driver shook his head, and sat back down.

Jonathan kept his sights on the driver and asked, "Have you a gun?"

The driver sat still.

"I asked you, have you a gun!?"

The cab driver sighed, then pulled a pistol from underneath his seat.

"Over the bridge please," Jonathan said, with a wave of his barrel.

The driver tossed it, and the gun vanished from view.

"Now, off."

The man hopped down from the carriage and onto the ground.

Jonathan's eyes darted back and forth between Nabil, thick lips, and the driver. "Stand next to Nabil and his friend there," he gestured to thick lips.

All the men, with the exception of Benny, who was still by the carriage holding his leg, were now standing in front of Jonathan. "Why did His Majesty send you?"

All he heard was the patter of rain on the bridge.

"Tell me!" His hand shook in anger.

"Figure it out yourself, detective," Benny said coldly, as he sat down on the metal step of the carriage.

"The hell with you all then!"

Jonathan released the two horses in the second carriage by slashing the leather straps that tethered them to the growler, then smacked them on the rump. They reared up with a whinny, and darted off down the road back to Cambridge. As Jonathan moved towards the first carriage's horses, he heard a gunshot ring out, and felt a sharp stabbing pain in his left shoulder blade. He convulsed forward, and fell to the ground.

"Jonathan! Jonathan get up!" he heard through the rain.

He turned his head and saw Gabriel with a leather helmet and goggles speeding towards him on his motorbike. Jonathan managed to his feet just as Gabriel's bike swept by, and he jumped on the back. Another shot was heard, and both boys ducked. Gabriel slammed his foot on the accelerator, and they sped off across the bridge and down the road.

They heard the men shouting and swearing behind them, but dared not look back.

"Can't leave you alone for one minute," Gabriel said through the howling wind, whipping around them.

"How did you know to follow me?" Jonathan said weakly, his shoulder throbbing. "And you could have been shot!"

"You said you were in danger, so I followed you. When I saw that carriage going in the wrong direction, I knew something was amiss." He looked back at Jonathan. "You're not the only one who can make deductions."

Jonathan hugged him tighter, painful as it was, and smiled. "Thanks, Watson."

"Right, don't get all emotional on me. That would be too out of character for a son of Sherlock Holmes."

"I killed a man," Jonathan blurted, "at least, I think I did..."

"Then he certainly deserved it."

Once they reached the Birmingham train station, Jonathan eased off the bike as Gabriel kept the motor running.

"You are certain there is nothing more I can do?" Gabriel asked.

"No, you just saved my life Gabriel, but I cannot put yours in any further jeopardy."

"I'll handle the girl's body then, what was her name?"

Jonathan painfully shook his head. "No Gabriel, it is too dangerous. She will have to wait. But it was Abigail. Abigail Hopkins."

Gabriel moved to speak, possibly wondering why they had the same last name, but then nodded. "Then just promise me you'll have that shoulder looked at first thing. I'd do it myself," Gabriel looked around, "but you haven't any time. Good luck, Holmes." He adjusted his goggles, then sped off down the road.

Jonathan stretched his neck to peer at his shoulder. He was still bleeding, and soaked to the bone. He shivered, and limped over to the ticket window.

"One ticket to London, sir," he said to the portly clerk. "Kings Cross Station, please."

"Eight shillings young man, and... oh my, are you all right, son?" the older gentleman asked, as he leaned over the counter and gawked at Jonathan's shoulder.

"Bit of a tiff with my brother. That is what I get for coming home to visit." He knew it was a pathetic lie, but he was in too much pain to think of anything better. Besides, the men could be seconds away. He handed the clerk the wet pound note.

The clerk shrugged, and handed Jonathan his ticket and change. "Train leaves in three minutes."

Jonathan managed down the pathway to the end of the train. He ached, like an old man. Before he boarded, he surveyed the periphery of the station for the men. None of them were there yet. His heart pounded as he forced himself into the train's last car. Finding an empty box seat, he flopped down with a cry, touched his arm, and winced as his fingertips were now stained with red. He would have to have the bullet removed, and soon, as his shoulder throbbed from the gunshot wound.

Those men were trying to kill me.

He shivered, then ducked away from the window, and closed his eyes. "Come on train, move, please move!" he trembled. Once the train began to roll, he opened his eyes and gathered the courage to look out the window. He saw Nabil huffing and puffing, with his hair a jumbled mess and his clothes sticking to him as he ran towards the train. Nabil paused to take a breath, rested his hands on his thighs, then glared up at Jonathan when he noticed his face in the window.

"Try and catch me now," Jonathan said, then stuck out his tongue.

But even with the train well on its way, he felt as if the man's piercing black eyes were burning through his confidence. He locked the door to the boxcar, curled up on the long seat cushion, and tried to sleep. His mother had been right. He had to finish this, before it finished *him*.

CHAPTER 33

A SAD RETURN

Jonathan disembarked the train and began his journey to the Diogenes Club to find Mycroft Holmes, the gentleman's club where his uncle was regarded as a permanent fixture. Just as he was about to hop on the underground, he had a sudden thought. Did Abigail's flatmates know she was gone? It had only been a day, so more than likely the news hadn't reached them yet. He would have to make a side trip to Hoxton first. Passengers stared at him as he entered the underground, and stepped away from him in apprehension. He must look a fright.

The train made a stop at Whitechapel and after a few minutes of remaining stationary, the train operator came walking through the crowd and announced that the carriage was down. They would have to jump train and take another line.

No, I'll walk.

A thick grey mist hung in the air as Jonathan wandered through the seedy streets of Whitechapel. He passed by George Yard Buildings, Hanover Square, and other illustrious locations that were chosen by the Ripper for killing his victims. Before, they had simply been locations he had passed through on his way to work or to the market, but now, they made him shiver. As he turned a corner, a cool wind picked up, and caused dust particles and loose papers to blow across the alleyway. The sky threatened to storm. *What were you thinking, Your Royal Highness? How could you behave so abominably?* The slight patter of rain began to sound on the cobblestones, and he closed his eyes in an effort to

402

comprehend what could motivate such rage, such anger, and felt that he *could* conceivably kill the person who had murdered Abigail.

Not realizing he had wandered over a blowhole, a large blast of steam emanated from the ground beneath him, and his eyes snapped open in terror. "I can never allow my mind to venture there," he shook his head.

When he reached his old neighborhood, the building where his rooms had once been located appeared to have been through some type of fire. The bricks were charred, the windows gone, and black soot remnants surrounded the building's foundation. Jonathan covered his mouth in horror.

He cautiously walked towards the rubble, and circled the base of the complex.

A young, red-haired girl sat on the steps of the adjacent building, playing cat's cradle.

"Excuse me," he pointed to the burned building, "but do you know what happened here?"

The little girl looked up terrified, violently shook her head, then raced inside and shut the door. Jonathan sighed. He was certainly a sight.

Could this disaster have been his fault? He stepped through the building's remains and peered inside. The floors had been burned through, leaving the interior virtually barren. Shards of wood still clung to the walls where the floorboards had once been.

He then noticed the blackened remains of an ornate oak chest peaking out through the wreckage. It was Abigail's. He felt his eyes grow moist as he pushed through the debris to reach it and dusted off the lid before lifting it open. There were a few scattered photographs inside, and several were of adults he didn't know posed with a younger Abigail, perhaps three years old. Could they have been her parents? The backside of the photograph read, *'Photographed by: Lang Studios, 225 Long Meadow Drive, Philadelphia, PA.'* Was Abigail an American? He took the photographs and shoved them in his pocket, then stepped back outside, trying not to trip over the piles of ruins.

Just as he was about to leave, a middle-aged woman dressed in black appeared in the doorframe of the other building where the little girl had run inside. She motioned for Jonathan to come closer, then pointed at the burned structure. "You the one asking about that?"

Jonathan nodded. "Yes ma'am. I... used to live there, a while ago. I was looking for my friends."

The woman wiped away a tear. "Burned it down, they did. Bloody bastards threw torches and firebombs through them windows. They pulled the children from one room, and shot 'em in cold blood. Said they 'ad done something terrible, and it were punishable by death. I think those blokes were lying. Never seen any of them do a thing wrong. Sweet lot they were," the woman sighed. "Don't know who they think they is, comin' in and murderin' innocent young ones. Always knew them was bad people. I never trusted no copper, not never. I'd like to give 'em a turn, I would!"

Bobbies don't *carry* guns, Jonathan thought. Whoever they were must have killed the others when they discovered where Abigail lived, even though none of them knew what Jonathan had been searching for.

"Did anyone get away?"

"Not that I knows of, no. You say you used to live there?"

"A long time ago," he lied. "One of the girls I remember, was Abigail Hopkins."

"She's a sweet thing. I never saw 'er that night, so maybe she did get clean away?"

"Maybe," Jonathan nodded, looking at the ground. "Do you happen to know if she was from America?"

The woman looked at him surprised. "She was. Don't you know 'er story? 'Er folks and 'er sailed to England when she was small, but 'er parents died on the trip over. That's how she came to be 'ere. She 'ad no one."

Abigail's distance and differences from the other End East girls made sense now. She *had* come from a better background, just as he did. He missed her even more now. He had become so wrapped up in his own past, that he never asked her about hers.

"Looks like you've had a time of things yerself, haven't you?" the woman gestured towards Jonathan's shoulder, snapping him out of it. "You could use some cleanin' up and fresh clothes. Besides, any friend of Abigail's is a friend o' mine. Name's Charlotte," she said, introducing herself with a handshake.

"Jonathan," he muttered back.

"Abigail used to watch little Kristen 'ere, so least I can do, is 'elp a friend o' 'ers. Come inside Jonathan."

Jonathan was concerned that he could be being watched, but he would only be more conspicuous looking as awful as he did, so agreed.

405

He carefully stepped through the doorway and into the dingy hovel as the woman went into the other room. She came back with a large heap of clothes.

"I found a clump that weren't burned yet inside your old building. Took 'em to wash and then give to the orphanage but why don't you pick something out from the lot?"

Jonathan grabbed up a blue striped shirt, a longer black overcoat, a pair of brown trousers, and a grey plaid duster cap. The coat looked enormous, the shirt had a few holes, and even though they had been washed, the smell of smoke still lingered in the fabric. However, he couldn't be picky right now.

The woman guided him into a smaller room to the left with a water basin and soap against the far wall. "You can change and wash up in 'ere. Sorry you 'ad to come back to this. Someone must 'ave got 'isself into some trouble, all's I can figure."

Jonathan cleaned the dirt from his skin with a facecloth as best he could with his one good arm, then turned to examine his shoulder in the small mirror hanging over the basin. It was crusted over with blood, and looked grotesque. It made him nauseous.

"How did anyone know what I was about?" he asked his reflection. He changed his clothes, pulled the cap as far over his eyes as possible, then looked through the dusty window, over at his old rooms. "When I discover who's responsible, I promise you, I will have my revenge."

Once dressed Jonathan thanked the woman, then headed for his uncle's club. It would be his first meeting with Mycroft Holmes, and he was dreading it, as one can only glean so much information on someone based on descriptions they've read in a book.

CHAPTER 34

DIOGENES CLUB

Jonathan knocked on the club's front door, and was greeted by a tall, white-mustachioed butler.

"Yes?" the man asked dryly.

"Please sir, I need to see Mycroft Holmes, it is terribly urgent."

The man eyed Jonathan's attire, and sniffed disdainfully. "This establishment is for members only. I am afraid I cannot allow you in."

"I understand, truly, but it concerns his housekeeper."

"I shall discuss with him," the man closed the door.

Jonathan hugged his large coat around him, half debating if he should leave when a portly, yet domineering man in evening dress opened the front door.

"This is about Abigail, isn't it?" the man asked sadly, "or should I say Amber Gaslight?"

Jonathan nodded.

"Please Jonathan, follow me to my office. What an awful mess this is indeed."

Jonathan gulped. This was apparently, Mycroft Holmes. He followed his uncle through the club and was eyed suspiciously by the various patrons as they sat smoking their cigars, saying nothing to each other. The quiet was disconcerting.

408

Once they reached the back office, Mycroft gestured for him to sit in the large red leather chair across from his desk, then closed the door.

Jonathan wrung his hands nervously, and sat down.

"Abigail is dead then, I may presume?"

Jonathan dropped his head. "Yes, yes she is."

Mycroft eased into his desk chair, then rubbed his cheeks thoughtfully. "I had guessed as much. I had hoped that her disappearance was due to you finding what you wanted from the journal. I would have preferred that outcome."

Jonathan sat forward. "Uncle, do you know what happened?"

"You would do best to consult your father, as it was apparently his journal that led to this."

Jonathan rolled his eyes.

"Does... that seem like an accurate assumption?"

Jonathan nodded.

"I take it you've read it then?"

Jonathan sighed, then nodded again.

"There must be some interest, if you would go to such lengths to steal it..."

"I wanted to learn about my mother," Jonathan snapped, "that was all."

"Yes, poor Scarlett. You are apparently in a bit of trouble yourself, I see," he nodded towards Jonathan's arm. "And there is little I can do, I am afraid. Sherlock is the only one who can figure this out as there are dangers present that even I am unaware of. You never should have got that girl involved. I knew she was working for you the moment I checked her fabricated records and heard all her questions about Sherlock, but supposed it was a way to possibly track you."

Jonathan rose to his feet. "You knew where I was? All this time?"

"No, as apparently, you had moved out of Hoxton just before we were able to investigate."

Jonathan felt like a fool for believing that Abigail had actually tricked his uncle, and if he hadn't got into Cambridge, he would have been in Holmes' clutches the very moment Abigail began working there.

"Taking the job was her idea..."

"Then I am sorry," Mycroft folded his hands atop his desk. "Now sit please."

"Who could have done this to Abigail?"

"For that, you must talk to your father, and I mean your birth father. And incidentally, Ellen Eaton is now deceased, if you cared to know. The sickness killed her not just a month ago."

Jonathan felt a brick in his chest. Of course he cared to know, and felt guilty that he had never bid her farewell. She hadn't been a bad person, but he'd been so consumed by his own problems that he forgot about her. "I am, sorry to hear that. I wish I could have said goodbye."

"Yes well, unfortunately you have cut off the Eatons for life and must now be taken for lost. It is too dangerous for them to continue any involvement with you, and you have wounded Francis beyond repair. However, he sends you his best, and hopes you find happiness. What happened to Abigail, and where?"

"It was at Cambridge--"

"Cambridge, eh?" Mycroft shook his head. "So much like your father."

"I--am *nothing* like my father. They slit her throat and left me a lovely little message written in blood on the wall behind her. I am certain it had everything to do with my discoveries on the Ripper case, given the method in which the warning was relayed..."

Mycroft sat up in his chair. "Dear God, you are not wrapped up in that, are you? Did Abigail take anything else of mine? Any other files?!"

"Yes, on Jack the Ripper."

"Where is that file now?!" Mycroft exploded. "Is it safe!?"

"It is safe, yes," Jonathan backed up, "I promise. At Cambridge, along with the box."

"The box?"

"My mother's letter box. I found it."

Mycroft sat back in his chair, and blew through his mouth. "Your life is in severe jeopardy if you now know what I think you do. Especially as *they,* are apparently aware you know as well." He shook

411

his head. "All the people your father has been trying to shield you from... oh nephew, even if I wanted to, I could not help you now."

"Well then," Jonathan moved towards the door and opened it, "I send my regards to Mr. Eaton and am sorry, as I never meant to cause him injury; but to Holmes on the other hand, I will make no such apologies. Good day!"

"Nephew, please! You cannot leave here in anger as it will impair your judgment and lower your defenses. Emotions inhibit our logical capabilities and especially now, you must be at your intellectual best. You have a brilliant mind boy, use it. Do not allow your vexation to consume you."

Jonathan knew he was right, so sighed and took his hand off the door handle.

"She will be very missed, Jonathan. Wonderful girl. Selfless, and kind."

"Just like my mother."

"Scarlett Tennyson was the only woman in this world who could have been a companion to your father. I had never seen a more perfect fusion of man and woman and I do not desire her fate to be yours. Though you refuse to believe it, your father loves you very much. He barely recovered from the loss of her, and losing you, well, it would destroy him."

Jonathan smiled wryly, his anger returning. "If only I believed you."

He banged the door shut and winced as it pained his shoulder, then stepped out onto the street and headed towards Regents Park.

There was no longer a choice. He would have to see... Sherlock Holmes.

CHAPTER 35

FATHER & SON

Jonathan took his time arriving to Baker Street. He stopped at a restaurant and begged for bread as he was more starved than he realized, and circled the streets around the apartment building several times before he was able to summon the strength to approach the front door. His stomach turned as he walked up the front steps and rang the bell. *Courage, Jonathan.*

Mrs. Hudson, the landlady, answered. When she asked the nature of his business, he said 'family troubles.'

"Now what might your name be, lad," she asked, as he moved into the vestibule, "so I may announce you to Mr. Holmes?"

"I would like to announce myself."

"Mr. Holmes doesn't like surprises," she shook her finger. "I have strict orders to..."

"Forgive me," he touched her hand, "but Holmes knows me. I do not believe a formal introduction is necessary, Mrs. Hudson."

Mrs. Hudson's eyes twinkled. She lifted an eyebrow. "May *I* at least have your name?"

Jonathan shook his head. "I would prefer not, but Holmes and I are old acquaintances."

Mrs. Hudson gasped, covered her mouth, then shook her head. "No, you could not be him. That's not possible. But then... your name's not... not Jonathan is it?"

Jonathan sighed. He truly hated having to lie to the old woman. "No."

Mrs. Hudson's face fell. "No, of course it isn't," she laughed lightly. "Well, no matter. I'll leave you to go up by yourself boy".

Jonathan stood at the base of the staircase, feeling terrible. For her sake, he wished he could have told her the truth. Obviously she had wanted him to be Holmes' lost son, but it was too dangerous to risk getting a woman emotional right now. He headed up the stairway to the second floor but before he could knock, the door opened, and Sherlock Holmes stood calmly in the doorway, wearing a grey dressing gown.

"I have been expecting you," Holmes greeted with a smile.

Jonathan bristled at the unanticipated welcome. "Have you now?"

"One cannot circle a building several times and not assume detection," Holmes explained.

Jonathan peered around the door and inside the room. "Where is Watson?"

"You have not heard? He is recently remarried. I am alone."

Jonathan breathed out. He couldn't have handled the two of them at once. It must have been extremely recent, as he had never heard his 'Uncle John' make mention of any women. Though, it had been five months since he'd seen him.

Holmes gestured for him to step inside. "Would you like to come in?"

Jonathan brushed past him and into the sitting room. "This is not a friendly visit Holmes, but I have nowhere else to go," he said coldly, as he looked around the room, "might I have a word?"

"Please," Holmes nodded, again encouraging him to sit.

"I'll stand."

"As you wish."

"Now Holmes, if you were indeed the world's first and foremost consulting detective, hell-bent on exposing the truth and always fighting for justice, why then, did you avoid solving the murder of your own wife? You knew the identity of the villain, Mycroft's file on Jack the Ripper revealed as much. You uncovered that The Prince not only killed my mother, but was also responsible for the murders of Jack the Ripper, based on the letters he wrote to my mother and your findings. Yet even in knowing that, you never brought him to justice. Why? Assuming you conveniently 'disappeared' to attain hard evidence against Albert Victor, or wished to protect me or yourself, when he died in '92, you still did not return for me. In fact, you waited another ten years *and* reestablished connections as a complete stranger." Jonathan's voice began to warble, and he was becoming unsteady in his emotions so he paused, and took a deep breath. "Why... why didn't you come back?"

Holmes folded his arms. "I will answer your questions, one at a time, on the stipulation that you will remove your coat, sit down, and permit me to--"

Jonathan pulled the coat tighter. "I am not yet through! You knew I was investigating all this, didn't you? About Abigail? About my attending Cambridge?"

"You assume too much."

"Then how is it that the moment I discover the truth, the one and only friend I have in the entire world who also knew is murdered? Who would have possibly known that *and* known where I was? Any ideas, Sherlock?!"

Holmes turned and walked towards the armchair by the fireplace. "If you are accusing *me* Jonathan, for heaven's sakes give me a bit more respect. I am not your enemy." He sat in the chair. "I had no idea you were at Cambridge, but congratulations on being accepted at thirteen. I see you inherited the gift of brilliance; splendid. But apparently," he leaned back and laced his fingers together, "you have also mastered the art of deception, as you have evaded us all rather well after leaving Hoxton."

Jonathan snorted.

"I am, however, sorry for the loss of your friend Abigail."

"How, then, did you know she was dead?" Jonathan pointed, but then cried out as the stretching had pulled his sore shoulder.

"Jonathan, you are a raving madman. You have greater observational abilities, so think before you speak and hurt yourself further," Holmes stood. "You mentioned that your one and only friend was murdered, and asked about Abigail. Put the two together. The most successful techniques are often times the most simplistic, my Cambridge student."

Jonathan shuffled his feet, and rubbed his arm. "Then who knew I was investigating the Ripper case? That is the reason Abigail's gone. Even Mycroft didn't."

"Are you sure you could trust her?"

"You are hardly one to question *anyone's* honesty, Henry Stevenson!"

Holmes sighed and faced the fireplace. "He is a dangerous man, Jonathan, with many loyalists. If you indeed feel she was trustworthy, then I believe you. Perhaps she did not disclose anything willingly."

"*Who* is so very dangerous? The King, protecting his tortured son? Is that whom you've been afraid of? People deserve the truth, and I intend to seek justice. I do not agree with you or Mycroft that the villain should remain nameless. If you truly cared a damn, you would help me."

Holmes spun towards Jonathan with a stern expression. It frightened him, so he stepped backwards.

"You want answers and I can give them, but you must first agree to behave like a rational human being. Now, will you please sit?"

"No I will not, and you cannot make me!" Jonathan shouted louder than he intended.

"Are you three, or thirteen Jonathan?"

Jonathan dropped onto the sofa, and ripped off his cap in agitation.

"That is better," Holmes said softly. "I will not help, as I do not condone this, Jonathan. I will not aid in what will be your demise if you pursue this."

Jonathan picked at the hat. "It will be my demise if I do not. They are already trying to kill me. The only chance I have of survival is to reveal the truth." He ripped a loose thread off the hat, then rolled it between his fingers. "And such a man deserves to be exposed, prince or not. If you had seen those letters he gave my mother in college..."

"You found her letter box?"

"I did, because I knew where to look. The entire reason she hid the box, and that she continued the relationship was out of fear, nothing more. I imagine she had every intention of retrieving it and destroying the letters once she perceived the threat was gone but clearly, she never had that chance. Her fear of exposing him for who he was led to her murder, and now, I will not make the same mistake."

"Exposing him will not solve your problems Jonathan, it would only increase them."

"You are wrong, and I would rather go out fighting than become a victim. Because of you and your world of lies and deception, an innocent girl was killed, and friends were forced into silence. Additionally, a murderer was concealed, and his legacy forever protected by his family and the few that knew." He then noticed the framed picture of a woman on Holmes' desk. Based on the photograph that Edith had given him, he knew it was of his mother. He stared at her face. "My mother came to me in a dream and demanded that I finish this and that I find you. I agree with her that there is no turning back."

419

"I think you misinterpreted the dream."

"Hadn't you told Watson that you wished me the chance of a normal life? When did that change?"

"I still wish that, but once you ran away from the Eatons, that became impossible..."

"Do not place the blame on me!" Jonathan stood. "You never should have come back," he moved towards the door. "You have complicated my life beyond what is fair, leaving more puzzles than answers."

"Jonathan, you will have your pieces to complete the puzzle if you will allow me to explain."

"If you will not help me, then I don't want an explanation. What I *do* want, is for you to stay away from me."

Jonathan turned to leave, but Holmes stepped between him and the door. "I know you think me a monster, and that I completely abandoned you," he placed his hands on Jonathan's shoulders, "but that could not be further from the truth."

Jonathan jerked away from him and stepped backwards.

"I understand you are angry..."

"*Angry?* A word has not yet been invented for how I feel, Sherlock Holmes, perhaps make that your next investigation," Jonathan said, shoving Holmes aside and opening the door, "to find a word that sums up years of resentment, sorrow and anguish, and means good night and good bye *for-ever!*"

Before he could reach the staircase, Holmes grabbed him by the arms, pulled him into the room, then slammed the door shut. Jonathan cried out in pain, then held his wounded shoulder as he sat on the sofa's arm with grit teeth, sucking in air.

"Jonathan, listen to me for once, dammit! You do not understand! You have identified the Ripper as the wrong member of the Royal Family. It was *not* Albert Victor."

"From your journal and Mycroft's files I know it was His Royal Highness. He was also at Cambridge when mother was, so who else could it have been?"

"Did I ever say it was a *current* student at Cambridge? Through descriptions, personality traits, and interests, you could not see?"

Jonathan looked at him confused. "What are you saying then?"

"You are correct that Albert Victor attended Trinity, but you are not in that he is the infamous 'Jack' from your mother's past. It was a *previous* student of Trinity, who was involved with your mother."

Jonathan felt his blood drain as the realization hit him, like a royal scepter to the gut.

"Before he was a King, he was a Prince. And while a Prince, he met Scarlett Tennyson whilst visiting his *son,* Albert Victor at Trinity, which was his alma mater. His mother..."

"Was Queen Victoria..." Jonathan said quietly as he collapsed backward onto the sofa. His body felt limp. "So then it was..."

"Not Prince Albert Victor but his father, Albert Edward, who was *then* The Prince of Wales, and is *now* Edward VII. Eddy had as much animation as a tailor's dummy and was about as bright. He had not the wherewithal to enact such doings without being apprehended."

Jonathan managed himself back up, but felt dizzy from the pain. "If you knew, why did you not reveal him? Especially before he became the king of our country?!"

"The dangers at the time were far too great. I was trying to protect you."

"But why not pursue him when you returned? I was assumed to be 'dead'. Are you still afraid?"

"If you target His Majesty Jonathan, he *will* kill you."

"I am not afraid of him."

"Stupidity is not bravery. Do not confuse the two."

Jonathan inched towards the door. "I have nothing and no one to live for, so what would I be losing if I do not succeed?"

"No one to live for?!" Holmes' voice was strained. "If you knew what I gave up to protect you."

"I don't think you care about anyone but yourself. Not unless it is convenient, and beneficial to do so," Jonathan opened the front door. "I wish I had never met you and I hate you. I never want to see you again."

Before Holmes could stop him, Jonathan stumbled down the stairs and out the door in a rage.

CHAPTER 36

LAST HOPE

Now that Holmes had denied Jonathan help, there was only one person left he could try. He walked through the main doors of Scotland Yard and up to the receptionist, who seemed very engrossed in the women's gazette that she was reading.

"Miss Whalley is in a meeting," she said suddenly without looking up. "But you can wait in her office if you wish."

"Thank you," Jonathan nodded. *Ah, I am a regular now.*

He stepped inside Celeste's office then partly closed the door. He surveyed the room's interior then paused to study a framed picture on her desk that he hadn't noticed before. It was of two young girls. One held a tortoiseshell cat, and the other sat in a wooden wagon. As he picked it up to examine it, Celeste rustled through the door wearing a royal blue satin French-fashioned skirt and blouse, with white lace ruffles around her neck. She was cursing, and grumbling under her breath but stopped in the middle of the room when she noticed Jonathan.

"Jonathan, aren't you supposed to be up at Cambridge?"

"Is this photograph of you?"

Celeste nodded. "And your mother. I always loved this picture," she said as she lifted it from his hands. "One of the few I still have of her. Seeing you prompted me to dig it out again."

Jonathan sat in the chair next to her desk with a sigh. "Abigail is dead."

Celeste replaced the frame to her desk, then ran over and closed the door. "My God, what happened?!"

"She was working for Mycroft Holmes, and the King's henchmen had her killed."

"The *King*?"

"*He* was the one who killed my mother, *and* all those women in Whitechapel."

"Why would he kill for his son?"

Jonathan watched her reactions carefully. Was she pretending not to know? "He didn't, he was the one in love with her."

"Oh dear me, King Edward!? Are you absolutely sure?"

Jonathan glowered at her. "Why so surprised, Celeste? Didn't you know she was seeing The Prince of Wales?"

"Whatever are you talking about?"

"I am referring to 'Jack'. She used you as an excuse to meet with him on countless occasions when she lived with Holmes. Surely she had to inform you to cover herself?"

Celeste sat down at her desk in shock. "I... honestly... did not know she was still seeing him after college. And she never once asked me to lie for her." Celeste's eyes began to tear, but she shook it off. "I... thought I was her dearest friend... but she used me." She chuckled sadly, "Maybe I wasn't then."

He was still not convinced. "Then what would you have told Holmes if he asked you about one outing or another? After speaking with you, he would know she had lied..."

"Then perhaps she was hoping to be caught! I know you are suspicious of everyone Jonathan, but I had hoped to be the one person you *would* trust."

Jonathan felt like an ass. "I am sorry, I assumed you knew."

"I should explain one thing, Jonathan. Holmes and I had such strong contempt for one another that we positively *never* spoke. Were he to happen upon me, and ask how an evening or afternoon was, I would have ignored him. Knowing that, she would never have need to explain to me in advance, anything she *pretended* to have done with me."

Jonathan sighed. "A private woman indeed."

"But Jonathan, Edward was already married to Alexandra when your mother and I were in school."

"I am certain you have heard what a philandering letch his Majesty has always been, so that part is not all that exceptional."

"Well, that certainly explains why Holmes refused knighthood. A paltry consolation indeed," Celeste shook her head. "What do you plan to do?"

"Go after him. His men have already tried to come for me once, and I barely escaped." Jonathan sat down and howled as his shoulder hit the back of the chair.

"Are you well?" Celeste asked, concerned.

He took off his coat, turned around, and lifted his shirt to show her the horrific gunshot wound. "When the King's men came to fetch me for His Majesty, I bolted."

"Dear Lord! Is the bullet still in you?"

Jonathan nodded.

Celeste grabbed her beaded Dorothy bag from her desk and her black velvet outing coat from the back of her chair, then took Jonathan's hand. "Come, I know a good doctor who will help you."

"His name is not Watson, is it?"

"You are in no position to be snide, boy," she helped him to his feet. "He is a friend at Charing Cross Hospital. He used to help with the scoundrels we brought in whilst he was still in training."

As they were leaving the office, Jonathan bumped into Mr. Ball, the Shoreditch Empire's owner. He was handcuffed, and in the custody of another officer.

"Mr. Ball?" Jonathan asked stunned.

Mr. Ball grunted. "Accusing me of murder, they is."

"Of who?"

"Abigail, saying I killed 'er because she broke 'er contract with me."

"That is impossible, she wasn't even working for you anymore."

"I know it, and I 'ave the documents she signed as proof, so I'll be fine lad. Besides, I was at the 'all the night before she was found up north. These bobbies," he shook his head. "I am sorry though, for you. Cannot imagine what you must be goin' through."

"Mr. Ball, may I ask you a question? How *did* Abigail manage out of her contract with you?"

Mr. Ball looked confused. "Didn't she tell you? The only condition of letting 'er break the contract early was if she were gettin' married. I assumed it was to you."

Jonathan gulped, and suddenly felt sick.

"I could 'ave sworn at the Christmas party..."

"You are a good man," Jonathan patted him on the shoulder, "and I am sure you'll be fine. Now if you will excuse me..."

He ran from the building and stopped a few hundred feet outside then fell to the ground, holding his chest. It had never hurt so much, and he had never missed Abigail more. He closed his eyes, then pounded his fist into the cobblestone. Just as Holmes hadn't seen Scarlett, and had been completely oblivious to the secrets and deep-seated anguish she had kept hidden, *he* hadn't seen Abigail, and the tortured heart she had been concealing. Her words, 'you are more like your father than you'd like to admit' now echoed in his mind.

Celeste caught up to him, out of breath. "What was all that about?"

"Abigail," he began to hyperventilate, "she.... she had wanted to marry me, or... told someone she did. Why would she do that?!"

Celeste squatted next to him, removed his hat, then stroked his hair. "Because I am sure she did. From what you told me, taking a job

427

with Mycroft, telling you to find your past, risking her life...she loved you, Jonathan."

Jonathan shifted away from her, and rested his head on the cobblestone. "We were friends, how was I to know.... how could I be so stupid!?"

"Men seem to have such a difficult time interpreting women. Do not judge yourself too harshly."

"Why cannot women just say what is on their minds? What is wrong with all of you?"

Celeste replaced his hat, and attempted to pry him from the ground. "We are different creatures, men and women, you will learn that as you get older. I know this news is upsetting, but we really must get you to a doctor and out of the open," she looked around nervously.

"But I am younger than she was," he said with a sniff, as she hailed a cab.

"Age is less of a factor than you think, Jonathan. You cannot control whom you love."

Dr. Mark Mathis at Charing Cross was a younger physician in his mid thirties, with light brown hair, a thin boyish face, and a slender physique underneath his white doctor's coat. He greeted Celeste with a hug, then shook Jonathan's hand who was now standing hunched over, as the pain was too great for him to be positioned otherwise.

"Now, what have we here?" Dr. Mathis asked, as he adjusted his amber framed glasses.

428

"The son of a very good friend," Celeste explained, "he has been badly wounded. Can you help him?"

"Of course, Miss Whalley, I've always the time to help you."

The two of them shared a moment as their eyes locked. Jonathan noticed the spark and for the first time, he observed Celeste in a different manner. Not just as his mother's friend, but as a vulnerable woman who also kept herself deeply hidden. With her blue eyes, long neck, and porcelain face, she was actually quite beautiful. He would have analyzed it further but at the moment, he was more concerned about the bullet in his shoulder.

"I was shot," Jonathan interrupted, pulling up his shirt and turning around.

"Dear me!" Dr. Mathis gasped. "What--."

"I am sorry, Mark," Celeste said quickly, touching his arm, "but we cannot discuss it."

"Ah, one of those. Understood 'Inspector' Whalley," he winked. "I'll have a look at him immediately."

Jonathan squeezed his eyes shut, and bit down on the cloth rag as the doctor extracted the bullet with a tiny pair of metal tongs. Though the pain was excruciating, only a single tear rolled down Jonathan's face.

"You certainly are a brave lad," Dr. Mathis praised. "What is your name, son?"

"Jonathan."

"Well Jonathan, it is not as bad as it could have been." He dabbed a wet cloth on Jonathan's shoulder. "I am applying some peroxide to prevent infection."

It stung like a rug burn magnified by ten.

"Your parents will have to change this bandage twice a day. Now, who *are* your parents?" he asked, as he wrapped Jonathan's shoulder.

"I... don't believe you know them, sir."

Dr. Mathis nodded. "Not to worry, I have long ago learned to not ask many questions of someone brought in by Miss Whalley."

Jonathan struggled with his shirt. "Why did you say 'inspector' the way you did?"

The doctor chuckled as he helped Jonathan button up the front. "She is not 'truly' an inspector by title, as women are not allowed. She is still regarded as a secretary. Most women would be appalled by such underhanded dealings, but Celeste, well, she is a different and special kind of woman," he patted Jonathan's head. "That should do you, Jonathan. Don't do too much running about for a spell, eh?"

"Thank you, Dr. Mathis."

Jonathan sat on Celeste's sofa and kicked his legs thoughtfully as he drank a cup of water. "Celeste, have you ever dined with Dr. Mathis?"

"Pardon?" Celeste asked, as she came into the sitting room carrying a stack of mail.

430

"I sensed a closeness between you. Has he ever asked you to tea?"

"He is simply a friend, Jonathan, nothing more," she said, as she separated out the bills and put them in a pile on her writing desk.

"Then you have a very *unique* friendship."

"Do not overanalyze everything like your father."

Jonathan sat forward, and put down his cup. "Come now, in the same sense that Abigail was a *friend?* Honestly, a five-year-old could have observed it. You don't really enjoy being alone, do you? Why not pursue a..."

Celeste slammed down the rest of the mail, causing a few envelopes to fall to the ground. "Because he is married!"

"I am... I am sorry," he gulped.

"And quite frankly, I am fine with my life as it is."

Jonathan thought otherwise, but decided it was best to keep his mouth shut. He needed her, and still felt terrible from the bullet wound.

Celeste looked over at him, and her face softened. "You look tired. Here, come lie down," she led him to her bedroom.

He sat on the bed and sank into the fluffy, white lace quilt. He had never felt anything so soft, and it was making him drowsy.

Celeste lifted the quilt, and helped him crawl underneath. "I think it is your bedtime, young man; you've had quite the day. May I get you anything?"

He yawned and shook his head, then rested down on the satin pillow and closed his eyes. He thought he felt Celeste kiss him on the forehead before she walked out the door. He smiled. For the first the time in a year he felt secure, comforted, and loved.

The next morning, Celeste came in carrying a grey boy's suit, a royal blue waistcoat, and black boots. "I do hope this will fit as I had to guess on the suit, but I grabbed one of your shoes and took it with me. Those at least should be correct."

Jonathan frowned. He was becoming attached to Celeste and that frightened him, as anyone he'd ever cared about had eventually been taken away from him. Should he pull back, or just enjoy this for as long as it could last? Not sure of the answer, he thought of someone he could ask. "Celeste, do you know where my mother is buried? I should like to pay my respects."

"She's at Highgate Cemetery. I will take you there."

"I'd... like to go alone if you don't mind."

"It is not safe for you."

"Then, I'll go in disguise. Have you any black shoe polish and brown makeup?"

CHAPTER 37

HIGHGATE CEMETERY

Once Jonathan arrived at Highgate Hill, he walked the ten minutes through Waterlow Park to the cemetery and made his way through the main entrance to Egyptian Avenue, and passed through the stone gates. Two huge obelisks, decorated with papyrus and lotus leaves, dominated the avenue on either side.

On the other end of a long row of tombs, there was a small clearing studded with Gothic monuments and sculptures that were overgrown with ivy. As he walked through the clearing he felt a slight chill, and heard leaves rustle as a gust of wind swept by, and knocked off his hat. He turned, sensing something, but found nothing was there. "Jonathan, you are being paranoid."

As he threaded his way through the massive oak trees, he paused when he came upon an ivory angel sitting atop a gravestone under a smaller cedar tree. The angel had a nameplate, and engraved in the pedestal underneath its feet it read, 'Archangel Gabriel'. Curious, Jonathan knelt down on the grass, and brushed aside a branch of ivy to read the inscription on the stone.

Scarlett Tennyson

"The woman who taught me to love, and helped me to live." -S. H.

He smiled, then rubbed the stone fondly.

"Mum, what should I do? Should I stay with Celeste? I am terribly afraid of losing her too, but I do not know if..."

433

The sound of footsteps crunched through dead branches not far away. Jonathan jumped up and hid behind a thick oak tree, then peered around the corner in direction of the noise.

A short, balding man with a bouquet of red roses walked towards his mother's grave, then carefully placed the flowers on the ground beneath it, muttering something inaudible.

"Why are you putting roses on Scarlett's grave?" Jonathan asked from behind the tree.

The man spun around. "What?"

Jonathan stepped from behind the tree. "Who are you?"

"I am Jamison, who in the bloody hell are you?"

"Her *son!*" he said, forgetting to be careful. "Now I demand to know why you are here."

Two men in police uniforms emerged from the shadows of a mausoleum as the man Jamison quickly scurried away. "We've been waiting for you, Jonathan," the smaller of the two said, who sported a carroty-coloured moustache. "Think we might 'ave some trouble 'ere," he pounded a beat stick into his palm.

"The King sent you, did he? Dirty Bertie cannot do his own crooked work?"

The two men looked at each other puzzled. "The King?" the larger man laughed, "'e's got nothin' to do with this."

"Who *are* you working for then? And how did you know I would be here?"

The larger man grinned, revealing a row of rotted, and chipped teeth. "The Guv'nor done told us..."

"You would do best to mind yer own business," the other man interrupted, as he tapped his pocket. "Just know your little girlfriend tipped 'im off as to what you was about."

"Tipped who off?"

"The Guv'nor she was workin' for."

"I believe you are mistaken sir, Mycroft would never..."

"Ain't never heard that bloke's name," the taller 'policeman' shrugged. "Oh... you didn't know 'er *other* Guv'nor..."

"What?"

"You see, 'er other owner, what paid 'er good, is in tight with the King. Once she told Mr. Esher who you was, it was our job to find you."

Jonathan now wondered if Holmes had been right about trusting Abigail, but he didn't want to believe that she had willingly betrayed him. "I don't understand."

"She was his mollisher, toffer, left handed wife, Dollymop, Ladybird, wife in watercolours..."

Jonathan closed his eyes and swallowed as he leaned on the tree for support. Now, everything made sense. The extra money, her queer attitude over the telephone, her 'appointment', the longer hours... he felt nauseous.

"And Esher don't like sharing much..." the taller man grinned, elbowing his partner.

Jonathan snapped his eyes open. "Abigail and I were not 'involved', if that is what you are implying."

"No matter, she knew more than she shoulda. I am sure you saw 'ow she was 'andled. Nobbled 'er blind, slit 'er throat, took 'er..."

"Enough!" Jonathan roared, as he pulled his revolver from his coat pocket and aimed it at the two men. "His Majesty's *friend* sent you then, did he? Tell *Esher* that Abigail meant nothing to me," he cocked the gun. "I... I am actually glad she's gone, the harlot!" he sniffed. In his heart, he didn't mean it, but he was devastated and didn't know how else to cope without breaking down.

Jonathan was suddenly assaulted from behind and pushed to the ground, which caused the gun to fire off. Jamison, having been the attacker, moved off to the side as the shorter man dove at Jonathan and pinned him to the ground. They wrestled in the frosted grass as Jonathan attempted to keep the gun out of the man's reach.

"Tom, some 'elp 'ere!" the short man shouted to his companion.

The taller 'policeman' then rushed at the pair and kicked the derringer out of Jonathan's right-hand arm. His assailant then rolled away to retrieve it, but not before whacking the boy smartly in the ribs, knocking the wind of out him. Jonathan gasped for air.

Tall Tom laughed maliciously, cracked his knuckles, then lifted Jonathan by the hair and smashed him in the face. Jonathan moaned as he fell backward and blood dripped down his nose. Tom moved to grab him again, but Jonathan darted to the side and sprang up on his feet.

Tom snapped a jackknife from his pocket with a growl. "You will be comin' with us now, young 'olmes."

"Not in your life," Jonathan managed, as he wiped his bloodied nose with his hand and looked around for a means of escape. A wrought iron gate was attached to one of the mausoleums so he sprinted towards it, leapt up, and climbed atop it to reach the rooftop with the two men fast on his heels. They missed him by a foot as he scrambled up to the roof and ran across, jumping from one building to another to keep as much distance as he could between him and the men on the ground.

"Marcus, 'e's getting away!" Tom shouted.

Marcus, the fat officer, fired a shot from Jonathan's gun, but missed. *One bullet left,* Jonathan thought. He looked up ahead and saw an oak tree. He tore across the roof of a massive stone building then flung himself onto one of the branches of the tree. He hid behind the trunk on the other side, and squatted down on one of the branches that was partially covered by leaves.

Trapped in a tree. Brilliant Jonathan. The bandages that covered his shoulder were becoming loose, and shifted uncomfortably underneath his new shirt. Now what?

A thick gnarled vine had wrapped itself around the tree's trunk, and Jonathan gave it a slight tug. It seemed sturdy.

"Where'd 'e go?" he heard Tom ask Marcus as they tromped through the grass beneath him. As the men came closer, Jonathan grabbed the vine, swung down on top of Marcus, and knocked the gun from his hand. He pushed himself to a standing position, albeit with some difficulty, and raised his fists. His chest hurt, and he felt dizzy, but he had to appear strong. "Come on then!"

Without warning, Tom rushed at Jonathan with the jackknife and inflicted a wound across Jonathan's chest. As Jonathan paused to hold his chest in agony, Tom punched him across the face with a force that caused him to lose his balance. He fell back with a cry, and smacked his skull on a tree stump. His head spun and he felt paralyzed, as the ground was cold and numbing. His forehead throbbed and his eyes struggled to stay open. His hands shook as he fought to move them, and as he touched his face, he felt a warm thick liquid covering his cheeks. Blood.

He looked up to see Tom towering over him like a Titan. He was barely in focus as Jonathan watched him aim the gun at his head.

"We was told if you gave us any trouble," Tom said, cocking the trigger, "it was up to our discretion to do what we fancied."

Jonathan felt like a wounded bull at the hands of a matador. *So this is how it ends*, he wept sadly. *I am so sorry, mum, I tried.* He wished he could have seen Celeste one more time. Gabriel too. Squeezing his eyes shut, Jonathan took a deep breath and held it, knowing it would be his last.

"Halt!" asserted a voice from the shadows, "I believe you should let the boy be."

Jonathan's eyes flickered open. He craned his neck to see who it was, and could barely make out the person's outline.

Tom took a few steps towards the figure. "And just who are you to get involved? This don't concern you."

"On the contrary. Anything involving this boy *does* concern me. Very much so."

Jonathan blinked as the figure became recognizable. "Holmes?"

"My good sir," Sherlock Holmes began, as he stepped closer and placed himself between the boy on the ground the monster attacking him, "we can settle this situation in one of two ways. Either you leave the boy be and go about your business, or we can resolve the matter with fists, which is most un-gentlemanly and base. Though I would surmise your preference to be the latter, the choice is entirely yours."

The two men snickered, then laughed as if they'd been threatened by a three-year-old girl.

"Blimey! You takin' on both of us?" Tom asked.

"You are not aware of whom you are dealing with, gentlemen," Holmes warned. "You have the peculiarity of a great many men in your profession who think numbers outweigh intelligence. And might I remind you of the illegality of impersonating a member of the police force?"

"I think you're in for a bit of trouble yerself, 'good sir', for meddling!" Tom snarled, punching his fist into his hand.

Holmes removed his coat, and tossed it over a gravestone. "If that is your choice, then I will oblige..."

Tom went after Holmes, then Holmes attacked him with the flat end of his hand, cross-hit him under the jaw, and sent him falling to the ground. Before Jonathan could see anything more, he lost consciousness, and the blurred figures slowly faded from vision.

CHAPTER 38

I THOUGHT I KNEW YOU

Jonathan awoke to someone dabbing at his forehead. It stung, so he winced.

"Ow! Leave off!" he waved Holmes away. "Can't you let me alone and stop following me?"

"Is that any way to thank me?" Holmes asked, as he sat back on the sofa. "Did I not tell you he would try to have you killed?"

"Did *I* not tell you, I didn't care? You've a lot of nerve!"

Holmes put down the wet cloth, which was stained with red. "For saving your life?"

Jonathan sighed and looked away. "Have you been following me all this time?"

"Not I, but I have many friends, Jonathan, in both high *and* low places. Someone who was very happy to hear you were alive, after thinking he'd seen a ghost at a Christmas party, has been my eyes."

Wiggins. I should have known.

"Now then, since I finally have you in a position where you are not at liberty to storm out, or run off to Cambridge, or sneak out the window..."

"Sneak out the window?" Jonathan shifted his body towards the back of the sofa, "How did you know... oh," he frowned, "from Watson's notebook missing."

"No, from the blonde hair you left by the windowsill, Mrs. Parker."

Jonathan cursed himself. Abigail and he had tried so hard to be careful with the fake letter and the break-in but apparently, Holmes had known the entire time.

"I would like to ask you..." Holmes sat forward, "how did you know I had a journal?"

"Abigail found it, and that is how I know everything."

"Indeed. Everything?"

Jonathan rolled his eyes. "Everything on every page, yes!"

"*Every* page? Are you sure?"

"Yes! Christ, Holmes! Well... there was one page missing, so *technically* not every page."

Holmes motioned to a cigar case on the second shelf of the glass cabinet against the wall.

"If you are able, grab that cigar case please."

Not wanting to argue, Jonathan weakly climbed off the sofa and walked over towards the cabinet. He opened the glass door, removed the box, then flipped open the lid. "And? What, do you want a smoke?"

"Look closer," Holmes nodded.

441

Jonathan examined the box. There were several old, cheap looking cigars inside, but as shallow as it appeared from the inside, the bottom extended far deeper than that of the average half-centimetre thickness of most cigar boxes. Jonathan removed the cigars and placed them on the shelf, them knocked on the box bottom. It appeared hollow. "Huh." He sandwiched his fingernail between the supposed bottom and the side, and found that it was removable.

In the true bottom of the box, there was a diamond ring with three diamonds in the centre surrounded by rubies, a silver locket, and a folded up, yellowed piece of paper. Jonathan rubbed the gold band of the ring, then picked up the locket and turned it over, fairly certain of what it was. His face softened.

"*S.T., avec affection, S. H.,*" he read aloud. "This is my mother's locket. You gave it to her on her birthday."

Holmes nodded.

Jonathan then picked up the worn piece of paper. "What is this?"

Holmes stood, walked to the mantle, and grabbed an amber stemmed pipe from the coal scuttle. "The missing page you were aware of," he said, filling the pipe with shag from the Persian slipper.

Jonathan put the box on the table, and carefully unfolded the letter as Holmes stood between the parted blinds of the bay window and lit his pipe, looking out onto the street below.

Jonathan began to read, then sat on the sofa as goose bumps covered his arms. He was suddenly filled with self-loathing.

~ ~

13th February 1891

"I have resolved to give up my practice of private detecting. My life with my wife and child is far more important. I desire a predictable work schedule so that I may have a more meaningful and scheduled existence with them. I shall take Jonathan for an outing this evening to discern the proper dialogue for revealing my plan to Scarlett.

I will now finally be honest about everything. How wonderful it will be to introduce Scarlett as my wife and no longer have to hide her, out of fear for her safety. To hear her addressed as Mrs. Holmes as she should have been long ago will bring me much joy, as will be saying of Jonathan, 'that enchanting and brilliant young boy is my son'.

This shall be my St. Valentine's Day gift to her, and unlike flowers that will fade in time, this gift will be the one that lasts forever. I hope she will be as excited for this news as I.

~ ~

"You wrote this before that night?" Jonathan asked, already knowing the answer.

Holmes nodded.

Jonathan looked at the floor, ashamed. A vision suddenly flashed through his mind as an entirely different rug now lay on the ground and he heard screaming. He looked up to see a beautiful, dark haired young woman in an aquamarine evening dress lying soaked in blood on the floorboards. A man was crouched over her, clutching her tightly in his arms, sobbing. It was Holmes. He looked over at Jonathan... then they were gone.

Re-folding the paper, Jonathan put it on the side table. He had never felt so terrible. As he watched Holmes standing by the window he was filled with regret. That was his father, but he had treated him like an adversary. He leaned his elbows on his knees, and noticed his reflection in the back of the small silver locket. With his shoe-polished black hair, thin physique, and worn expression, he was exactly the younger version of Holmes.

"But you are Sherlock Holmes," Jonathan sniffed softly, "the world's greatest detective. You could not simply quit."

Holmes slowly turned and a cloud of smoke followed him. "But I was not. I was not the Holmes that everyone had wanted and needed. I had grown into a different person entirely. I wanted a new life with your mother. One that would allow me to be a true husband to her and father to you, as I felt I hadn't been."

"And you were to finally tell everyone?"

Holmes blew smoke through his nostrils and nodded.

"Why did you tear out this page?"

"Because it was something that could never be."

Holmes picked up the piece of paper from the side table, carefully placed it back in the cigar box with the locket, and returned it to the shelf. "Part of me died with her that night," he said, as he rubbed his temples and closed his eyes. "If I hadn't left her alone..."

"You cannot blame yourself, Holmes--"

"But I do. Every day. And with the added threat of The Prince, I knew that I could never safely have a life with you, which is why I had no choice but to let you go."

"He wanted to kill me too?"

"No, he wanted something that would have been a far worse torture. When I began to build a case against His Majesty; His 'Royal Highness' at the time; he threatened to take you away from me and claim you as his own."

Jonathan was speechless.

"Yet even when I desisted in the investigation he had made up his mind to take you. Apparently, he'd long ago expressed interest in having children with your mother so in his warped and twisted mind, he somehow felt entitled. When I brought to his attention that I had witnesses who could testify you were my son, he quickly found ways to eliminate the more verifiable ones.

"I then had but Celeste, Watson, and Mrs. Hudson to vouch for you, but none of them had been there for the birth. Who would the court believe? The few of us, or His Majesty with his hired entourage of 'bystanders'? I knew then that the only way to save you from becoming a Prince of England, the son to a man who murdered your mother, was to arrange for your disappearance. Only Watson was allowed the truth, as he had to protect you until Francis could take you from his custody."

"Why did you tell him you never wanted to see me?"

Holmes puffed thoughtfully, appearing to relive the entire tragedy. "Had any one of His Majesty's allies seen me with a small boy, it would have immediately aroused suspicion, Jonathan. It was the most difficult decision I ever had to made."

445

"Oh Holmes, I am so sorry!" Jonathan began to cry, "how awful I have been to you!" He then curled forward, embarrassed by his emotional outburst.

Holmes set his pipe on the mantle, then sat down next to him and put a hand on his shoulder.

"Jonathan I..."

Jonathan sniffed loudly, then jumped onto Holmes, wrapping his arms around him as tears continued to flow down his already damp face. Everything he had been missing in life, everything that hadn't made sense now finally did, and he could see Holmes for who he truly was; someone who loved him, and someone who had wanted to do the best for his family, even if it meant possibly never seeing them again. It was worth everything Jonathan had gone through to embrace his father with love, this one time.

Holmes lifted Jonathan's chin with a smile. "With the Eatons, you had a chance at a normal life, and one that I could still somehow, be a part of."

Jonathan inhaled deeply. "You mean, as Stevenson?"

Holmes' eyes sparkled. "Not just as Stevenson, Jonathan." He pulled a handkerchief from his jacket pocket, and wiped Jonathan's eyes. "I found ways to be in touch with you, every step of the way. Do you remember your tutor, Professor Sherwood in Downe?"

"Yes?"

Holmes patted Jonathan's knee. "You were always my brightest pupil."

"*You* were Professor Sherwood!?"

Holmes nodded. "Indeed. I was able to see you every day during the week. I had to take what precious hours I could to see you without being obvious. If you recall, you also had a fencing instructor, Boucher, and a tailor, Geoffrey. You were as quick a study with a sword as your mother, with exceptional form and coordination. There were several others, little characters I would pull together, but it was always to see you. It was more difficult to hide my feelings as Stevenson for you were older then, and seeing you practically every day... well, I simply wanted so much to be part of every aspect of your life. I became careless, and let my attachment show, which was why Francis sent me away. I was too close to you, beyond what was appropriate, he said."

Jonathan leaned against Holmes' shoulder. "I cannot apologize enough for how I treated you." He sat up. "Yet, even after all the atrocious things I said, you came back for me last night. Why?"

Holmes laughed. "Words cannot destroy a father's love for his son. That is, if I may call you that."

Jonathan nodded, and hung his head. "Yes of course, you are my.... my... father, after all. Part of me always hoped that you cared."

Holmes rubbed Jonathan's right shoulder fondly. "You did not have the knowledge base necessary to make an accurate appraisal of the situation, and neither did I, apparently, about The Prince. Now how did you find the trinket box?"

Jonathan looked across the room at the picture of his mother on the edge of the desk. She appeared to be smiling at him, as if happy for their reunion. He smiled back, and proceeded to tell Holmes where he found it, what was inside, and the conclusions he made.

447

"I would have surmised the same," Holmes nodded, taking it in. "I feel now as though I knew her not at all, and was never truly let in."

"What *do* you remember of her?"

Holmes whimsically stared at her picture. "I remember how every morning she awoke with a smile. I remember how soft her hair was, how smooth her skin, and how every moment with her was precious. Oh, what a woman, Jonathan! I would have gladly given my life for hers. I felt very fortunate to have her love."

"Then, if she was so wonderful, she deserves to be avenged."

"Revenge is sweet, but has short-lived satisfaction." Holmes placed both hands on Jonathan's shoulders. "However, I know you are a very determined young boy and I presume that there is little I can do to dissuade you," he rose from the sofa, "but you must be very careful," he warned as he relit his pipe, "for now that he has been alerted to your being alive, I am certain he is making every effort to track you. The King has many spies; how else did he know your mother's and my every move? To avoid suspicion, on my part particularly, he would have needed a much larger ensemble of loyalists. The flower girl on the street, the barman in the pub, the cabbie of the hansom you hail," Holmes paused, as if reading Jonathan's thoughts, "even, the girl *you* befriended."

Jonathan frowned, remembering the conversation in the cemetery. "Perhaps you were right. Apparently, Abigail was involved in some sordid affair with a man named Esher."

"Lord Esher?" Holmes asked concerned.

"I suppose? They did not say, except that he was 'in good with the King."

"Hmm..." Holmes puffed thoughtfully, "he is the advisor to His Majesty. A very dangerous, and unscrupulous man. I doubt that any involvement your Abigail had with him was enacted upon freely, as I do not know many who trust him. He hardly seems to know what is important or moral from what is not, which is why His Majesty relies so heavily on his counsel. They are creatures of the same standards."

Jonathan stood, then began to pace the room. "As he is a Lord, is Esher a member of the Diogenes Club? I know Mycroft tends to consort with such high socialites." He looked over and saw Holmes grinning. "What?"

Holmes shook his head. "As Mycroft is chairman of the board of governors, he would not allow such a man to be a member. Oh, and well done for giving me at least one satisfaction concerning my brother."

"Which is?"

Holmes jumped to his desk, slid open the top drawer, and ripped out a piece of paper. "For the first time in my life, you found an instance in which Mycroft had guessed incorrectly." He held up the page. Yesterday's date had been hastily written across the top, and it read 'Mycroft was wrong!' in big red letters. "He is not so very perfect, after all," he slipped the paper back into the desk.

"About Albert Victor being Jack the Ripper?"

"Indeed. He was able to surmise that your mother had a previous involvement with a member of the Royal Family but as I refused him specifics, he created his own theories. In opposition to my silence, he declined to reveal his assumptions. I was happy to hear he was wrong."

"But Lord Esher --"

"Do not even contemplate going after him. I know you are angry about Abigail but you must pick and choose your battles, for you cannot win all of them. You must be more vigilant if you wish to continue with this. Your life may seem insignificant to you, but there are those who love you dearly."

"I do not doubt that now," Jonathan nodded.

"Where will you stay, meantime? You have seen the dangers of being alone."

"With Celeste." Jonathan's eyes then went wide. "Dear God!" he leapt off the sofa, "she must be worried sick; I never came home last night! I must leave immediately!" He looked down and just now noticed that his new suit trousers were grass-stained and muddy, and his once shiny black shoes were dulled and caked with dried mud. "And, she will be properly angry with me for ruining my clothes."

Holmes' face fell. "Then, give her my best?"

Jonathan coughed on a suppressed laugh.

"I do mean that Jonathan. I have forgiven her over the years, though I do not imagine her opinion of me ever changing. She never approved of me, not from our first encounter."

"She doesn't hate you," Jonathan turned to leave, "I just don't think you ever gave each other the occasion to try and be friendly."

"Perhaps not, and Jonathan?" Holmes followed after him, "I do not feel comfortable with you travelling to Mercer Street alone, even with Wiggins trailing you and especially in your condition."

"But--"

"You should go in disguise, for your safety and for hers. Your mother would occasionally don a man's suit at times, therefore..."

Jonathan scrunched up his face. "I should dress as a woman?!"

Holmes laughed. "That *would* be the least obvious."

Jonathan sighed. "Bloody hell." He wasn't entirely in favour of the idea, but Holmes had a point.

Holmes left the room then returned with a long black velvet coat, a light pink tea dress, a hatbox, and a blonde wig. "Throw it on over," Holmes suggested, as he rested the articles on the chair.

"Mum's?" Jonathan asked, as he slipped the dress over his head. "This is absolutely absurd," he muttered through the cloth, as his head was stuck in the arm of the dress.

"Indeed," he heard Holmes say, as he rescued Jonathan from the clutches of the dress's arm, "and you look darling."

Once Jonathan had been properly fitted into the entire outfit, Holmes embraced him and handed him the hatbox. "Please be safe."

Jonathan questioningly held up the box. "Why do I need this?"

"Keep the wig in one piece, please," Holmes winked.

CHAPTER 39

FORMULATING A PLAN

"Hello?" Celeste said, as she opened the door with bloodshot eyes. "Who are you, and what do you want?" she asked the female version of Jonathan. She clearly hadn't slept as she was wearing her biscuit-coloured taffeta gown trimmed with pale blue from yesterday, and it was as wrinkled and disheveled as she was.

Jonathan brushed the wig's blonde strands of hair from his eyes. "I am sorry, Celeste, but I was detained."

"Jonathan!?" Celeste's clenched her teeth and looked as though she would slap him, but then she wrapped her arms around his neck and hugged him tightly. "Where have you been?" she began to cry, "I was out all night looking for you! And why are you dressed as a woman?" she asked, as she pulled him inside and closed the door.

Jonathan proceeded to chronicle the previous night up to the following morning, explaining how he was fairly unconscious until recently.

Celeste dropped to the sofa in dismay. "Holmes was going to quit?"

Jonathan nodded, then took off the cloak and wig and made a face as he felt his matted hair. "He also said to give you his best."

Celeste snorted.

"He meant it," Jonathan perched next to her. He reached for the hatbox to replace the blond wig inside, but when he pulled off the lid there was a small stuffed brown bear inside, with a blue ribbon around its neck. "Hello, what's this?" he picked it up.

Celeste looked over with surprise. "Where did you get that bear?"

Jonathan shrugged. "Holmes, apparently. I suppose it is mine?"

"It *is* yours, I gave it to you!" Celeste grabbed the bear from his hands, and inspected it. "He kept it? All these years, he's kept it?"

Jonathan pulled the bear from Celeste's fingers and moved aside the blue ribbon around its neck. Some of the stitching in the back had come undone. Puzzled, he examined the fur along the neck seam with his finger, and touched upon the smooth edge of a rolled-up piece of paper buried inside. He dug through the bear's neck to pull it out, then began to read the page with a smile. *You knew I'd find this, didn't you?*

Celeste looked over his shoulder. "What is that?"

He handed her the note. "Something you should read."

~ ~

I had gathered the last bits of evidence to condemn The Prince, including the Naval log books that proved he was in London on the dates he claimed to be at sea with his son George. I had him for sure, but then, I received a telegram from the palace. His Royal Highness wished to see me. I would rather have accepted a warrant for my arrest, or the parcel of cloth sent to George Vicars in Eyam during that fateful August but as it was a formal invitation, I could not refuse. He knew I was attempting to trap him.

I was to bring every last shred of evidence, and burn it before him. If I did not, my son would be taken from me. What choice had I? To lose Jonathan as well? I did as he instructed, and after destroying the proof I had so desperately struggled to obtain, The Prince confessed that over the course of the previous night he had decided to take Jonathan regardless, but now, to claim him as his own. He had already reached an accord with Alexandra, and she would accept a bastard child of his in exchange for increased influence in his court.

I reminded him that there was a doctor and midwife at his birth, as well as other witnesses to verify Jonathan's identity. He invited me to ask them, and I could only imagine the reason for his confidence.

Dr. Daniels had been found dead in his home that morning, and the midwife had mysteriously disappeared. The two people who could have proven Jonathan's parentage were gone. There was only one option. I had to let him go, but *not* into the hands of The Prince of Wales. I therefore needed someone I could trust, to become the parent I could not be.

A friend of Mycroft's from Cambridge was my only hope, and truthfully, with the pain and anguish I am currently experiencing, I *also* need an escape. From London, from Baker St, from the emptiness that now consumes and haunts me. I therefore will make it my life's work to pursue to the death my arch nemesis, Professor James Moriarty.

Perhaps this adventure will kill me, but in truth, I no longer care. Should I return, somehow, someday, I hope to be a part of my son's life. But, will it ever be safe to do so as Sherlock Holmes?

~ ~

Celeste rubbed her face with her hands and let the note flop to her side. "It was wrong of him to hide you, but his heart was in the right place. This will take some getting used to. This... not loathing him and all, for my emotions blow hot and cold on the matter."

Jonathan took the paper, rolled it back up, and replaced it inside the bear's neck. "Everything takes time. Who is George Vicars?"

"George Vicars had a cloth sent to him from London that brought bubonic plague to the village in the 17th century."

"Morbid," Jonathan shivered, as he placed the blonde wig and bear back inside the hatbox, then closed the lid, "but I understand the metaphor."

"What do you plan to do now?" Celeste asked.

"Get out of this dress for one," he lifted it over his head, "but ultimately, seek revenge."

"Dear Lord, *look* at your new suit!" she gasped. "Jonathan, killing the King of England will only get you hung. You do realize that, don't you?"

Jonathan threw the dress to the ground, feeling guilty about the suit. "What does that matter now?"

Celeste picked up the dress, then held it out. "This your mother's?"

Jonathan nodded.

Celeste hugged the garment close. "I know we've only recently become reacquainted, but I do care for you Jonathan, very much so. I do not wish for you to disappear again, this time forever."

456

Jonathan rubbed his neck. "I appreciate the sentiment, but if I can have my revenge, whether it kills me or not, I will at least feel as though I have accomplished some type of overall retribution for those innocents who were murdered."

Celeste gently placed the dress on the sofa, and folded her arms. "I do not view dying as an accomplishment."

"This is my quest, my revenge. I am not asking for help."

Celeste smiled. "Well, you will have it."

Jonathan was shocked. "But, what about your sister?" he pointed to the picture on the wall. "Or any other family members? How would they feel if–"?

"My sister and I are as distant as America and Europe. I haven't spoken to her in years. The rest of my family, well, since I took my current position at the Yard, none of them approved, so they have abandoned me as well. As Scarlett was my dearest friend, it is the least I can do."

"This could be setting forth into a battle we will likely lose."

"I could not live with myself knowing I had let you walk into this alone, no matter what the outcome with His Majesty."

Jonathan hugged her. "Celeste, why are *you* alone? Even my father, who's a very singular creature, has Watson."

"I almost married," she said, as she slid open the top drawer of the secretary desk and pulled out a small round box, "but he died in the Boer War in South Africa." Inside the box was a gold ring with several green gemstones. She carefully lifted it out, examined it fondly, then sighed and replaced it. "I vowed never to love again. I could not endure such pain a second time."

"Before, I would have agreed with you, but I now know that everyone needs someone. It is better to have them, even for a short while, than to never have anyone at all."

"Even if he ends up being a murderer?"

"Did you know the King? Would he remember you from Cambridge?"

"I never met him. He wouldn't know a thing about me beyond my friendship with her, not even what I look like."

"Brilliant."

After a few days of coaxing, Jonathan was able to convince Celeste to write the King a letter, saying that she'd found helpful information on finally solving the murders of Jack the Ripper. But, Scotland Yard required a higher authority's permission to continue. As it was a delicate matter, she wanted a personal audience to ensure that the information did not fall into the wrong hands. Only she and a few others were privy to this information, and she'd like to keep it that way.

As she finished the letter, Jonathan instructed her to give only her last name, and not even her title.

"Also, we will need to find a floor plan of the palace," he said.

To keep a low profile, Jonathan continued his charade as a girl and they searched the London Public Library for blueprints. By using her Scotland Yard credentials, they were allowed access to a locked room where they found James Pennethrone's 1860 floor plan of Buckingham Palace. They hoped that proved recent enough for their purposes. Jonathan took meticulous notes on room locations, names, exits and entrances, and overall dimensions.

Afterwards, they walked down The Strand to find sustenance. As they stepped through the doors of Simpson's restaurant, Jonathan wondered if Celeste knew the historical significance of the location, or if she had just picked it on a whim. If she did not know that Simpson's was where Holmes had taken Scarlett on their engagement night, he certainly didn't plan on telling her.

He glanced across the street, and several pairs of eyes seemed to be following them as they entered the restaurant. A chill ran down his spine. He adjusted the blonde wig, took a deep breath, then hovered closer to Celeste as he took her hand.

Once they were seated in one of the dark wood booths in the back, Jonathan relaxed. He gave the dining room a quick scan and everything seemed normal, everything except, an elderly lady with a pooch on her lap who was feeding the dog small bits of food from her plate.

Jonathan waited until the server had taken their order, then whispered the plot he had been formulating to Celeste. He would dress as a servant boy, enter through the servant's entrance, and once inside the kitchen area, find a way to the stairs and up to a guest room. From there, he could scale the outside wall up to the roof, then lower the rope and slide down to the balcony of the Green Room, directly outside the

Throne Room. Most likely, Celeste would have her audience in there, so she would need to ensure that the door was somehow left open for him.

Celeste grabbed a roll from the wire basket in the middle of the table, and ripped it in half. "He might still be looking for you. Therefore, I think you should continue as a girl."

Jonathan snatched up the other half of the roll, leaving his napkin on the table, and grabbed up a knife to swipe a pat of butter from the dish. "You are correct," he buttered the roll, "then I will play it up as best I can."

"Your napkin belongs on your lap, young lady," Celeste said with a grin.

Jonathan groaned then ripped it off the table and threw it on his lap.

"You must also be open to the chance that he may not respond. Then what?"

Not really having an answer, Jonathan bit into his roll.

CHAPTER 40

AN AUDIENCE

"Miss Whalley," called one of the Yard's policemen, as he entered Celeste's office, "you have a telegram." He was in his late twenties with a ruddy complexion, and was rather heavy set for his short height. He reminded Jonathan of a potato. He was wearing one of the newer single-breasted uniforms of blue serge with the five white Victoria Crown buttons down front and two outside pockets, each with a smaller version of the same button. A pity it didn't fit him better.

"Oh? How interesting," Celeste feigned surprise, as he handed her the envelope.

"It just arrived for you. Oh, hello there little girl!" the man waved to Jonathan.

Jonathan was seated on the floor in the pink tea dress surrounded by a sea of folders and papers. He smiled politely, but then rolled his eyes the moment the officer looked away. 'Who is that?' the policeman mouthed to Celeste.

"A friend of mine had to travel out of town unexpectedly. She's just with me temporarily," Celeste answered sweetly. "That will be all, Reginald," Celeste nodded.

"Of course," he bowed, turning to exit. "Oh, and Miss Whalley," he spun back around, "have you heard from that Damer Dawson woman again? One looking for a secretary position?"

461

"Yes. But I surmise she's really only interested in the new Detective Training School, and women aren't allowed. Tell Gregson I don't believe she's Scotland Yard material, regardless."

"Quite right," Reginald nodded, then left.

Jonathan lifted himself up and stood next to Celeste, examining the telegram. "Are you going to open that?"

Celeste's fingers flew to her top drawer where they retrieved her letter opener. She cut through the envelope with a forceful swish. "Patience is a virtue. Ever hear that expression?" She pulled out the index card.

"Miss Whalley. Very interested to meet with you. Thursday six o'clock. We may discuss. Come alone if you please. You know where to find me. They will be expecting you. Regards, Edward.

"Well, this is what we wanted," she said half-heartedly. She put a hand on Jonathan's shoulder. "Jonathan, I... I don't want you to do this," she said softly. "Don't go after him. I can simply ignore his request."

"I cannot be hunted the rest of my life Celeste, or wonder if I could have brought her and the others some sense of finality--" Though part of him was *also* having second thoughts.

"We could leave, Jonathan- go to America. I have friends at the Pinkerton Agency, I could ask William and Leverton to--"

Jonathan held up his hand.

"There is no talking you out of it, is there?"

He shook his head.

462

"You are so much like your mother, stubborn as an ox. Very well then, we continue as planned."

"If you have changed your mind..."

"As *you* pointed out, I did not even have the courage to be with the man I loved. I knew Mark Mathis long before he met his wife, but I was too afraid of being hurt again to let him in, so... he gave up. I want to be there with you."

Jonathan kissed her cheek.

CHAPTER 41

HIS MAJESTY

On Thursday evening, Celeste headed to Buckingham Palace. Meanwhile, dressed as a girl, Jonathan made his way to the servant's entrance. He sneaked through the lavish gardens of St. James Park and stopped at the front gate as a parade of servers and housekeepers were leaving for the day. As they streamed out of the massive doors Jonathan stood to the side, waited for the right moment, then slipped past the group with his picnic basket. He thought he had succeeded in being undetected when he accidentally bumped into an official looking man, blocking the pathway into the kitchen. "Where do you think you're going, miss?"

"My sister asked me to bring a change of clothes for her, as she has an appointment," Jonathan said in his best falsetto.

The man narrowed his eyes. "What's her name?"

Jonathan froze. *Think quick, think quick.* "Mary."

"Hurry up, she should be off within the hour," the man waved him through.

Jonathan sighed with relief. He continued through the enormous, deserted kitchen, where copper pots and pans and ladles of every size imaginable hung from above, or lined the walls.

Once past the kitchen, Jonathan crept upstairs, and locked himself in one of the royal guest bedrooms. He removed the wig, dress, and cape then rolled down his pants and shirt sleeves. He opened the basket, pulled out a grappling hook tied to a rope that Celeste had 'borrowed' from Scotland Yard, a wet cloth, and his gun. He stuffed the clothes inside the basket, then stood in front of a large, silver framed square mirror.

"How can women stand wearing this stuff?" he said, nearly pulling off his face as he removed the red blush from his cheeks with the wet cloth.

He looked out the window and seeing the coast was clear, he slowly pushed it open, then stared upwards at the roof. The wind blew furiously, whipping his hair as if it were angry with his intentions.

There were several parapets just above him that could easily catch the grappling hook, so he took the hook by the rope, then swung it around and around and threw it up in the air. It caught on something with a loud 'CLANK!' Jonathan grimaced. "That was loud." He peered out the window to see if anyone had noticed. No activity.

He listened for a moment longer, then tugged on the rope. It seemed secure. He took the picnic basket and swung it over his shoulder like a handbag, then shoving the gun into his belt, he proceeded to scale the wall of the palace. He had never been so terrified in his life, and the icy breeze that snapped at his cheeks chilled him from the inside out.

Once he reached the rooftop, he extracted a carefully folded up piece of paper from his front pocket, and studied the palace floor plan. "The throne room should be by the green room to my... left," he nodded, still slightly winded from the climb.

A gust of wind spontaneously swept past him, and nearly wrenched the paper from his hands. Panicked, he tucked the page inside his shirt pocket and inhaled nervously.

He draped a rope over the side of the palace by the green drawing room's balcony, and cautiously slid down. As he hopped onto the balcony, he noticed that the window was unlatched. He stepped through, and listened outside the large throne room doors, straining to hear the conversation between Celeste and King Edward.

"So, Miss Whalley," he heard the King, "You say you have some... evidence about the Ripper murders you think I might be interested in?"

"Yes, Your Majesty."

"And might I have your Christian name Miss Whalley? You curiously omitted that from your letter."

"One cannot be too careful with such private information, Your Majesty. It is Celeste Whalley."

Jonathan peered through the crack in the doorway, just in time to see the King's reaction. Edward was evidently aware of who she was, based on his raised eyebrow and slight smile. The king was even larger in girth than he imagined. His skin was pale, and his beard and hair showed signs of grey. The gold medals and decorations that covered his outfit appeared to be weighing him down, so much so, that he wondered how the man stood erect. *This* was whom Holmes had feared for thirteen years?

"And actually Your Majesty, the truth is, I am here because of Scarlett Tennyson."

The King folded his hands over his chest. "Scarlett Tennyson? Cannot say I know the name."

"Think, think hard Your Majesty. Trinity College, visiting Albert Victor, a beautiful girl with black hair, to whom you wrote several letters?"

"Newham College girl? The one I wrote to on behalf of my son, Albert Victor, who had expressed interest in her? That was ages ago, whatever does she have to do with the Ripper murders?"

"You had an affair with Scarlett, am I wrong?"

The King bristled. "I do not feel as though I need to answer that."

"She loved you, so how can you shrug her off and pretend you barely knew her?"

"I have not seen nor spoken to her in fifteen years, Miss Whalley. I could not even tell you where she is now."

Hearing enough, Jonathan burst through the doors, and aimed his gun at His Majesty's head. "You know where she is," he said angrily, "six feet under, seeing as how you killed her!"

"Who are you?!" the King bellowed.

Jonathan cocked his gun. "Jonathan Alexander Holmes!"

The King was unmoved by the gun. "Who?" he laughed. "Is there something I am missing, boy?"

"The son of Sherlock and Scarlett Holmes."

"I am afraid that none of this is ringing a bell, son."

"You had *wished* I were your son, but whether you choose to acknowledge me or not, *I* know who *you* are."

"Then you must also be aware that you are trespassing on private property of the Royal Family, a penalty punishable by life in prison."

Jonathan felt his anger rising, like a teakettle about to boil. "I think murdering women in Whitechapel is a much higher offense, and punishable by *death* if I have comprehended *your* laws correctly, JACK!"

The King stiffened, then burst out laughing. "So, you think *I* am Jack the Ripper?" he turned to Celeste with an evil grin. "Is this a game you find amusing, Inspector? Does the Yard know of you engaging in such mendacities? Perhaps I should inform them." He turned to Jonathan, and folded his arms over his wide chest. "Well then, what proof do you have? I would venture... none."

"There are the naval log books saying that you were spending time with your son George, when actually, he was still at sea; the confessional letters to my mother..."

"I do believe those are no longer in existence boy, but why not ask your father?" the King smiled triumphantly.

"Then what about the letters you wrote to my mother in college? 'Jack' and 'Bean' jar any memories for you?"

Edward's hands shook as his face turned red with rage. "How could you have those letters!?" The king exploded. "They were destroyed with Elizabeth Jackson!"

"Not the ones in her trinket box she had hidden at Cambridge. Nor were the 'favours' you had given her."

The king paused, knowing that he had betrayed himself.

"So you *admit* to having Elizabeth Jackson killed for deciphering who you were," Jonathan stepped towards him.

The King's pale colour returned as he smoothed out his beard. "I admit nothing, young Holmes. Where are those letters?"

"They are safe, and you'll never see them again, except printed in the papers for all the country to read."

The king stared at Celeste with fire. "Have you any idea whom you are dealing with?"

"Besides a murderer?" Celeste fought back, "I am sure the Yard would *love* to be informed of that!"

"Your time is done, Your Majesty. No one will ever be hurt again," Jonathan cocked his gun. "Either you confess to your crimes and accept the punishment, or, you will die."

"If you kill me, what do you suppose will happen to you? To Celeste?"

"Once you're dead, nothing else will matter."

The king walked closer to Celeste. "Then she is of no consequence to you?" His eyes gave her a once over but then he pulled a jeweled decorative gun from the holster on the inside left of his jacket, and fired it into Celeste's chest. She gasped and convulsed forward, then collapsed on the ground.

"No!" Jonathan screamed, as his arm dropped to his side.

The King squatted down next to Celeste, and he lifted her limp head in his arm. "Miss Celeste Whalley, Scarlett's closest friend. You had told her to leave Holmes as well, didn't you?" he stroked her cheek with the gun. "Apparently, she refused to listen to either of us. Shame really, or this would have ended very differently. Such a waste." He shifted his gaze back to Jonathan. "I should thank you, Jonathan, for finding me the last piece of the puzzle. I had not the slightest where to find the elusive Celeste of Scarlett's college days, but *you* brought her right to me." He chuckled quietly. "Not quite as bright as your father now, are you?"

"She was unarmed!" Jonathan cried. "How could you?"

"So, my little friend," the King said, "I suppose she is of consequence then?"

"How will you explain this?"

The king tucked his gun back into the holster, and covered it over with his jacket. "I will say you did it. If she's dead, who are they going to believe? Me, or the boy who dropped in unannounced with a gun? Perhaps she was about to disclose something to me which you did not approve of, so you followed her here and killed her?"

As he fought back tears, Jonathan raised his arm and pointed the pistol at the King's chest but his hand was shaking, so his aim would be off. He only had one shot. If he missed, it was over.

"Or," the king approached him slowly, "you were sent here against your will, a poor, abandoned boy with no one, living in the East End, who was only trying to earn money for survival by taking the job. If I say that I pardoned you as an act of charity, with the condition that you stay here under my watch to be reformed, then we can forget all this.

470

Things could work out very well for you Jonathan, as they might have years ago when you couldn't make that decision on your own."

Jonathan's mouth stood open, and he blinked his eyes in shock at the King's ludicrous proposal.

"It's a very fair offer, Jonathan. Think of the life you would have."

Jonathan's shaking stopped. "You are a vile, evil man, and I will enjoy killing you!"

The King frowned, then moved towards the throne. He grabbed a French gras rifle bayonet off a coat of arms on the wall, slid the scabbard to the floor, and pointed it at Jonathan. "If you will not listen to reason, then let us fight as men."

Jonathan nodded and pocketed the gun. He raced over to a different coat of arms holding a pair of sabre foils, and yanked one down. "You are too old, and too fat to fight me. This shall be quick indeed!" Jonathan took up the defensive position. "You have managed to remove everyone I have ever cared for. I want your death to be as drawn out and painful as possible!"

The King raised up his sword and his eyes went dark as a vacant, faraway look entered them. "I gave your mother the chance for a last word," he said in a low, eerily calm voice, "so what will yours be?"

"Do not underestimate me."

Jonathan dove at him with the sword. The King shifted his weight to the left to dodge Jonathan's cut, but only by inches. With Jonathan's next attack, the King parried his blade but wasn't quick enough to avoid the rebuttal, which resulted in a slash being torn across

471

his jacket sleeve. Blood seeped through the torn fabric, leaving a red streak across His Majesty's shoulder.

The two broke into a fight, shifting back and forth across the room as if it were a choreographed dance. Initially, the King seemed to have the advantage as Jonathan's rage was affecting his ability to fight, but then Jonathan remembered Mycroft's warning; to remain level headed at all times; so he was therefore able to rein in his feelings and take control, trapping the King in a corner.

"Have *you* any last words?" Jonathan panted.

The King said nothing, simply glared at him.

Just as Jonathan was about to drive his sword through the King's chest, Edward slipped a small derringer from his side pocket, and pointed it at Jonathan. Jonathan backed up in surprise. His Majesty moved to pull the trigger but another gunshot whizzed through the air, knocking the pistol from his hand. They both turned to see Celeste sitting upright, and holding a smoking revolver in her hand.

Jonathan ran over and hugged her neck with his free arm. "Celeste, you're alive?!"

Celeste rubbed her head where it had hit the ground, and shot venomous glances towards the King. "I knew his Majesty wouldn't fight fair, so I took precautions," she unbuttoned the top part of her green velvet dress, to show a padded interior. "Padded steel plate," she tapped it with her gun's barrel. "I've learned a thing or two over the years... Jonathan look out!" Celeste cried.

Jonathan felt a deep searing pain as a dagger lodged itself between his neck and shoulder blade, not far from the bullet wound. He dropped his sword then fell to his knees.

472

The King unstrapped the dagger's gold sheath from around his boot cuff, and threw it to the floor with a grunt. "You two are a lot of work to kill."

Celeste leapt to her feet and aimed the pistol at the King. "You bloody cheat!"

"No one gets what they want playing fair, Miss Whalley. You of all people should know that," the King folded his arms. "However, if you would like to be charged with killing an unarmed King..."

"No," Jonathan said, as he managed to his feet, "it will not be on your head, Celeste." He carefully pulled the dagger from his shoulder, and grabbed the gun from her hand. "This is my fight, my family, and my final play."

The King raised his hands in surrender, obviously out of tricks. "This is the end then. For us both."

Jonathan knew what he meant. Killing the king would have him arrested and sentenced to death, but right now, he was willing to make that sacrifice. He threw the bloodied dagger to the floor, and aimed his gun. "You are damn right it is."

"I would like to offer another solution," a voice echoed from the other end of the room. They all turned to see Sherlock Holmes standing in the middle of the two large doors at the room's entrance.

"Holmes! What are you... *how* did you get in here?!" the King roared.

Holmes pointed to the doors then shrugged. "Through those, and is that any way to greet an old friend? I may have just saved your life. Now there is a twist of irony." He nodded a cheery, "Evening, Miss

Whalley," to Celeste, then stepped next to Jonathan. "Hear me out before you act, just this once," he said sternly, pushing the gun's muzzle to the floor.

Celeste's eyes locked with Holmes' then Jonathan's. She nodded for Jonathan to lower the gun. Jonathan sighed, and dropped his arm.

Holmes pulled a thick handkerchief from his coat pocket and applied it to Jonathan's bleeding shoulder. "You should not have yanked that out so quickly, as you have most likely wounded yourself further."

The King pulled on a purple velvet cord to his left, possibly summoning the guards. "I thought you knew better than to venture here Holmes, apparently you've grown rusty with your powers of the mind if you cannot remember that."

"I rarely do as I am told, as you have discovered," he smiled. "Now then, since I have everyone's undivided attention and we are all standing at ease, I would like to inform His Majesty of one thing. Should any one of us not venture from here alive or be arrested, your secrets, your crimes, and your alias will no longer be safe."

The King tilted his head. "Oh? I stood there and watched as you obliterated any shred of evidence over ten years ago. You have nothing."

"On the contrary, for you see, I had burned the wrong year of log books," Holmes said smugly. "It is a rather simple task to turn a 'seven' into an 'eight'. Therefore, the year of 1887 is destroyed, yes, but that does you little good as you murdered those women in 1888. Hence, the dates you *supposedly* spent with your son George, you can quite

474

clearly see, were a lie. In addition, the letters you sent to my wife admitting your identity as the Ripper, I had forged, therefore, you received false copies, and the real letters are still in existence. And, as Jonathan mentioned, the notes from Cambridge you sent to Scarlett are also still intact. I made charted copies of everything I uncovered before our audience, and 'obliterated' as you say, the duplicates. I have colleagues in waiting, so that in the event that Jonathan, Miss Whalley, or myself do not return this evening, they will release all items to both the press and Scotland Yard. You will be committed and hung for the Ripper murders, as well as for the murder of my wife." Holmes folded his arms with a smile. "However, if that is the fate your wish for yourself and your country..."

Jonathan blinked. Was he bluffing?

"Suppose *I* tell everyone that you have a wife and child, Holmes, for I had tactfully mentioned such facts in my 'confessional letters'. You see, we both have our secrets."

Jonathan also now realized why his mother had kept the letters a secret from Holmes. The King was threatening to reveal *their* life together, so she had been left in a very difficult position.

"*Had* a wife thanks to you, and my secrets will not have me condemned."

The King was visibly perturbed, but not yet out done. "Suppose I release you. Who is to say you will not have the information sent to the public as revenge? That is too much of a risk."

"I always keep faith, Your Majesty. *I,* unlike you, do not seek revenge on someone who has wronged me. I *can* however, ensure it does not happen again. In return for our silence, and your evidence never surfacing, the lives of the three of us must never be in jeopardy. For if one of us is to be missing, dead, or severely wounded, the information will be handed over to the authorities. No questions asked, no explanation accepted. Are we clear?"

"What if something happens I cannot control? For example, being struck by lightning?"

"Then I suppose you'll have to start playing God, which shouldn't be much of a stretch, as you already consider yourself exempt from the law or any other moral responsibilities."

The King huffed. He opened his mouth to speak, but Holmes held up a finger.

"And, I am not yet finished. Additionally, for my wife's sake, you must completely fund the remainder of our son's education, and any other financial exploits he embarks upon until he has completed his schooling, whether that encompasses four or forty years."

The king mulled this over, perhaps knowing that time was short and a decision had to be made of what his story would be before the guards arrived.

Jonathan pushed Holmes hand off his shoulder and removed the handkerchief. "I don't want anything from him, father. What I *would* want, he could not possibly offer." He looked up at the King. "You had countless affairs over the years, so why? Why single her out for refusing you?"

"I met her whilst visiting Albert Victor at Cambridge. He admitted to loving a girl he saw from afar at Newnham. When we crossed campus, and he wished for an introduction, she expressed no interest in him, but was all too willing to speak with me. After only a few moments, *I* too, fell in love with her. I would have made her my queen if she had let me."

"She would have been nothing but another mistress," Holmes interjected.

"I would have divorced Alexandra to marry her. In her college days I knew her to be too young. I was being patient."

"Your Majesty is too fickle, too restless, and too self-indulgent to ever remain faithful to one woman. Soon, you would have tired of her as well. And might I jog your memory as to the ruin of Sir Charles Dilke, due to the scandal of his divorce? I understand your popularity with the people your Majesty, but such an act would have created a stir large enough to bring about the downfall of the monarchy. Your philandering nature aside, you could not have married outside the crown. The English people would not have accepted a Queen of common birth. You would have had to step down from the throne. Obviously, you had not considered that."

"I had been working on just that with Lord Esher," the king's eyes focused on Jonathan, "whom I believe was acquainted with your dear, Abigail Hopkins?"

Jonathan's face turned red. He made a step towards his Majesty only to have Holmes put a firm hand on his shoulder, holding him back.

"He was constructing a title and lineage to give her the proper authentication to be my wife. I had also prepared an entire wing of Sandringham for her. After her final refusal, I had the floor burned. I could not stand the sight of what might have been."

"She never would have accepted those conditions," Holmes said.

477

"Forgive me if I am wrong, but wasn't your entire relationship based on deception? No one was to know of your marriage, or even your *son?*" the King stepped towards him.

Holmes stood firm. "The woman she was would have vanished in your shadow. I kept her identity a secret to protect her, whereas you would have flaunted it."

"Holmes," Celeste tugged on his sleeve, "we haven't much time."

"Your Majesty?" Holmes asked.

The King pulled on his beard, and watched the door. He took a deep breath, and nodded.

"You have my word for scholarly investments, and your safety."

Jonathan opened his mouth to speak but then sighed, realizing this was the best option. It was also the only one that would ensure Holmes' and Celeste's safety. All his life he had only thought of himself, and now, he had to think of them.

"I accept," he nodded quietly, pocketing the gun. "Otherwise, I would be no better than he."

A loud knock suddenly pounded on the outside of the door.

"Enter!" the King commanded.

Celeste quickly scoped up the bloodied dagger and stuffed it in her skirts before the double doors pushed open, and a handful of guards entered the doorway.

"Everything well, Your Majesty?" bowed the first in line, a tall, older gentleman with greying hair and moustache. The rank badges on his collar and epaulette, indicated that he was a Captain. He frowned as he noticed Edward's bloodstained sleeve.

"All is well, Captain Musker, thank you. Got a bit too exuberant with swordplay," Edward chuckled. "My guests were thinking of an extended visit at the palace but have since changed their minds, stating that they have urgent business to attend to. You may go," the King commanded. "As will I."

Celeste breathed a sigh of relief.

Holmes took Jonathan's hand. "Miss Whalley? Shall we?"

"Celeste, is just fine Holmes," she nodded respectfully.

"Thank you for helping Jonathan."

"You are welcome," she smiled.

Jonathan looked from Celeste to Holmes, then Holmes to Celeste. He was grateful that the two people he cared about most no longer had such animosity towards each other. They might even be friends one day; who was to say?

As they stepped through the doors, the King paused in front of Holmes. "Evidence of trust begets trust." Holmes nodded in comprehension as the King made his way down the hallway with his guards.

As Holmes, Celeste, and Jonathan passed by the Green Room, Jonathan noticed the picnic basket lying on the ground of the balcony outside, and the rope dangling from above. He snatched up the picnic basket and stared at the rope.

"Leave it," Celeste said, "our work here is done. Let him figure out an explanation."

"What about the dagger?" Jonathan pointed to her skirts.

"A souvenir."

CHAPTER 42

BACK TO CAMBRIDGE

After spending a few days with his father, Jonathan decided he would return to Trinity and continue his education.

As they stood on the steps of Kings Cross Station, just as he had done with Abigail not months before, Jonathan took a deep breath. "So it's over then?"

Holmes nodded. "As long as His Majesty keeps his word, then yes."

"Do you think he will?"

"He has no alternative. As he's one of the most well-liked monarchs since the 1600's, he cannot allow anything to tarnish that belief in his character. He's far too conscious and desirous of the people's approval. Furthermore, his status as Monarch does not guarantee him impunity."

"Killing him would have solved nothing, except my own desire for revenge."

"I was relieved when you demonstrated your understanding of that concept. It is not easy to deny yourself the immediate gratification of a retaliatory act; especially one so deserved." He put both hands on his son's shoulders. "Are you going to be all right, Jonathan?"

Jonathan looked to the ground, and shuffled his feet. "I think so. At least I haven't the hunt for my past to distract me from my studies."

Holmes lifted his chin with a smile. "I am pleased you are returning to school. Best thing. Do you see a future in detecting? You have quite the mind, son."

Jonathan laughed and shook his head. "Like father, like son? No, I should say not. I've had enough adventures to last a lifetime. Though I *am* considering pursuing the school of medicine, as someone at Cambridge has inspired me," he chuckled, thinking of Gabriel. "But one never knows. Besides, the world can only have one man like Sherlock Holmes, and I am proud to say that he is my father."

Holmes hugged him closely.

"Here I thought I was in search of my mother, but I believe I was really searching for myself and you, all along."

"Well, you found us both," Holmes winked. "I am grateful you bear me no ill will at this juncture. I could not be certain if you would ever truly forgive me."

"You did what you thought was best." Jonathan's mind then wandered back to Abigail. "You never realize what you have until it's gone."

"I am sorry about Abigail." Holmes said, as if reading his mind, "her memorial was well done."

"Thanks to Celeste. Abigail deserved better than a pauper's grave. In her honour, I would like to keep my name Hopkins, as it has been at Trinity. You--have a reputation to uphold, and I have a lot of studying ahead of me," he rationalized. "It is... best to leave things as they are. Case solved."

Holmes' mouth twisted into a grin. "On the subject of solving cases my young detective, may I have my journal back? It is after all, very precious to me."

Jonathan nodded. "You mentioned that mum kept a journal as well. Does that still exist?"

Holmes folded his arms with a mischievous expression. "It does, yes."

"Might I read that as well, sometime?"

Holmes sighed, and shook his head with a laugh. "Jonathan, I believe there are some things that are best kept secret," he patted him on the shoulder. "*That* is just for me."

"And you shall continue as usual I suppose?"

"I am considering retiring. Perhaps I shall take up beekeeping. Far less taxing to the body and mind, and ensures that I will still be around if my son ever wishes to visit me."

The train whistle blew, signifying that it was time to go.

"I'm sad to leave father, but I am glad I have you."

"And I'll always be here, Jonathan, whenever you need me," Holmes said, as Jonathan hopped up the stairs and head into the train.

As the wheels began to roll and the train picked up speed, Jonathan appeared through one of the windows, and waved. He lifted open the glass. "Oh, and take care of Celeste," he called, "she needs someone too!"

Jonathan watched Holmes pull out his gold cigarette box, grab a stick, then light it with a match from his pocket. He inhaled deeply, and nodded to Jonathan with a smile.

CHAPTER 43

THE CHOICE

Biarritz, France, 1910

Torrential rain poured down, and the afternoon Biarritz sky was filled with smoke coloured clouds. Jonathan took a last sip of coffee, and daydreaming, stared through the window of the French café. A patch of sky was suddenly illuminated by an erratic lightning bolt passing through the clouds. It snapped him back to consciousness. He looked at his watch. Five minutes to eight. He set down the cup, stood from his breakfast table, then threw on his long jacket over his white doctor's coat.

A petite waitress with tight brown curls swept by to claim Jonathan's coffee cup, and scolded him for not eating more of his quiche Lorraine. Jonathan grabbed the fork from his plate, and placed it upright in the middle of his half-eaten pie.

The waitress giggled.

"Now, now, it is a very serious experiment," he said with a wink, then tossed her a coin. He picked up his homburg, pulled it down over his ears, then adjusted his bow tie and high collar before pushing open his umbrella and exiting the front door.

As he trotted down the street, the bottoms of his black trousers quickly becoming soaked with rain. He hoped it would be a relatively easy day at the hospital, as he had plans for the evening, important plans, and didn't wish to get sucked into another double shift. It was one of the prices he typically had to pay for being among the more favoured physicians.

As he approached the Hospital de Biarritz, the wind whipped up from the cobblestone street, and threatened to blow his umbrella inside out. He grumbled, and grabbed the silver tip of one of the umbrella's ribs closest to him, to keep the canopy in place.

An elderly nurse in a white knee length frock held open the hospital's front door as Jonathan stepped inside, shook out his umbrella, and dropped it into the stand. He smoothed back his hair, but then jumped backwards, startled, as Gabriel Adams had suddenly materialized in front of him like a magician does through smoke. His face was twisted into what might have been either an angry expression, or a troubled one. His lips trembled.

He cleared his throat in a hesitant manner, and looked down at the tiled floor as he said, "Dr. Hopkins, a patient needs your attention, he's... he's in bad shape."

So much for an easy day.

"Well then, let's get to it!" Jonathan said, throwing off his coat and tossing it on the coat rack. "Take me to him, Dr. Adams."

Gabriel gripped Jonathan's left upper arm tightly. "You don't know who it is."

Jonathan attempted to pry Gabriel's fingers from his coat, but then paused. Something made his skin prickle. "Is there an issue?"

"I tried to get them to assign someone else, I swear it Jonathan."

Now Jonathan was worried.

"Gabriel, *who* is it?"

Gabriel gulped. "It... it is King Edward."

Jonathan felt time move in slow motion as the words dropped from Gabriel's lips. He was one of the few people who knew what that name meant to him.

"Dear God."

The room felt as though it were collapsing around him, caving in, like being crushed from the outside by some colossal giant. He couldn't breathe. He felt his heart beat faster, and his throat constrict. He gasped for air and seized Gabriel's arm, leaning on it for support as his legs gave way beneath him.

"Jonathan," Gabriel helped him to his feet, "you are the only doctor available at the moment with the proper knowledge to handle him... I... I.... tried to take it from you, but they said I was refused."

Jonathan took a deep breath and closed his eyes. "Has he been told?"

"That you are his doctor? Unlikely, for he was unconscious when they brought him in."

Flashbulbs of images shuffled through Jonathan's mind, like a series of plate photographs. Abigail, his mother, Celeste, and Holmes. His brow furrowed, and he clenched his teeth. He breathed out in anguish, pushed passed Gabriel, and flew out of the front door into the rain.

As he entered the downpour outside, he ran until he collided with a street post, then paused, and pounded his fists into the cold black metal. He stopped when he noticed his knuckles were red and bleeding. He cried out in pain, then spun around and slammed his back into the post. Inhaling deeply, he looked up at the dark clouds, and repeatedly blinked as raindrops entered his eyes. He covered his face with his throbbing hands, and his fingers trembled.

"Give me strength," he whispered, then stared down the narrow street. "What would you have me do?" he asked the empty air, "save the very man who killed my mother?" His only response was the patter of rain against the stone street, and the sound of running water as it ran down drainpipes and into the sewers. Jonathan shook his head, wiped his knuckles against his white coat, then mechanically walked back into the building. He grabbed a towel from the counter of the nurse's station to wipe his hands.

"Are you... alright Hopkins?" Gabriel asked, noticing his hands.

Jonathan dried off his face. "Where is he, Gabriel?"

Gabriel nodded, gripped Jonathan's shoulder, then walked with him down long hallway.

The normally inviting white walls now seemed eerie, haunting, and unfamiliar, and the shiny polished floor glowed with the ghostly images of the flickering lights overhead. The journey down that skinny corridor seemed like an eternity, and with every footstep that echoed across the stone floor, Jonathan felt his confidence, calm, and courage, quickly crumbling. Sudden bursts of lightening pierced the high, narrow hospital windows, creating grotesque shadows on the walls. Thunder clapped, and Jonathan jumped involuntarily.

They stopped at the third room down on the left. As he stood in front of the open doorway, he poked his head inside and peered around to the right. The great King Edward of England, confined to an ordinary hospital bed, covered with a plain white sheet like any other patient, rested motionless in the small empty room. His eyes were closed, and his breathing labored. Jonathan muttered "*primum non nocere*" before stepping through the room. He approached the elderly, greyed monarch, and stood next to his bedside, his eyes burning with hatred.

"Why you? Of all people, why in God's name were you sent here to haunt me?"

The King's eyes jerked back and forth beneath his eyelids, but they did not open.

Jonathan inhaled deeply, rubbed his temples, then walked back to the door and closed it. He took an oath, a promise, to not discriminate between, or against patients, but he never anticipated that his commitment would include the monster before him. His mind and heart battled over the decision as he paced the floor. What would Holmes do? He found himself asking. The conflict was killing him. At thirteen, he had found the courage to walk away, and even in the heat of a vengeful rage, had lowered the gun, realizing he'd be no better off by killing a murderer. Why now, was he struggling as an adult, when he should be infinitely wiser, more mature, and be able to see things from an outside perspective? Instead, his anger felt deeper, stronger, and more alive than ever. Though he'd had years of separation from the King, his intrusion into Jonathan's life yet again, made him hate the man even more.

He stopped to grip the metal-framed footboard and closed his eyes. He knew this was his choice to make, his alone, and he would have to live with the consequences of whatever option he selected. Which would haunt him least? He took a deep breath, opened his eyes, and made his decision.

CHAPTER 44

HOLMES' EPILOGUE

6th May 1910

On the 6th of May 1910, King Edward VII, the King of Great Britain & Emperor of India, was dead, and all the world mourned. That is to say, all the world, save for myself. He was said to have had several heart attacks that day, and previously suffered bronchitis. That was given as cause of death. I however, had other suspicions. In the last two months of his life, while visiting Biarritz, France, King Edward had ended up in hospital in Bayonne for his bronchitis.

The main medical physician in his ward at that time...was Jonathan. With my boy's extensive knowledge of medicine, which of course could include anything both helpful and harmful, Jonathan could have very well taken his revenge, and over a period of time, slowly poisoned the King with what he would have thought were antibiotics.

I knew my brother Mycroft had connections with the Crown, so asked if he was familiar with the Royal Physician in Ordinary, Sir Francis Henry Laking. He said he was not, but knew Thomas Horder, the extra physician to the king. I asked if I might speak with him briefly over the phone, as I had one important question I needed answered.

Mycroft arranged the call, and I had but a moment's time with him, which was all I needed. "Mr. Horder, you were the extra physician to Edward VII, correct?"

"Yes, yes I was."

"Upon the King's death, was he on any medications of note?"

491

"None, save for his antibiotics for his bronchitis, but he was too far gone at that point for it to have had any real effect."

"I see, and you prescribed those to him?"

"No, his doctor in Biarritz did, when he was in France."

"Do you remember the doctor's name?"

"Vaguely. Hopper, Hopkins, Hodgins? Despite his youth, he is well esteemed in Bayonne, so I trusted him completely. He probably aided in actually prolonging his Majesty's life while under his care, if I am not mistaken. In March, we feared he would last less than a week. Perhaps we should have left the King with him longer, who is to say if he would still be around?" Mr. Horder said sadly.

"Indeed," I mused softly.

"Mr. Holmes, is anything the matter?"

"Just wanted to rule out any possibility of medications interacting, but how foolish of me, you, of course, would have been aware of that. I apologize for taking up your valuable time," I expressed.

"No need to apologize, but glad I could clear things up for you. Good bye," he hung up the phone.

"Good bye, Mr. Horder," I muttered to the dial tone.

I then paused. Did Jonathan honestly try to save him? Or did he slowly kill him in retribution? I decided I never wanted to know the answer.

CPSIA information can be obtained
at www.ICGtesting.com
Printed in the USA
BVOW08s0010051217
501912BV00014B/522/P